Greyla

PINK S[

'O. Douglas' was the pseudonym of Anna Buchan (1877 – 1948). She was a daughter of the Manse, busy aunt to her older brother John's large family and ran the household for her younger brother Walter. With the added stimulus of her literary family background, she was well placed to write the 'mild domestic fiction' which made her world famous.

She was born in Fife and moved to Glasgow when she was eleven, when her father was called to the John Knox Church in the Gorbals. She and her brothers spent their long summer holidays with their grandparents in Broughton, in the Borders. After the birth of her youngest brother Alastair, she left school to be useful at home and to work in the parish.

When in 1906 Walter was sent to take over the family legal and banking business in Peebles, Anna, aged 29, went with him and here they both stayed for the rest of their lives.

From this fairly restricted life bound by family duty, she drew inspiration for all of her books. Set variously in the Borders, Fife and Glasgow that she knew so well, the twelve novels are peopled with sharply observed characters very often drawn directly from her family and acquaintances. Though they are "Nice Books", she does not shy away from tragedy and loss, and the "pink sugar view of life" is seasoned with dry Scottish wit and shrewd good sense.

BY THE SAME AUTHOR

Olivia in India
The Setons
Penny Plain
Ann and her Mother
The Proper Place
Eliza for Common
The Day of Small Things
Priorsford
Taken by the Hand
Jane's Parlour
The House that is Our Own

PINK SUGAR

O. DOUGLAS

Greyladies

Published by
Greyladies
an imprint of The Old Children's Bookshelf

© Anna Buchan 1924

This edition first published 2009
Reprinted 2014
Design and layout © Shirley Neilson 2009
Foreword © Deborah Stewartby 2009
Preface © Shirley Neilson 2009

ISBN   978-0-9559413-8-2

All rights reserved. No part of this publication may be
reproduced, stored in or introduced into a retrieval system, or
transmitted, in any form or by any means (electronic,
mechanical, photocopying, recording or otherwise) without the
prior written permission of the above copyright owners and the
above publisher of this book.

Set in Sylfaen / Perpetua
Printed and bound by Berforts Information Press Ltd.

Contents

Foreword, "Because of Bill"
by Deborah Buchan, Lady Stewartby   vii

Map of Broughton / Muirburn   x

"Her Own Beloved Border Country"
Anna Buchan's Peeblesshire   xi

Pink Sugar   1

TO
JOHN AND SUSAN BUCHAN

BECAUSE OF BILL

"Because of Bill"
Foreword by Deborah Buchan, Lady Stewartby

A very small girl remembers being carried into a room with a big marble fireplace, conscious of the rough tweed of her father's jacket against her bare legs. In the corner the little girl notices an old lady with piercing eyes. This is my only memory of my Great Aunt Anna Buchan – the novelist O. Douglas – and I am glad to have that link between me, O. Douglas and my father William Buchan, who in the character of 'Bad Bill' played such a large part in *Pink Sugar*.

My Great Aunt Anna started writing her novels when she was going nearly mad with grief following, over a period of years, the loss of her Violet, who died aged only five, the death of her father, the unexpected sudden illness and eventual death of her brother William, and her mother's long and debilitating illness. Although she declared that she liked to write about "pleasant people, whose lives simply meandered on," there was much more to her books than that. Her own life was not devoid of tragedy and her writing conveys a sympathetic understanding of the grief and boredom, poverty and anxiety that 'pleasant people' could suffer from, not dwelt upon but not ignored.

"O. Douglas" came into being as my great-aunt didn't want to be thought to be taking advantage of the Buchan name, made famous by her brother John. Olivia Douglas was the heroine of her first book, *Olivia in India*, so the world has explained her pseudonym from that. However, there is a family tradition that the name came from a family dog, rejoicing in the name of Black Douglas. As is often the case in families where the children are highly disciplined, the animals were not – and his exuberant mischief provoked constant wails of "Oh! *Douglas!*"

Pink Sugar was dedicated to my grandparents, John and Susan Buchan, "Because of Bill" and my father did indeed bear a striking resemblance to him. The characteristics which appear in the book stayed with him throughout his life – he remained "a pattern of neatness" and those piercing blue eyes, uncomfortable if you were detected in a misdemeanour but welcoming if not, were only dimmed in ninety years by blindness.

His vivid imagination – the "Russian-refucheese clown" and "That's not Aunt Fanny, that's the sheep in 'Alice', the sheep what sat in the boat and knitted," and neat turn of phrase – "Oh, what a long preach! I thought he was going on till Monday," were transformed into the most elegant prose in the books he later wrote.

In one episode in *Pink Sugar,* Bill's siblings, Barbara and Specky, are asked out to on an adventure and Bill is to be left behind. "Bill stared fixedly at the tablecloth. Kirsty knew he was on the point of crying, a humiliation which would have vexed his proud soul, and without looking at him she slid her hand over his small clenched fist . . ." Was O. Douglas firing a warning shot across my grandparents' bows that Bill felt then, as he did all his life, that being the middle of three boys was an unhappy and neglectful place to be? But perhaps what sums up for me the characteristic that so defines the person into which Bill grew, is when

Kirsty returns from a visit to London and Bill immediately takes her off to show her the little garden he is making. That love of, and talent for, gardens stayed with my father until the very end. And what distinguished the grown-up Bill from the "Bad Bill" of *Pink Sugar* was the most perfect good manners and innate courtesy, which transformed him from a child frank to the point of rudeness to a most delightful companion.

Anna Buchan believed that she had traduced my father's character in *Pink Sugar* and, to make amends, promised him a farthing for every copy that was sold in the first year. My father remembered receiving a cheque for £30, which at four farthings to the penny and two hundred and forty pennies to the pound made for a tremendous number of copies sold. I am sure that this re-issue of *Pink Sugar* will have the same appeal today as it did in 1924.

Deborah Stewartby
Broughton, 2009

(William Buchan, 3rd Lord Tweedsmuir, Bad Bill in *Pink Sugar,* was the second son and third child of John and Susan Buchan. JB was a novelist, lawyer, soldier, statesman and, ultimately, Governor-General of Canada.)

Map of Broughton / Muirburn and district

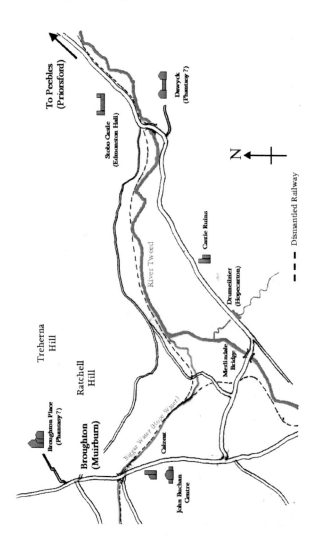

"Her Own Beloved Border Country"
Anna Buchan's Peeblesshire

Anna Buchan quite clearly loved the Borders. When she was growing up in Glasgow, she and her brothers spent their summer holidays with their grandparents in Broughton. In her late twenties she moved to Peebles to run her brother Walter's household when he took over the family business of Writer to the Signet, Procurator Fiscal, banker and Town Clerk. And there she stayed, at the very heart of the town, for the rest of her days.

Anna used the locations she knew and loved as the settings for the books she wrote as O. Douglas. She often used real place names taken from the surrounding area but moved them to different locations entirely. In *Pink Sugar* she gave Broughton the name of Muirburn, taken from a nearby farming community. It is a thin disguise, maybe only adopted to show that Anna Buchan's Broughton and O. Douglas's Muirburn are slightly different places.

The main street in Broughton even in 1924 had very few shops, and Muirburn is no different. Mrs Dickson's general shop with its onions and paraffin barrels is the social centre of the village but Muirburn's inhabitants still have to rely on vans from Priorsford for many things, such as the "divine sponge cakes" that Davidson the carter brings to Little Phantasy. Present day Broughton still has a village shop, a few doors down from the teashop which used to be called "The Thirty Nine Steps".

In O. Douglas's Muirburn there are two Presbyterian churches, cheek by jowl. The Muirburn Parish Church is at Calzeat at the southern end of the town. It is where the young Buchans would have worshipped and was for several years the John Buchan Centre. Robert and Rebecca Brand's Muirburn Manse with its "singularly ugly dining room" is across the road, over a burn and through the trees along the narrow 'Minister's Path' at Easter Calzeat.

The much grander Netherton church, "with its pipe-organ and genteel society" is more or less next door, with several contenders for its "absurdly large manse in an absurdly large garden", ideal for the McCandlish's annual Garden Party with the Priorsford band playing in the shrubbery.

Standing guard over the whole village, are the Border hills. Anna would have spent much of those childhood summers in the hills and glens around Broughton and in *Pink Sugar* she describes them at some length. "That funny little heathery hill is called the Hill o' Men. That plain faced one is Ratchell. Hasn't it a threadbare look as if generations of schoolboys had slid down it and worn off all the nap?" Then there's Treherna and big humped-backed Cardon.

These hills keep their own names – and haven't been moved – but the "green glen" of Hopecarton is another matter. Hopecarton glen in real life is only a few miles south of Broughton, but in *Pink Sugar* ("six houses and a shop that sells more acid drops for a penny than a shop has ever been known to do") it is quite clearly Drumelzier, on the road to Dawyck. Anna's left and right directions are a little confusing, as is the position of the bridge, but you can follow the burn for a hundred yards or so, and "you will find yourself in the 'greenest glen shone on by the sun'."

"To this glen one shining day in the beginning of June Kirsty Gilmour brought her household to hold high revel."

Nearby too is Merlin's Haugh, where Robert Brand proposed another picnic. The present day Merlindale bridge crosses Tweed just west of Drumelzier. "Isn't it odd to think that there is nothing changed in this green glen since Merlin sang his wild songs in the morning of the world?"

Unsurprisingly Muirburn station, through which the little train from "the Junction" (Symington on the main Euston – Glasgow line) ambled its way to Priorsford, has now vanished. You can still see the contour of the embankment in the centre of Broughton, and the bridge, but the line, meandering through Stobo and Lyne on its way to Peebles, was closed to passenger traffic in 1950.

Bad Bill, on a trip to the barbers in Priorsford with Kirsty, chose as his treat going to watch the train turn round.

"Priorsford" is of course the small market town of Peebles, one of the gems of the Borders and Anna Buchan's home for 42 years. It first appeared in her third book, *Penny Plain,* with the warmly enticing first line, "It was teatime in Priorsford."

The Buchan home was the Bank House at the west end of the High Street, next to the Sheriff Court and the Old Parish Church. Incredibly, in view of its history, half of the Bank House was demolished in 1984 to widen the road and the Cuddy Bridge.

The landmark square tower is there no longer, but the red front door was kept and moved round to the side. Bank House is now a furniture boutique with its offices upstairs.

Some of the shops Anna would have known are still there. Opposite the Bank House is Whitie's, newsagent, stationer and bookshop (though Anna seems to have bought all her books from The Times Book Club.) From Whitie's book-room at the back of their shop, you can also see the dormer window of the room Walter Buchan rented for his sister to write in, undisturbed by everyday domesticity and callers to the Bank House.

Veitch's, an old Peeblesshire name used in *Pink Sugar,* was a rather old-fashioned draper and ladies' and men's outfitters, probably unchanged since it first opened. It has closed now but its name and the large plate glass windows remarked upon by Peter Reid in *Penny Plain* are still there. Scott Brothers the ironmongers and The Medical Hall chemists still have their original old shop fronts and some fittings from Anna Buchan's time, though not the bakers who supplied the "divine" sponge cakes for Kirsty and her Aunt Fanny to enjoy every evening with a glass of hot water.

These settings are generally agreed upon; it is when we come to locating the houses of the main characters that there is more room for debate and opinions do differ, especially over Phantasy itself.

Phantasy, with its dower house Little Phantasy, was set in a park with Japanese deer at the end of a long drive that wound through the trees and crossed and recrossed the Hope Water. Little Phantasy stood very close to Hope

Water and Specky liked to fish "between the little waterfall beyond the house and the bridge where the stream meets Tweed."

The one immovable location in this description is where Hope Water (generally agreed to be Biggar Water) met Tweed. The bridge that marks the meeting was mentioned fairly often – Kirsty could see it from her bedroom window and Colonel Home rested his arms on the parapet to admire the view. But there is no bridge anywhere around.

In her book, *Anna Buchan and O. Douglas*, Wendy Forrester suggests that Phantasy was based on nearby Dawyck, the grounds of which are now open as a major botanical garden.

It is indeed a beautiful old house, the garden is famous for its rare trees, and there are deer and a burn with a waterfall though not near the house. Although she says there are no possibilities for Little Phantasy in its grounds, there are in fact several, including a lodge and converted stables.

Broughton Place, a handsome imposing house at the north end of the village, stands at the top of a long wooded drive and is beside a "cheerfully brawling" trout stream, which could very well be Hope Water. But when *Pink Sugar* was written there was no house there at all. The original was burnt down in the 19th century and it wasn't rebuilt until the 1930s. This location moves Hope Water well away from Tweed, but Lady Stewartby nevertheless believes that this was the origin of Phantasy, hence the name – the house was Anna's fantasy.

I think it's most likely that Anna took certain features

from several houses – and, indeed, from her imagination – and transposed them all into one Phantasy. This is exactly what she has done with the "bear" gates to Phantasy, which famously belong to Traquair House several miles down Tweed, near Innerleithen.

Anna quite often did this. Though there is a small ruin of a castle at the meeting of Tweed and Hope Water where Hawkshaw is in *Pink Sugar*, the descriptions of it are clearly of Neidpath, near Peebles. Behind it were the remains of a walled garden. "Grim in the August heat stood the Castle with its few deep windows, mere slits in the depths of the walls, mute, remote, like one who has outlived his time."

Edmonston Hall is another instance of Anna's confusing use of place names. In real life it is on the Edinburgh road north of Biggar. In *Pink Sugar* it is placed within walking distance of Little Phantasy – Kirsty walks the three miles in order to have time to herself to think – and could well be based on Stobo Castle, near Dawyck. It is now a luxurious health spa; in the book it was the home of Sir Andrew and Lady Carruthers and was a grand affair with extensive gardens requiring six gardeners and "a most ornate gateway with gilded railings."

"I suppose these are what are known as 'gilt-edged securities' Kirsty told herself, and laughed a little at her own joke."

Could Anna Buchan still be laughing gently, seeing us all tied in knots trying to sort out her version of Muirburn and district? Exploring real life Broughton and its surroundings gives much enjoyment and many ideas for discussion, but wherever the precise origins of her houses and glens, they all have the distinctive flavour of the Borders country she knew and loved so well.

Shirley Neilson
Edinburgh 2009

PINK SUGAR

CHAPTER 1

> "Now Mercy was of a fair countenance and therefore
> the more alluring." *The Pilgrim's Progress*

"I DESCRIBED myself as a spinster without encumbrances. I don't know quite what I meant by it, but I thought it sounded well."

Kirsty Gilmour stood in the window in the spring sunshine, arranging daffodils in a wide bowl, and laughed.

Blanche Cunningham, lying back comfortably in a large armchair, looked at her friend appraisingly.

"How old are you, Kirsty?" she asked lazily, choosing with care a chocolate from an opulent-looking box that lay on her knee.

"I'm thirty," said Kirsty, "but you shouldn't make me say it out loud like that."

"How would you like to be forty, my dear? That's what I'll be on my next birthday. But you don't look thirty, child. You can stand in that glare of revealing sun and work with spring flowers and fear nothing. You're rather like a daffodil yourself, now that I come to think of it, with that green frock and cloud of pale yellow hair—your eyes are green too. Did you know that?"

"Of course," said Kirsty, attempting to make a weak-kneed daffodil stand upright, "that's why I'm so fond of jade . . . Now, isn't that pretty? They look as if they were growing in the moss. I like best the small single daffodils that grow almost wild, they have such an eager look."

"Very pretty," Mrs. Cunningham said, glancing carelessly at the bowl of flowers. "But, Kirsty, it's absurd that you should be a spinster. How have you managed it?"

"I wonder! Blanche, you married so young that, as I've often told you, you've acquired the male attitude of mind. No man ever allows himself to believe that a woman is single from choice, and, in your heart, neither do you."

"Pouf!" Mrs. Cunningham waved the imputation aside and searched diligently in the chocolate box. "I'm afraid I'm making a dreadful mess of your chocolates. I'm looking for a hard one, and I've squashed all the soft ones pinching them . . . You forget, my dear, when you accuse me of unbelief that I was on the spot and saw at least two aspirants to your hand—at Cannes, you remember? There was the hidalgo from the Tyne (I've forgotten his name), just baroneted, with all his blushing honours thick upon him. How red the back of his neck was! And there . . ."

"Blanche," Kirsty was smiling, but there was a note of appeal in her voice. "*Need* you talk about ugly things the first real day of spring? I've had no luck in suitors—let us leave it at that . . . You really aren't behaving very nicely. I've looked forward so to your visit, and, instead of giving me a week as you promised, you are only staying a miserable few hours—you arrived at luncheon-time and you say you must leave by the early train tomorrow morning. I've so much to tell you and to show you, and you don't seem interested . . . it's very disappointing."

Blanche Cunningham sprang up impulsively, upsetting the box of chocolates in her haste, and attempted to grab Kirsty, and the bowl of flowers she was carrying, in her arms. "But I *am* interested, Kirsty dear," she cried; "I'm dying to see every corner of this delectable place. How did you find it? *Little Phantasy.* I love the name."

"Just see what you've made me do!" said Kirsty, carrying the flowers to a place of safety, and proceeding to mop up the water spilt on the floor with her handkerchief. Then she sat down on the arm of her friend's chair and tried to dry her wet fingers with her wet handkerchief.

"It was the name that fascinated me," she said. "As soon as I read the advertisement I knew I simply must live here. But I'll tell you about that later—To begin just where we are, do you approve of this room?"

She looked proudly round the gay white room with its wide windows of small-paned glass, and before her friend could reply, went on: "You don't think the chintzes too bright, do you? I like a lot of colour in a country room, and I thought the white-panelled walls could stand the tulips and the parrots. Isn't it luck that there should be such a good oak floor when we have so many rugs? I collected them for years all over the place, hoping that some day I might find a use for them. That Bokhara one is my special find. When I showed it to Mrs. Paynter—you remember the delightful American lady?—she took it in her arms and hugged it and said, 'I don't care how much you paid for this, it couldn't be too much'."

Blanche laughed. "Yes, but I like best the big one in the middle. It makes me think of a meadow of bright flowers . . . But it's all charming: the dark old mahogany, and the white walls, and the bright chintzes, and the gentle colours of the rugs. Somehow I'm surprised. I never seem to have thought of you as a homemaker."

Kirsty shook her head rather mournfully.

"You see," she said, "it's the very first home I've ever had, though I *am* thirty."

Blanche was silent, remembering the Kirsty she had first known, a rather listless girl, dragged from one smart hotel to another by a valetudinarian but sprightly stepmother. Change had been the breath of life to Lady Gilmour. Plaintively seeking health, she had moved from one to another Pool of Bethesda, where in very truth she "troubled the waters."

Thinking of Lady Gilmour, Blanche was conscious again of the hot wave of dislike that had so often engulfed her when she had come in contact with that lady in life. She remembered the baby-blue eyes, the appealing ways, the smooth sweet voice that could say such cruel things, the too red lips, the faint scent of violets that had clung to all her possessions, the carefully thought-out details of all she wore, her endless insistent care for herself and her own comfort, her absolute carelessness as to the feelings of others. Blanche told herself that she had done more than dislike Lady Gilmour, she had almost hated the woman—chiefly on Kirsty's account.

She had first met Kirsty and her stepmother ten years before at an hotel in Mentone where she was recruiting after an illness in India. She had been interested at once in both of them, the pretty fragile mother and the young daughter with the cloud of pale gold hair and grave green eyes. They made a charming picture, she thought, but they were so constantly surrounded by a crowd of admirers, both male and female, that it was some time before an opportunity came to speak to the girl. When it came she found her shy and, for such an attractive creature, oddly grateful for attention and responsive to kindness. When she heard that Mrs. Cunningham was Scots she cried, "But so am I, through and through. Kirsty Gilmour—that sounds Scots enough, doesn't it?"

"And you live in Scotland?" she had asked.

"No. You see my stepmother hates Scotland. It makes her ill, she says: so draughty and cold. We seem to go everywhere but to Scotland. D'you know, I haven't been home—to Scotland, I mean—since I was eight. Not since my father died."

Blanche had laughed at the woeful droop of the girl's soft mouth and said, "What part of Scotland do you belong to? The Borders? Ah well, you must see that you marry a Scotsman and make your home there."

Later on she had been introduced to Lady Gilmour, and had found her sweet and friendly and quite intolerable. For the sake of seeing something of Kirsty she had tried to dissemble her dislike and make one of the admiring crowd that murmured at intervals, "Dear Lady Gilmour, *so* frail, *so* touching;" but at all times Blanche dissembled with difficulty, and Lady Gilmour had herself seemed to feel the antagonism and return it with interest. She had done her best to wean Kirsty from her new friend, but Kirsty was staunch, and she and Blanche had corresponded regularly and met at intervals all through the ten years.

Lady Gilmour had been dead about six months, and Kirsty had come, like a homing bird, to the Borders.

"Kirsty," Blanche laid her hand on her friend's arm. "However did you stand it all those years? What an intolerable woman she was!"

Kirsty sat looking in front of her.

"She's dead," was all she said.

"Well," Mrs. Cunningham retorted briskly, "being dead doesn't make people any nicer, does it?"

"No—but it makes them so harmless and unresentful."

"As to that, Lady Gilmour wouldn't be harmless if she could help it, you may be sure of that. I never met a woman with such a genius for mischief-making . . . You were a model of discretion, my dear, the most dutiful of stepdaughters, but you aren't naturally stupid—you *must* have seen."

Kirsty looked out to the wild garden where the daffodils danced in the April sun. All the light had gone out of her face, the very gold of her hair seemed dulled. She was again the listless girl who had followed apathetically in the train of her egotistical stepmother.

When she spoke her voice too had changed: it dragged tonelessly. "Oh, don't you see? If I had ever even to myself put it into words, I couldn't have stood it another day. I never let myself say to myself how I hated it, I just went on—dreary day after dreary day. And after all, Marmee was all I had, she needed me, and perhaps she did care for me a little in her own way, though she couldn't help always stinging me like a gadfly. I've been thinking since that my misery was greatly my own fault. If I had been a different kind of girl I might have enjoyed the life very well. To many it would have been rapture to go from one gay place to another, to have their fill of pretty dresses and dancing and tennis, and no domestic cares or duties. But to me it was anathema. The fact is, I was born out of due season. I should have lived in mid-Victorian days."

Kirsty stopped to laugh at herself, and Blanche said:

"Yes, I know what you mean. You would have enjoyed what somebody calls 'the comfortable commonplaces, the small crises, the recurrent sentimentalities of domestic life'."

Kirsty nodded. "I would indeed. I would have rejoiced in nurseries of bashful babies, brothers and sisters, warm family affection. But I was set solitary in the world with no mother and a very busy father. I suppose, poor innocent, he thought he was doing his best for me when he married again; and when I was eight he died . . . My stepmother didn't care for children, and I stayed at school until I was seventeen. Then she sent for me, and took me about with her everywhere, made me call her 'Marmee,' and liked people to say that we looked like sisters. She loved hotel life, and I loathed it from the first—the publicity, the abiding smell of rich foods and cigars, the rooms with their expensive furniture and utter lack of homelikeness or individuality; the people who sat about fatly in fat armchairs, the way they gloated over their food, their endless efforts to keep themselves entertained."

Blanche nodded comprehendingly, and Kirsty went on:

"It wasn't only the hotels I loathed—indeed I might have enjoyed them if they had only been an interlude in a life filled with other things. But it was the way we behaved in hotels. I don't know what my father did to be given a knighthood, but whatever it was, I wish he hadn't. It complicated matters so. A title—even a very little one—has a wonderful attraction for certain people, and those people swarmed round Marmee like wasps round a honeypot. I remember one idiot saying to me, 'How *gracious* dear Lady Gilmour is'—and poor Marmee lapped it all up like a hungry cat."

Blanche cracked a hard chocolate with her strong white teeth, and "I can see her," she said.

"And we were such snobs ourselves," Kirsty went on. "We always pursued the worthwhile people—Marmee had a wonderful keen eye for the best people—and very often we were snubbed for our pains. It served us right, of course, but it was pretty ghastly. Happily we never stayed long in one place. Nearly always we quarrelled with someone, and Marmee lost taste for her new friends and left."

"Yes," Blanche said, "she was like the lady in one of Elizabeth's books whose new friends liked her, and who had no old friends."

"Poor Marmee," said Kirsty.

"No, don't pity her. She was the most accomplished egoist I ever came across . . . But you were greatly to blame, Kirsty. Why were you so weak? Surely you had the right to live your own life. Why didn't you break away?"

"Well, you see"—Kirsty looked at her friend deprecatingly—"after I was twenty-one most of the money was mine, and I couldn't very well—I mean to say it would have crippled her a lot, and she liked to do things well, and—Oh, I know I sound frightfully feeble, but I can't help it. I simply hate to hurt people's feelings or make them feel uncomfortable. It's the way I'm made . . . I did try once to break away as you call it. It was the second year of the War, and I suddenly felt that I simply could not go on doing nothing but knit socks and make shirts and give subscriptions. I went off, after a wild scene, to work in a hospital. I hadn't well begun when I was sent for. Marmee had had a heart attack, and the doctor—a new one—blamed me severely for having left her. Oh, it was no good, Blanche. I was bound. She wove a web round me."

Blanche moved impatiently. "Heart attacks wouldn't have bound me," she said.

"The War years," Kirsty went on, "were the worst. We had no one even to be anxious about. I envied—yes, I did—the haggard-eyed women devouring the newspapers. It is awful to be left out of everything . . . And having borne no part in the War, we had the impertinence to be among the first who went to look at the battlefields. Marmee liked to say she had done things before the herd rushed in, so we motored from Paris by Amiens, through the Somme country to Arras. She was soon bored—there was so pitifully little to see. 'Shocking,' she said, as we saw shattered towns and villages, blasted trees, miles of mud. You see, it was nothing to us. We weren't reconstructing it all in our minds—we weren't saying to ourselves, 'So it must have looked when *he* saw it.' 'Here perhaps he stood.' . . . On the road from Albert to Arras our chauffeur stopped at a hillock near the roadside. This, he told us, was the famous *Butte de Warlencourt*, which men had died by thousands to take and hold. I got out and walked across to the hillock. It was an April day, with blinks of sun between wild beating showers of rain. My feet sank in the mud—*Somme mud*, how often I had read of it! There were tin hats and long trench boots lying about, and here and there stood a frail wooden cross. Every inch of the ground had been black with the blood of our men—I could hardly put one foot before another as I thought of what each step must have meant to them as they struggled up against pitiless fire. On the summit there were three tall crosses—like Calvary . . . A party of four, two women and two men, had got out of a car and were walking over the ground near me. The men evidently knew the place of old, and one said to the other in tones almost of awe, 'D'you see? There are *cowslips growing in the shell-holes.*' The women were in mourning—a mother and daughter I thought, very pale and quiet. One the men turned to them and said softly, 'It was about here,' and they stood still, their hands clasped as if praying. I crept back to the car and Marmee . . . Oh, it's wretched of me sitting here, talking like this, making myself out a creature of fine feelings, and blaming a woman who can't answer back. I daresay I must often have irritated her when I felt superior and showed it. If I had known she was going to die I would have been so much nicer."

"You were amazingly patient."

"Perhaps I seemed so, but I often wasn't. There is one thing that comforts me, though, when I think of her. In her last illness she was surrounded by admiration and affection, and she knew it. She was only ill for a few days—really ill, I mean, for she was always delicate—and I think she knew it was the end, and the odd thing was she didn't think about herself—she thought of others, she thought of *me*. I was so touched. And the nurse told me with tears in her eyes that she had never nursed a more delightful patient, and that evening when she slept peacefully away the doctor said, and his voice sounded really moved: 'A very sweet woman.' I was so thankful to hear them speak so."

"And thankful that the illness was a short one," said Blanche dryly, "so that they could speak so. Ah, forgive me, Kirsty; I sound a brute, I know, but you are such an incurable sentimentalist. You find everything and everybody 'touching.' You spend your time wrapping up ugly facts in pink chiffon: you see life like a picture on a chocolate-box. Yes, I know I'm being horribly rude, but who is to tell you home-truths if not an old friend?"

Kirsty walked to the fireplace and bent over the log basket to replenish the fire.

Presently she said, lifting a flushed face to her friend:

"I don't mind home truths, and I daresay I am sentimental, but please try to forget what I said about Marmee. All that part is finished with. Now I can make what I will of my life. And I mean to make just as many people happy as I possibly can." She stopped, glanced at Blanche, and added, "Now I mean to live for others."

At this announcement Blanche sat bolt upright.

"My dear," she said in a shocked voice, "I'm afraid Lady Gilmour has done more than spoil your youth. I'm afraid she has destroyed your sense of humour. *Live for others*. You say it in cold blood, just like that."

Kirsty laughed. "I admit it sounds pretty bad—priggish in the extreme; especially when you say it in that frozen clear voice of yours. But why should you be so shocked? Surely it is a most laudable intention? Now stop eating chocolates (you don't deserve to have a sound tooth in your head), and come and see the house. I shan't spare you a cupboard, and it will be much better for me than talking about myself. I'm sick of the subject, anyway."

Blanche rose lazily and looked at herself in the narrow gilt mirror above the mantelshelf.

Then she turned and took Kirsty's face between her two hands, smiled at her, and said obscurely:

"Froggy's Little Brother."

CHAPTER 2

"Dr. Johnson (said I), I do indeed come from Scotland,
but I cannot help it." BOSWELL

"YOU SEE," Kirsty explained, "the dining-room opens out of the drawing-room. It has another door, of course, which you reach by going through the hall and down a passage; that's how we'll go when we have a dinner party (if ever we have one); it's more impressive."

She opened the dining-room door as she spoke.

"And because the other room is such a riot of colour I've kept this one golden-brown."

"Like a beech wood in autumn," said Blanche. "The other is like a midsummer garden—What luck to have all this panelling!" She walked to the window and looked out. "Why, what's this stream?"

"That," said Kirsty, joining her, "is the Hope Water—a very delectable stream."

"I daresay, but aren't you a little too near it? I prophesy that some wet morning you will find the Hope Water coming in to meet you at breakfast."

They went through the wide low-ceilinged hall and up the shallow staircase.

On the first landing Blanche paused. "This is really very pretty," she said approvingly, "the powder-blue carpets and the grey walls. By the way, have you electric light?"

Kirsty smiled at the notion. "Of course not," she said, and

sniffed. "Lamps. Can't you smell them? I always think paraffin oil is such an innocent smell. It goes with dimity and potpourri and faded samplers.

"Idiot! I never heard anyone praise the smell of paraffin before. But you seem determined to be pleased with everything in your country cottage."

"Please, not so superior," Kirsty begged. "This is such a queer uneven house. One is always going up a few steps or down a few steps. 'Upstairs and downstairs and in my lady's chamber'." She opened the door of a room all white and blue, with touches of black. "Mine," she said, looking eagerly at her friend for approval. "I *swithered* between pale grey and orange, and blue and white, but I'm glad I decided on this. I do so love blue: it's a happy colour . . . and a bathroom of my own next door, made out of a dressing-room—all black-and-white-striped like peppermint rock."

"How amusing!" Blanche said, sitting down on the edge of the bath and looking round. "Black and white walls, black and white tiled floor, black and white curtains, and rose-red rugs. This is rather clever of you, Kirsty. It would please my friend Joyce Parker. (You've heard me talk of her?) She has been in India for more than twenty years, and looks it, and when she was last home she told me a most mournful story of a visit she had paid to some people who have a cottage somewhere on the Thames. She had a luxurious bathroom for her own use, snow-white from floor to ceiling, with a window through which the sun streamed, and a cherry tree in full blossom just outside. The cherry tree was the last straw. The poor dear said she had never realized quite how faded and finished she was until that May morning, in that white bathroom with the flaunting cherry tree outside. It quite cast a blight upon her visit."

"Dear me!" said Kirsty. "I never thought before about a becoming bathroom. My cleverness is quite unintentional, but it is a hint to me to be tactful in details—if ever I do entertain."

They went into Kirsty's bedroom and sat down on the wide window seat.

Kirsty pulled aside the chintz curtains.

" 'The warm west-looking window seat'," she quoted, and pointed over the flower garden and across the park. "That, you see, is Phantasy proper. We are actually in the grounds. I suppose this is a sort of dower-house."

Blanche knelt on the window seat to look at the grey house among the trees.

"And who owns the place? Are they pleasant people? Because if they aren't, it won't be very comfortable for you to be so near them, almost in their lap."

"Well," said Kirsty, "there isn't any 'they.' I mean to say the owner is a single man—Colonel Archibald Home."

Blanche pretended to conceal an exaggerated yawn.

"Oh, what a dull tale your life is going to be! I can see the end from the beginning. *Of course* you will marry Colonel Home. What is he like?"

Kirsty flicked the cord of the blind impatiently.

"Blanche, you really are absurd. Vulgar, too. You've read so many silly novels on those constant voyages of yours to and from India that your mind has gone quite mushy . . . I've never seen Colonel Home. He's probably seventy, and crippled with gout. I gather that he has a pretty bad temper from the way the factor spoke, and his desire to make sure that I was a harmless person. I told you that I described myself as a spinster without encumbrances to satisfy him. I don't suppose he will trouble me, and I certainly shan't trouble him. I am too happy simply to be allowed to live in Little Phantasy." She stopped, and after a moment said rather wistfully, "You don't know what all this means to me, you who have always had a home. It's what I've dreamed of all my life, a little plain house in an old-fashioned garden near running water . . . Always my life has been full of rich things—great purring cars, expensive shops, meals with out-of-season dainties, show, glitter. Now I want the exact opposite. I want life at its simplest: plain meals, no smart servants . . ."

Blanche nodded and patted Kirsty's hand.

"I know, and I'm glad your dreams have come true. I believe you are one of the people who really love simplicity . . . By the way, what kind of servants have you? That was a stern virgin who waited on us at luncheon."

"That was Miss Wotherspoon," Kirsty said.

Blanche raised surprised eyebrows. "*Miss* Wotherspoon?"

Kirsty explained. "You must know she isn't an ordinary parlour-maid. She kept house for her brother, who is a minister, until he married, and then she had no home. She feels it a dreadful comedown after being mistress of a manse to come here as parlour-maid. She stipulated that I would call her 'Miss.' I feel as guilty, when I see her wearing a cap, as if I had branded her as a slave."

"Touching, do you find it? No, but seriously, is she an educated woman?"

"I'm afraid not, poor dear. It was only that her brother was clever and educated himself. But Miss Wotherspoon feels that her short reign in a manse so gentled her condition that she can now afford to look down on Easie Orphoot, decent woman—"

"Who is that?"

"Easie is the cook. She has lost three husbands; at least, two died, and one went off to Canada and has sent no address. But, as Miss Wotherspoon says (rather bitterly), 'it has never ca'ed the down off her,' meaning that her losses have left her quite calm and cheerful. Easie is the most imperturbable creature in a house, large, laughing, and easy. And we have a young girl called Nellie Sym, who is supposed to help both Miss Wotherspoon and Easie. Her energy is positively destroying. The way she goes panting about her work reminds me always of a goods train coming out of a tunnel, and her words come out like small explosions, but she is a most willing child. I have nothing to complain of—it sounds a most ridiculous thing to say, but you don't know how envious I was when people I met travelling with Marmee regaled me with tales of their servant troubles. I actually longed to have servant troubles."

"My dear Kirsty, if any one heard you they would refuse to believe you sane. Servant troubles are as little desired by ordinary mortals as a near view of Jerusalem the Golden."

"Yes," said Kirsty, "I know I'm daft. I was daft for a home, and now that I've got it I'm daft with joy. To have had no roots all my life—just a weed floating on the stream: and now to find myself at home, in Scotland! The blind fury that used to fill me when I heard people talking lightly about going to Scotland, and making jokes about the awful weather they were likely to have—mere English people who should have been thankful for the chance of seeing Scotland in any weather! What right had they to go to my Scotland at all when I was shut out?"

Blanche looked at her friend and shook her head.

"What a child you are, Kirsty, in spite of your thirty years! You make me think of my niece Barbara, Isla's girl—I wrote to you about Isla's illness and death."

"Oh, my dear, you did. I was so dreadfully sorry for you, but I didn't like to speak about it first—every one takes trouble differently, and I didn't know whether you would want—"

"I was glad of the letters you wrote me. No, I don't care to talk about things that come very near to me, except to the one or two who understand. There were only the two of us, and distance didn't separate us at all. I can hardly bear the thought of India without Isla's letters. But I was with her at the end, that is something to be thankful for . . . She was only thirty-five, and she had a lot to leave—three small children and her husband. What is to be done with the children I don't know. If only it had been five years later, Tim and I would have been settled at home, and only too glad to have them."

"But what about the father? Doesn't he want them?"

"Oh, poor Alan! He is absolutely lost without Isla. She mothered him as much as she did the children. He is a charming fellow, a most likeable fellow, but he needs somebody to lean up against. He will marry again—I hope he will marry again—but one can hardly expect that he will find another Isla, and I can't bear the thought of Isla's children—However, what I was going to say was that your passion for Scotland is shared by my niece and nephew. Barbara and Specky love Scotland with a quite pathetic intensity, and at present they are living in Clapham with an old governess of ours who has a house on the Common. It is a pleasant, airy place, and they are most comfortable, but they regard having to live in London as a studied insult."

"Oh, poor lambs!" Kirsty cried. "I know exactly what they feel. All those years I was at school at Eastbourne— What ages are they?"

Blanche thought for a moment. "Barbara must be ten, and Specky eight; and Bill—Bad Bill—is between five and six."

"Why is he bad?" Kirsty asked.

"I think because he can't help it. No, I'm not maligning him. He really is rather a terror, old Bill. He passes over his sister and brother like a Juggernaut, leaving them flattened but furious."

Blanche smiled as if at some recollection, and Kirsty said, "But why have they to live in Clapham? Where is Mr. Crawford?"

"Oh, he couldn't endure the house after Isla died. He has got rid of it and stored the furniture, and is now preparing to wander about the world indefinitely. You know what men are! They fly from trouble, while women sit patiently at home learning to bear it, and in Alan Crawford's case the natural selfishness of man is complicated by the artistic temperament. You know he is an artist? No, not very good, but he has a private income . . . But all this is a great waste of precious time. There are so many things I want to know. Tell me, you don't mean to live alone, do you?"

Kirsty stopped twisting the cord of the blind.

"Didn't I tell you? Aunt Fanny is coming to me tomorrow evening—you just miss each other. No, I don't suppose you ever did hear of her. She is my father's only sister: unmarried and about sixty-five, I should think. I haven't seen her since I was a child, but I have always kept somewhere in the back of my mind a recollection of something soft and comfortable and soothing that was Aunt Fanny. She has let her house for a year, and is going to try what living with me is like. I hope she won't be dull. She knits a lot—white woolly things."

"People who knit are never dull," Blanche said wisely. "I'm glad you are to have Aunt Fanny." She rose to look out of the window. "Now tell me, please, the lie of the land. What hills are those I'm looking at?"

Kirsty rose eagerly. "I've only just learned their names. Away over there are the hills round Priorsford—Cademuir, the Black Meldon, Hundleshope. Now come to this window. D'you see that bridge? That's where the Hope Water meets Tweed. That funny little heathery hill is called The Hill o' Men. That plain-faced one is Ratchell. Hasn't it a threadbare look, as if generations of schoolboys had slid down it and worn off all the nap? I'm going to climb them all some day soon. And now, my great treasure"—Kirsty seized her friend's arm in her excitement. "Beyond the bridge, to the right, high on the brae, a grey tower—d'you see? That is Hawkshaw Castle, and there Mary Queen of Scots once stayed. Did you ever know anything so thrilling? It's like living in a ballad . . . Over the top of the trees you can see the chimneys of the village, our village—Muirburn. Netherton, the next village, is a very absurd one, because, being itself about two miles away, it has its church in Muirburn, almost cheek-by-jowl with the other church. It complicates matters very much, for, as Easie puts it, 'They are baith one sex.' Then there is a tiny Episcopal church, St. Mark's, which is worked by the Priorsford rector. So you see there is a plethora of kirks."

"Which will you go to?" Blanche asked.

"Not to the Episcopal, anyway. I have bowed long enough in the House of Rimmon. The choice lies between Muirburn and Netherton. The latter has a pipe-organ and a large and very urbane minister, called the Rev. Norman McCandlish, B.D. He and his wife have already called. The Muirburn church has only a squeaky harmonium, and is altogether much less genteel. But the minister, a long lean lad called Brand, fought all through the War, and he hasn't called on me, so I think I shall go there. Imagine, three ministers and no doctor. They seem to expect one to be more soul-sick than body-sick. The nearest doctor is at Priorsford, nine miles away."

"And what about neighbours?" Blanche asked.

"There are some, I think," Kirsty said vaguely, "but I haven't seen any of them yet. After all, we only got into the house a fortnight ago: there was so much that needed doing. The house is ready for callers now, but I must tackle the garden seriously. I've great schemes . . ." She gave a long sigh of content.

About nine-thirty that evening, sitting by the fire in the lamp-lit drawing-room, Kirsty broke a silence with: "We've talked ourselves almost hoarse—there was need, when the talk must last us two years! But there is something else I want badly to say—and I don't know how to say it."

She left her chair and knelt on the hearthrug before her friend. "I'm so afraid you will think me pushing and impertinent. You won't, will you, Blanche? It's about your sister's children, Barbara and her brothers. The idea leapt into my mind this afternoon, and the more I think of it the better I like it. Why should they stay in Clapham with strangers all summer when I am here with a house and garden that cry aloud for children? Do you know there are bars on the windows in one of the bedrooms?—the one that is called 'The Stable,' because it is papered with pictures of horses. Bad Bill would like them, I'm sure. It would be better for the children to be in the country, and it would make Little Phantasy perfect for me . . . Of course I know you must consult Mr. Crawford, but please, please try to get him to give the plan his favourable consideration."

Mrs. Cunningham at first looked perplexed, then she laughed. "Kirsty, you are sitting there like a wistful dog. I expect all your life you will beg humbly for what no one else would take as a gift. Who but you would want to be bothered by three troublesome children? (You didn't think I was hinting, did you?—for such a thing never entered into my head.) I'm afraid you don't realize what you are offering. It is all very well to see children for an hour when they are at their best; but having them planted on you for months is quite another thing. They have a good governess—quite a young girl but wise—but even so, I'm afraid you'd get very weary of them."

Kirsty gave a laugh that was almost a sob.

"Well, all I ask is a chance to weary of them . . . I've planned it all, indeed I've thought of little else since you told me of them. Barbara will have the primrose room next to mine, and we'll have two little beds put into the Stable for Specky and Bill. The governess will have the pink room. That just fills up the house nicely. Aunt Fanny, of course, has the only really imposing room, being Aunt Fanny . . . Oh, it isn't fair that I should be so happy, and that you, poor Blanche, should have to go away out to India at almost the worst time of year. But you are going to Tim."

"And," said Blanche, "I'll probably get nothing but abuse from Tim for coming. He will be sure to say that he is perfectly well, and that I was an idiot to worry."

At that moment the door opened and Miss Wotherspoon entered, wearing her usual ill-used expression and carrying a kettle. She laid the kettle on the hearth and left the room, appearing again with a tray which she put on a table beside Kirsty. Then she sighed deeply and said:

"Easie says Davidson's forgot the spongecakes the day, and the cart'll not be round again till Tuesday."

Kirsty glanced at the tray.

"Oh well, there's one for tonight, anyway," she said cheerfully. "Goodnight, Miss Wotherspoon. I hope your headache is gone."

Miss Wotherspoon rocked a little as she stood, making her slippers creak dolorously.

"Ma head's worse than ever. I don't suppose I need go to ma bed tonight, for I'll never sleep a wink. But I'm used to suffering . . . Goodnight, Miss Gilmour. Goodnight, Mrs. Cunningham."

"Goodnight, Miss Wotherspoon."

Kirsty shook her head as the door closed behind the gloomy retainer.

"She always says she never sleeps. I wonder."

She put the kettle on the fire, and measured some tea from a little silver tea-caddy into the pot.

"Here's the cup of weak China tea that I know you like at night, Blanche. Anything to eat?"

"No, thank you. The tea is delicious. Aren't you having any?"

"This is what I have every night—a glass of hot water and a sponge-cake. I began it when I came here, and I love it. Priorsford spongecakes are divine. I can hardly forgive Davidson for forgetting to bring them in his cart today."

She took a bit of spongecake and waved her glass at Blanche.

"You can think of me when you are in the Gorgeous East, sitting happily at my own fireside drinking hot water and eating spongecakes and . . ."

"And living for others," Blanche put in dryly.

"Oh well," said Kirsty, and was silent for a minute. "You needn't think," she went on, "that I would consider having the children living for others. It's pure selfishness makes me want them; they would be such a delight to me. Blanche, *I'm going to be so happy.*"

Mrs. Cunningham looked rather sadly at her friend. "My

dear, I hope so. I do hope so. But I'm afraid you think now that you are free and in Scotland that the millennium has come. It hasn't. People can be just as selfish and tiresome and ungrateful in Muirburn as in any other place. Little Phantasy, charming as it is, won't be a serpentless Eden. *Don't* expect too much, and don't try to do too much for people."

"Oh," groaned Kirsty, "what depressing advice!"

Blanche sipped her tea and looked into the fire.

"I don't believe," she said darkly, "that people like being lived for."

CHAPTER 3

> "A pickle plats an' paths an' posies,
> A wheen auld gillyflowers an' roses:
> A ring o' wa's the hale encloses
>   Frae sheep or men:
> An' there the auld housie beeks an' dozes
>   A' by her lane."   R. L. S.

THE Rev. Robert Brand and his sister Rebecca sat at breakfast in the singularly ugly dining-room of Muirburn Manse.

Looking round it, Robert Brand told himself that the only pretty things in it were the April sunshine and the big blue bowl of kingcups that stood in the middle of the table.

There was certainly no beauty in the worn carpet, the horsehair furniture, the solid Victorian sideboard with its burden of salver and fluted biscuit-box grown yellow with constant cleaning, or in the black marble clock on the shabby black mantelpiece. Except for a Shakespeare calendar hung on the bell, the room was almost exactly as it had been six-and-thirty years ago when the Rev. Ebenezer Brand had been inducted to Muirburn and had taken to himself as wife Lizzie Telfer—and very fine they had thought it.

The stipend of Muirburn was small, and Ebenezer Brand, having been entirely without worldly wisdom, had married a girl as penniless as himself; but they had struggled along light-heartedly, pinching and scraping to educate their two children, making jokes about their poverty, finding amusement in the fact that the carpets had lost all pattern and were "like the road." They had been abundantly happy, and when, after a long illness, his wife left him alone, Mr. Brand for six months tried to live without her, "liked it not, and died," and his son Robert reigned in his stead.

Rebecca sat opposite her brother, facing the windows, with the April sun lighting her round red face and mouse-coloured hair. She wore a serviceable but unbecoming brown woollen jumper, and a most uncompromising expression. Lizzie Brand had often looked at her daughter with a ruefully affectionate smile. Where had she come from, this solid, dumpy little person with her practical ways, her sledgehammer common sense, her gift for peeling the gilt from the gingerbread? She was certainly utterly unlike either of her parents, who had been dowered with good looks, wit, and a pretty fancy, but in whom practical talents had been somewhat conspicuously lacking.

Robert was like his father, tall and thin, with a gentle, rather long face and a shy manner. This morning he wore an old tweed coat and a pair of ancient flannel trousers. It was evident from his extremely clean and well-brushed look that he did not belong to the type of clergyman who forgoes the morning tub, contenting himself with "a nice wash," and who spends the greater part of the day frowsting in dressing-gown and slippers.

Rebecca was supping porridge with evident enjoyment.

"These porridge are very good," she said, "though I made them myself. Jeanie has never turned up this morning. I suppose she will say that her mother is ill again, but it's more likely to be the thought of the washing that has kept her away."

Her brother nodded absently as he carried his porridge plate to the sideboard. He took the cup of tea Rebecca had poured out for him, and stood meditatively holding it in his hand.

"Bec," he said, "I've been thinking we might make some changes in the papers we get for the Magazine Club. What's the good of always getting the same ones? Couldn't we take for a change the *Times Literary Supplement*, and the *Spectator* or the *Outlook?*"

Rebecca put down her cup with a cluck of impatience. "Rob, what's the good of talking like that? Do go and sit down in your place, and not stand about in that lost way— Of course, I know you would prefer literary papers, but for one who could read the sort of papers you like thirty get pleasure from the present ones. Can you see old Robert Stark, who pores for hours over *Chambers's Journal*, finding anything to read in the *Times Literary Supplement?* What does he care what new books are being published, or how brilliantly the first article is written? And would you deprive Mrs. Stark of the *Sunday at Home*, which she has read every Sunday for goodness knows how many years, and offer her the *Spectator* instead? You're simply selfish, Rob; that's what you are."

Rob sighed.

Rebecca continued: "And it isn't as if we were at all ill-off for good reading. There's the library at Priorsford; you can bicycle down any day; and you know how good the librarian is about saving you *Blackwood's* and the *Cornhill.* And Merren Strang is always lending you new books—"

"Oh, I know." Rob took a scone and buttered it slowly.

Then he said rather shamefacedly, "A paper like the *Literary Supplement* coming always at the end of the week is something to look forward to."

"Rob, you baby!" Rebecca cried, but her voice softened as she said, "Well, I daresay we need something to look forward to now as much as when we were children. You and I haven't been exactly smothered with the good things of this world. I wonder often what it must feel like to have money to buy things that aren't necessary, only pretty; to be able to renew a house when everything seems to be going done on your hands. And just fancy being able to go into a steamboat office and take a ticket to India and China! Except for the three years that I went to school in Edinburgh I've hardly ever been away from Muirburn. I've just made beds, and swept rooms, and polished floors, and washed dishes, and cooked, and attended church services, and taught in the Sunday School, and collected, and given out magazines—and now I'm thirty-five."

Rob nodded.

"I know. You've had the worst of it, Bec. All the time I was at the War you were having the really hard job at home—watching Mother die. And then Father . . . I wish you had an easier life."

"Oh, I don't know." Rebecca gave her head an odd little self-conscious jerk, a habit with her when she found herself the topic of conversation. "I've a lot to be thankful for. I might have had to live in a mining village or a dismal big town. If I have to stay always in one place I couldn't find a prettier place than Muirburn, and it was nice of the people to elect you in Father's place. Oh, I know you think you ought to have a harder job, but say as you like, Rob, you aren't fit for hard work yet. I doubt if you ever will be. It will take years anyway before you get over the wounds and the gassing. If you insist on trying to get a slum church you'll crock up, that's all you'll do."

"But I feel such a slacker," Rob complained.

"Father was happy here for nearly thirty-five years," his sister reminded him.

"Ah, but Father was different."

"How 'different'?"

"Well," said Rob, "for one thing he was the very man for a country charge. He loved the changes of the seasons: the garden was the delight of his heart; the hills were his friends; what is it Wordsworth says?—'The sounding cataract haunted him like a passion.' And then he could occupy his spare time with writing—it wasn't remunerative work, but it gave him pleasure. And you must remember that he and my mother were bound up in each other, and the purpose of both their lives was fulfilled in the mere fact of being together. That was wonderful and beautiful."

"And very uncommon," Rebecca said, pouring herself out a second cup of tea with a brisk air.

Her brother cast an amused glance at her, but only said, "Well, as you say, there are worse places than Muirburn, and after all we never know what a day may bring forth. Any morning the postman may hand to us a letter that will change the whole course of our existence."

"He passed yesterday without calling," said Rebecca.

Even as she spoke the latch of the garden gate clicked,

and the postman was seen wheeling his red bicycle along the winding narrow drive, brushed by the tassels of the flowering currant, and shaded by the laburnums, green still, and waiting for their golden days.

Rebecca sped to the door, and came back with a letter.

"For me," she said breathlessly. "Rob, it's from London, and it's good paper."

Rob sat with a piece of bread and butter halfway to his mouth while his sister opened it, but in a second she let it fall on the table with a "Tuts" of disgust.

" '*Special offer of Worcester Corsets!*' They oughtn't to be allowed to send such alluring-looking letters as advertisements. I'm positively shaking with excitement."

Robert laughed, and ate his bread and butter.

"Poor old Bec! Never mind, some day it will come."

Rebecca returned to her seat behind the breakfast tray, shaking her head dejectedly.

"Not in Muirburn. Nothing ever happens in Muirburn. The primroses and daffodils come up and flower; then the lupins and the Canterbury bells and the columbine and the roses; then the autumn flowers; then whirling winds and winter again. That's all. The people are always the same—more or less. Children grow up, and the middle-aged ones get old and deaf and blind, and now and again one is carried round the corner to the churchyard, and there is generally a new baby somewhere . . ."

"Dear me, Rebecca, when you babble of flowers things are pretty bad. But something has happened at Muirburn now. Colonel Home has come back to live at Phantasy, and Little Phantasy is let for the first time in the memory of man . . . D'you remember, Bec, what a hero we made of Colonel Home when we were little?"

Rebecca nodded, and her brother went on:

"To us he was no ordinary mortal, he was a knight straight out of a fairy tale—the young laird of Phantasy. I suppose he would be about sixteen when I was six. I know he seemed to be larger than human—tall and straight and blue-eyed. I was convinced that he wore shining suits of mail in his more exalted moments. We used to haunt the gates of Phantasy on the chance of seeing him. There was romance in the very way the heavy gates creaked, and the stone bears seemed to me to guard some fairy pleasaunce. Sometimes—you remember?—he gave us sweeties and a pat on the head, and we almost expired under such a weight of honour. I hate to think of him as middle-aged and maimed and rather poor, such a shining figure as he was to us."

Rebecca sat looking at the bread she was crumbling on her plate.

"Yes," she said, after a minute, "and I hate most to think of him having to let Little Phantasy. The Homes always kept themselves apart, and to have to admit strangers within their very gates must be galling. And if it had been taken by a sensible couple who would have been company for him—this Miss Gilmour is just a girl, I don't believe she is more than five-and-twenty, and—"

"Have you seen her?" Robert asked with interest.

"Yes, she was in Mrs. Dickson's shop on Saturday when I went in. I forgot to tell you. Pretty? Oh yes, I suppose you would call her very pretty, and *beautifully* dressed. Such suitable clothes. A knitted green dress and hat, and hand-knitted grey silk stockings, and grey suede brogues, and long grey gloves. She had a big basket on her arm as if she were playing at housekeeping, and she has that silly way of going on in a shop—you know —'Now, suppose I take this and this' Mrs. Dickson, under the impression that her advice was being asked, got quite coy and kept saying, 'Oh, I'm sure I don't know. It's for you to say—' But she seems a friendly sort of girl. She looked at me as though she would like to speak, but I kept well back among the onions and the paraffin barrels. When she went out Mrs. Dickson was full of her; I could hardly get out of the shop. She asked, if we had called yet (knowing full well we hadn't!) and added, rather rebukatively, that Mr. McCandlish had called at once. Poor Mrs. Dickson! She is very anxious that we should lure this wealthy newcomer to the church. As if we had any chance against Netherton with its organ and its genteel society!"

"I don't see why you should say that," Rob complained. "Ours is a pretty little church, and I don't see anything wrong with the harmonium. I don't say I'm much of a preacher, but I'm no worse than McCandlish."

Rebecca smiled pityingly at her brother.

"My dear," she said, "you are a much better preacher than Mr. McCandlish (though Mrs. Stark complains that you stop much too suddenly, 'like a cairt cowpin'), but you can never hope to compete with him, he has such *affable teeth*. I expect his smile and his jovial manner have already made a deep impression on Miss Gilmour, and she will immediately stumble into his fold—unless, as is most likely, she is an Episcopalian."

"Oh well," Robert Brand shrugged his shoulders, and having finished his breakfast got up to go to his study. He stopped at the door.

"By the way, I forgot to tell you that I met Lady Carruthers yesterday, and she told me a long story about some scheme she is involved in, something Russian, I gathered, but not the Famine. Anyway, she ended by asking me to subscribe. I suppose we must?"

Rebecca, who had begun to collect the breakfast dishes, stopped with a porridge plate in her hand, and said in tones of concentrated fury, "*That woman!* What imbecile scheme has she got into her head now? Probably to send gramophones to soothe the savage breasts of the Bolshevists! We can't give less than one pound. Oh, it's too bad, Rob. It will have to come off what I had saved up for your new suit. That's the worst of being poor, you can't refuse. Rich people would refuse without a thought, or give her five shillings and tell her to go away, but we can't."

"Never mind, Bec. My suit isn't so very green, and, anyway, who cares?"

"And we need coals," Rebecca went on. "I thought I could make them last till May, but they won't, and coals are such a ransom here. But I don't grudge the coals as I grudge one pound to Lady Carruthers . . . The last time she came I had been spring cleaning and starching curtains till my hands were stiff, and she sat there wasting my time, and then had the impertinence to tell me that what I needed was to get on to the Higher Plane."

Robert sat down on the arm of the sofa and laughed aloud, while Rebecca with a circular swoop collected the butter, the marmalade, and a plate of scones.

"Stop laughing, Rob. There's little to laugh at. This week's begun badly with that woman and coals, and a big washing and Jeanie not turning up. I'd better just set on the boiler fire and start myself. Rob, I do try to be as saving as I can, but what's the good of saving? If I could only make some money! To think of Merren Strang being able to make money by writing! I'm sure you might try, Rob. You're almost sure to have inherited it from Father, and—"

Rob laughed again and said, " 'Treason is not inherited, my lord,' nor, I fear, is the art of writing. Besides, I don't remember that Father ever made any money to speak of."

"Oh no," Rebecca said hopelessly, "we're not the kind of people that ever could make money."

She went over to the fireplace to pull the daily leaf off the calendar.

"This is Holy Week," she announced. "St. Mark's people will be busy. There won't be an arum lily left in the district when they've done decorating that little church of theirs. I wonder who makes up these calendars." She tweaked off the leaf impatiently. "They have the most inappropriate quotations. For weeks I've had nothing but remarks about kings—'Comets usher forth the death of kings,' and such like, things that can interest no one but the Royal Family."

"What's the one for today?" Robert asked.

His sister held it out to him with a twinkle in her small grey eyes.

" 'Sweet are the uses of adversity'," she repeated, and the brother and sister laughed together before separating to their several duties.

CHAPTER 4

> "She is an excellent sweet lady; . . . and out of
> all suspicion she is virtuous."
>
> *Much Ado about Nothing*

IF LIFE had been pursuing its usual comfortable course with Miss Fanny Gilmour when her niece's letter arrived asking her to make her home at Little Phantasy, it is doubtful whether she would ever have considered the proposal for a moment.

For thirty years—since the death of her parents—she had lived placidly in her own house, Harelaw Lodge, in Harelaw village, tended by a cook who had been in the Gilmour family for nearly fifty years, a housemaid who had been almost as long, a parlour-maid who was regarded as quite juvenile at forty-five, and a groom-gardener who was a teetotaller, a non-smoker, and an elder in the church. Thus buttressed and supported, Miss Fanny had listened calmly to the tales people brought to her about their domestic trials, thanking kind heaven for her own blessed state.

But a sudden and swift decay fell on the household at the Lodge. Janet, the cook, took influenza and died; Mary, the housemaid, was seized with neuritis, and retired on a pension; Agnes, the parlour-maid, went to keep house for an uncle who had money to leave; and James Smith, the groom-gardener, surprised and disgusted his mistress by marrying, at the age of fifty-two, a girl of one-and-twenty, and sailing for Canada.

"If the foundations be destroyed, what shall the righteous do?"

Miss Fanny, terrified by the tales she read daily in the newspapers, dared not engage new servants, who would probably give faked references and decamp in the middle of the night with all her valuables. Confused and frightened as a lost lamb, she could only shut up her once so safe and comfortable house and fly for refuge to a fashionable hydropathic.

It was in this unhomely place, surrounded by strangers loud in voice and manner (they might almost have spoken a different language, so alien did they seem to the gentle old lady), stranded and lonely, that Kirsty's letter reached her. No wonder that the thought of Little Phantasy and a home with her own niece, Andrew's girl, seemed safe and sweet—a haven, she called it to herself.

Miss Fanny had now been a week in her haven, and sitting this afternoon by a bright fire (the April wind was cold), knitting one fleecy white shawl and wrapped in several others, she smiled happily to herself. She was really a very contented woman. Given a comfortable chair well out of draughts, a bright fire, good regular meals, plenty of light but pure literature for weekdays and the life of a missionary or philanthropist for the Sabbath, she asked little more of life. All these she had found at Little Phantasy.

For the rest, she thought her niece a bright creature, if somewhat given to rash speaking; her bedroom looked south and was the largest in the house, the cook seemed to be capable and amiable, and Miss Wotherspoon was a superior sort of woman with sound ideas about church attendance and the keeping of the Sabbath.

Miss Fanny was now sixty-five, and had, on the whole, enjoyed her life very much. She had a horror of clever books, so she had never had her feelings harrowed by reading of the "frustrated" lives of spinsters, and had no idea that she ought to be miserable. She had never even heard of Freud. The only thing that troubled her about life was the thought of having to leave it. Death was a fact that she could not reconcile herself to: "a step in the Dark," she called it sadly. She knew well that this fear was very unbecoming in a professing Christian, and she strove hard to overcome it by reading many hymns and comforting booklets. She was reading one now, a little white and gold thing called *Gleams from the City*.

Kirsty had come in with her hands full of flowers, and was chattering gaily while she arranged them.

She was very pretty, Miss Fanny thought, this niece of hers, pleasant to look at and to listen to. Miss Fanny was not paying much attention to what she was saying, nor was she paying much attention to the good words in the little book; she was knitting mechanically, and thinking that tea would soon be coming in, and vaguely hoping that Easie had baked some of her delicious currant scones. If it had been Harelaw someone would probably have dropped in to tea; she missed her friends dropping in, but one can't have everything.

"Muirburn people are in no great hurry to call on newcomers," Kirsty said suddenly, as if she had read her aunt's thoughts. "So far no one has called but one minister and his one wife. Perhaps this isn't a sociable neighbourhood. I'm sure I shan't mind. When the children come I shan't have time to give a thought to neighbours."

The children! Miss Fanny had forgotten about the menace which hung over the peace and comfort of Little Phantasy. To her the thought of three wild creatures let loose in the quiet household brought no rapture. Of course it was sad that they had lost their mother. The father, Kirsty had told her, was going to travel and get over his grief; surely it would have been better if he had stayed at home and looked after his children, rather than fling them in this haphazard way into the arms of a stranger, while he fled to far seas to seek consolation.

She was musing thus when Kirsty, her eyes on the outside world, cried: "A man coming down the drive—a caller. Who can it be?" and in a minute Miss Wotherspoon answered the question by announcing in the tone of one breaking news of the worst kind—"Colonel Home."

It may be said at once that Colonel Home was not there without great effort. He knew that he must call some time or other on his new tenant, but the disagreeable duty had been put off from day to day. To tell the truth, he had been something less than pleased when his factor had broken to him the fact that Little Phantasy was let to a single woman who, when seen in the flesh, turned out to be quite young and exceedingly pretty, and he had resolved to shun her like the plague. He would call once—courtesy demanded it; he would ask her if the house were to her liking, and tell her to see the factor about anything she wanted; he would send her some game occasionally. What more could be expected from a morose bachelor landlord?

Kirsty by this time knew that Colonel Home was not, as she had assured Blanche Cunningham, "seventy and crippled by gout." She had made friends with some of the village people, and had heard here and there a significant sentence which had given her a fairly accurate idea of her landlord. She thought it only too probable that as tenant of Little Phantasy he regarded her with deep distaste, and a demure smile turned up the corners of her mouth as she rose to greet him.

Miss Fanny sincerely admired her niece that afternoon. She herself belonged to a type that simpered before men when they were affable, and sat in frightened silence when they were difficult. Colonel Home, haggard and rather grim, barking out abrupt sentences, and disagreeing at every point where disagreement was possible, was certainly no lady's man, and made Miss Fanny draw her shawls nervously round her for protection.

But Kirsty made the tea, talking and laughing in the easiest way. She was, her aunt noticed, a most adroit hostess. Many subjects were discussed in the way strangers casually discuss subjects over the teacups, epoch-making events were passed over with a word, and whenever the visitor appeared to be going to get fractious Kirsty glided serenely to something else.

"Quite a woman of the world," said Miss Fanny to herself.

Only once did she feel uncomfortable. The talk had turned on the manners of modern youth, which Colonel Home considered deplorable.

"Yes," said Kirsty musingly, the sunlight bright on her hair, both hands clasped round one knee. "Yes, I suppose they are deplorable, terribly off-hand and casual. And such meaningless slang! And yet," she turned grave green eyes on the visitor, "when the modern youth makes love in the meaningless slang, don't you think it means as much to him and to the girl as the most florid declaration or the most delicate languishments? 'Old bean' is perhaps what his lips say, but his heart is singing, '*Thou art all fair, my beloved; thou hast doves' eyes*.'"

To quote the Song of Solomon to a gentleman! It seemed to Miss Fanny the height of indelicacy. She made up her mind to speak to Kirsty about it, and also about hugging her knee in that unladylike way. It all came, she was afraid, from roving about the world with a flighty stepmother.

She was glad when the conversation was interrupted by the entrance of Miss Wotherspoon with a telegram, which she handed to Kirsty.

Telegrams were almost as alarming as bombs to Miss Fanny; she trembled like an aspen when she had to open one, and she noted with amazement the careless way Kirsty glanced at the contents of this one.

"From Mr. Crawford," she said. "He suggests coming here tomorrow to talk over the plans about the children."

She looked at her landlord; then she addressed her aunt.

"Do you think, Aunt Fanny, that this is an auspicious moment to break it to Colonel Home about the children?"

Miss Fanny gave a scared look at the visitor and retreated without a word into her shawls.

Kirsty bent forward earnestly.

"I'm not sure that I've played fair with you, Colonel Home. When I took the house I told the factor I was a spinster, and I'm afraid he let me have it because I sounded a quiet tenant. But things have changed—No, don't look so startled, I only mean that I've offered to take charge of three children for the summer. Would it bore you to hear about it? Their mother died some months ago—she was the sister of a great friend of mine—and the poor lambs are boarded in Clapham because there are no relations in this country to take them—"

"What about their father?" Colonel Home asked. "Isn't he alive?"

"Oh yes," said Miss Fanny, suddenly emerging from her shawls.

"He's alive," said Kirsty, "but very broken, you know. So he is going away to travel or take a voyage or something—"

As her landlord made no comment she went on:

"Perhaps I ought to have asked your permission, but I was so fearfully keen to get them. It isn't quite fixed yet, but this is a wire from Mr. Crawford (that's the father) saying he will come here tomorrow and talk it over. I think he leaves England next week."

"Does he?" said Colonel Home drily.

"So—you don't really object to children being here, do you?"

"As to that, I don't suppose they'll bother me, but keep them out of the woods, please, or there will be rows with the keepers."

"Oh yes," Kirsty promised blithely. "Out of the woods in case of traps, and out of the Hope Water in case of drowning—you and I will be kept busy, Aunt Fanny."

Miss Fanny sighed resignedly, and Colonel Home said:

"As a matter of fact I don't think there has ever been a lot of children at Phantasy. I was an only child, my father was an only child, and so on—away back. But I should think it would be quite a good place for children. I know I was very happy, only child as I was."

"Oh, I'm not afraid of them not being able to amuse themselves," Kirsty assured him. "They are country children, and I should think the joy of being in Scotland and away from London would be almost enough for them. And then there is this jolly garden, and the water, and the donkey. Are there any children round about they could play with?"

Colonel Home thought for a moment. "I don't believe there are," he said at last; "it's a very middle-aged neighbourhood. I'm afraid, Miss Gilmour, you've let yourself in for an uncommonly dull time here."

"That's what I want," said Kirsty, and, seeing his incredulous look, she added: "No, I'm not posing. I've always lived among a great many people in so-called gay places, and I want to see what a really quiet country life is like. So far I haven't seen any of the inhabitants of Muirburn except the Rev. Norman McCandlish."

"You've seen him, have you?" said Colonel Home.

Kirsty waited for further comment, and when none seemed to be forthcoming, continued: "Who else is there to see?"

Colonel Home stared at the fire and appeared to be thinking deeply.

"There's young Brand," he said, "the other minister, and his sister. They've been here all their lives, for their father was minister of Muirburn. And the Anthony Hays at Cherrytrees. What? Yes, it's a nice name for a place . . . And some people bought Edmonston Hall some time ago—Carruthers is the name, the man was knighted in the war; they roll in money. I've never seen them . . . And that's about all the people around Muirburn that are ever at home, except of course Mrs. Strang at Hopewaterfoot. She's a connection of mine through my mother. Her boy was in my battalion. He was killed. Her husband was killed in the Boer War. She writes books."

"Oh!" cried Kirsty, "this *is* interesting! Do you hear, Aunt Fanny? Someone who writes books living quite near. What kind of books does she write? Novels?"

"I believe so." Colonel Home rose to his feet in a determined manner as if to indicate that nothing more was to be got out of him. As a matter of fact, he felt very satisfied with his visit. He had stayed nearly an hour, and it had not been as bad as he had expected. His tenant seemed quite an intelligent young woman, and, as far as he could judge, would not be likely to obtrude herself on his time or attention. He liked the frightened lady in the fleecy shawls, and altogether it might have been much worse. So he limped through the garden, basking in the peace that the doing of a disagreeable duty brings.

Kirsty looked after him rather sadly.

"So that's your landlord, Kirsty," said Miss Fanny.

"Poor soul," said Kirsty.

Miss Fanny looked rather shocked. "Of course he's lame,"

she said, "but still—"

"That's the least of it," Kirsty said.

When Miss Fanny failed to understand she asked no questions but turned her thoughts to something else. She now mused on the coming of Mr. Crawford, and asked suddenly:

"Will he stay the night?"

"Who? Colonel Home?"

"Oh no, Mr. Crawford. Didn't you say he was coming tomorrow?"

"Yes, I expect he will stay the night. I must remember to tell Miss Wotherspoon to get a room ready. We must put our best foot forward, and send him away with a good impression of Little Phantasy. It's lucky you are here to give the place an air of respectability. Colonel Home looked quite reassured when he saw you."

"Perhaps," said Miss Fanny, as she took up her knitting, "but I would have enjoyed Easie's scones better without him. He's not what I call a pleasant man."

CHAPTER 5

"There's nothing so queer in this world as folk."
An Old Wife's Tale

MR. CRAWFORD arrived the next day in time for luncheon.

Easie in the kitchen, resting after her labours in cooking and dishing an excellent meal, asked Miss Wotherspoon if the guest had seemed to enjoy it.

" 'Deed did he," was the reply she got.

"Weel, we're getting on," said Easie. "The Laird yesterday, and Mr. Crawford the day! It's hertsome, and Miss Kirsty's a braw lass."

Miss Wotherspoon drew down her long upper lip as she laid a dish of custard on the table.

"Some folks' minds are aye running on the one subject," she observed acidly.

Easie was unabashed.

"This yin lost his wife no lang syne," she said cheerfully.

Miss Wotherspoon sniffed. "Ye wadna think it to look at him. He's as brisk as a bee. Now the Laird might have lost half a dozen by the look of him."

"Oh ay, he's a soor-lookin' cratur," said Easie. "But a body canna be aye mournin'. We've got to bear our troubles and keep a bright face."

"Ay, and it's weel kent that to some folk losing a husband is no worse than a dinnle on the elbow," Miss Wotherspoon observed drily.

Miss Wotherspoon was consistently provocative, but

Easie refused to fight. Now she only gave a fat, good-natured laugh and said:

"Weel, c'wa' and get yer denner. Nellie's been waitin' on us for the last ten minutes—"

Miss Fanny was delighted with Mr. Crawford. He was exactly the kind of man she liked. He picked up her ball of wool and sat down beside her, and in a few minutes she was telling him all about Harelaw—the comfort of it, the central heating, the way the windows fitted, the never-failing supply of hot water. Of Janet the cook she told him, and her sudden call; of Mary the housemaid and her neuritis; of the unexpected worldly-mindedness of Agnes the parlour-maid; of the disappointing lapse from sanity of James Smith the groom-gardener. It was long since Miss Fanny had found such a good listener.

"What a doctor he would have made," she thought regretfully, "or what a minister!"

There was certainly something very engaging about Alan Crawford. He had such a kind, interested way of talking to every one. He deserved to be popular, for he had the gift of being able to say nice things that were also true; he had the knack of finding some attractive trait in unattractive people and bringing it into notice. And he was exceedingly good to look at.

It was astonishing how quickly he made himself at home at Little Phantasy. He was hardly in the house when he was walking about exclaiming over this treasure and that. He noticed at once all the things Kirsty was most proud of, and complimented her upon her taste. Never was there a more appreciative guest.

In half an hour Kirsty and her aunt felt as if they had known him all their lives. Before luncheon was over he was chaffing Miss Fanny about the number of her shawls, and that timid spinster was bridling like a Victorian maid.

When Miss Fanny settled herself by the fire to rest, Kirsty took her guest to explore the gardens. If he had been delighted with the house, his enthusiasm about the surroundings was ecstasy.

"Tell me the names of the hills," he said, "so that I can say them over to myself when I'm at the other end of the world. That noble fellow is Cardon, didn't you say?"

So Kirsty, nothing loth, named over the heights that guarded Priorsford—Cademuir, Hundleshope, the Black Meldon.

"And those are our own Muirburn hills—Ratchell, so bare and rubbed-looking, and Treherna leaning against it, and Hill o' Men, and big, hump-backed, solemn Cardon. There's a rhyme an old woman said to me about the Hills. I wonder if I can remember it? It's something like this:

> Bonnington lakes and Crookston cakes,
> Cademuir and the Wrae;
> Hungry, hungry Hundleshope,
> An' scawed Bell's Brae.

And there's another about the farms round here:

> Glenkirk an' Glencotho,
> The Mains o' Kilbucho,
> Blendewing an' the Raw,

Mitchell-hill an' the Shaw,
There's a hole abune Thriepland wud haud them a'."

Kirsty said her rhymes with triumph, and Alan Crawford was delighted.

"Jolly they sound, these placenames. Pictish some of them. They remain while the generations crawl about a little and are gone. I say, this is a jolly stream—what d'you call it? The Hope Water. That's jolly too. Won't Specky be out of his mind with delight when he sees it? He'll want to fish all day, Miss Gilmour. You never saw such a patient little chap. He never gives up, no matter how little success he meets with."

"I want to ask," said Kirsty, "why you call him Specky. Surely that isn't his christened name?"

"No." Mr. Crawford laughed. "His christened name is John Montgomery, but when he was quite small he developed astigmatism in one eye and they made him wear spectacles, and he called himself Specky. He won't have to wear them when he grows up, that's one blessing but they've ruined his looks as a child—and he's a good-looking little chap."

It appeared that Kirsty need have had no apprehension about Mr. Crawford not allowing his children to come to Little Phantasy. From the first he seemed to take it for granted that the thing was settled.

Kirsty found him quite surprisingly expansive. He told her much about the children, more about himself, and a good deal about his wife, whom he called "my poor girl." Kirsty was not at all sure that had she died and left a husband she would have liked him to allude to her as "my poor girl."

"Anyway," she thought, "it's better than the fat man I sat next to at meals on the *Caledonia*, who talked of 'my late wife.' But I'm sure the best thing is not to talk at all, just think."

They decided together where would be the best spot to erect a swing, and what hours the children should spend over lessons, and Kirsty said she was sure Mr. Crawford would like to see the rooms prepared for them.

They went first to the Stable, complete now with two little white beds with gay counterpanes.

"This is where the boys will sleep," Kirsty said "You see they look out on Ratchell Hill."

"Bill will want to climb that," said Bill's father. "He always wants to see over the other side." He walked over to the window and stood for a minute. "They'll fall asleep to the sound of the Hope Water—I haven't tried to thank you, Miss Gilmour. There is nothing I can say; your kindness is beyond words. Only—if you knew what it means to me to think of them here . . ."

"Dear sir," said Kirsty, "it is I who ought to say thank you. If you knew what it means to me, the thought of having children in the house! All I ask is that you will spare them to me as long as you can . . . Now I'll show you Barbara's room. You see they are all quite near each other, and near the governess . . . Oh, I do hope they will be happy."

"They are lucky little beggars. I shall envy them many a time . . . Would it be too much to ask you to write to me sometimes and give me news of them? Miss Carter always sends me bulletins about their health and behaviour, and Barbara writes quite a decent letter, but I would like to hear your account of them. You will? I say, that is good of you. I wonder what you will make of old Bill? Barbara and Specky are naturally quite gentle and amenable to reason, but Bill can be a holy terror when he likes."

"Poor Bad Bill," said Kirsty.

Two days later Kirsty began a letter to Blanche Cunningham:

". . . I have waited to write till I could collect some news, for I know that you would consider details about my gardening (my daily occupation) merely dull. Now I can tell you about Aunt Fanny, give my first impressions of my landlord, and describe to you the visit of your brother-in-law, Mr. Alan Crawford.

"First, Aunt Fanny. Blanche, she's a *dear.* If I could have had my pick of a world of elderly aunts I am sure I would have chosen her. She might be described as a perfect specimen in the Aunt World. (I am remembering how when we were once buying rugs the man said as he fondly stroked a choice one, 'I assure you, madam, in the Rug World we consider this an almost perfect piece.' What a delicious place a Rug World must be, so soft and warm and cosy!) But to continue, Aunt Fanny is the sort of person that makes a room look comfortable. Only a few people have the gift. I don't in the least know how it is done, but I have known people who could sit in a railway waiting-room or an hotel drawing-room, and by the mere fact of their presence make the place look home-like: haven't you?

It has something to do with being elderly and rather fat and fond of knitting. I thought the drawing-room at Little Phantasy nearly perfect (you know how you laughed my pride in it!), but you can't imagine what a difference it is to go into it now and find a pretty, pink-cheeked old lady in a striped grey silk dress and layers of white shawls—if she wears so many in spring, in winter she will be more like some round woolly animal than an aunt—sitting in the big armchair with the 'lugs,' a small table beside her with a collection of tortoiseshell spectacles, for she continually loses them, a bottle of smelling-salts in case she feels faint (she is perfectly healthy), and a pile of small religious books which she reads diligently. She also keeps a pile of storybooks beside her. She is very particular about her fiction, and in these days it is difficult to supply her with the sort of book she likes. To begin with, it must be 'nice,' that is to say, it mustn't discuss any unsavoury subject; it must of course end well, for Aunt Fanny is easily depressed; but it must also begin well, for she cannot endure those modern books which launch the reader into unknown seas, without chart or compass. She likes the sort of book that begins: 'The Surbiton family sat together in the drawing-room of The Laurels one stormy December night. Mrs. Surbiton, a stout, sweet-faced woman of about sixty summers, chatted pleasantly with her husband, a well-preserved man of seventy. Janetta, the eldest daughter, sat at the piano . . .' and so on and so on.

"Then she knows where she is, and can keep a firm grip of the characters until they are all married or dead.

"She likes me to read the books that she is reading, so that we can compare notes. At present we have left this restless age, and have taken a long step backwards into *The Wide Wide World*. It was in a box of childish belongings of my own that I have always clung to. I had forgotten how exciting it is. D'you remember when Miss Fortune dyed all Ellen's white stockings a dirty grey? And oh! the delicious priggishness of Mr. John!

"I do enjoy these evenings. There is something so restful about the way Aunt Fanny's conversation flows on, and you would laugh to see us discuss together glasses of hot water and Priorsford spongecakes at nine-thirty of the clock!

"She is funny—Aunt Fanny, I mean. On the principle that what the eyes do not see the heart does not grieve over she refuses to hear of, or think of, or read of anything sad or terrible. A picture of starving children she passes over with, 'Yes, dear, but we'll hope it isn't true.' And when I tell her something in the papers that has shocked me she says, 'Try not to think about it.' It is certainly one way of getting comfortably through the world. I'm afraid I worry her a good deal. It is odd that I, who have always been considered by myself (and by you) the dowdiest and dullest of Victorians, am now regarded as quite dashingly Georgian. She positively shrinks into her shawls at my indelicate remarks.

"Well, this has been a red-letter week in our lives—our landlord has been to call!

"He isn't as old as I thought he was—a little over forty, perhaps, rather handsome in a gaunt way, with fierce blue eyes. He is the very *angriest* man I ever came across. There is hardly one thing happening on the face of this globe that doesn't simply infuriate him. I think he is one of those people who care almost too passionately for their country, and who are bound to suffer when they see things ambling placidly to the dogs. He has been a soldier all his life, and has been pretty nearly all over the place, and the British Empire stands to him before everything. For all the world he is like *Blackwood's Magazine* walking about on two feet: alas, no, only on one foot; he was terribly wounded in the War. I think most of his friends are gone, and he rather wonders why he remains behind; for him 'nothing is left remarkable beneath the visiting moon.' I know you object to me finding people 'touching,' but I did feel heart-sorry for Colonel Home.

("Talking of my habit of finding pathos in things, I came across a sentence in one of Alice Meynell's essays which you will enjoy. She objects strongly to some 'fugitive writer' saying that he found pathos in Christopher Sly, and finishes: 'And Lepidus, who loves to wonder, can have no better subject for his admiration than the pathos of the time. It is bred now of your mud by the operation of your sun. 'Tis a strange serpent, and the tears of it are wet.' ! !)

"If you had been here when my landlord called you would have realized the utter absurdity of your prophecy. The idea of this angry soldier falling in love with me is ludicrous in the extreme. He only called because his stern sense of duty sent him, and when he thought he had stayed long enough, he went with the alacrity with which one escapes from the dentist's chair. He scared Aunt Fanny almost into fits; he is what Easie calls 'a soor-lookin' customer,' but he has a sudden and rather delightful smile. So much for Colonel Home . . .

"Your brother-in-law has just left us. He wired that he was in Edinburgh and would like to come out, and of course we were delighted to see him.

"You didn't prepare us for such good looks. Aunt Fanny, who, like all spinster ladies, loves a man, has been remarking at intervals on the beautiful way his head is set on his shoulders.

"He is certainly, as you said, very likeable, and so extraordinarily easy to know. We couldn't have had a more appreciative visitor, and he seemed to like the thought of the children being at Little Phantasy. He is perhaps a little bit too facile, but he won the hearts of Aunt Fanny, Easie Orphoot, Nellie, and even that grim virgin, Miss Wotherspoon, at the first time of asking, so to speak. It is a blessing, for Aunt Fanny and Miss Wotherspoon are none too pleased at the thought of the children coming; but now when the poor things are tiresome and naughty (as they are bound to be sometimes) I hope they will remember what a delightful father they have and forgive them. It is absurd that such a boyish person should be the father of quite big children. He seemed so fond of them, and spoke so feelingly about them, that I couldn't help wondering how he could go away and leave them for eight months. But men are queer.

"My dear, everything is ready for the children. The little beds look so expectant, and there is a big box of toys and picture books for them to dive into if they are inclined to be lonesome at first. They come on Tuesday, by the ten train from Euston. I shall write you after they arrive.

"I was very glad to get your letter from Port Said, but sorry you found the passengers such a boring lot. Consider, though, that it is hardly the moment for high spirits, the voyage out to India in the hot weather. I daresay by this time you have made many friends—You will be nearly there by now, and I shall wait anxiously for news of Tim. If you find him better you won't mind the 'abuse' you so confidently expected—as if Tim ever did anything but lie at your feet!

"Miss Wotherspoon continues to have headaches when anything happens to put her out. Nothing puts out Easie. I find the kitchen has a fatal fascination for me with that woman in it. Her jests sometimes almost border on the Rabelaisian; but with two such ladies in the house as Aunt Fanny and Miss Wotherspoon I feel can stand a somewhat broad humour. Nellie still pants and puffs like a shunting train over her work. I came in muddy the other day, and she rushed for a brush and volunteered to tidy me up. I felt exactly like a horse as I stood patiently while Nellie 'shushed' under her breath as she brushed, directing me at intervals to 'Stand still, will ye!'

"I may as well confess I haven't begun to live for others yet; indeed there seems little opportunity for such a thing in Muirburn. I've made friends with some of the people in the village; they are tolerant of me, but not excessively welcome.

"But oh, Blanche, such catkins by the Hope Water, and curly young bracken on the hillsides!—Yours,

"KIRSTY."

CHAPTER 6

"O most gentle pulpiter!"
As You Like It

THE MANSE at Netherton was a striking contrast to the Muirburn Manse. The Brands existed in a spate of advanced shabbiness; the McCandlishes were grand beyond belief, with rich carpets, brocade curtains, heavily carved and most solid furniture; the very window blinds were trimmed about a yard deep with lace.

The father of the Rev. Norman McCandlish had not been a poor scholar but a rich Dundee manufacturer, who had always felt it to be a marked condescension on the part of his son to choose to be a minister of the Gospel. It was such a poorly paid job, with very little to offer an ambitious young man in the way of advancement.

It would be difficult to say what had turned young Norman's mind to the Church, for, though he had what may be described as a gentlemanly approbation of religion, he was hardly conscious of a "call." But in many ways he made a very successful minister. He had a fine voice, a good presence, an urbane manner, and a reverence for things as they have always been, and Netherton, which owned an absurdly large manse in an absurdly large garden, and needed someone with a large private income, had never regretted its choice.

Mrs. McCandlish was a genteel little person with short legs, rather a pretty face, and most tidily done hair. Her behaviour was circumspect to a degree. Never was there such a miracle of discretion as the wife of the minister of Netherton. Scandal died in her presence, slain by the prim set of her mouth as she changed the subject. Even mere good-natured neighbourly interest was dismayed by her high ideal of what constituted conversation, and as a consequence she was not very popular at local tea-parties, where she was apt to prove something of a killjoy.

She always spoke of her husband as "Mr. McCandlish."

She had a fortune of her own.

On the day of which I write the McCandlishes walked in their garden in the cool of the evening. Mr. McCandlish was genuinely fond of growing flowers, and inordinately proud of his rock garden, which he had largely made himself, and which would soon be at its best. Every day in this May month he spent at least an hour brooding like a Providence over each little clinging plant. The herbaceous borders promised well too, the lawns were shorn to a velvet smoothness, and the owner, wearing a light grey suit, and a very white, very high clerical collar, and smoking an excellent cigar, looked (and felt) the picture of a prosperous and contented country minister.

"Lovely evening, Aggie," he said, complacently surveying his domain.

"Lovely, Norman! As warm as June." Mrs. McCandlish took a large mouthful of each word, putting, as it were, every word into italics.

Her husband removed his cigar from his mouth, looked at it affectionately, and said, "The little place looks well, Aggie."

"Indeed, yes. I am glad you insisted on getting those large

stone vases. I thought them an extravagance at the time, but they really look very well." She folded her hands in front of her. "In another fortnight we shall be looking our best, and we must be thinking of sending out invitations for the Garden Party."

The minister nodded. "Ah yes, our annual Garden Party."

Netherton Manse Garden Party was one of the features of the summer season in the district. When you received your invitation you knew that summer had really come, and that the Manse lupins were now at their best.

"Order a good day, Aggie," the minister jocularly suggested, and then looked suddenly grave as if he felt he had not spoken in the best of taste. "We have no control of the weather," he finished rather obviously.

"As a rule we are very fortunate," his wife said placidly. "June is generally a dry month . . . I am just wondering, Norman, if we ought not to have it purveyed this year? From Priorsford, or even from Edinburgh. As you know, up till now we have always prepared everything in the house, with a little outside assistance, but since we got the car we have extended our calling-list wonderfully. We owe hospitality to quite a number of people in Priorsford—all motor people—and I'm sure they would appreciate our little party. But if we have it on a larger scale I would not like to attempt the refreshments. We would need to have several kinds of sandwiches, and a variety of small cakes, and even ices. And we would need extra waiting, everything a little more elaborate. The question is whether it would not be better to have it all done from Edinburgh."

"I'm sure," put in her husband, "Priorsford cakes are hard

to beat."

"Oh yes, Priorsford in some ways is just as good as Edinburgh, and certainly less expensive; but we are all so accustomed to Priorsford cakes that it would be more of a treat to get Edinburgh ones. And McVitties' puts a little flag on each plate of sandwiches, naming each variety, and that is so *chic*."

As Mrs. McCandlish made this long speech she was stepping sedately towards the house by her husband's side, while he smoked, and nodded, and looked at the flowers. Now she paused, standing on the smooth turf, and looked at the house, trying as it were to see it through the eyes of the guests to be, especially the new friends in Priorsford.

Surely a house to be proud of! The Manse itself had been freshly *harled* in the early spring, and looked almost painfully clean; every lace-trimmed blind hung with mathematical precision; the sash curtains (Mrs. McCandlish had a weakness for sash curtains) were crisp and fresh; the conservatory, which at their own expense they had built on to the drawing-room, was glowing with colour.

Mrs. McCandlish nodded her head gently in approbation.

"A lovely night," said Mr. McCandlish, and threw away the stump of his cigar. The scent of it hung on the still air as the minister and his wife entered the drawing-room by the conservatory.

Mrs. McCandlish sat down on a small hard chair. All the other chairs and the large chesterfield had fat down cushions which needed to be plumped up every time they were sat upon, and she did not care to disarrange them. Her husband, for the same reason, sat on the piano stool.

It was rather like a show drawing-room in a furniture shop. One almost expected to see the price-ticket attached to each article. The fireplace glittered with the latest thing in steel fittings. The whitest and furriest of rugs lay here and there on the thick pile carpet. The wallpaper was pale blue, and looked like watered silk. Large majestic vases stood about. One or two books, obviously wedding presents, lay on polished tables. Mrs. McCandlish did not care for many books lying about—nothing, she thought, gave a room such a littered look; so such volumes as the house contained were confined strictly to the study, where smoking was also allowed. The drawing-room was seldom used, except to impress visitors. At intervals the minister and his wife gave a dinner party, and then the company sat solemnly sunk in the large chairs, admiring the wonderful polish and perfection of the room.

The study, or, as Mrs. McCandlish preferred to call it, the library, was not so grand as the rest of the house. It was restfully shabby; indeed, it was almost the only room in the house that had a used look. There were comfortable, worn chairs, and a large, plain writing-table, and books. Not so many books when all was said. Mr. McCandlish was not a great reader, he had no passion for books, and one bookcase held all his belongings. There were many volumes of sermons by popular clergymen, and "Aids to Preachers"; several shelves were filled by well-bound editions of standard authors, but the minister evidently distrusted his own taste in modern literature, for whether in biography or poetry or fiction it was but poorly represented.

This evening when Mr. and Mrs. McCandlish had sat for

a few minutes surveying the room that was the crowning glory of their house, Mrs. McCandlish rose to pick a dead leaf from a plant. Her husband rose too, and presently they found themselves, as if propelled by invisible hands, walking towards the study.

There Mrs. McCandlish settled herself into her own particular chair, crossed her feet, and said, "Well, now, Norman, we must decide who all are to be invited."

Her husband lit his pipe, and prepared to consider the question.

"All the usual people, I suppose—the Carruthers, and the Hays, and Mrs. Strang, and the Brands, and . . ."

"Yes, of course, dear, but this year we will go farther afield. Our friends in Priorsford, the new people at King's Houses, and, of course, Colonel Home of Phantasy. It's the first time he has been in residence since we came to Netherton—and Miss Gilmour at Little Phantasy. By the way, she hasn't returned our call, and I never see her in church—"

There was a pause, and Mrs. McCandlish was evidently thinking something rather scathing about Miss Gilmour's manners; but her better nature prevailed, and all she said was, "She has lived so much abroad—"

Mr. McCandlish turned his large, kind, meaningless face on his wife and said, "Quite so."

Mrs. McCandlish calculated in silence for a few minutes, and then announced, "I think, Norman, we must invite at least fifty. There will be tennis and clock-golf for the young people, and the older people enjoy talking and seeing the kitchen garden. I've been wondering—do you think,

Norman, it would be wise to engage the Priorsford Band? They might play in the shrubbery (music among the trees would have a nice effect), but I don't want to do it if you think it would be ostentatious or in any way unbecoming to our position. We must remember that we are clergy people, and keep ourselves in check."

Mr. McCandlish nodded gravely.

"It's quite true, Aggie. Personally, I think a band would be a very cheery addition to the party, but one can't be too careful. To rouse envy would be a bad thing. When one thinks of the poor fellows who enter the ministry with no private means, and when they get a living have their manses to furnish. What a struggle it must be for them all the time. I don't know how they manage at all. It makes one almost ashamed to be so comfortable—a car and all— That reminds me, we must send some peaches whenever they are ripe to the Brands."

Mrs. McCandlish sighed.

"I just wish Miss Brand was a more appreciative person. She really has the most ungracious manners—but, poor thing, what can you expect? Always so poor, and her youth gone, and never any decent clothes. I am sure that would sour any woman—the clothes, I mean. Anyway, there will be no peaches ready for quite a time." (This last thought appeared to give the good lady satisfaction, as if she thought Miss Brand's manners might possibly have improved by the time the gift was made.) "By the way, Norman, someone told me that the Little Phantasy people are going to Muirburn Church. They have been seen coming out two different Sundays."

Mr. McCandlish knocked his pipe against the mantelpiece and got up.

"It's a good thing they go to some church, my dear. There is nothing I deplore so much as the lax ways young people are so apt to fall into as regards church attendance . . . Well, I'll just have time to see old Laidlaw before the dressing-bell goes. I hear he is ailing. *Au revoir*, my dear."

His wife, left alone, sat still for a little thinking about the garden party that was to be. She wanted it to be a really successful affair, and decided finally that it must be purveyed by McVitties'; the little flags on the sandwiches carried the day. And she would ask particularly for some of their delicious little citron cakes. McVitties' strawberry ices were always a treat. She did hope it would be a fine warm day. Would it really be ostentatious to engage the band from Priorsford? Surely not, if they played in the shrubbery. Besides, what possible difference could it make to any one whether or not the McCandlishes (known to be people of means) had a band at their garden party? Besides, the members of the band had been put into new uniform (she had helped at the bazaar that raised money for them), and looked very smart. Of course, if they were to remain in the shrubbery their appearance did not much matter. Still, they would emerge for tea, after the guests had finished and were engaged elsewhere. Anyway, she was determined that all the expenses of the party would be borne by herself. Norman had bought the car—such a handsome one, the very best make—and the chauffeur was a big extra expense, though he did do odd jobs as well as look after the car . . . How good Norman was, and how contrary of any one to prefer Mr. Brand—an estimable young man, doubtless, but so abrupt. Uncouth, was that the word? And his sister rather worse. Hardly a word of thanks when they tried to show them kindness, and Lady Carruthers said she found the same thing.

Mrs. McCandlish looked at her watch—a quarter to seven. There would just be time to finish a story she was reading in the *People's Friend*. She took the paper from a satin-lined workbasket (she did not care to leave it lying about in case any one thought the *Friend*, as she called it familiarly to herself, frivolous reading for a minister's wife), and in a second she was absorbed.

CHAPTER 7

> "And there were no visitors, only chocolate ladies, and
> tall white lilies." *A Child's Dream*

THE DAY before the children were due to arrive turned out to be a receiving day at Little Phantasy. All the neighbours who had tarried in their welcome to the newcomers chose to appear that sunny day in May.

"It's always the way—a hunger or a burst," Miss Wotherspoon remarked to Easie, as she went to answer the third ring at the front door bell.

Kirsty had never given a thought to the possibility of callers that day, and was devoting herself to the garden.

She had come in at the window to talk for a minute with Miss Fanny, who was apt to feel neglected if left long alone, when Lady Carruthers was announced, and a tall woman of about fifty-five came into the room.

In the country Lady Carruthers affected somewhat bizarre raiment. This afternoon she wore a very short skirt of many colours, a jumper of a single violent hue, checked stockings, and shoes so exaggerated in the way of tongues and heavy soles that they made her seem feather-footed. As she never walked a step if she could help it, there seemed little reason for such sporting attire.

Kirsty, looking at her with interest, decided that the visitor must have been a good-looking woman before her face had grown so soft and puffy that it seemed as if a dent must remain if it were touched. She had wandering brown eyes, a wide, slack mouth, and a somewhat affected manner. In her time she had gone through many phases. Just lately, when in London, she had met a stately lady whose serenity had greatly impressed her; so Muirburn was being treated to the sight of Lady Carruthers with her hands folded and a faraway expression in her eyes, murmuring at intervals, "All is well." Her husband felt it to be almost the most provoking of her phases, so far as they had gone.

People who met Sir Andrew and Lady Carruthers for the first time invariably put them down as New Rich, but in that they were wrong. Sir Andrew was a decent dull man who had inherited a fortune from his father. True, he had doubled it in the War, and for so doing had been given a K.B.E.—an honour that he had not much use for, except that, as he put it, "it pleased the wife." He was a plain man to whom life held little of interest. The country bored him; he was of those who would rather hear the mouse cheep than the lark sing; he disliked shooting, and hated entertaining housefuls of guests. He liked to go off for a day with a rod, not because he wanted to catch fish, but because he wanted to escape from the necessity of talking to people. A fortune was thrown away on Sir Andrew. He would have been quite happy working in a city office fifty weeks out of the fifty-two; to him £500 a year and a semi-detached villa would have been "paradise enow." Lady Carruthers was the daughter of a wealthy manufacturer. She had been a bright particular star in the suburb in which they had first pitched their palatial tent. There she had been content to devote her energies to bazaars and philharmonic societies and reading-clubs, but looking back from the eminence she had attained, it all seemed to be pitifully provincial. Now that she was "county," the thought of the villa-people she had once been satisfied to call her friends made her shudder. Not that she was a snob, she would have told you, far from it; but now that she knew what real refinement meant, chasms seemed to yawn between her and the good-natured but unintellectual friends of her younger days.

Edmonston Hall, which her husband hated with all that it meant of servants and guests and such worries, was her Mecca. Here she could live as she felt she had been meant to live, surrounded with beauty and taste. And her husband, looking back on the Maggie he had married (he still called her Maggie though she had been Margot to herself for many years), hardly recognized that hearty, simple creature in the much-mannered woman with an English accent, who lisped and posed, and discussed things out of books which, as he would have told you, he had never even "heard tell of."

Lady Carruthers was a great talker, and this was the more courageous of her as she had a very uncertain grip of the pronunciation of the English language. When to use a broad A was an unsolved puzzle to her; indeed, so confused had she become as to whether gas should be called "gās" or "ges," that she had given up alluding to that useful commodity altogether. Africa was another difficult word, and Arran hopeless.

As Lady Carruthers came into the drawing-room at Little Phantasy she stopped, and, with her head on one side, said archly:

"This is so exciting. Now, do let me guess which is Miss Gilmour. You, I *think*—" and she half knelt before Miss Fanny.

"Yes," said that lady in the congratulatory tone in which one tells a child playing at *Hunt the Thimble* that it is "warm." To tell the truth, she was more than a little surprised at this behaviour on the part of such a large and (apparently) sensible person. She put out her hand to help to raise the visitor, and said kindly:

"I mean, of course, I'm Miss Gilmour of Harelaw, but it is my niece who lives here. Kirsty, my dear . . ."

It seemed very unfortunate to Miss Fanny that Kirsty should have chosen to garden that afternoon, and that she should have to receive visitors in a large pinafore and a shabby felt hat pulled over her hair. But Kirsty came forward unabashed, thrusting her gardening gloves into a large pocket, and surveying her hands doubtfully.

"I wonder if my hand is clean enough to shake! I've been poking about in the border out there. It's such fun not knowing what's in it. The whole garden is a sort of lucky bag to me."

As she spoke she shook hands and pulled forward a chair into which the visitor sank, crying:

"A garden! What a joy it is! You must see our gardens at Edmonston Hall. They are very extensive, and require six gardeners! A lot of glass, you know."

Lady Carruthers had a curious way of avoiding the eyes of the person she was addressing. It gave her a furtive look, which accorded ill with her foolish but perfectly honest face.

Now she hitched herself up in her chair—it was one of those low chairs with loose, down-filled cushions into which heavy people sink in a way that leaves their legs exposed to a critical world—and, with her eyes wandering round the room, she continued her conversation:

"And how do you like this place, Miss Gilmour? Phantasy—isn't it a strange name? Almost like a joke! From what I hear there is precious little phantasy about the owner. Have you met Colonel Home, Miss Gilmour? He has never called at Edmonston Hall, but then, he is lame, poor man. Of course he could drive. But," lightly, "perhaps he doesn't care for calling. Some men don't. Sir Andrew, now, would sooner do anything. When I do get him to go with me he's such a picture of misery that he makes me feel quite unwell. I didn't urge him to come today seeing that there was no gentleman here for him."

"No, indeed," Kirsty agreed, "it would have been a thousand pities to make him miserable. Have you been long in this neighbourhood?"

"About five years, Miss Gilmour. It's what you would call a dull, neighbourhood socially, I mean no society—to speak of; but happily," here Lady Carruthers tried sitting forward on the treacherous down cushions, thus gaining more control of her legs, "happily, Miss Gilmour, I'm not at all dependent on neighbours."

Kirsty smiled at her visitor.

"You mean you are good friends with yourself! I know. There is nothing pleasanter than having a lot of time to oneself. I suppose you read and garden and . . ."

"And think about Life," said Lady Carruthers. "Life is so

interesting, isn't it? Have you read a book called *Nothing Doubting?*"

"I don't think so," Kirsty said. "Who wrote it?"

"Oh," said Lady Carruthers, sinking her voice, "it comes from the Other Side."

"America?" said Miss Fanny brightly.

A pained look passed over the visitor's face. "No, no," she said, "I mean it comes from the Unseen—spirits—you know. It is so wonderful, you learn from it to trust. It is so nice to think that whatever happens in the world is right."

Miss Fanny sighed, and Kirsty said, "Yes," somewhat doubtfully.

"Don't you feel that?" Lady Carruthers asked. "But you *must*. It's all a question of getting on to the Higher Plane. I used to worry. Wore myself out about the way the servants went on, and all that, but now I have such a beautiful feeling of serenity. I just fold my hands and say, 'All is well'."

Kirsty looked at her visitor, a somewhat ludicrous figure perched on the edge of the chair, her pillar-like legs rather far apart, a foolishly benign smile on her face.

"But," she objected, "all *isn't* well. To read the newspapers—"

"Oh," Lady Carruthers said airily, "I never read the newspapers, except the Births and Deaths and the Court News."

"That explains it," said Kirsty. "You can't feel very serene when you read that there are thousands and thousands of men out of work, and children not getting enough to eat."

"My dear Miss Gilmour," Lady Carruthers said, "that is all

the effect of this absurd dole. The men don't *want* to work."

Kirsty opened her mouth to say something, and shut it again firmly.

"Yes," the good lady continued, "I know everything will work out right. A little patience is all that is needed. Human nature is so *fine*, when one really looks for the good."

"I'd like to believe that," Kirsty said, "but sometimes one despairs. Did you notice lately in the papers—ah, but you don't read the papers, I forgot—that a woman left in charge of three little children while their father was at sea so ill-used them that two of them died. She starved them and beat them with sticks that had nails in them . . . little soft creatures, so easy to hurt."

Kirsty's face was white and her eyes dark with horror at the thought of this beast of prey.

Miss Fanny knitted rapidly, for she felt uncomfortable.

"Try not to think about it," she said soothingly.

Lady Carruthers was looking genuinely shocked, not so much at the tale as at Kirsty for having told it.

"But surely, Miss Gilmour, it is rather an unhealthy taste to care to read about horrors. It is very dreadful of course, but there will be some explanation. They must have been low people. Don't dwell on it. Think rather of all the children who have happy homes, dear little well-kept children in warm nurseries."

And Kirsty, feeling herself to have acted like a fool, said, "Yes, I am sure you are right—Ah, here comes tea. Aunt Fanny, I know you have been longing for it. Lady

Carruthers, do come to this chair by the tea-table. That's better."

They were halfway through tea when the Brands came in.

They had had tea early, and walked slowly up to Phantasy hoping that tea would be over there. "And if Miss Gilmour's out, so much the better," Rebecca had said hopefully; so it was with a glum face that she found herself seated by Lady Carruthers at the tea-table, buttering a scone, while that lady spoke volubly.

Kirsty was glad to see the Brands. After half an hour of Lady Carruthers, Rebecca's grim face was like a tonic. One could see that she was no facile optimist; life was evidently a struggle to Rebecca.

Kirsty had gone for two Sundays to Muirburn Church, and had enjoyed the ministrations of Robert Brand, and now she found that "the long lean lad," as she had christened him, seen close at hand, was an attractive person, with the light of humour in his eyes and a cleft in his chin.

She put him beside Miss Fanny, who was much refreshed to see a minister again, and immediately launched forth into inquiries about the congregation, the size of the Manse, the givings to Foreign Missions—subjects calculated to set any parson at his ease.

As she poured out tea for the newcomers Kirsty listened idly to the conversation of Lady Carruthers and Rebecca. Lady Carruthers was relating the marvellous effect the reading of some article had had on her, while Rebecca listened, supremely uninterested.

"I think it was in the *Fortnightly*, Miss Brand. Yes, I'm

almost sure it was in the *Fortnightly*. I shall send it you. It gave me quite a spiritual uplift."

"Thank you," Rebecca said, without enthusiasm, "but I haven't much time for reading just now. With one small girl as sole servant there's a lot to do in a house, and when I do have a minute I like a good story to take me out of myself. But I daresay Rob might enjoy it: he would read anything."

Lady Carruthers looked somewhat crushed, and turned to her hostess for comfort.

"You read, I am sure, Miss Gilmour," with a glance round at the bookshelves which lined the room. "Now, I wonder if you follow any course of reading. I think that is so helpful."

"I'm afraid I don't," Kirsty said, pouring some water into the teapot. "Just now I'm reading *The Wide Wide World*. Did I hear you say, Miss Brand, that you run the Manse with one small girl? I'm so interested, for I have only just begun housekeeping. Let's talk about servants. Do you mind? I think it is the most absorbing subject."

Both the visitors looked at their hostess. The big chintz pinafore and rakish hat gave her the look of a schoolgirl; her face was all alight with interest. Both ladies disapproved of her, and each had her own reason.

"Affected," thought Rebecca.

"Mindless," thought Lady Carruthers.

"I make such mistakes," Kirsty went on, "about ordering things, you know. I do wish you would give me some hints."

Rebecca swallowed a bite of scone quickly and said:

"My hints would be very little use to you, I'm afraid. My system of housekeeping is doing with as little as possible. It's no fun at all, I assure you."

"We have a housekeeper at Edmonston Hall," Lady Carruthers said rather loftily. "A capable woman. She stands between me and all the sordid details of housekeeping. Such a relief! It leaves me free to devote myself to my books and my garden. I don't like to be worried wondering why they eat so many kippered herrings in the servants' hall."

Kirsty began to laugh. "I'm so new to it," she explained, "that the kipper question would interest instead of worry me. I'm afraid I'm a trial to the servants. Miss Wotherspoon, the parlour-maid, often fixes me with a disapproving eye."

"Do you call your parlour-maid 'Miss'?" Lady Carruthers asked.

"Oh yes, that's no effort. I would call her 'Your Grace' if it would make her feel happier."

What reply Lady Carruthers would have made to this will never be known, for at that moment Miss Wotherspoon announced: "Mr. and Mrs. Anthony Hay," and Kirsty, jumping up, saw enter the room a couple that might have walked out of mid-Victorian days. Both were over seventy, both were high-coloured and white-haired; they brought with them such an air of jollity and good humour that every one in the room had to respond.

Mr. and Mrs. Anthony Hay thought it only fitting to dress with some ceremony when they paid a first call. They belonged to the days when people had "best" clothes. Mrs.

Hay wore black because, she said, it was the only becoming wear for a woman of her years, black silk and fine lace and spotless white gloves, and very delightful she looked.

Miss Fanny, looking at her, comparing her with Lady Carruthers of the gaudy stockings and short skirts and violent jumpers, felt vaguely pleased and proud. Lady Carruthers was twenty years younger, and represented what she thought was the last word in modern fashion; but what an unpleasing spectacle she was with her puffy white face and sloppy, loud clothes compared with this daintily-clad, wholesome-looking old lady.

And how truly delightful, thought Miss Fanny, were the manners of the Victorian couple. The quiet dignity, the rather formal phrasing of their welcome to the newcomers, combined with the real warmth and kindness of their eyes, pleased her mightily. Modern people and their modern manners confused and frightened Miss Fanny; she so seldom had any idea what they wanted to be at. This Lady Carruthers, for instance—what nonsensical ways she had! And her conversation was the most tiresome thing, Miss Fanny thought, that she had ever listened to.

Mr. Anthony Hay was talking to Kirsty, asking really intelligent questions about things that mattered: central heating (so essential), a good kitchen range; the danger of damp from the water. Miss Fanny nodded her head in profound agreement, and even ventured a remark or two; and soon Mr. Anthony Hay, in his dark blue suit and white-spotted tie (Miss Fanny did like a man to look fresh and well brushed), had drawn his chair up beside her and was telling her tales of the countryside and its characters, and laughing at his own jokes. Not only that, he was making the other visitors join with him in his interest and amusement. Mr. Brand capped his stories with others, and Rebecca forgot that she hated paying calls on rich, affected young women, and laughed her surpassingly pretty clear laugh. Lady Carruthers said, "Oh, but how amusing," and presently got up to go.

"I'm an old-fashioned wife, Miss Gilmour," she explained, "and I don't like to leave my good man too long alone. When I have been away for a day he says it has seemed like a month. Quite touching, isn't it?"

It may have been touching, but it was certainly untrue. Lady Carruthers had no intention of being untruthful, but living with the unresponsive Andrew had bred in her the habit of putting into his mouth the pretty and polite speeches he ought to have made but never did make. Sometimes she even did it in her husband's presence, and it was awkward for the guests when that maligned man burst out: "Me! I never said such a thing!"

Kirsty noticed that after the departure of Lady Carruthers Rebecca Brand's glance became much less baleful, and she sat down beside her and sought to please her by praising Muirburn, and the church, and the preaching of Mr. Brand. But all the flowers of flattery she offered her seemed to wilt under the disconcerting gaze of Rebecca's small grey eyes. She had the air, Kirsty thought, of not believing a word that was said to her, and it was with something of relief that she saw her rise to go.

The Anthony Hays stayed, comfortably talking, for a little while, and then departed, pressing invitations on the two

Miss Gilmours.

"Well, have you enjoyed your afternoon?" Kirsty asked her aunt as she came into the room after speeding the departing guests from the doorstep.

"Oh yes, dear. It does one good to see people now and again. They seem pleasant people. Mr. and Mrs. Hay are specially nice—Dear me! Isn't that the bell again?"

It was, and the last visitor of the afternoon appeared— Mrs. Strang of Hopewaterfoot.

"I oughtn't to come in," she said. "You've had the whole of Muirburn, it seems, this afternoon, and I'm afraid I'll prove the last straw. But may I just stay and look at this room for a minute? I've been away, or I would have been here long ago. I was so excited when I heard that Little Phantasy was let—it's easily the nicest house hereabout, and I was afraid . . . Now that I've seen this room I know you're just the right people to live in it. Lady Carruthers is capable of hanging 'The Soul's Awakening' above that fireplace. No, I'm not really unkind. I like Lady Carruthers in lots of ways, but she has a most unstitched mind, now hasn't she?"

As she spoke Mrs. Strang looked full into Kirsty's face, and laughed so infectiously that Kirsty had to laugh too. She had a small impudent face with freckles on the somewhat tip-tilted nose, and a wide red mouth. She was straight and slender, and had a rather boyish, gallant look about her.

"I'm only going to stay ten minutes, I promise you, so please be kind and tell me about yourselves. You," nodding at Kirsty, "are Miss Gilmour, I know, for someone pointed you out to me yesterday in the village."

"And this is my aunt, also Miss Gilmour, who is so very kind as to live with me. We are very interested to see you, because of your books."

"Have you read any of them?" Mrs. Strang asked.

Kirsty, taken aback, blushed and stammered, and Mrs. Strang laughed cheerfully.

"It's not a question any nice-minded author would ever have asked you. The proper thing is to be very coy about one's books and allude to them as 'One or two little things. Of course you won't have heard of them.' But I'm frankly disgusted when I find people in a state of complete ignorance about my immortal works. I've written several books. Jean Hill I call myself. My best known book is *The Penny Whistle*."

"But I've read it," Kirsty cried in great excitement. "I love it. Aunt Fanny, you know I was telling you about it only the other day, and wondering how you had missed it. I always keep a copy, but it seems to have been lost in the general *mêlée*. I must send for another at once, and we'll read it aloud. Imagine you being Jean Hill."

"Now, that's more like the thing," Mrs. Strang said encouragingly. "I'm not going to stay a minute longer. When will you both come to see me? Tomorrow? Wednesday? Thursday? I've just got back, so I've no engagements. Do come to luncheon tomorrow?"

Kirsty explained, while Miss Fanny crept into her shawls to escape this so precipitate lady, that the next day would be wholly given over to preparations for the coming of three children from London.

"I hope they will be here all summer," she added.

"Then you must bring them all to Hopewaterfoot and we'll have a picnic. We'll just seize a good day and arrange it all in a minute. That will be fine . . . By the way, how do you get on with Archie?"

"Archie?" said Kirsty.

"Your landlord, Colonel Home?"

"Oh, quite well. We hardly know him; he has been very kind," Kirsty stammered.

"That's good. Well, I'm off."

Kirsty and her aunt looked at each other after Mrs. Strang had driven off in the pony-cart.

"Don't you think, dear," Miss Fanny said gently, "that people who write books are always, well—just a little peculiar? I'm afraid Mrs. Strang must be what they call Bohemian?"

"Oh, don't you like her? She reminds me of my friend Blanche Cunningham; something of the cheeky schoolboy about her, but frightfully straight and honest. It's very amusing, isn't it, meeting new people? I'll go to Hopewaterfoot and Cherrytrees with joy, but I doubt if we are quite up to the standard of Edmonston Hall, you and I, with its six gardeners, and housekeepers, and kippers in the servants' hall. What do you think?"

CHAPTER 8

"Have you heard the news?" said the Moor Wife.
"The Will-o'-the-Wisps are in town."
                                        HANS ANDERSEN

THE DAY had come.

At least twenty times Kirsty had wandered through the rooms prepared for the travellers and gazed with delight at all the arrangements made for their comfort. There were no ornaments to break, no toilet covers to crumple and worry. Solid chairs, comfortable and squat, a shelf of books which she guessed children would like (or at any rate *should* like): *Alice, The Jungle Books, Treasure Island, The Wind in the Willows*. It had given her infinite pleasure to put them there, and she had dipped into each one as she put it on the shelf.

The Primrose Room, Barbara's room, was a little "paradise of dainty devices." Barbara was ten. Did girls of ten like dainty things? Kirsty tried to remember across twenty years; anyway she thought Barbara would like her room. It had pale primrose walls and a soft grey carpet. The furniture was pale grey, very simple in design, and the chintz had a demure, old-world pattern of bunches of primroses on a grey ground.

Kirsty had taken particular pains with Miss Carter's, the governess's room, and had filled it with flowers to give it a welcoming air. The preparations had been pure delight. Never, Kirsty thought, had she been so happy.

It was not till she sat down to lunch with Miss Fanny that distrust began to lay hands on her, and she sank into silence. Miss Fanny was always rather quiet at meals, for she took them seriously. She ate as if she thoroughly enjoyed every bite, but always wore a resigned air as if she were saying to herself, "Dear me, this is a very good dinner, but who knows how long I shall have health to enjoy a meal? It's an uncertain world."

Kirsty peppered a baked egg, and looked at her aunt musingly.

"I've just been thinking," she said, "that I know absolutely nothing about children. I've only dreamed about them, and read about them, and I'm afraid I'm going to be distressingly shy of the actual. What shall I talk to them about? Suppose they take a hate at me whenever they see me?"

Miss Fanny laid down her fork—her egg had been exactly right, not over-baked and not too soft—pulled a shawl closer about her shoulders and sighed.

"You can never tell with children," she said. "They like the most extraordinary people. I remember your father as a child had a perfect passion for tramps; he would have followed one anywhere. They very rarely like really nice people. I can't help thinking it shows a lack of discrimination."

Kirsty laughed. "Then, if they don't like me, I may take it as a kind of a compliment, as Smee said?"

Miss Fanny sighed again, and helped herself to a beef-olive from the dish Miss Wotherspoon was holding out to her in the grimly disapproving manner in which she always waited at table, a manner which meant, "Is this what I have come to? I'll do my duty, but if things were rightly ordered I know who would be doing the waiting."

Miss Fanny was silent until her plate was empty. She made the tidiest of plates. To see her eat a chop was a revelation, and Kirsty, who always found a great many things to leave, felt thankful that the children would find at least one example to follow.

"The worst of children"—Miss Fanny stopped and looked at the open window, shivering ostentatiously—"the worst of children is that they are a constant irritation—Do you think, dear, it is quite wise to keep the window so wide open when we are at meals? There is always a cold air from the water."

"Oh, do you think such a little air can do us any harm? It's such a lovely day . . . Oh well, close the window, will you, Miss Wotherspoon, please? . . Don't you like children, Aunt Fanny?"

"I like well-behaved children quite well, but all children have such uncomfortable ways. They lean up against you and whine, or else they tear about upsetting things, which is worse, and if you don't happen to know where they are they are certain to be in mischief, and as they get older they get impudent—"

It was Kirsty's turn to sigh.

"Aunt Fanny, you're not at all reassuring, and today I need to be reassured, for I feel that I have attempted something rather beyond me. How can I go to the station tonight and meet three possibly hostile children who won't want to live with me? What will Miss Carter do all day? What is there for any one to do? Oh, this is dreadful—"

"They'll fall in the Hope Water for one thing," Miss Fanny said. "Why any one would build a house at the very water's edge I cannot understand. So dangerous for every one, rheumatism and children drowning and mists in the evening."

Miss Fanny's determined pessimism began to have its usual effect on her niece. From where she sat she could see the sun shining on the Hope Water through a willow which "grew aslant the brook," dipping its grey velvet pussy-pads into the shining ripples. Above, the ground rose steeply in a tangle of larch and rowan trees—larches for the spring, and rowans for the autumn. There was comfort in the sight, and she cried:

"Oh, aren't we the lucky ones to have a house beside running water? And you know, Aunt Fanny, it would be a very small and inert child that could drown in the Hope Water. Our children are large. Why, Bill the baby is nearly six."

Miss Fanny buttered a bit of toast with care.

"The worst age!" she said. "No sense, and always sticky. However, I hope it will be all right."

Punctually at six-thirty that evening the train which brought passengers from the junction sauntered into Muirburn station.

Kirsty stood on the platform eagerly scanning the passengers. A girl got out and walked demurely away. Two schoolboys tumbled out, laughing and pushing each other.

Two "business gentlemen" who owned houses in Muirburn and travelled daily into Glasgow, got out, to be greeted by wives and daughters. No one else. Had they not come? Kirsty felt slightly relieved, and at the same time vastly, achingly disappointed.

Then a door burst open and a tall young woman got out, hurriedly followed by a girl with two long plaits of shining hair, and a boy struggling with a fishing rod and basket and other impedimenta of the sportsman.

"Come on, Bill," Kirsty heard the tall young woman say, and she saw standing, half in and half out of the carriage, a small figure in a blue jersey and short blue trousers. It was a very small figure, but there was something oddly commanding about it.

Bill's head was large and covered with tossed yellow hair which defied the brush. His eyes were a lovely sea-blue with golden lashes. His nose was short and inclined to turn up, he had a long upper lip, a wide curly mouth, and a heavy jowl. "Like a bloodhound," Kirsty said to herself, and although it seems improbable that a golden-haired little boy should even remotely suggest a bloodhound, yet the likeness was there.

He stood placidly, unmoved by the appeals of his family, refusing firmly to leave the train until he had seen all his special belongings landed on the platform; then he descended, in time to meet Kirsty, who had come shyly up to the group.

"I think you must be Miss Carter," she said to the tall young woman. "I am so very glad to see you. And Barbara? And Specky? And this, I think, is Bill."

Barbara came forward and held up her face to be kissed.

Specky grinned bashfully, and disentangled a hand to shake, but Bill stood staring, with an unsmiling face, until Miss Carter took his hand and laid it in Kirsty's.

Kirsty, feeling very shy under this unwinking scrutiny, picked up a large untidy paper parcel and made a move towards the waiting wagonette—having no conveyance of her own, she was dependent on this vehicle, which could be hired from the husband of Mrs. Dickson at the shop. But no sooner had she touched the parcel than she was startled by a shout of rage from Bill.

She at once dropped it, while Barbara said, "You mustn't touch that, please. It's Bill's melodeon."

"It's my melodeon," echoed Bill. "I carry it myself."

"Then be quick about it," Miss Carter said briskly, "and don't keep Miss Gilmour waiting. Specky, you might take that bag of books, and Barbara, you can manage the wraps."

The porter had meantime carried the trunks to a waiting cart, and soon they were all on their way to Little Phantasy. The children sat silent, while Kirsty and Miss Carter exchanged civilities.

Miss Carter was a pleasant-looking girl with dark hair and eyes and a good-natured mouth. It relieved Kirsty greatly to hear that she loved the country.

"I love out of doors," she said. "I'd never enter a town if I could help it."

"Yet you have just come from London," Kirsty reminded her. "Have you been long with them?" She nodded towards the children, who were absorbed in the passing of some sheep and lambs.

"Two years. I'd suffer more than living in Clapham for their sakes. Besides, I promised their mother—"

"I never knew her," Kirsty said softly. " I'm glad they have you. I know you will help me to make them happy."

"You needn't worry about *that*. They are naturally happy children, and they have been nearly demented at the thought of getting back to Scotland. Bill has packed and unpacked his little case every day for a fortnight. I do hope you won't think I have let him get out of hand, but he is often so stubborn and makes such a noise that, for the sake of peace, I sometimes pass over things."

"Six big mother sheep, seven white lambs, and a black one," reported Bill, who had been hanging his head over the side of the carriage. "I didn't see a sheep near all the time I was at Clapham."

"Bill broke all the blinds on the London train," Barbara said cheerfully and irrelevantly.

"Surely not them all?" said Kirsty.

"Well, the two in our carriage, and I *think* the one that was nearest to him in the dining-car."

"Yes," said Bill complacently.

Miss Carter looked at him severely. "It's nothing to be proud of," she said.

"I thought you hadn't come," Kirsty broke in. "Why were you so reluctant to leave the train?"

"Because," said Miss Carter, "we didn't realize that it was our station. We couldn't make out what the porter said, and we saw no name-board, and I jumped out on the platform to ask. What would have happened if we had been taken on?"

"Nothing very deadly," Kirsty assured her. "You would just have gone on to Priorsford. But I got a bad fright when I thought you hadn't come."

"Then you really wanted us," Miss Carter said in an undertone.

Kirsty nodded. "You may be very sure of that."

The wagonette passed through the gates that guarded Phantasy, and turned down the winding road that led to the dower-house. As the Hope Water, cheerfully brawling, came into sight, Specky rose to his feet, his fishing rod clasped to his heart, his face as the face of one beholding the Promised Land, gazed at the burn, then sank back in his seat with a long, satisfied sigh.

His governess, who had been watching him with an understanding smile, turned to Kirsty and whispered:

"Fishing is his passion, but never in his wildest dreams did he imagine anything so ideal as to live close beside a trout stream."

Kirsty laughed happily as she jumped out of the wagonette and proceeded to lift her children down.

"Here we are at home," she cried. "Ring the bell, Specky, and Miss Wotherspoon will come."

CHAPTER 9

> "Is thy name William?
> William, sir.
> A fair name." *As You Like It*

THE MOMENT of waking at Little Phantasy always gave Kirsty peculiar pleasure. To look through the wide open windows and see Ratchell humped against the dawn-flushed sky, to lie and listen to the sounds of a new day beginning, and remember that she was in a Tweeddale glen, in a home of her own, these were delights new-born every morning.

On the children's first morning in their new home she woke very early and lay wondering for a little what was the difference she felt in the house. The usual early morning stillness—Miss Wotherspoon and Easie were not inclined to be early birds—was broken by a soft rustling and whispering, the sound of the padding of small naked feet, stifled trills of laughter.

Kirsty looked at the little clock by her bedside. Five o'clock. Ridiculous! Breakfast was not till nine, the children would starve. She foresaw all manner of complications if this sort of thing went on. Breakfast would have to be put forward an hour, which meant that the servants would have to rise an hour earlier, and she sighed as she thought of the tempers that would be smashed in the process. And as she sighed she thrust her feet into moccasins, threw her dressing-gown round her, and opened her bedroom door.

All was quiet in the passage.

Barbara's door was slightly open, and she looked in.

Barbara, at any rate, was no disturber of the peace; she lay in profound slumber halfway down the bed, her long plaits nearly touching the floor.

Kirsty softly shut the door, and went down some steps and along another short passage to the Stable.

The carefully-planned chamber was a scene of wreckage. The two little beds, white and inviting with clean fair linen, into which she had tucked the boys the night before, were pitiful now, the sheets crumpled into wisps, the pillows reposing on the floor, which was also strewn with boots and toys and garments and the picture-books they had taken to bed with them. It seemed impossible to Kirsty, who had never known small boys, that such a mess could have been made of a room in so short a period of time.

As she opened the door there was a sudden rustle and a hush.

Bill's bed was empty; but there were two humps in the other bed, and when Kirsty said, "Where's Bill, Specky?" a head emerged from under the bedclothes and explained:

"He's in my bed. He says he's a Russian refucheese, and he's got nothing on."

Then Kirsty saw among the many articles scattered on the floor a diminutive sleeping-suit which somehow had a look of Bill.

"Bill!" she said sternly.

A hump at the foot of the bed moved, and presently the culprit crawled out.

Kirsty started when she saw him. Not only was he naked, but his nose was a bright carmine, a hectic patch adorned each round cheek, while on his chin and forehead were dabs of black. His yellow hair stood fiercely on end.

"What on earth—" Kirsty began, when Specky again explained:

"You know the toys you gave us last night?" Kirsty had been so afraid that the children might feel homesick that she had lavished all the treasures she had accumulated on them at once—"There was a paint-box, and Bill wanted to paint when he woke up but there was no painting-book, so he did his own face." Specky regarded his brother rather proudly. "He looks like a clown, I think."

"I'm a Russian refucheese clown," Bill said, and smiled broadly.

Kirsty hardly knew what to say. It seemed a pity to begin the first day by scolding, such a "sunshine morning" as it promised to be. Already the sun was bright on Ratchell, while the mist lay in soft swathes in the glens. She recalled the gardener's weather prophecy—

> "If the mist takes the howes
> There'll be drouth for the knowes..."

But the young ruffians could not go unreprimanded. She bent and, picking up the sleeping-suit, handed it to Bill, telling him in dignified tones to put it on at once. To her relief Bill seemed rather impressed, and obediently wriggled into the garment; then he awaited developments.

Kirsty went to the washstand and took a sponge which

she found there, and rubbing it well with soap, proceeded to scrub the disfiguring marks from Bill's face. He stood it well, only remarking, "If you rub soap on sponges, you make them slimy, but that's Specky's sponge, so it's all right."

Specky, careless as to the state of his sponge, was standing on his head in the bed.

Soon Kirsty had them both tucked up, and was lecturing them kindly but firmly on the necessity of small boys remaining peacefully asleep until their elders and betters chose to bestir themselves.

"What time is it?" Bill demanded.

"Only about a quarter-past five," Kirsty told him in shocked tones.

"Well, that's a good time to get up," said Bill.

"And we could have breakfast at six," said Specky, "and that would give us a fine long day. I'm hungry now. Bill woke me hours ago, before the light had quite come."

"I never needed to wake up," Bill boasted, his yellow head jumping up from the pillow as if worked by a spring. "I've been awake all night like the sheep and the cows."

As Kirsty had seen them both fast asleep before she went to bed she was not impressed by this statement.

"Could we have something to eat?" Specky asked politely, and "I want my breakfast," said Bill.

Kirsty looked vaguely round. What could she get them to eat at this hour—two and a half hours away from morning tea? She was still very ignorant about household matters. Where did bread stay when it wasn't mealtimes? She might attempt to raid the pantry, but Miss Wotherspoon was addicted to a certain fearful looking for of burglars and had a passion for locking up places, so it would probably be no use. However, there might be something to eat in the big cupboard in the dining-room.

"I'll look for some biscuits," she said, and, pulling her dressing-gown round her, prepared to sally forth on the quest.

"Let me come too," said Specky, and Bill bounded like a ball on to the floor, and slid his hand into Kirsty's.

With Specky capering in front they stole softly downstairs.

How odd and unfamiliar the house looked in this curious light of sunshine and drawn blinds. Behind closed doors people were sleeping. It seemed to Kirsty that the furniture too looked as if it were asleep. Through the day it seemed alert and interested; now it was terribly inanimate.

They found the key in the cupboard lock, and soon they were all inside, for it was a big square cupboard, almost like a small room.

If Miss Wotherspoon allowed herself to be proud of anything it was of this cupboard, and she kept it in a state of intense neatness. Here had she ranged on the shelves the more sprightly form of stores—gaily coloured tins of fruit, boxes of dates, tins of biscuits.

Kirsty seized a box which bore the legend *Rich Mixed* and, the children eagerly watching, tried to open it by running her thumbnail along the edge of the lid; but it seemed to be very securely papered down, and after hurting her thumb she was forced to look for a knife.

This meant opening every drawer in the sideboard, and

the boys got so excited in the search that caution was forgotten, and Bill's voice shrilly upbraided Specky for having got before him before Kirsty could silence him.

The box was forced open at last, and there was revealed to the enraptured gaze of Specky and Bill rows of richly decorated biscuits. Kirsty, viewing them doubtfully, said, "They look much too sugary for early morning. Only two, Bill, and two for Specky, and take the plainest."

"I'll take one with a sugar curl on it," Bill said, brooding over the box, "and one of those long ones, for they are the biggest."

"Don't breathe on them so," Specky advised him. "I'll choose now."

They were, all three, so absorbed in the biscuit-box that they did not hear the dining-room door open, and were aware of nothing until a voice said, *"Mercy!"*

Then they looked up and saw a shattering vision.

Miss Wotherspoon stood in the doorway armed with a poker. Her head was muffled in a grey Shetland scarf, and she wore, draped over her nightgown, a bright red cashmere shawl that had belonged to her mother. She was a sufficiently arresting sight, and Kirsty and the boys cowered before her in silence.

"What's all this?" she demanded, still gripping the poker threateningly.

"It's all right, Miss Wotherspoon," Kirsty said soothingly. "We're not the burglars you expected. The boys woke early, and I came down to get them some biscuits."

Bill, after a glance at Miss Wotherspoon's face, quickly bit the sugar curl off his biscuit, as if determined that, whatever happened, he would make sure of that.

"Sugar biscuits at this time in the morning!" Miss Wotherspoon's voice was bitter in its scorn. "It's well seen you ken nothing about bairns, Miss. If ye had looked ye would have seen digestive biscuits in the next box. I suppose ye never thought ye would file the puir lambs' stomachs? I doubt we'll all pay for this morning's work. I can feel ma head beginning already—such a fright as I got!"

"Go back to bed, then," said Kirsty, rising from her undignified attitude on the floor. "You've more than an hour before you need think of getting up."

But Miss Wotherspoon shook her head with a martyred air. "When I'm up, I'm up. I'll just get dressed, and get on with ma work. Goodness knows there's enough to do," and she stalked away, her shawl trailing and the poker held like a sceptre.

Kirsty withstood an impulse to giggle, and Specky said in his gentle voice, "Who is that lady?"

"That," said Kirsty, "is Miss Wotherspoon. She helps with the housework, and she isn't very strong, so you must try not to worry her, or give her extra work. Come along now," as she saw more questions coming, "back to bed you must go, and after this you shall have bread and butter in your room in case you waken early. Now let's see which of us will go upstairs most quietly—like mice—"

Kirsty did not attempt to sleep again. She sat by her window, and saw the world all shining with dew, and watched when the sun first struck the ripples of Tweed as it flowed to the old grey bridge. She heard the first stirrings of life in the village—the *tinka tinka tink* from the smiddy, the lowing of the cows going to be milked, the clatter of cans as they were brought to the back door, and Easie's gay voice in badinage with the lad who brought them, all the cheerful morning sounds. She smelt the wood-smoke from newly kindled fires, and the incomparable freshness of a May morning. The day seemed a long time begun when she went down to the nine o'clock breakfast.

Miss Carter was already in the dining-room with her three charges, bright-eyed, with shining hair, all agog for whatever the new day might hold for them. She looked her best in the morning, with her clear skin and frank brown eyes, and her slim, square shoulders held very straight. Specky was hanging out of the window, gazing rapturously at the Hope Water, while Barbara, anxious little sister, clung to his legs in case he fell out.

When Miss Fanny came into the room. Kirsty glanced at her somewhat anxiously as she gave her good morning.

Things had not gone too well the night before when the children arrived. They had been taken into the gay white drawing-room where Miss Fanny sat knitting, wrapped as usual in fleecy shawls, and Barbara and Specky had at once gone to her and greeted her politely. But Bill, Bad Bill, had lived up to his name. Seeing him hang back, Kirsty had thought him shy, and had said encouragingly:

"That is Aunt Fanny, Bill; go and shake hands with her."

But it was not shyness that troubled Bill.

"That's not Aunt Fanny," he said, "that's the sheep in *Alice*, the sheep what sat in the boat and knitted."

Barbara and Specky had stared at poor Miss Fanny, then turned horrified eyes to Kirsty, as if to say, "It's dreadful of him to say it, but you must admit in fairness that he's right;" and Kirsty, looking at her aunt's kind, long face and rather bent, fleecy back, couldn't but own that the likeness was there.

Miss Fanny had, happily, not understood the allusion (she thought *Alice* either *in Wonderland* or *Through the Looking-Glass* only fit for imbecile minds), but she had mistrusted Bill at the first glance. The unwinking stare of the sea-blue eyes, the untidy yellow hair, the heavy jowl gave her an uncomfortable feeling. Barbara and Specky were nice children, good-looking and with pretty manners, but she determined that she would see as little as possible of Bill.

"Porridge!" said Barbara. "Now I know I'm in Scotland. We didn't get right stuff at Clapham; it was thick and had knots, not smooth like this."

As Bill finished the last spoonful of his porridge he looked at Kirsty and announced, "I shall call you Pie."

"Why Pie?" asked Barbara and Specky together, while Miss Fanny paused in the act of buttering her toast and regarded him suspiciously.

Bill refused to give a reason.

"Then I must call you Pudding," Kirsty said.

Bill took a drink of milk.

"You will call me William," he said, turning his head away in a final manner. "May I go out now to the garden?"

Kirsty said she would take them out that morning while Miss Carter unpacked and got things in their places. Every other morning, except Saturday and Sunday, they would have lessons for two hours.

"Bill rests at eleven," Miss Carter told Kirsty as they were leaving the house."

Bill turned on her angrily. "Why did you tell Pie that? Don't you know in Scotland nobody rests?" and he flew after Specky, who had gone, as if drawn by a magnet, straight to the shining Hope Water.

CHAPTER 10

"An' naebody for dacency but barely twa or three."
R. L. S.

WITH punctilious politeness Kirsty returned her calls the week after they were made.

One bright afternoon she ordered Mr. Dickson's wagonette, regretfully watched Miss Carter and the children start for a walk without her, impressed on Miss Fanny the fact that she was very lucky to be let off paying calls and allowed to sit comfortably at home, put on a new coat and skirt and a pair of clean gloves, and mounted the high step of her chariot as if it had been a tumbril.

Mr. Dickson was a wizened little man, with a coat much too large for him, and a passionate craving to know what church every stranger he met belonged to. He took a wide view of a coachman's duties, and Kirsty found that he attended less to his horse than to her. By way of amusing her he related the family history (so far as it was known to him) of the inmates of the different houses they called at, turning half round on his seat to do so. If snubbed in his amiable efforts to entertain he was apt to fall asleep. The horse, a sedate animal (James by name), did not seem to mind much what his master did.

The first call was at Netherton Manse.

As they drove up the drive Mr. Dickson waved his whip condescendingly.

"Ay, McCandlish has gotten his place rale doss. Nae credit

to him—wi' twae gairdeners. His faither left him an awfu' siller, ye ken; he's mair like a laird than a minister. He canna preach ava, puir soul, but he stands up and maks a fine noise, an' his folk are quite weel pleased. They dinna ken a guid sermon when they hear it." Mr. Dickson leant over towards Kirsty and said impressively, "I whiles even doot if McCandlish kens what conversion means."

"Really?" Kirsty said, feeling miserably ill at ease, and casting apprehensive glances at the windows of the house.

There was no one in at the Manse, so they proceeded on their way to Edmonston Hall.

"New folk," said Mr. Dickson, as James slowly climbed the steep drive. "Rich. That's aboot a' ye can say o' them. I whiles see Sir Andrew (as they ca' him) slinkin' aboot—a rale hame-ower wee body. The first time I saw him I said to ma wife, 'Dinna tell me that that wee pepper-pot's laird o' Edmonston.' The wife's a muckle strappin' wumman, but I tell ye what it is, things are come to a bonnie cripis when folk like that get titles an' ca' themselves gentry."

He let his whip play angrily in the air round James's patient head.

"Ma word, if Robbie Burns was here to make a song aboot the new gentry! That wud sort them!"

He stared superciliously at the butler who opened the door, and was obviously delighted when he heard that there was no one at home.

"Juist as weel," he remarked to Kirsty, when once more she had climbed to her uneasy seat. "Whaur'll ye try next?"

"Take me to Cherrytrees, please," Kirsty said, with dignity.

"I will that." Mr. Dickson flapped the reins so smartly that James actually broke into something resembling a canter. "Whoa there. Canny noo, James. Ye're ower croose, ma man, when ye're visitin' the gentry; ye'll hae to come doon to the cairt again the morn, mind that."

Mr. Dickson leant over to Kirsty. "He's an awfu' happy horse, James," he said; "ye canna help likin' him. But he hes nae gumption, kinna senseless. No like Bob. Bob had a' the sense in the wand. Eh, he was a fine beast, I miss him yet. When he de'ed I wrote a—a—what d'ye ca' thae things on gravestones? Ay, a epitaph. This was it:

> "Here lies Bob,
> He de'ed on the road
> Comin' frae Skarlin' Fair, b'Goad."

What d'ye think o' that for a epitaph?"

"Very good," said Kirsty. "I suppose it was true—that he died on the road, I mean?"

"True as daith . . . Ay."

He was silent until they drew near Cherrytrees, when he began to give Kirsty some of his ideas on the Anthony Hays.

"Ay, the Hays, faither and son, hev been at Cherrytrees a lang time, an' this yin (Mr. Anthony, he's aye' ca'ed, though there are nae mair o' them leevin') an' his wife are weel-likit folk. Deed, I whiles think that in the next warld they'll get the 'woe' that comes to ye when all men think well o' ye. It wud hardly be fair, to ma thinkin', to let folk hae sic a comfortable downsettin' in this warld, an' guid health and length o' days, and then gie them a place far ben in Heaven."

"But why," said Kirsty, "why, if they live so as to deserve an entrance into Heaven, should the fact that they have been comfortable in this world keep them out?"

"Because," Mr. Dickson said, "it's fine an' easy to be guid if ye're comfortable."

"Is it?" murmured Kirsty uncertainly, remembering Becky Sharp's remark that she could be good if she had £2,000 a year. "I don't quite see that. If one is very poor and ill and miserable this world can't mean much to one, and Heaven will shine all the more alluring, whereas if one has everything this world can give it's only a vexation to think of leaving it."

Mr. Dickson regarded Kirsty condescendingly.

"Of coorse it's no to be expeckit that ye can understand muckle aboot religion, you that's lived maist o' your life in furrin pairts. There's only wan thing that'll get ye into Heaven."

"Well, why shouldn't rich people have it as well as any one else?" Kirsty asked.

"Weel, ye ken fine that the Bible says it's as difficult for a rich man to get into Heaven as a camel to get through the eye of a needle—an' that juist means it canna be done. James, here, couldna get through the eye o' a needle, let alane a camel . . . Of coorse, if a man sells a' that he has—but he could hardly be expeckit to dae that aither. I've aye hed a guid deal o' sympathy wi' the Rich Young Ruler—"

"Well," said Kirsty, feeling that she had erred in allowing herself to be drawn into such a profitless discussion, "it isn't for us to judge our neighbours, rich or poor."

But Mr. Dickson was not so easily quelled. He gave his whip an airy whirl and said, "Whae's judgin'? They can a' gang whaur they like for me—Weel, here's Cherrytrees... The man wha keeps the gate-hoose is mairrit on a cousin o' ma wife's. I'm sure I hope ye'll get in here. We could baith be daein' wi' a cup o' tea."

But again Kirsty was rebuffed on the doorstep.

Mr. Dickson's face as he saw her turn away from the door was a study. Kirsty was guiltily aware that he had counted on putting up James and having a good tea and a talk with the man who had married his wife's cousin, and she hardly dared look at him as she said with what spirit she could muster, "I would like to go to Muirburn Manse now, please."

"Muirburn Manse!" said Mr. Dickson. "Ye needna bother. I saw Mr. Brand wi' ma ain een this verra day gaun awa to Priorsford in the nine train to attend the Presbytery meetin', an' Miss Brand wi' him."

"Oh—well, I want to go to Hopewaterfoot."

She bundled into her seat, and went off in the swaying wagonette, feeling like a pea in a drum.

At first she was left to her own meditations, for her charioteer was evidently too disgusted at the non-success of their afternoon outing to indulge in any more theological discussions; but in a little he said, without looking round, apropos of nothing that had gone before:

"I've kent Miss Merren (that's Mrs. Strang) a' her days. This while back she's ta'en to writin'," (He says it, thought Kirsty, as if it were an evil habit), "but she's no a bad body for a' that. I mind her when she was wee Miss Merren Stair, fleein' aboot on her powny like a wild thing. She mairret when she was but a lassie, an' her man was killed in the Boer War, an' syne she came back to Hopewaterfoot wi' her laddie, a bairn in airms." Mr. Dickson turned round, and looking sternly at Kirsty continued, "It's a maist confounded thing war . . . I was fond o' that laddie. He cam' to the shop to spend his pennies. He was terrible camsteerie, but there was nae ill in him. I used to help him to howk wurrums in oor midden—he was daft aboot fishin', of coorse . . . He cam' to see us the nicht afore he gaed awa' to France. He had been that feared that the War wud be feenished afore he got oot, an' he was neither to haud nor bind aboot gettin' awa'. He stood up to show us his uniform, his buttons that new and bricht . . . He went oot to Maister Erchie's regiment (that's the laird, ye ken), an' the first day he was in the trenches he was shot through the heid . . . When they buried him the buttons hedna got time to dim . . ."

"Poor, poor Mrs. Strang," said Kirsty.

"Ay. She never said onything, but she must ha' missed him sair. I ken *I* missed him—D'ye want oot here, or wull I gang roond by the drive?"

They had come to the wicket gate in the high beech hedge, which was a short cut through the garden to Mrs. Strang's house.

"Oh yes, please let me out here," Kirsty said. "And you might wait for a few minutes to see if I get in, and if I do, just go home. I shall walk. Thank you very much." Without waiting to see the effect of this command, she walked up the flagged path through the rose garden, and tirled on the knocker of the door.

Mrs. Strang was giving tea to Robert Brand when Kirsty was shown in, and she rose to greet her visitor with real pleasure, crying, "I was just wishing someone would come in, and first came Mr. Brand, and now you, the very people I would have chosen."

Kirsty sank into the chair offered her.

"You couldn't have a more grateful visitor," she assured her hostess. "I feel exactly as the dove from the Ark must have done when it could find no resting-place. I have paid three calls, and been turned from the door at each place."

"Returning calls, are you? Good child. You must be exhausted. But, on the other hand, you might have been more exhausted if you had found every one in. Anyway, it was luck for me that they were out, or you would never have got my length. Robert, push Miss Gilmour's chair nearer the table. That's better. How did you come?"

Kirsty began to laugh. "In Mr. Dickson's wagonette. And he treated me to his views on the life and character of every one we called on. I didn't mean to get a conveyance of any sort, but Mr. Dickson will drive me to it."

"Dickson's a great fellow," Mr. Brand said. "He's one of my elders, you know, and he keeps me toeing the line. I simply dare not preach an old sermon. He sits in the front seat, and fixes me with an eye like a hawk."

"I can see him," said Kirsty. "By the way, he told me you were in Priorsford today, when I threw out a suggestion about calling on your sister."

"So I was, and Rebecca too, and we wouldn't have been back yet if Colonel Home hadn't brought us up in his car . . . How are you liking us, Miss Gilmour? I mean the countryside and the folk of it."

"Well—"

"That sounds dubious."

Kirsty smiled. "You're not quite what I expected you to be, I confess. All my knowledge of country people has been got out of books, and I think I expected to create more of a sensation than I seem to have done. I mean—I thought a newcomer would arouse interest, some curiosity perhaps; but no. I don't think my coming made even a tiny splash in the Muirburn pool. And the village people aren't like book village people. I think I thought I would find a Jess and a Leeby in every cottage, but so far I've come across nothing but very stolid matrons. They seem to want nothing from me, not even a visit! But perhaps as I get to know them better—"

"Aren't you thinking of getting a car?" Mrs. Strang broke in. She was pouring out the tea, and not listening to the conversation.

"No," said Kirsty, making room for her cup on the table. "I don't want a car—it would spoil things so. If we had a car we would need a chauffeur, and to give him something to do we would have to be flying all the time about the countryside, worrying people for luncheon and tea, and all our quiet life would be spoiled. Besides, my aunt doesn't care for motoring."

"I'm afraid," Mrs. Strang said, "that I like rushing about the countryside. I'd order a car at once if I could afford it.

Wouldn't you, Rob?"

"I'd order two," said Mr. Brand recklessly.

"As a matter of fact I have ordered one," Mrs. Strang confessed. "I went to the motor show in Glasgow, simply to look—and I fell. But it's a very little one, and I shall drive it and clean it myself. Have a scone—"

Kirsty took a scone. "I hadn't thought of that," she said. "I might get a small one and be my own chauffeur. It's such fun to do things for oneself."

"There speaks the person who has always been waited on," said Mr. Brand.

"Oh, I know, but if you had spent most of your life travelling about and living in hotels and having everything done for you, you too would find pleasure in the most ordinary things that seem to other people pure weariness . . . Yes, I should like some jam."

"Oh," cried Mrs. Strang suddenly, "have the children come?"

Kirsty beamed. "They have."

"And what are they like? As nice as you expected?"

Kirsty shook her head. "I daren't begin about them in case of boring you to the bone. You see, children are new to me too—What I want to say is that this is the first time I have ever had tea with an author, and I feel it to be a great occasion."

"So it is!" Mr. Brand assured her.

"I won't be mocked," said Mrs. Strang. "Robert, I don't believe you ever even attempt to read my works." She turned to Kirsty and pointed a finger at the minister. "Mild domestic fiction he abhors; the more vivid forms of crime are all he cares about."

Robert Brand protested. "It isn't true, Miss Gilmour, believe me. I could pass an examination on any one of Mrs. Strang's books."

Merren Strang went on as if he had not spoken.

"I once knew a bishop who cared for nothing but reading the most lurid 'shockers.' And, after all, it is only natural that the clergy should like highly coloured fiction. It brings a brightness into their lives—"

"Otherwise lacking," Robert finished. "But it's true—not only about tuppence-coloured. I simply don't know how a country parson can exist who doesn't love books and gardens—gardens for the spring and summer, books for the winter."

"I suppose," said Kirsty, "living in the country in winter you do get through a lot of books?"

"Ah, you don't know anything about it yet. Wait till you see the doors shut and the lamps lit by four o'clock. You need to be pretty good friends with yourself, I can tell you, to live in the country in winter."

"Then do you read all the evening?"

"Three evenings of the week I'm out, but every other evening I work till eight-thirty, which is suppertime. I'm trying to write a sort of history of Upper Tweeddale in my spare moments. After supper I give myself to enjoyment for an hour or so. A clear fire, a bright lamp, a galloping yarn, and 'I wadna ca' the King ma cousin,' as they say about here."

"Oh, I know," cried Kirsty, her eyes sparkling. "I'm so looking forward to my first winter in Little Phantasy . . .

D'you remember Robert Louis' description of reading by lamplight? coming in from a patrol on the hills with the shepherd, and sitting down to a long evening by the fire with the *Vicomte!* And he tells how every now and again he would rise from his book and pull aside the blind, and see the snow and the glittering hollies in the garden, and the moonlight on the white hills, then he would turn back to the crowded field of life on the page of his book— Somehow that gives me a most happy feeling. It's so lovely to think of all the sunshine and laughter that can lie between the two boards of a book."

The minister nodded. "But what I object to is the small allowance of either given us in these days. Each book seems drearier than the one before."

" *'The brightest things in Baudelaire are anything else but gay'*," Mrs Strang quoted. "Have some more tea, Robert? No? Don't you know that it is hopelessly out of date to write as if there was anything decent left in the world? You simply must not let either your characters or your readers be happy."

"But your books are happy," Kirsty objected.

"Oh, but I don't pretend to count. Are you going, Robert? Tell Rebecca to come and see me when she has time. I shall be able to take her to Priorsford to shop when I get my little car. Yes. Take any books you like."

Robert Brand went off happily with two new books under his arm, and Merren Strang looked after him affectionately.

"There goes a good fellow," she said. "A righteous man, if ever there was one."

Kirsty nodded. "I think so too. And he preaches so well. . . . Isn't it odd that he should be satisfied with such a small place?"

"*Is* he satisfied? He knows he hasn't strength at present for anything very strenuous. And this isn't a small place. His visiting often means cycling or walking twelve miles. And he doesn't spare himself. He has a weeknight service every week up the Moors as well as in Muirburn. And he is doctor and lawyer and everything to the shepherd folk—as his father was before him. It's amazing what a minister can mean in a country place! But come and be cosy and let's have a talk. You don't need to go yet awhile, need you?"

"I don't want to go," Kirsty said truthfully . . . "I expect you are sick of having people gush about your books, but you don't know how thrilled I am to be here." She looked round the pleasant, homely room. "Is this where you write?"

"Oh, I write anywhere."

"But—I thought authors needed perfect quiet, and a large writing-table, and shelves of books for reference, and that sort of thing."

Mrs. Strang laughed. "Perhaps real writers do. I'm afraid I'm dreadfully disappointing. I do wish for your sake that I had been a real literary lion with a wonderful writing-room filled with signed photographs of other writers, and all manner of things that would have impressed you. I'm only an author by chance, so to speak. I feel the merest amateur."

"What made you begin to write?—This sounds like an interview."

Merren Strang lay back in her chair and smiled at Kirsty. "I'm sure I don't know what made me write. It was in the War. I did what work I could, but I had some spare time when one simply did not dare to have spare time—and the thought came to me to write a book, something very simple that would make pleasant reading—you see there's nothing of Art for Art's sake about me. I thought of all the sad people, and the tired and anxious people, and the sick people. Have you ever had anyone lie very ill in a nursing home while you haunted lending libraries and bookshops for something that would help through sleepless nights for him? If you have, you will know how difficult it is to get the right kind of books. Merely clever books are no use, for a very sick person has done with cleverness. You need a book very much less and very much more than that. So I tried my hand and produced *The Penny Whistle*. I had no thought of money or anything else when I wrote it, and because it was a real cry from my own heart it touched the hearts of quite a lot of people. So I went on writing. I have only the smallest talent—about as much as would lie on a threepenny-piece!—but if I can give pleasure to some I'm glad and grateful."

Kirsty sighed. "I think it must be the most delightful thing to feel that you give pleasure to people. Do you get letters from grateful readers? I expect you do."

Merren nodded. "The world's not as full of clever people as you would think, it's only that the few there are are very vocal. The world is full of simple plain people who like plain things, and who are often very bewildered and unhappy. Perhaps my books are a sort of soothing syrup: I don't know. It's a stupid subject anyway. Tell me about the household at Little Phantasy."

"That will keep," said Kirsty. "Won't you please tell me some books to get? The novels sent from the library are a menace. Aunt Fanny was almost in hysterics over the last lot, and has gone back today to a book she had in her childhood, *Anna Lee, the Maiden, the Wife, and the Mother!* I never tire of the old books myself, and I have just gone back to Jane Austen. We get all the Lives that come out—Aunt Fanny feels safe with them—but I ordered a novel I saw raved about by the reviewers, and it is the grimiest thing I've ever read."

"How was it reviewed?" Merren asked with interest. "When you read that a certain novel deals with a subject in a 'courageous yet delicate manner,' you are pretty safe to give it a pass."

Kirsty laughed. "I wish I had given this a pass. It is diabolically clever, but it slimes over things like a snail. But I'm sandwiching it with *Crossriggs*—do you ever sandwich books?—and I find that a most excellent plan. It's like coming out with hot, tired eyes from being steeped in heavy scent and blinded by lights and deafened by garish noises into clean salt air."

"I know. I know. I know *Crossriggs* almost by heart. I read it once a year, and am always desperately sorry when I finish it."

"And," Kirsty went on, "it isn't as if the Findlaters were in the least mawkish or miss-ish. They can beat the 'courageous but delicate' writers at their own game. Did you ever get such a feeling of the utter *badness* of a woman as those two spinster ladies give you of the girl, Dolly Orranmore, that poor Van is jockeyed into marrying?"

"It's amazing. But they make you hate nastiness, while the other kind of writer buzzes round it—like a bluebottle round tainted meat. I often wonder if our strong novelists really meet the people they write about—the ape and tiger sort of people. I must have led a dreadfully circumscribed life, for I've only met decent people. It is very cramping to a novelist only to know one side of life. I read a review the other day which began, 'This is a book about good, gentle, scrupulous people who live on the bright side of life.' Those are the sort I have always known, and I'm afraid if I tried to make the other kind 'out of my own head,' they would be the most unconvincing villains."

"Tell me," said Kirsty, "aren't you frightfully nervous when you bring out a book what the critics will say?"

"I am rather—it is like sending a poor little unprotected child into a cold world. But, on the whole, the critics have been wonderfully good to me, though I'm not an interesting person to review. After you've said my books are pleasant there isn't much more to say, is there?"

"Lots. But don't you think it must make a great difference where and how a critic reads a book? If the cook has influenza, and the dinner is bad, and his wife cross, he can't be in a good mood, and the book will suffer in consequence."

"One would think so," Merren agreed. "And then, of course, there is always the danger of a book falling into wrong hands. A budding Bolshevist gets an old-fashioned, rather prim story—he rends it, naturally; a prim-minded gentleman with a love for order and decency gets a 'courageous' book, and with a howl of rage he flies at it."

"I see," said Kirsty, beginning to pull on her gloves. "It's all very difficult, but if critics would read the books in bed they would always find something good in them. I don't know how it is, but even a book which I didn't think much of by the light of day, when read in bed reveals all sorts of excellences. I read in bed every night for half an hour by the clock, and every book I read seems a masterpiece. Now I really must go. I've stayed an unconscionable time. Would you have been writing?"

"Not I." Merren whisked the very idea airily away: "I never write if I can help it. I welcome every interruption. . . . Listen to me, child. I want you to come here very often, and I want you to bring the children. And do you think you would persuade Miss Fanny to come? I've fallen in love with her, woolly wraps and all!—If you wait a second I'll get my hat and walk home a bit of the way with you."

CHAPTER 11

" . . . Gie me a Border burn
That canna rin wi'oot a turn."
J. B. SELKIRK

OF ALL the lovely glens in the pleasant land of Upper Tweeddale there is none more lovely than Hopecarton. To reach it you must leave the high road at the beginning of Hopecarton village (it consists only of six houses, and a shop which sells more acid drops for a penny than a shop has ever been known to do), turn to your left, and cross the bridge, pass the school and the schoolhouse, follow the burn for a hundred yards or so, and you will find yourself in the "greenest glen shone on by the sun."

It is narrow to start with, and the hills rise steeply on either side, but as you follow the burn the glen widens, and there are stretches of emerald turf running into the heather, banks of fragrant thyme, and one white hawthorn-tree which now, in the sweet o' the year, stands snow-white, enchanted.

To this glen one shining day in the beginning of June Kirsty Gilmour brought her household to hold high revel.

There was no special reason for having a picnic. It was nobody's birthday, nobody had been specially good, nobody had done anything brilliant in the way of lessons; but on the other hand nobody had been specially bad, the sun was shining on the Hope Water, turning it to molten gold, and Kirsty felt that something was due to the glad earth, and proposed a day by the Hopecarton burn. Having said it there was no turning back.

With a shout Specky cast his books on the floor and fled to see that his fishing tackle was in good order. Barbara threw her arms round Kirsty's neck, crying "*Darling* Pie," while Miss Carter with alacrity began to tidy up.

Bill had hardly begun to take lessons seriously, he only toyed with them for an hour at a time, and this morning he was accompanying Tod, the gardener, as he went about his work in the sunny garden. Here Specky found him and told him of the picnic.

To expect enthusiasm from Bill was to court disappointment. He rarely showed any feeling except, perhaps, rage. When Bill was angry the whole house was aware of it. But Miss Carter assured Kirsty that he was really improving. He had been three weeks at Little Phantasy, and had only made two bad breaks. Once, roused beyond endurance by some fancied slight, he had bitten Specky, and another time he had thrown his mug at Barbara, missing his mocking sister and deluging poor Miss Fanny. That lady had been much shaken by the incident.

"Won't it be fine, Bill?" said Specky coaxingly. "Pie says it's a lovely burn."

"Will you give me a turn with your rod?" Bill demanded.

"Yes," Specky promised rather ruefully.

Easie, when interviewed, flung herself with enthusiasm into the thought of a picnic; indeed, she was so high-flown in her ideas that Kirsty had to hold her to the ground. When the offer of roasted fowls had to be declined owing to the impossibility of procuring and roasting anything in the space of one hour, they finally decided on cold lamb, a salad, plenty of bread and butter and fruit; and Easie promised that Nellie would bicycle over in time for tea with a baking of scones and pancakes.

They drove in Mr. Dickson's wagonette, Specky beside the driver, deeply interested in all he could tell him of the trout in the different burns. Bill (his melodeon by his side) sat between Kirsty and Miss Carter. Whenever their attention was engaged he leaned over and rattled a stick between the spokes of the wheels. Barbara and the lunch occupied the opposite seat.

Miss Fanny had declined to accompany them. She loathed picnics, and could see no enjoyment in eating out of doors. It seemed to her little short of imbecile to leave a well-cooked meal in a comfortable dining-room to perch on a tuft of heather with some cold meat. She had seen the party leave with a feeling of satisfaction: there would be peace for a few hours, anyway.

Not, she would have told you, that she disliked the children, poor things, but she was too old for the restless atmosphere that stirring children give to a house. They wearied her. Specky was her favourite; there was a gentleness about Specky that endeared him to everyone. Barbara, with the best possible intentions, was something of a destroying angel in the house. What she touched she generally broke, and her belongings were thrown about in a most admired disorder. Miss Fanny would have been the first to admit that she was a most affectionate and warm-hearted child, but she dreaded her embraces. When Barbara rushed to hug her, the poor lady retreated from her as from a charging bull.

As for Bill, Miss Fanny avoided his society whenever possible.

By five o'clock in the afternoon the picnic was approaching a conclusion. It had been a highly successful outing. The cold lamb and salad washed down by ginger-beer had been excellent; and after it they had played a new and thrilling game. Barbara was a fervent Jacobite at this time, and as Specky subscribed to all his sister's opinions, it followed that he was the same, and they decided that "Jacobites" was the only game for this glen of glens.

At first there was some friction between Barbara and Specky as to who would play the coveted part of the young Prince. Specky claimed it by right of sex, but Barbara overbore him by the weight of the arguments that she brought forward as to her superior height and strength and agility, and Specky, who ever in his right hand carried gentle peace, meekly gave in, merely remarking, "I don't see why you can't be Flora Macdonald, when you're a girl anyway."

"Ho! Flora Macdonald!" said Barbara disdainfully.

It was finally decided that Specky would be the gentle Lochiel, while Bill was offered the somewhat ungrateful part of Murray of Broughton.

"Bill, will you be Murray of Broughton?" Barbara asked, murmuring quickly to Kirsty, "Don't say anything about him being a traitor."

It is doubtful whether Bill had ever heard the word "traitor," and certainly he had never heard of Mr. Secretary Murray, but he gravely nodded his acceptance of the part.

"Shall I be Mrs. Murray?" Kirsty suggested helpfully, only to be promptly put in her place by Barbara, who told her, "You can't be her. You and Carty must be the abominable English soldiers looking for the Prince."

So they played, and found it a most pleasing game for a sunny afternoon on the hillside, that pitiful, beautiful story of love and loyalty.

After much lurking among heather bushes, and crossing and recrossing the water, hotly pursued by the brutal and licentious soldiery, tea was a very grateful thought. In the Prince's camping-place a fire was already lit, and Specky and Bill squatted beside it feeding it carefully with twigs, while Barbara took the kettle some distance away to fill it at a well she had discovered which bubbled out crystal-clear water.

When Nellie arrived, hot and important, with Easie's contributions to the feast, the kettle was just "coming through," and she was invited to remain to help to eat the feather-light scones and pancakes. Miss Carter, being an expert with picnic fires, looked after the tea-making. Kirsty, watching her quick, deft movements admiringly, thought what a capable creature this girl was. She had settled at once into her place at Little Phantasy. She was never in the way, but always there when she was wanted. The children liked and respected her, Miss Fanny found her sympathetic, the servants admitted that instead of making extra work she was a help to them. And she was pretty and young and lighthearted, altogether a very delightful addition to the household.

"I can't call you *Miss* Carter," Kirsty told her. "May I call you Stella?"

"No, please don't. I hate my name, really. Stella Carter sounds so theatrical somehow. If you'd call me 'Carty' as the children do I would like it."

So Carty she was to them all.

They had tea by the burn at the point by the white hawthorn where it widened into a shallow, glittering stream.

Just as they were beginning Specky pointed out two figures coming down the glen.

"Shepherds probably," said Kirsty, buttering a scone for Bill.

"Fishers perhaps," Specky said hopefully, but when the men came nearer it was seen that they were neither shepherds nor fishers, but Colonel Home and the Rev. Robert Brand. They stopped as they came up to the picnic party and greeted Kirsty, who immediately asked them to have some tea.

"We have two extra mugs," she told them hospitably, "and the tea isn't very badly smoked. Miss Carter, may I introduce Colonel Home—Mr. Brand? Colonel Home, these are the children I told you about . . . you remember? Barbara, Specky—and this is Bill."

"I've seen them from a distance," her landlord said as he shook hands. "I really don't think I can wait for tea, thanks very much. I told Watson to bring the car to the bridge at four-thirty—it's that time now."

He stood leaning on his stick, and Kirsty saw that his face was grey with fatigue. "Tired to death," she thought to herself, "pretending that he is a whole man and can walk the hills as well as ever he could." Aloud she said, "It won't hinder you long to drink a dish of tea, and Easie, our cook, has baked all sorts of fine things. See, this is a most convenient boulder to sit on. I'm sure Mr. Brand wants his tea."

"I don't deny it," said that gentleman, and Colonel Home had perforce to remain.

"Have you come a long way?" Kirsty asked him, when he was comfortably seated with his back against a young rowan tree.

Only over the hills, he told her, from Phantasy—nothing of a walk—at least once he would have thought it nothing. He had found Mr. Brand paying a pastoral visit to the shepherd's cottage at Hope Head, and they had come down the glen together.

"Is this still Phantasy?" asked Kirsty.

"Yes, this side of the glen; the burn is the march."

"I see," said Kirsty, thinking that people who only answered questions put to them and volunteered nothing were extraordinarily difficult to converse with.

"We've been here all day," she told him. "Isn't it a perfect place for a picnic? . . We've been playing at 'Jacobites.' Barbara was Prince Charlie, and I had the ignominious part of an English soldier."

She stopped.

Colonel Home said, "Indeed!"

"The uninterested creature!" thought Kirsty. She looked round at the others. Mr. Brand was talking to Miss Carter. Specky had mounted a shaky wooden bridge that at this point spanned the burn, and was being fed by Barbara and

Nellie, who hovered near him like the ravens of Elijah.

"You can't think how good things taste up here," he told them. "Throw me up another chocolate biscuit. It's a pity the bridge is too shaky for more than one at a time. Look out, Barbara, can't you? You nearly had me over."

Bill was sitting under a red parasol belonging to Kirsty, wiping his fingers delicately on a handkerchief.

"You'll fall into the stream," he warned Specky.

"*Stream*," jeered Barbara. "Can't you say bur-r-n, you horrid little Englisher?"

Kirsty laughed and turned to her companion. "Barbara is the most perfervid Scot. It comes from living in England. Poor Bill with his stream!.. I do love a burn, don't you? Especially this kind of burn that twists and turns, sometimes so narrow that you can hardly see it for heather and ferns, and then widening out, sparkling and rippling."

She stopped and softly quoted:

> "... Gie me a Border burn
> That canna rin wi'oot a turn.

How utterly heart-breaking to read that in a foreign land with no prospect of getting home!.. This is my first spring in Scotland for twenty-two years."

"But surely," said Colonel Home, "you can have had very little recollection of Scotland. You must have left it as a baby."

"I was eight, so you see I'm a very mature person now. It does seem grim to talk of years in twenties! But twenty-two years in England simply made me more of a Scot—and now

I'm home . . . You have been a great deal away too, haven't you?"

"Yes. India, then South Africa, then India again. Then the War—But we creep back in the end, those of us who survive."

His tone was so bitter and hopeless that Kirsty found nothing to say in reply, and they sat and looked at the burn in silence.

But the beauty of the glen, the sound of the water, the crying of birds, and the sweet-scented air moved Kirsty to sudden anger against the man beside her who, it seemed to her, was not grateful enough for the good things God had given him. She turned impulsively and cried:

"You talk as if it were a hardship to come home to this. How can you! I don't say the dead weren't the lucky ones—they made a great finish—but think, won't you, about all the poor men still lying in hospital, blinded men, the men who lost their reason—and others trying to earn their bread and failing to find work. They were all willing to give their lives, but they were asked to do a much harder thing in these days—to live. And here are you coming back to a place like Phantasy, the home of your people, with eyes to see this green glen, and—and—Oh, you should be down on your knees thanking Heaven fasting—"

Then the spurt of anger died down, and with cold horror she realized that she had been scolding an almost perfect stranger, her landlord to boot, a man of years and honours.

"Oh, forgive me!" she faltered. "I know it's no earthly business of mine. I can't think what made me talk like that."

In her confusion she longed to rise and fly and hide somewhere her diminished head. She saw with envy Stella Carter in deep and evidently most amiable conversation with Mr. Brand. Every one appeared to be having a good time but her luckless self and her moody companion. She dared not look at him to see how he had taken her tirade, but her relief was great when presently he said, " 'Down on my knees thanking Heaven fasting.' Perhaps you're right; I hadn't realized that I was grousing." He was looking down as he spoke, picking some sprigs of wild thyme. "It's a good thing at times to have one's faults pointed out to one, Miss Gilmour. Thank you."

"Oh," said Kirsty with a gasp. "Thank *you*. You're such a—a naturally angry person anyway, that I thought you might never forgive my outrageous rudeness. I don't make a habit of it, really I don't. I may very likely never be rude to you again."

Colonel Home actually laughed, and Kirsty, feeling very much as the lamb must have done when it found itself on sociable terms with the lion, turned in order to create a diversion, and suggested to the company that it was time to pack up and go home.

"I told Mr. Dickson to come to us to the village about six," she said.

"But it doesn't feel as if it were time to go home," Barbara, complained.

"No," said Robert Brand, looking at his wristwatch. "In the Sight of God it is only a quarter to five, but it's a quarter to six summertime."

It did seem a pity to leave, for the air was still warm, and drowsy with the humming bees, and sweet with the scent of thyme, and the sun was still high.

Bill had come and seated himself by Colonel Home, his melodeon laid carefully beside him, and he now said confidentially, "Besides big Tweed I've seen four wee Tweeds today."

"You mean," Archie Home said gravely, "burns that run into Tweed."

Bill nodded, and then said, "Tell me a story, won't you?"

"I'm afraid I don't know any stories."

"Oh yes," Bill said confidently, "you're sure to."

Round them the whaups were crying "*Pooelie, Pooelie.*" In desperation, hypnotized by the steady blue eyes fixed on him, Colonel Home began, "Have you ever heard the story of the Respectable Whaup?"

"Tell us," said Barbara, casting herself at his feet.

He cleared his throat nervously. "I'm afraid I'm no hand at telling a story, but . . . Well, one day, in this very glen, a shepherd was coming home from church, and he found the place full of whaups all crying *Pooelie, Pooelie*, as they are doing today, only the place was thick with them. They flew so low that they brushed against him, and their wailing irritated him so that he shoo'ed them away with his arms. But they only seemed to mock him and whistle in his very face, so he waved his stick at them, and threw bits of rock at them, and at last in desperation cried, *'Deil rax the birds' thrapples.'* In a moment all the noise was hushed, and the glen was empty. Only one bird was left, standing on tall legs before him, its head bowed, and its beak touching the heather.

" 'What bird are ye?' the shepherd asked, and the bird answered, 'I am a Respectable Whaup,' and went on to tell the shepherd that he had broken in on the whaups' family gathering. 'Once in a hundred years,' he said, 'we forgather for decent conversation and here we are interrupted by a muckle swearin' man—"

Colonel Home stopped. "Go on. Go on," Barbara cried, "what did the whaup do next?"

"Did it peck him," Bill asked hopefully, "peck him with its long beak?"

Colonel Home turned desperately to Kirsty. "I say, you know, there's no use in me going on with this. I've just realized that it's very long and involved, and I can't remember the end . . . It's called *The Rime of True Thomas*."

"Oh," moaned Barbara, "*couldn't* you remember just a little bit more?"

The harassed storyteller suddenly had an idea. "I tell you what," he said. "I have the book at Phantasy. I'll give it to you, and you'll read it for yourself."

"That will be better," Kirsty agreed; but Bill said coldly that it would not be better, and that if he couldn't hear the story now he never wanted to hear it at all.

"We'll read it aloud," said Kirsty, ignoring the malcontent, "if Colonel Home will be kind enough to let us have it. Now we must go."

"Let poor Bill play once," Barbara begged, keen for anything that would delay the departure.

"Well, once."

Bill took his melodeon, and succeeded in producing some

weird and startling noises; then he looked up at the blue heavens, and, as if inspired by what he saw there, he began to chant:

> "Oh, you never saw the likes of it
> When the sky was set."

"The sun, you *mean*," corrected Specky.

"When the *sky* was set," Bill repeated firmly.

Archie Home's eyes met Kirsty's.

"Don't dare to laugh," she whispered, "it's as much as your life's worth."

Happily Bill's song went no further. "Stand up now," he commanded. "It's *God save the King*," and again he drew forth some discordant sounds, watching keenly the while to see that the whole company stood at attention.

After that everybody picked up something in the way of baskets and kettles, looked to see that no unsightly paper had been left lying about, and proceeded slowly towards the village. Nellie went first on her bicycle, then came Barbara and Specky laughing together and tugging at a basket containing the teacups, which they dropped more than once with an ominous crack which boded ill for the contents.

Bill had attached himself to Colonel Home, and had bestowed on him the melodeon to carry. He insisted on holding the hand of his new friend, and also keeping firm hold of Kirsty's hand. Robert Brand, walking with Miss Carter, watched Bill with amusement.

"Funny chap," he said. "I like his odd little face. It is as if someone had brushed it up from the chin when it was soft. D'you see? His mouth turns up, his little blunt nose turns up . . . Isn't it Theocritus who talks about the 'blunt-faced bees'?"

"Is it? I'm afraid I don't know Theocritus, but it's deliciously true of Bill. He is a little blunt-faced B . . ." She turned and looked back to the glen. "What a day of days this has been. I don't think I'll ever forget it . . . I do think there is something enchanted about this place."

"There is," said Robert Brand. "Don't you know that Merlin once lived here, Merlin the Wizard? Some day we must have another picnic, to Merlin's haugh . . . This place is full of fairy lore. Isn't it odd to think that there is practically nothing changed in this green glen since Merlin 'sang his wild songs in the morning of the world'?"

Stella Carter looked up at him and laughed.

"It's almost too much," she said, "to come straight from Clapham to *this!*"

CHAPTER 12

> "One may be happy to a good degree, I think, in a faithful friend, or moderate fortune and a retired life; further than this I know nothing to wish, but if there be anything beyond it, I wish it you." *Letters of Dorothy Osborne*

THE NEXT DAY Kirsty wrote to Blanche Cunningham:

" . . . I feel ashamed of the letters I have written to you lately—hardly more than 'All well: how are you?' But you know what it means to have children in the house; half the time is spent simply standing round, listening. I never tire of it; but I get nothing else done.

"I hope this is going to be a real letter. The children have gone off with Miss Carter and Nellie to climb Ratchell Hill. They have tea with them, and won't be back till nearly bedtime. It adds greatly to their pleasure to have Nellie accompany them, and there is nothing Nellie likes better. The merest hint, and cap and apron are thrown off and she is ready for the road. I'm afraid they will have rather a hard pull up, for there is a strong wind blowing. Indeed, it is cold and grey, like November, a dismal change after a fortnight of glowing sunshine.

"It is quite a day for a fire, and Aunt Fanny is enjoying it, and enjoying, also, wearing an extra shawl. She has been reading diligently since luncheon at little books, but now her specs are off, and she is having a quiet sleep. It is odd how old she is at sixty-five; some women are quite girlish at that age, anxious to share in all the fun, but she is content with the chimney-corner. It amazed me to hear the other night from Aunt Fanny's own lips that she had once been engaged to be married. I don't know why I should have been amazed, for she is a pretty, at least a pleasant-looking, woman now, and forty odd years ago she must have been an absolute duck. What did people wear forty-five years ago? Bustles and chignons and things like that? I can picture Aunt Fanny, with a dress very tight about the waist and humpy behind (like the pictures in an old *Punch*), and her hair all curled and puffed, and a locket round her neck, being very sweet and gentle and a little coy to a young man with a frock-coat and whiskers.

"She was vague about why the engagement had been broken off (I verily believe she has forgotten!), murmured something about a hasty temper, and 'no reason for jealousy,' and owned that perhaps she had been 'flighty.' Somehow I can't help thinking that it was rather a good thing Aunt Fanny did not marry. I am sure a husband would always have been to her more of a nuisance than anything else; and there is no doubt she has no real liking for children. When the whiskered gentleman left her I feel sure she promptly forgot him and 'took comfort to be her spouse'!

"It's great luck to have a household of old and young. Aunt Fanny and I alone together would be happy, I daresay, but very sober and staid and slow-paced. As it is, we never get time to settle. I don't know if Aunt Fanny quite likes it, poor dear, but it certainly is doing her good: she has become years younger and more active these last three weeks in her efforts to avoid old Bill. And neither of us would enjoy our quiet evenings as we do, were they not the peaceful end of strenuous days. I feel surprised at the change in myself. Was I ever really listless and quiet and lifeless and all the other things you used to taunt me with? Anyway, now I'm not. I talk all the time. I'm getting quite 'forritsome' in my manner. I fish, I climb hills, I play football as if I were seventeen instead of thirty, *and*—the children think me quite young. Aha!

"Specky paid me such a nice compliment the other night when I was saying goodnight to him.

" 'When are ladies allowed to marry, Pie?' he asked. "I thought a minute, and said seventeen was about the age.

"Could you marry, Pie?' he asked next.

"Having satisfied him on that point, I said, 'What age do you think I am?'

'I thought about seventeen,' he said gravely.

"I felt highly pleased, for most children assume their elders to be hovering about eighty, and are surprised that they don't remember the battle of Waterloo and Mary Queen of Scots.

"I must not rave about Specky's gentleness and goodness or you will think that he has suddenly turned into a priggish Little Lord Fauntleroy. If he thought about it for a minute he would scorn to be good. It is just that he doesn't think about himself at all, and is *naturally* good. Lessons are what he dislikes. Pen and ink are an abomination to him. For his writing exercise (his writing is shocking) we said he might write a letter to his father. He managed to scrawl about two lines, and when Carty protested he said plaintively, 'I know Daddy's a nice person, but I've got worms to dig.'

"He would like to spend every minute of the day out of doors—fishing, for preference. We dare not let him go to Tweed alone, but he is very content with the Hope Water. He fishes from the little waterfall beyond the house to the bridge where the stream meets Tweed. We can watch him from the dining-room windows, moving like an elf in his slim grey jersey. He is the eternal figure of your true fisherman—patient, hopeful, happy. He has worn a track right along the bank with his steadfast feet!

"For the first fortnight he fished, literally, all day, and caught nothing. It got on all our nerves. At first we went out to meet him and asked gaily, 'Well, have you caught anything?' but the answer was so invariably in the negative that we got quite shy about asking. In vain did Tod (the gardener) help him to dig the most tempting bait, in vain Specky threw his line into every likely pool—nothing happened. We got so annoyed at the trout. So much so that Miss Wotherspoon said vindictively, 'That laddie'll catch a fish if I've to tie one on to the line.' However, there was no need for such extreme measures. One evening Specky came in triumphant, carrying a minute trout, weighing I should think about one ounce.

"We all said we were so glad, and what a noble fish it was, and all was well until Barbara rushed in to see the first catch. She looked at it, and promptly burst into floods of tears, and sobbing out, 'He's gone and killed a poor baby,' rushed from the room.

"Specky, very crestfallen, ate his supper, his catch clutched in one hot hand.

" 'It's all very well,' he said, 'for Barbara to go on like that, but even the babies are very hard to catch.'

"We tried to cheer him, but he went rather heavily upstairs to bed, after having entrusted the trout to Easie, who promised to fry it in oatmeal for his breakfast.

"Half an hour later I went up to the boys' room. Bill was sitting on his bed half-undressed, solemnly chanting to himself some low ditty, while at the other bed knelt Barbara and Specky, the tears still wet on their faces, clasped in each other's arms, saying their prayers together.

"I always thought I didn't care much for little girls, but I make an exception in Barbara's favour. That child has the best intentions in the world, and it isn't her fault if she generally forgets them in the stress of keeping her end up with two brothers. Few people have such a gift for living as Barbara. She just seems to fling herself headlong into the sunshine and joy of these summer days. Desperately careless and untidy, scoldings worry her not at all. She is deeply penitent—for a minute! Then off again. She is never at a loss for something to amuse herself with: animals are her passion; she beseeches me to keep a pig! So far we have only a donkey, and a cat which the children have christened Percy. Easie pronounces it Pearcy, and Miss Wotherspoon Perzy.

"I don't like to talk to the children much of their mother (I don't feel I have any right to, and they might resent it), but I can see that Barbara tries (when she remembers, poor lamb!) to take her place with Specky and Bill. I find that she goes in every night and reads the Bible to them, as her mother did.

" 'What shall I read?' I heard her ask the other night.

" 'Oh,' said Specky, who is always polite, 'you might read a psalm, one of the nice little short ones, or Daniel and the lions' den, or the men in the furnace, or—"

"Then Bill, seated on his pillow, said languidly, 'You may read me about Jono,' but whether he meant the heathen goddess or the prophet it was hard to say

"When Barbara has read some verses carefully, she continues reading softly, running the words together to make a soothing effect.

" 'I'm murmuring,' she told me; 'that is what Mummy always did to put us to sleep.'

"Bill is a 'card': a most surprising fellow.

"He is naturally naughty, as Specky is naturally good, and he is never repentant. That is Aunt Fanny's great charge against him—that he won't say he is sorry; but after all, what would be the good of saying it when he obviously isn't sorry.

"Yesterday when I was round in the back premises looking for Tod I heard voices. Aunt Fanny was inspecting the greenhouse, and had found Bill squirting water from the tank over the plants and over himself. Having reprimanded him for that, she went on to other offences.

" 'Who,' she asked, 'turned on the tap of the paraffin barrel and ran out all the oil?'

" 'Mr. Nobody,' said Bill, insolently swaggering about.

"Waste almost breaks Aunt Fanny's heart, and this seemed to her an awful crime. She continued:

" 'Don't you know, you bad boy, that Someone was looking down at you when you did that?'

" 'Someone up the loft?' Bill asked, rather interested.

" *'God saw you,'* Aunt Fanny said solemnly.

"Bill looked at her as if he were sorry for her ignorance.

" 'Ho, don't you know? God's at Clapham. He saw me steal a lump of sugar there. Carty said He did. He didn't see me eat it, though, for I went under the table.'

"Carty says that when Bill was small he refused utterly to greet visitors, but now he has developed a sort of fierce politeness which is very disconcerting. He grabs their hands, and says rapidly, without looking at them, 'Howdyoudo. Quitewellthankyou,' and retires, feeling his duty done.

"Barbara and Specky are careless about their appearance; neither of them ever possesses a clean handkerchief, and they have to be sent back constantly to brush their teeth or hair. Bill is always a pattern of neatness. No one ever saw him with dirty hands (when he feels them sticky he wipes them on the clothes of whoever is nearest to him), and he keeps his hanky always in the fold. When it is rumpled he throws it away. He likes to wash in my bathroom and use my special soap ('It smells of you, Pie'), and he adores having scent on his handkerchief. My lavender water is too mild for him, but Nellie went to Priorsford for the day, and brought him a bottle labelled 'New Mown Hay,' most offensive stuff, which he uses regularly. *Sweet William with his homely cottage smell!*

"Specky, as you know, hates pen and ink, but Bill 'hears the sound of pens writing.' Already in staggering capitals he prints stories. He is struggling with one now, called *The Brave Prince*. It is all about dragons and other fearsome things, but when I read it last night the last half-finished sentence ran, 'something soft touched his hand—' 'What was it, Bill?' I asked, and he turned to me and gave, like the interpreter, 'a wonderful innocent smile,' and said, 'it was a pussy.' The gentle imaginings of Bill!

"Well, that's all about the children. It's odd, but I can scarcely believe that there ever was a time when I wasn't at Little Phantasy, and hadn't the children to enjoy. All the rest of my life seems like rather a dull story about somebody else.

"Do you remember a book you liked very much, *The Penny Whistle?* Well, the author of it lives near here—Mrs. Strang of Hopewaterfoot, a relation of my landlord. She has been to see us, and I had tea with her the other day, I liked her whenever I saw her; chiefly, I think, because she reminded me of you. She is dark and very slim (there is something boyish about her, though she can't be young. How old would you be, if you were married in the Boer War?) and has an impudent little face—like you! Her husband was killed in the Boer War, and her only child in France, so she is quite alone. It is frightfully sad, but she isn't the sort of woman you could offer pity to: she never speaks of her losses. She doesn't seem to think it is at all clever to be able to write, and rather laughs at herself as an author . . . I would like you to meet her. We have other delightful neighbours, the Anthony Hays of Cherrytrees. They are elderly, and frankly Victorian, and much thought of by Aunt Fanny.

"I like the parson we 'sit under,' Mr. Brand. He is frightfully keen on books, and so poor that he can't even afford the *Times Literary Supplement*. I am going to take in every paper and magazine that I think he would like and cart them along to him. I wish I could do something for the sister, she is so hard working and conscientious, and seems to have such a dull time. But I don't think she likes me, she is so prickly when I try to be nice to her.

"I don't believe I have ever mentioned Miss Carter! She is all you said she was and more. She is as good as can be with the children, and she is most companionable and pleasant in the house. She tells me she has a stepmother and several younger sisters, and isn't wanted at home, so I suppose she will have to go on teaching for always unless she marries. What fun it would be if she married Mr. Brand! He is the only eligible bachelor about here, and perhaps 'eligible' is hardly the word. Of course there is Colonel Home, but any one can see he is a confirmed bachelor. Blanche, I did a fearful thing yesterday. I squirm when I think of it. We were having a picnic at Hopecarton Glen, and the landlord and Mr. Brand came walking past on their way home from somewhere, and of course we had to ask them to have tea. I was trying to make conversation with Colonel Home, and he said something, I forget what it was, that sounded as if he were sorry he had been spared to come home from the War, and I quite suddenly lost my temper and scolded like a fishwife. It was most uncalled for, and I simply can't think what he must have thought of me. The odd thing was that instead of being furious he was quite patient under my rebuke. He really has a very nice smile.

"I had a letter from Mr. Crawford the other day from somewhere in Spain. He seems fairly cheerful.

"Will you give Tim all the nicest messages you can think of from me? It is splendid to hear he is so much better. Seeing you would put new life into him. I'm glad he has you, but I wish I could have you too!

          "Love from
             KIRSTY."

CHAPTER 13

"Hark! I hear the sound of coaches."
The Beggar's Opera
"Be pitiful: be courteous."
ST. PAUL

WITH ANXIOUS EYE the Rev. Norman and Mrs. McCandlish watched the barometer as the day fixed for their annual garden party drew near.

For a fortnight the weather had been perfect, and it hardly seemed possible that it would hold out for another two days. Every morning Mrs. McCandlish sighed and said, "If only we had fixed it for today; it would have been just as convenient, but how could we tell?" And her husband replied with the easy optimism that is so hard for wives to bear, "It will be all right, you'll see. There is no sign of the weather breaking."

The day before the event was grey and cold and windy, and threatened rain.

Mrs. McCandlish's face remained pink and white and placid, her hair perfect in its elaborate waves and curls, everything about her person was as rigidly neat as ever, but her husband knew that she was seriously perturbed by the way she moved restlessly about, touching things aimlessly, and answering in an absent way when spoken to.

He himself felt more than a little anxious. If the rain did pour, what a fiasco the afternoon would be! Every one herded into the house, no one admiring the garden, all the carefully thought out plans lying in ruins. But aloud he said, "No need to worry. This is only a confirmation of the drought, the sun will shine tomorrow," and he hummed, very flat, two lines of a hymn:

> "We expect a bright tomorrow,
> All will be well!"

"I hope so, dear, but it is a very anxious time. I'm sure I don't know what makes us attempt a garden party. The uncertainty about the weather takes years off one's life. But, somehow, you forget from one year to another how miserable the weather makes you. And, of course, we never have had a bad day, and the garden is beautiful. Except for size, it is quite as fine as Edmonston Hall." She stopped and looked out of the window at the smirr of rain drifting over Ratchell Hill, then observed despondently, "But even the garden is hardly worth it . . . If it rains outright it will be bad enough—we will know the worst then and make the best arrangements we can—it will just be a large dull tea-party in the house—but if it is neither one thing nor another what is to be done? Suppose we put out all the tables and the rain comes on and soaks everything? And then, oh, Norman, the Band! I had forgotten about it."

She sat down weakly on a chair and stared at her husband. "Why did I ever think of such a thing? Outside it would be quite impressive, in the house it would be simply *ludicrous*. They would need to play in one of the spare bedrooms." Mrs, McCandlish laughed almost hysterically.

"Well, well, it hasn't happened yet," her husband told her

soothingly. He tapped the barometer—they were never far from the barometer in these anxious days. "Ah, if anything, inclined to rise." In his relief he became quite jocose. "A Band in the house, Aggie, would be like the Highlander's idea of Heaven, 'A sma' room fu' o' pipers' . . . But that won't happen. No, no. All will be well."

And his faith was justified. The next day broke cloudless.

"A perfect day," Mrs. McCandlish said, as she stood in her neat morning frock watching the maids carry the plainest and strongest chairs the Manse possessed into the shrubbery to support the Band. "How thankful we ought to be! I hardly liked to pray about it, for a garden party, being a secular function, isn't like a Sunday School picnic—I always pray about the weather for things like that . . . Oh, Norman, will you see if Murray understood about going to the station to meet the things that are coming from Edinburgh? Yes, dear, he had better take the car . . ."

"A perfect day," grumbled Kirsty Gilmour. "What a waste to go to a garden party! You will come, won't you, Aunt Fanny, seeing it is such a good day? The grass can't possibly be damp, and it might amuse you to see the people."

Miss Fanny drew her shawls about her. Even on this warm June day she wore a shawl or two.

"I think not, dear," she said. "I never did like garden parties, and I'm getting too old for new people."

"Well, I'm not going alone, that's certain. Carty, you must come with me. Oh, do. Aunt Fanny will keep an eye on Bill"—Miss Fanny here murmured something—"and you won't be bored, because I believe everything interests you, even people at a garden party. I always think human nature is at its lowest at that form of entertainment . . . Perhaps Mrs. Strang will be there. That's something to hope for, anyway . . . Be ready at four o'clock, will you, Carty? Shall we have the wagonette, or walk? Which would be worst, to arrive among all the smart cars mounted high in that chariot, or walk and appear flushed in the face and dusty about the feet? I'm afraid we shall have to get a car. Or we might compromise on a pony-cart. What do you say, Aunt Fanny?"

Miss Fanny shook her head. "No, dear, I don't care for pony-carts—a victoria for the summer and a brougham for winter is what I have always been used to . . . Kirsty, dear, I think I shall lie down this afternoon, if you will be so good as to tell Miss Wotherspoon to bring my tea to my room about four o'clock. I have a slight headache."

Kirsty expressed great regret to hear of her aunt's headache, and strongly advised her to rest.

"Nellie will have tea with the children in the wood. That will be a treat for them all, and they won't disturb you." She added ruefully, "It would have been a treat for me too, if only the McCandlishes hadn't been so hospitably inclined. However—"

The garden party was in full swing. Every one who had been invited had arrived, and an imposing assemblage of vehicles crowded the stables and overflowed into the drive, from the newest Rolls Royce to the wagonette of Mr. Dickson in which Kirsty and Miss Carter had made their modest entrance.

The heart of Mrs. McCandlish swelled within her as she stood on the lawn and watched the scene. From the shrubbery the Priorsford Band discoursed sweet music. She was glad now that she had been bold enough to have it. She had had many qualms about it (especially when she woke in the night), but standing in the bright sunlight, watching the groups of smartly dressed people enjoying a tea that was simply sumptuous—six different kinds of sandwiches, a rich profusion of small cakes, and *ices to follow*—she felt that she had been justified. This was no ordinary occasion.

Never, she thought, had the garden looked more beautiful, the lawns like velvet, the wide borders gay with every sweet old flower—columbines and Canterbury bells, lupins and sweet-williams, pansies and peonies. A chestnut grew at one side of the lawn, holding up hundreds of waxen blossoms, like some great decorated Christmas tree. Behind, the hillside rose steeply, and a group of tall dark pines threw up effectively the whitewashed house.

Mrs. McCandlish was glad to see that every one seemed to be chatting freely with every one else. Soon the young people would begin to play tennis, and the older people clock-golf. She gave a thankful little sigh, and turned to a vacant seat.

Kirsty found herself seated at a table with three people she had never seen before, two women and a man. Mr. McCandlish had introduced her, murmuring names that meant nothing to her, and had immediately flown off to greet some newcomers. The man was a clergyman, and the younger of the two women was evidently his wife; the other woman had small restless eyes like a ferret, and a hat covered with paradise plumes. Most uninteresting, all three, Kirsty decided; and, as they seemed to have nothing to say to her after a few murmured civilities, she amused herself by picking out the few people she knew among the occupants of the other tables.

Carty was quite near talking to Mr. Brand, who seemed in a sprightly humour and amused by his companion. Miss Rebecca Brand was at another table, eating an ice with an abstracted air, in the company of two old ladies in bonnets. She wore a tweed coat and skirt, and looked hot in spite of the ice.

Mr. Anthony Hay waved a greeting from another table, and she noticed Lady Carruthers talking very vivaciously to a group of people, but those were the only faces she knew in the crowd. There were some pretty girls and a very few young men; most of the people were middle-aged or frankly elderly.

She turned from contemplating them to listen idly to the conversation going on at her own table.

The ferret-like lady with the paradise plumes was speaking. "What I dislike about your service, Mr. Wood, is that there is so much getting up and sitting down about it: you never get a rest. And then you hardly ever have a sermon. I think that is a great pity. I must say I like a sermon. One needn't listen unless one likes, but there is something very satisfactory about a sermon. I've thought out many a household detail during a sermon, I can tell you. Oh, it's all very well being an Episcopalian—it sounds well, and I admit it is smarter—but there's no doubt if you've been brought up a Presbyterian you take ill with it."

Mr. Wood flushed. He was a boyish-looking person, with a round face—no match, obviously, for the determined lady who was giving him her views about the Episcopalian form of worship. His wife, who had also a round cheery face, seemed to urge him with her eyes not to make any retort.

Kirsty wondered at the resemblance between the husband and wife. Had they grown like each other since they married, or had the likeness attracted them in the first case? She felt very sorry for them both, but hardly knew how to break into the conversation.

"You are very High Church, Mr. Wood," continued the lady, "and perhaps you can't help it; but what I say is, why not be a priest right out? Of course, there would be no Mrs. Wood" (her tone seemed to imply that that would have been no great loss, and the poor little woman wilted under it), "but you would have full freedom to cut all the capers you liked in the way of dressing up, and confessing, and carrying on . . . By the way, is it you that gets the Easter offering? It is? No wonder you were anxious that it should be a big one."

Again Mr. Wood flushed, and that flush and his round boyish face were too much for Kirsty. She broke in with, "Isn't this a delightful garden?" addressing the clergyman and his wife, and ignoring the other occupant of the table.

Mr. Wood started. "Quite, quite," he said. And again, "Quite, quite;" and the little wife added, "And there is such a nice stretch of turf."

"Talking of turf," said the ferret-like lady, turning her back on the couple and addressing Kirsty, "talking of turf, you should see our lawns at The Towers. Do you belong to the neighbourhood? Or have you only come with someone? I don't seem to have seen you before, and of course I know every one—county and otherwise."

Kirsty had succeeded in turning the attack on herself.

"Do you?" she said gently. "How very nice!"

The restless eyes of the lady went all over Kirsty, priced her gown, valued the string of pearls round her neck, noted the way she wore her things, and her voice, when next she spoke, was almost silky.

"I expect you're staying at Edmonston Hall. I know Lady Carruthers very well. What does that poor husband of hers do with himself all day?"

"I don't know," said Kirsty truthfully. "What do most husbands do with themselves?"

"Well, mine made money." The little lady gave a short laugh. "Yours, Mrs. Wood, occupies himself with Popish practices. And yours," she turned to Kirsty, "what does yours do?—if you have one."

Kirsty looked at her with large wistful eyes.

"Alas! I haven't one," she sighed, and added:

> "She hath no loyal knight and true,
> The Lady of Shalott."

The clergyman and his wife cast uneasy glances at her, while the ferret-like lady said, "What did you say your name was? I didn't catch it."

"I didn't say it. But I shall now. My name is Gilmour, Kirsty Gilmour."

No one looked either impressed or enlightened, and with a sniff the lady went back to the subject of Edmonston Hall.

"Has Lady Carruthers a large party just now? She is a great entertainer, but I daresay she feels that she must amuse herself somehow in this out-of-the-way place. It's different with us in Priorsford. We have quite a giddy round of gaiety in summer. Tennis, you know, and—and one thing and another. Is this your first visit to Edmonston Hall?"

Kirsty raised her eyebrows, and said patiently, "But I'm not staying at Edmonston Hall."

"Then why did you say you were?"

"I think it was you who said I was. You didn't give me time to undeceive you."

"Well," said the lady very crossly, "where in the world are you staying?"

"In my own house," said Kirsty meekly. "I've taken Little Phantasy on a lease. Perhaps you know it?"

"*Little* Phantasy! There's a Colonel Home of Phantasy. He has never been at home since we came to this district, but now that I think of it I did hear he had come back to settle down."

"Colonel Home lives at Phantasy proper," Kirsty explained. "We have a much smaller house in the grounds."

The little lady's small eyes were bright with interest.

"Then you'll know Colonel Home? What kind of man is he? What age, I mean. And will he be a help socially?"

Kirsty thoughtfully bit a sandwich, surveying the while the eager eyes of her questioner.

At last she said, "I've only seen Colonel Home twice, but

he didn't strike me as the type of man to be a social success. He was badly wounded, perhaps you know, and is lame. He seemed to me rather inclined to be a recluse."

The ferret-like lady struck the table impatiently with her little hard hand.

"Isn't that like the thing?" she said bitterly. "A neighbourhood almost devoid of men, and when one does come to settle down the first thing you hear is that he is a *recluse?*"

She looked so balefully at the little clergyman that he instinctively moved his chair away from her.

"Oh," said Kirsty soothingly, "it may not be as bad as that. Colonel Home will probably find that he must entertain and be entertained a certain amount. But I'm afraid there will never be anything of the 'giddy round' about him . . . Is this really a very manless neighbourhood?"

"Manless!" the lady snorted.

The clergyman's wife here ventured a remark.

"Of course, when you say there are few men, you mean eligible men. There are lots of middle-aged married men, and some nice elderly bachelors who don't mind going out to tea."

"Well, they must have been eligible once," Kirsty said cheerfully, as if determined to look on the bright side. "And, anyway, what does it matter?"

The ferret-like lady looked at her darkly. "Wait till you give a dance," she said.

"But there is nothing further from my intentions," Kirsty assured her.

"It's odd that you, a comparatively young woman,"

(Kirsty smiled), "almost a girl, should want to settle down in this lonely place. There must be some attraction . . . Did you know Colonel Home before you took the house?"

"*No*," said Kirsty, and rose to her feet. "Oh, pardon me, but I see someone I must speak to," and she ran eagerly to meet Mrs. Strang, who was coming towards her.

"I did hope you would be here," she said as they shook hands.

Mrs. Strang nodded to the occupants of the table Kirsty had just left, and said as she walked off with Kirsty, "How did you get into that circle?"

"I was put at that table by Mr. McCandlish. Tell me, is that the clergyman who comes to St. Mark's every week—Mr. Wood?"

"Yes. He works it along with the Priorsford church. Rushes between the two on a motor bicycle. He is a nice fellow, and a good cricketer, and I like his wife. She has a gift that almost amounts to genius for managing fowls. Her hens don't die in debt, which is such a blessing, for they are rather badly off—Well now, what do you think of this for a garden party? Isn't it well done? The tea is purveyed from Princes Street, the Manse garden is like Prospero's Island—full of sweet noises that give delight and hurt not (in other words, Priorsford Band brought at great expense in a charabanc), and our host and hostess are as pleased and proud as they can be. I've suffered tortures of anxiety in case it would rain ever since Mrs. McCandlish told me about the Band. I never really cared much for the lady (it's difficult knowing what to say to her after you've discussed the price of food and how to make rock cakes), but I shall like her always now; it was so sporting of her actually to compass the Band . . . Dear me, there is Archie Home. Well, he *is* trying to do his duty by his neighbours, poor dear fellow. Come and speak to him."

"Wait a moment," Kirsty said, clutching her companion's arm to stop her. "Do tell me who that is I was sitting beside? No, not the Woods, the little sandy-haired woman with the ferret's eyes and the paradise plumes?"

"My dear, be careful, please, how you allude to that lady. That is no less a person than Mrs. Duff-Whalley of The Towers, Priorsford. (That's her daughter, that pretty, bored-looking girl in the green hat.) What did she say to you? Oh, here she comes, bearing straight down on us . . . How d'you do, Mrs. Duff-Whalley? I haven't seen you for a long time. Have you been away?"

"Of course," said the lady, her paradise plumes wagging, "Priorsford's impossible in the early spring. Muriel and I always go to the Riviera. Then we paid some visits, so we're not long back . . . Have you been writing any more books?"

Mrs. Strang laughed gently at the humouring tone, and murmured something about "always writing a little."

"I'm sure," said Mrs. Duff-Whalley, "it's a nice pastime for you. And people who know you are quite pleased to buy your books . . . I was telling Muriel the other day I believed she could write if she liked to try. Her letters are really awfully good. She has that kind of interesting style, you know, lots of dashes and exclamation points. Racy you call it. And then she sees so much of the world, and meets so many interesting people. Nearly everybody in the hotel we were in had some sort of title, and there were two divorced Peers and a black Prince!!" Mrs. Duff-Whalley paused to note the effect of this statement and finished, "Some of them were queer in spite of their titles."

"I daresay," said Mrs. Strang; "a title is no guarantee of sanity. This is Miss Gilmour, Mrs. Duff-Whalley; she has come to live here."

Kirsty received a nod from the lady, who said, "We were sitting at the same table—is Colonel Home here, Mrs. Strang? He's a cousin of yours, isn't he? I should like to get to know him, and show him some civility. It must be very lonely for him, and a cheery evening at The Towers would raise his spirits, him lame and all."

"It would," Mrs. Strang cordially agreed. "There is Colonel Home over there talking to our hostess. Shall I go with you . . ?" but the energetic lady was halfway across the lawn before the sentence was finished.

"Who is she?" Kirsty asked excitedly, as she watched her march, paradise plumes waving, to start her crusade against Colonel Home's possible dullness.

"She's a wonderful woman," said Mrs. Strang; "she knows what she wants and goes straight for it. Poor Archie!"

"I don't think I want to see much of her," Kirsty said.

"You won't, if she doesn't consider you worthwhile. If you have made a good impression on her (I mean by that if she thinks you are rich enough to be worth knowing) she will arrive in a very large and opulent car and shower cards on you (I never saw any one so lavish with cards—she leaves positively stacks of them), and then she will invite you constantly to dinners, lunches, tennis parties, dances—there is simply no end to her hospitality."

"She was being very rude to poor Mr. Wood."

"Oh, I daresay. She considers him and his wife fair game . . . I wonder who that pretty girl is with Rob Brand?"

"Why," said Kirsty, "that's Miss Carter, the children's governess. Do come and speak to her. She is so interested in you, and she knows nobody here—but perhaps you ought to be speaking to other people? I expect you know everybody."

"Not I. Mrs. McCandlish has thrown her net wide this time. And I would like to meet Miss Carter. When are you going to bring the whole household to Hopewaterfoot?"

"We're just waiting to be asked," said Kirsty, with engaging candour.

"That's all right. Shall we say next Tuesday? Every one of you, remember, and do try to persuade Miss Fanny. Tell her I'm really much nicer in my own house . . ." Then Mrs. Strang was engulfed by a group of people she knew, and Kirsty wandered away by herself and sat down beside Miss Rebecca Brand, who was watching two clergymen and their wives play clock-golf.

"It's a good thing it's keeping fair," said Rebecca.

Kirsty was amused at such a mild description of a perfect day, but she merely smiled her agreement and asked her companion if she cared for garden parties.

"No, I don't," was the uncompromising answer, "but it's an easy way of entertaining if you've got a good garden, and I don't blame Mrs. McCandlish. They give one every year. They began very simply—just a cup of tea outside and a walk round the place—but they've grown and grown, and now—" Rebecca waved her hand impressively.

"It *is* smart," Kirsty agreed. "And such a lovely setting for a party, the garden and the hills behind. You must be very fond of this countryside, you and your brother. Muirburn has always been your home, hasn't it?"

"Oh yes. We like it well enough. New people rave about it, but when you've always lived in a place you never think much about its beauty."

"Perhaps not," Kirsty said, "but I don't think one ever gets used to ugliness."

Kirsty looked about, pulling down the wide brim of her hat to shade her eyes. It was quite amusing to watch the people. "I could almost tell," she said to herself, "which are the 'worth while' people by Mrs. Duff-Whalley's behaviour. She is all smiles and honey to some, others get a jerky nod and a mechanical smile, the rest are ignored entirely. I do hope she will consider me beneath her notice."

There was no trace of Miss Carter, and presently, with a word to Rebecca Brand, Kirsty got up and sauntered away to look for her. The lawn was covered with groups of people busily talking. Lady Carruthers waved a greeting to Kirsty, and Mr. Anthony Hay came up to inquire anxiously if she had had enough to eat, and asked if he might walk round the garden with her.

"All those people must be strangers to you, Miss Gilmour; indeed, many of them I don't know myself. I hope you haven't felt it dull. I always think myself that a garden party is a meaningless form of entertainment—not that it isn't exceedingly kind of Mr. and Mrs. McCandlish to have us here . . . Your aunt didn't come with you? Ah yes, she and I belong to the same school of thought! Come and look at Mr. McCandlish's rock garden."

Half an hour later Kirsty found Stella Carter, still accompanied by Robert Brand, in the vegetable garden.

"Is it time to go?" Stella asked, and seemed surprised.

"Well," said Kirsty, "the Band is playing *Will ye no come back again?* which looks to me like a broad hint . . . Have you enjoyed yourself, Mr. Brand?"

"Amazingly," said Mr. Brand.

Kirsty laughed. " 'Amazingly' is good. You mean, much more than you expected to enjoy yourself?"

"Just that," said Robert Brand.

Everyone was gone now; the piles of dishes were washed, the lawn was cleared of seats and seemed surprisingly little the worse of the tramping it had received, the chairs had been brought in from the shrubbery, and the Band was safely on its way to Priorsford. It was nearly seven o'clock.

Mr. and Mrs. McCandlish, flushed, tired, but very happy, stood together in their garden talking.

"They stayed so long, Norman, they *must* have enjoyed themselves."

"No doubt of that, my dear. It was a most successful party."

"Norman, even Mrs. Duff-Whalley owned that it was a sweet garden, and she mentioned the sandwiches with the little flags on them."

"Did she, my dear?" said Mr. McCandlish. "And Colonel Home said very kind things about our lupins. I was taken with him, Aggie. There is something very pleasant about his smile."

"Yes, dear." (Mrs. McCandlish would have found something pleasant in Apollyon at this happy moment) . . . "Did you hear what Mrs. Strang said about the Band? She stood before me and said in that very definite sort of way she has, 'It absolutely made the afternoon,' and quoted something—poetry, I think (you would have known what it was)—and then she said so warmly, 'Dear Mrs. McCandlish, it was an inspiration'."

Mr. McCandlish stooped over a broken flower. "So it was," he said. "So it was."

"I'm always rather afraid of Mrs. Strang," his wife continued; "I've an idea she is given to laughing at people, but I really liked her today. She quite set my mind at rest." Mrs. McCandlish sighed happily.

"Well, well, Aggie, all our fears have been disappointed. Last night, you remember, we were very anxious." Mr. McCandlish straightened himself and took a long breath as if he felt a burden removed.

"Norman," his wife said solemnly, "I said to myself last night, if we get over tomorrow decently at all, I shall never risk another garden party—but tonight I'm not so sure."

"Of course we'll have another (that is to say, if we are spared), but you'll never surpass this effort, my dear . . . Dear me, is that the gong? I must say I'll be glad of a bite of dinner. I got no tea for talking . . . Come away in, Aggie."

And they turned from the scene of their triumph and went into the house hand in hand.

CHAPTER 14

"Thus have I had thee, as a dream doth flatter,
In sleep a king; but waking no such matter."
Sonnets of William Shakespeare

REBECCA BRAND stood in her bedroom dressing to go out. She had put on a muslin blouse and a tweed skirt, and had just decided that it was much too warm to put on the tweed coat that belonged to the skirt.

"Not that I like going out with a blouse," she told herself, "there is something so unfinished about it, but I haven't a washing dress fit to be seen."

She looked discontentedly into the little mirror on her dressing-table and thought over her small stock of summer frocks, all so washed out and shrunken as to be quite hopeless. Then she sighed: "Of course, if I had clever hands I could make myself a new one for very little, and knit dresses too—but I'm a donkey, I can't even knit a jumper."

Again she regarded herself in the looking glass, and what she saw there seemed to give her small satisfaction. The frilly collar of the muslin blouse framed unbecomingly the round red face, and her hat had a way of tilting back on her head, which gave her a slightly rakish look.

She turned herself about before the inadequate glass, pulling down the skirt, patting the blouse to make it lie better, then she shook her head. "Nothing on earth could make a blouse and a tweed skirt becoming. If I had one of those dresses that Miss Gilmour wears, slim clinging sort of things with long lines, I believe I might have quite a decent figure; but as it is, I'm a dumpy object."

She left the glass—at no time did she spend much time before it—and pulled out a drawer to get a pair of gloves.

It was a neat, fresh room, every drawer tidy, every bit of furniture well polished, but there was no attempt at prettiness or decoration. The room was practically the same as it had been when Rebecca first began to use it. The dressing-table stood in the window as it had stood for more than thirty years. It was of walnut with curved legs and ball feet, and on it lay four thick crochet mats. They were ugly, they were useless, but they had always been there, and Rebecca saw no reason why they should go. On two of them stood glass bottles filled with coloured salt set in patterns, which were believed to have come originally from Brighton. The looking-glass was small and damp-spotted, and was apt to tilt violently backwards unless propped by a shell-box which had been bought at the Crystal Palace in the 'seventies.

Her brushes and hand-mirror had been a wedding present to her mother, and were of ivory.

On the top of the chest of drawers was stacked tidily a pile of books, the books Rebecca loved best and kept always near her. They were an odd mixture—the Bible and Marcus Aurelius, Shakespeare and *Little Women* and *Good Wives*, Burns and Christina Rossetti, Browning and *Brucy, A Little Worker for Christ*.

The room had two windows. One looked to the front of the house, and commanded a view of the lawn and the short drive fringed by lilac and laburnum trees, the white gate and the highroad; the other looked west over the kitchen garden with its gooseberry bushes and rows of potatoes, over the fields where the Highland cattle grazed, over the Hope Water to where among the trees Phantasy stood.

Phantasy was Rebecca's one touch of romance. As a child she had worshipped the young laird: he had seemed to her all the heroes of legend and fairy tale come to life. Phantasy itself was enchanted ground. To enter the gates had been high adventure. The Lodge with the honeysuckle, the long drive that wound away among the trees and crossed and recrossed the Hope Water, the park with the Japanese deer, the garden that lay all a-growing and a-blowing in the shelter of its high walls, the shaven lawns that ran up to meet the heather and the bracken of the hillside—all had a glamour in Rebecca's eyes.

She had sometimes gone to lunch at Phantasy with her parents when old Lady Ann was alive, and one always-to-be-remembered day the laird himself had been there. It was a party, and Rebecca had felt hopelessly out of place among a lot of people whose language she did not seem to know, and who viewed life from an entirely different angle. She had been sitting silent and lonely when Colonel Home came up to her and asked if she would care to see the garden. He had shown her everything he thought would interest her, and had talked to her in his rather slow, grave way, and later had himself driven them all home to the Manse in his motorcar, then a new and fearful innovation in Muirburn.

Rebecca had not enjoyed the afternoon (at best it had

been a kind of pleasing torture, for she had longed to be witty and amusing, and could think of nothing but the most empty commonplaces), but since then her heart had been at Archie Home's feet. Not that he knew it was there. It is doubtful if he had even given Rebecca another thought. He had simply been sorry for the plain, shy girl, and had tried to make the time pass pleasantly for her, and was most thankful when his task was over. Hidden away, unconfessed, he had an odd tenderness for the neglected things of this world—stray mongrels, homeless cats, unwanted children, plain, unattractive women.

Rebecca herself had no illusions. "How could I ever be anything to him?" she asked herself in scorn. "He probably hardly realizes my existence." But all the same Phantasy and its owner stood for all that was vivid in her grey life.

Through the War she had prayed ceaselessly for his safety. In her desk, tucked securely away, was a photograph cut from some picture paper when he was awarded the D.S.O. and the Croix de Guerre. She had mounted it (rather clumsily) on pasteboard, and this she looked at night and morning.

She had been happy in her dream, but now that Archie Home had come home to Phantasy she had tried to put it from her. She felt that it was not possible to dream even innocent dreams about being allowed to serve and look after a man, when she was liable to meet the said man any day walking about with his dogs.

She had spoken to him only twice since his homecoming: once when Rob had brought him in to tea (as luck would have it she had neglected to bake that day, and the bread was stale and there was no cake), and once when he had driven them in his car from Priorsford.

Rob went a good deal to Phantasy, for the library was an irresistible attraction to him, but he could tell his sister little of what she wanted to know—if the servants looked after their master well, if his lame foot bothered him much, if he was content to be at home.

"How should I know?" Rob protested when asked those things. "He's comfortable, of course. My word! I wish I had his books . . . I don't see why he shouldn't be contented. He will always be lame, but he can hobble about on the hills wonderfully, and he has more to live for than most men. I don't suppose he has ever had much time for thinking of such things, but now that he's settled at home he ought to marry. It'll be a thousand pities if he doesn't . . . I've been thinking, wouldn't it be rather odd if the laird married the tenant of Little Phantasy?"

Now, often had Rebecca said to herself, "He will marry, he must marry," and had tried to picture to herself the woman to whom the wondrous honour should fall. But to hear her brother casually suggest a bride—a girl she knew, a girl she did not particularly admire; pretty, Rebecca admitted, yes, and rich and kind, but oh! not good enough for Archie Home—filled her with bitter wrath. She was thinking of her brother's remark as she looked out of the window towards Phantasy; then she pushed in a drawer, and glanced round to see if she were leaving the room quite tidy.

Going downstairs she saw through the open door Rob, bareheaded and without his coat, running the lawnmower vigorously.

"I'm going out, Rob," she called, "to do some visiting. Jessie will give you your tea."

Robert Brand left the lawn and the mower and came towards his sister, wiping his brow.

"That's warm work! I'll have a bath when I finish it, and, like you, do some visiting. I'll be sure to get tea somewhere, so tell Jessie not to bother."

Rebecca looked at her brother. "You're great at going out to tea now. I've seen the day when wild horses wouldn't have dragged you, but Miss Gilmour has worked a charm."

Robert's hot face got hotter.

"Oh, I may not go to Little Phantasy," he said, with an air of great carelessness. "But I did promise to run in and show Specky how to dress flies, and he will be looking out for me . . . I may get tea at the Hopehead; I've got to see the shepherd's wife there. Where are you going?"

Rebecca finished buttoning her glove. "I'm going to the Castle. I haven't seen the Starks or the Taits for an age, and Jessie tells me that Nannie Tait isn't well, and that her mother—Jessie's mother—thinks it may be the same trouble as the other had."

The minister's honest face grew troubled. "Surely not. Jessie's mother is an old ghoul. It's probably nothing but a little cold . . . Well, are you off? Look here, why not go into Little Phantasy for tea? I'll meet you there."

"Oh, I don't think so. But I'll see. Goodbye just now."

While Rebecca was gazing at her own reflection in her small greenish-hued mirror, Kirsty Gilmour was standing at the toilet-table in her blue and white bedroom.

All the windows stood wide open, and the chintz curtains swayed gently in the warm wind. The room was dainty with spotless muslin covers and cushions. A great bowl of roses stood on the dressing-table. Kirsty herself was a vision of delight in a soft white dress and a shady hat trimmed with roses.

She was not thinking of what she looked like as she stood there before the mirror. She was smiling reminiscently at something Bill had said, and thinking of the hundred little pleasant things that went to make up her day—ordering meals, consultations with Carty, hours spent with the children, hours in the garden, talks with Aunt Fanny, Miss Wotherspoon's moods, Easie's imperturbable good-humour, Nellie's willing but violent service.

She sighed, sighed not because her heart was heavy, but because it was satisfied.

"I'm almost too happy," she thought. "I feel as if I should be touching wood all the time . . . And I'm not doing what I meant to do; I'm always turning aside and doing things I like instead of disagreeable things like calling on people I don't know. But today I shan't put it off. Today I'll do it." She nodded defiantly at herself in the glass. "I'll go to the Castle and see the people Mr. Brand told me about."

She pulled on a pair of gloves and ran downstairs.

It was a delightful walk from Little Phantasy to Hawkshaw Castle: down the garden by the side of the Hope Water to the bridge, a little way along the dusty highroad, and a short steep climb to the old keep. There was a cart-road which made a more gradual ascent, but Kirsty preferred the little path through the whins and the bushes of broom, green broom.

The Castle stood on the brae looking down on the meeting of Tweed and Hope Water. A few very old yew trees running eastward showed where once the avenue had been, and behind it were the remains of a walled garden. Grim in the August heat stood the Castle with its few deep windows, mere slits in the depths of the walls, mute, remote, like one who has outlived his time. At one end were a few out-houses and the cottage of the shepherd, Robert Stark. The forester, Tait, lived in the Castle itself, which, though ruinous, had for a hundred years housed the Hawkshaw forester.

Kirsty always suffered miseries of shyness when she set out to call on her poor neighbours.

"I'm not really pushing," she told herself as she approached the shepherd's door. "I'm only calling to show an interest. It's horrid to live near people and not know them. They'll be quite nice to me, I'm sure."

The door of the Starks' cottage stood wide open. A stone passage, sanded in an intricate design, led evidently to the kitchen, from whence came the sound of voices.

Kirsty knocked.

"See whae that is," someone said, and presently a young man emerged and stood speechless in the doorway.

"Is Mrs. Stark in?" Kirsty asked.

Instead of replying, the young man shouted, "Mither," and retreated into the kitchen. His place was taken by an elderly woman, bent but carrying herself with dignity, with a stern face and grey hair brushed firmly back under a black lace cap. She looked inquiringly at Kirsty, who explained that she had come to live at Little Phantasy, and wished to make Mrs. Stark's acquaintance.

"Ye'll be Miss Gilmour? Come in."

She led the way into the kitchen and, nodding towards an old man who was sitting in an armchair by the fire, said, "That's ma man. And that's ma son William. He's juist back frae the lamb sales at St. Boswells."

William was the tall young man who had come to the door. He was standing now before the fire being questioned by his father, the head shepherd, a tall, loosely-built old man with a long face, a permanent pink flush on each high cheek-bone, and a thatch of white hair.

He took his pipe out of his mouth for a minute when Kirsty came in, gave her a nod, and went on talking to his son.

". . . What did ye say he offered ye?"

William stared at the fire, and said in his slow, sweet voice, "Oh, he said, 'I'll tak them at thirty shillings the piece'."

"Ay, an' what said ye to that?"

"I said," Willie said gently, "I said that I wud raither tak them to hell."

The old man smoked in silence for a minute, then replied, "Ay, Wullie, faur better, faur better."

Mrs. Stark motioned Kirsty to a chair. She herself was seated before a small table in the window which held a workbasket and a pile of mending.

"I'm nae guid at makin' claes," she told Kirsty as she proceeded to put a large patch on a pink-and-white striped shirt, "but I can aye mend."

Kirsty sat down beside her and tried to think of something to say. As a beginning she remarked that it seemed to her very romantic to live beside an historic castle, but Mrs. Stark refused to see anything romantic about it.

"It's a terrible steerin' place," she complained, "near the road and the shop." (It was a good half-mile from either.) "We've only been here aboot ten years. Afore that we were miles frae a'thing, scule and kirk and shop and station. It was faur nicer—peaceful like."

"Still," Kirsty began, when steps were heard outside and a youngish woman entered the kitchen. She had a long, mild face, and wore a blue print dress with a white sprig. She carried a large brown paper bag, and looked hot.

Mrs. Stark's greeting to the newcomer surprised and startled Kirsty. Fixing her with a cold eye while she bit off a thread, she said, "Three-quarters of an hour, Agnes, to run to the shop for sugar!" Then, with slow, thoughtful bitterness, "*I could thrust a sword through ye.*"

Agnes flushed deeper and looked deprecatingly at Kirsty.

"Mrs. Dickson wanted to show me a bedcover she's finished, and there were a lot of customers. I couldna get away, Mother."

"Tets! I wud like to see the body that wud keep me if I wanted awa'. Ye're puir cratur, Agnes Stark, hingin' an' gossipin' in a shop. Eh, lass, ye are unlike yer mother."

"Well, well," Agnes ejaculated, smiling forgivingly at her stern parent. "There's no much harm in taking ma time over a message on a bonnie summer afternoon, an' Mrs. Dickson's rale guid company." She turned to the visitor—

"Ye'll be Miss Gilmour? Ay. I've seen ye at the kirk. I hope ye're pleased wi' our minister?"

"Oh yes, indeed," Kirsty said, much relieved to have a subject to talk about. "I think he's an excellent preacher, and such a nice man. And Miss Brand must be a great help to him."

"She's a' that," Agnes agreed, but her mother demurred.

"What Miss Brand should dae is gang awa' an' tak a situation, an' let her brither tak a wife. It wud be faur better for the congregation, for she hes nae way wi' the folk."

"But, Mother," Agnes expostulated, "Miss Brand's rale kind an' well-meaning. If there's sickness or trouble she's aye there, an' she's a teacher in the Sabbath School, and collects . . ."

"Oh ay, but for a' that I dinna like her." Mrs. Stark stroked her face with her hand, a curious habit she had, as if she were stroking away the deep wrinkles round her mouth. "She hesna a bonnie face, an' ye see fine when she comes to the hoose that she feels she's daein' her duty. I've seen her screw her face when I was speakin' as if I was a dose o' castor-ile . . . No' that Mrs. McCandlish is ony better—waur if onything. She's as perjink as a dancin'-mistress, an' I canna stand her way of speakin', it's terrible angersome. An' it maun tak the wumman hours to pit up her hair—sic a curls an' twists! There's one thing aboot Miss Brand, she disna gie a preen what she looks like. If her an' the ither yin were cairded through each other they micht mak one wise-like wumman."

The good Agnes looked at Kirsty and shook her head,

sayin "Ma mother disna mean a' she says."

"Div I no'?" her mother retorted wrathfully. "I mean faur mair. I could tell ye ma opeenion o'. . ."

"Please, Mrs. Stark," Kirsty broke in, "don't tell me your opinion of myself. I couldn't bear it."

"D'ye think I've nae mainners?" asked Mrs. Stark, much affronted, while Agnes tried to create a diversion by asking her brother if a certain man had been at St. Boswells.

Robert Stark answered for his son. "I've been speirin' that at him, but he says he disna ken . . . An' he disna ken wha bocht the Cor Water lambs." He took a pinch of snuff, and finished, "I'm rale vexed for Willie: he kens nocht."

Kirsty got up to go, feeling that this household was almost too much for her.

"Doesn't someone live in the Castle?" she asked as she was leaving.

"Ay, the Taits," Agnes told her. "Mistress Tait's a rale nice body, but it maun be eerie in that auld castle at nicht."

"Has she a husband? And children?"

"Tait's the wudman," said Mrs. Stark. "They hed three lassies, but they've only the yin left. Juist when they got to be aboot eighteen they fell into a decline. Ay, an' I'm no' sure aboot Nannie. She's ower pure a colour, an' she gies a nesty short cough whiles. But ye daurna say that to her mither, she's fair fierce ower Nannie, and spiles the lassie. Wadna let us say a word when she cam hame frae her situation in Glesgae—she was a typewriter—an' we a' kent . . . Weel, weel, a toon wi' its temptations is nae place for a bonnie glaiket lassie. But it was a sair affront to her faither and mither, for they're dacent folk."

"Oh, *Mother!*" Agnes murmured, and Kirsty made her escape.

At the gate she met Rebecca Brand.

"Are *you* going to call on Mrs. Stark?" she cried.

"Isn't she awful?" said Rebecca, with simple directness. "It's a positive penance to go" (Kirsty recalled Mrs. Stark's apt simile about Rebecca's face and the dose of castor oil), "but it would never do to visit Mrs. Tait and leave her out. She's a rude old woman. I always leave her with a lowered opinion of every one in the neighbourhood . . . Rob likes her—would you believe it?—and she is never nasty about him."

"I expect," Kirsty said, "Mr. Brand stands up to her, and she likes it . . . I am going now to the Castle."

"I've just been there—you'll find Mrs. Tait very different from Mrs. Stark. Well . . ."

"Come in to tea on your way home," Kirsty urged, but Rebecca would not promise.

Kirsty went through the courtyard to the front entrance with its six half-circular steps. The heavy nail-studded door stood open, and led into a hall with doors opening from it; but there was no sign of the place being inhabited, and when she pushed open one of the doors she found the room within empty and unfurnished.

She climbed the stair and came to a landing with two doors. One she pushed gently open, and saw that within was a finely proportioned room panelled in white, now very cracked and grey. A tub of clothes soaking for the wash stood on a stand, some brushes hung on a nail, and at the far end of the room was another door from behind which came the sound of voices. She walked across to this door and knocked, and it was opened almost immediately by a gentle-faced woman.

"Ay," she said in response to Kirsty's inquiring "Mrs. Tait?" "Come in. I ken ye fine by sight. You're Miss Gilmour at Phantasy. Nannie, here's a visitor. This is ma dochter, Miss Gilmour. She's hame for a holiday."

The room, a kitchen, was long and narrow, with a window at either end. Even on this blazing August afternoon it was shadowy, and Kirsty wondered what it could be like in winter. It was panelled like the other room, but a brightly flowered paper had been plastered over the wood. Along one side of the room were two fixed-in wooden beds valanced with turkey-red. A door near the fireplace opened into another smaller room, which was Nannie's bedroom. A dresser with dishes stood near one window, and in the other was a round table laid for tea. Out of the shadows came a girl, and Kirsty at once thought of *Evelyn Hope:*

"Why your hair was amber I shall divine,
 And your mouth of your own geranium's red . . ."

She held out a slim hand to Kirsty, brought forward a chair, and smiled without speaking.

Her mother gave her an anxious look, but said brightly, "Nannie hasna been juist that awfu' weel this while back; bloodless a wee thing, mebbe, but the doctor's gi'en her a tonic, so she'll sune be a' richt."

"I'm quite well," said Nannie, and gave a short cough.

She had nothing of her mother's broad Border accent: her speaking was colourless and correct.

Kirsty turned to her. "How glad you must be to come home to this lovely place. Is your work in a town? Rather nice to come from the roar of traffic to lie and listen to Tweed."

Nannie looked over her shoulder to where, through the narrow window, she could see the silver water running between green banks, and shivered.

"It's a lonely sound," she said. "I'm afraid I like the town best. Glasgow's awful bright, and always something to do, picture houses and places to dance—a girl need never weary."

"Oh, Nannie lass," her mother sighed.

"But it's quite true," Kirsty agreed. "It is dull for a young girl who naturally wants dancing and fun. But after working all day in an office or in a shop it must be terribly tiring to dance for hours. No wonder you needed to come home for a rest, Miss Nannie. I expect you both work hard and play hard."

"Oh well, I don't know. I'm fearfully fond of dancing." She gave a laugh and a cough and looked at her mother. "Mother thinks it's wicked to dance. She doesn't admire my silver slippers." She nodded towards an old wooden chair with arms on which stood a pair of slippers. "I bring them out to look at them sometimes just to mind me that I used to have some fun. It's such a short life, I don't see why we shouldn't enjoy it as we like."

"Wheesht, Nannie . . . Miss Gilmour, wud ye tak a cup o' tea? Nannie and me were just gaun to sit doon."

"Oh, have I been keeping you? I'm so sorry. No, thank you very much, I must go home to tea. I have a household to look after."

"Ay, they tell me ye have bairns in the hoose—They'll be freends—relations?"

"No, no relation. Their mother is dead, and their father is abroad. I am so enjoying having them . . . Do you care for reading, Miss Nannie? Wouldn't you come down and get some books, and see the children? They might amuse you."

Nannie shook her head. "I don't go far from the Castle. It's such a pull up to get home, and I can't be bothered walking much. Thanks all the same."

Mrs. Tait went with Kirsty through the white-panelled outer room, down the stairs to the door.

"Nannie's no' ill, ye ken, Miss Gilmour. Ye dinna think she looks ill?"

"She is lovely. I've seldom seen such hair and eyes, and such a complexion. No wonder the child loves gaiety. She is meant to be admired."

"Dinna say that. I wud rather she had been as plain-heided as Agnes Stark than what she is. Beauty's a snare, I tell ye . . . Weel, I'm glad ye came, Miss Gilmour. Good day to ye."

When Kirsty went through the doorway into the light she was almost dazzled by the brightness of the afternoon. Blinking she took her way across the courtyard, and as she went through the crumbling archway she saw two figures just before her. They turned at her approach, and she saw that they were Rebecca Brand and Archie Home.

"Is the whole of Muirburn visiting today?" she asked, as

she greeted them. "Miss Brand, what was Mrs. Stark like to you?"

"Very _sneisty_," said Rebecca.

"That's a good word," said Colonel Home. "It's long since I heard it, and it exactly describes our friend."

"Oh, you have little to complain of," Rebecca told him. "She positively fawned on you. I was thankful when you came in."

Archie Home laughed. "I enjoy a talk with old Stark. I like his soft, slow speech, and he's a sound judge of both men and sheep."

"He was very rude to his poor son," Kirsty broke in, "as rude as Mrs. Stark was to her daughter. How came it that such caustic parents produced two such gentle creatures as Agnes and Willie?"

"They are almost middle-aged," Rebecca said, "and they allow themselves to be treated like children. Poor Agnes hardly dares go an errand without her mother's consent, and Willie isn't allowed to smoke."

"I suppose," said Colonel Home, "they are too peace-loving to make a fuss about it and get their own way. I remember my mother used to tell me about the Stark children. When they lived up at Cor Water they had to walk eight miles to school at Muirburn. One day my mother met them and asked Willie, a little white-headed boy, what his name was.

" 'Wullie,' he said.

" 'And what more?'

" 'Nocht mair'."

They had reached the highroad. Kirsty turned to Rebecca

and urged her to come to tea. "Visiting Mrs. Stark is such thirsty work," she pleaded, "and Little Phantasy is so near. Colonel Home, you will come too."

"Thanks, I'd like to," said the laird.

But Rebecca shook her head.

"*Do* come." Kirsty's voice was urgent.

"Not today," said Rebecca firmly. "I have still some of my district to collect for the 'Highlands and Islands,' and this is a chance to do it;" and she turned, leaving Kirsty and her landlord standing together, and took her way along the dusty white road.

CHAPTER 15

> "As I gaed east by Tarland toun
> I heard a singin 'neath the mune:
> A lass sang in a milk-white goon
> Aneath a hawthorn tree.
> The sma' green trees bowed doon till her,
> The blooms they made a croon till her,
> I was a graceless loon till her,
> She frowned and scorned at me."
> MARION ANGUS in *The Lilt*

KIRSTY TURNED, somewhat unwillingly, from watching Rebecca's retreating back to walk home with her landlord. She wished Rebecca had not been so firm in her refusal. What was to hinder her, when she was so near, going on to Little Phantasy? Then she, Rebecca, would have made conversation with Colonel Home, while she, Kirsty, would have enjoyed the walk. It was so difficult knowing what to say to her landlord—unless she scolded him. Her face flushed as she cast a side-glance at her companion, wondering if he remembered against her the impertinent onslaught she had made on him the day of the Hopecarton picnic. That day seemed a long time ago now, and she had met her landlord frequently since then at various small festivities, and in her own house, but she had never been alone with him. Anyway, it was no good trying to talk, she decided. Her crumbs of conversation seemed despicable surrounded by his large silence. It was easy, after all, to behave like a post and say nothing. She would be silent too.

They walked on together, neither speaking until they came to the bridge over Tweed, when they both turned back to look at the Castle. Surprisingly enough, it was Colonel Home who spoke first.

Folding his arms on the parapet of the bridge he said, "This is the view I like best. You get the sweep of the river in front, and the green hillside with its grey boulders and whin bushes, then Hawkshaw, battered but undefeated, with its bodyguard of ancient yews—don't they look like the straggling remnant of an army?—and behind the Hawkshaw woods."

Kirsty nodded. "They were clever people who planted that wood with its contrasts. The larches seem to laugh among the solemn pines. I never realized till today how very old and eerie it is . . . You know the people who live in it, of course? The man, Tait, is the forester, I think. I went to see Mrs. Tait this afternoon. Have you ever been inside the Castle, I mean in the rooms the Taits use? The ground floor seems to be used only for storing things, at least I could see no signs of habitation. I climbed the stair, and on the first landing there was a door standing open. I looked in and found what must once have been a reception room, a lovely room, white-panelled. There was nothing in it but a tubful of clothes and some brooms, but at the far end there was another room—the Taits' living-room. Such a queer room, long and narrow, with slits of windows: it must always be twilight there . . . Have you seen Mrs. Tait's daughter Nannie?"

"Not to my knowledge," said Colonel Home.

"She is the loveliest thing. In that dusky room she was

like a flame. I could do nothing but look at her. But I'm afraid she is ill. She coughs, the child; and her mother sits with such an anxious little face, always her eyes on the girl, but never caught looking. The woman with the tongue next door, Mrs. Stark, told me that Nannie is all she has left; she had two other girls who died of consumption."

"Yes. I remember hearing about it; my mother visited them . . . But surely something should be done at once. If she went to a sanatorium now she might be cured. Has a doctor seen her?"

"I think so," Kirsty said. "But, you see, the difficulty is that the poor mother won't own to herself that the girl is ill, and every one else seems so apathetic, so fatalistic—the sisters died, so this child is doomed . . . Something, of course, *ought* to be done, but it is so difficult to know what is best. So many people have a horror of sanatoriums: they cling to their homes, such as they are, and would rather die comfortably in a frowst than linger on exposed to all the winds of heaven—and I don't know that I wouldn't prefer it myself."

"But that is hardly the point," Colonel Home said, his arms still folded on the parapet, his eyes on grey Hawkshaw. "The girl ought to be given a chance of life. She doesn't know what is best for herself. If she stays here shut up in a stuffy kitchen, in a mouldering old castle, the winter will kill her. I must see Brand about it, and ask him what can be done. The parents need be put to no expense."

"You're kind," said Kirsty, looking at him as if surprised, "but do you mind letting me try first what I can do? I'm so anxious to help people, and no one seems to want my help."

She laughed a little ruefully. "I went there today quite by chance, so it almost looks as if I had been *meant* to help. But I don't know what I can do. I hope I'll be 'guided,' as Miss Wotherspoon, our parlour-maid, would say. To take a young girl away from her home, from the surroundings that seem poor and stuffy to you, but to her are dear because they are familiar, and place her among strangers where all is bleak and alien—well, it's a risk."

"Yes, but if she can be persuaded that it is for her own good—"

"Till I came here," Kirsty continued (she seemed to have forgotten her resolution to be a post and silent), "I didn't know much about how people lived, but in Muirburn, now that they have got used to me, they let me go in and out of the cottages, and I've been amazed to see a mother lying very ill in the kitchen-bed with the family life going on all about her—the children washing themselves in the sink, having their meals, doing their lessons by the fire. And I've wondered if illness isn't easier for those women than for better-off women who are shut away in a bedroom with a nurse, or in a nursing-home, with nothing round them but reminders of their illness, the world far away from them, no noise but the whisper of the nurse's dress . . . I know I would rather be the poor woman and lie in the kitchen-bed, and have wee Tommy come to see me to ask if his sum is correct, and lean on one elbow to tie Jeannie's hair ribbon, and give advice about frying potatoes. And if death comes it must lose some of its terror, surely, coming to the familiar kitchen, with the schoolbooks scattered about and the tea things on the table . . ."

Kirsty stopped, suddenly ashamed to find herself talking at such length.

"Shall we walk on?" she said. "It must be teatime."

They turned down the little path at the end of the bridge which led to Phantasy grounds.

"It's chagrining to me," said, Kirsty, looking up at her companion, "to find myself talking so much. I meant to say not a word; to match you in silence." She laughed. "How do you manage to say so little, if it isn't a rude question?"

Archie Home's brown face flushed slightly.

"I'm afraid I'm a very dull person, he said stiffly, "but at least I can appreciate the eloquence of others."

"And that settles me," Kirsty said impudently. "Oh, do just look at the foxgloves!"

At the edge of the wood was a knoll covered with them, standing high and proud with their heavy bells, purple and white. Kirsty sank down on the moss the better to admire their beauty.

"Isn't it a queer mixy-maxy world?" she said after a minute, bending a white foxglove to her face as she spoke. "Shadows of sadness and age in the old Castle, shadows of bright youth coming quick to confusion, and out here the summer sun and foxgloves . . . How I wish there was no sadness in life! I do think if I had been making a world I would have arranged that every one should be happy."

Colonel Home did not answer. He stood leaning on his stick, watching her kneeling there among the foxgloves in her white dress and wide rose-trimmed hat. Her hair was honey-coloured, he decided. With her green eyes and delicately tinted face she made him think of some old tale of Faery. Even so, he thought, might the Queen of Elfland have looked to mortals, who, seeing her once, never more found earthly rest.

They were walking on towards Little Phantasy when he said suddenly, "You must always have been happy." It was a statement more than a question.

"Must I?" said Kirsty. "Do you mean because I've always had money and good clothes, and a fairly decent face, and seen a good bit of the world? But I don't think these things make you happy at all. Happiness is a gift, and people who are born with it have it always, no matter what happens to them. I haven't got it—at least, if I have it it hasn't revealed itself. You see, it is no credit to me to be happy now, when I've got every single thing in the world I want."

"Every single thing?"

Kirsty nodded. "Well, pretty nearly."

"Lucky woman!"

Kirsty looked at him. "You sound very unbelieving. Don't you think we were meant to be happy? Or are you like Charlotte Bronte, who complained that life was 'bitter, brief, and blank'?"

" Did she say that? I suppose it is true—for many people."

"But," Kirsty protested, "isn't it largely their own fault? One finds what one looks for. I'm a sentimentalist, I suppose. You are a serious thinker, and the difference between us is that you like to stare piercingly at all the terrible things in life, while I turn away my head and look at foxgloves. I believe that things are bound to come right in the end in spite of so much that is ugly, while you rather hope they won't so that you won't be proved wrong."

Colonel Home deigned no reply to this speech, but after a minute he said, "There is something to be said for the pink sugar view of life."

"Pink sugar!" cried Kirsty, and laughed a little. "It's odd that you should say that . . . When I was a child I was taken once to a market held in a little town. I was allowed to ride on a merry-go-round and gaze at all the wonders—fat women, giants, and dwarfs. But what I wanted most of all I wasn't allowed to have. At the stalls they were selling large pink sugar hearts, and I never wanted anything so much in my life, but when I begged for one I was told they weren't wholesome and I couldn't have one. I didn't want to eat it—as a matter of fact I was allowed to buy sweets called *Market Mixtures*, and there were fragments of the pink hearts among the *curly-doddies* and round white *bools*, and delicious they tasted. I wanted to keep it and adore it because of its pinkness and sweetness. Ever since that day when I was taken home begrimed with weeping for a 'heart,' I have had a weakness for pink sugar. And good gracious!" she turned to her companion, swept by one of the sudden and short-lived rages which sometimes seized her, "surely we want every crumb of pink sugar that we can get in this world. I do *hate* people who sneer at sentiment. What is sentiment after all? It's only a word, for all that is decent and kind and loving in these warped little lives of ours . . ."

"Quite so," said Colonel Home, and Kirsty was silenced.

As they neared Little Phantasy they met Barbara, or rather they saw her in a tree, and she shouted to them:

"Pie, what do you think? Miss Wotherspoon fell over Bill with a tray and broke all the lunch things. And she's got a heart attack, and so has Aunt Fanny."

Barbara told her news with immense gusto.

"But where was Bill," Kirsty asked, "that he managed to trip Miss Wotherspoon?"

"Well," said Barbara, hanging dangerously by an arm and one foot from a branch, her long plaits touching the ground, "he was being an alligator just inside the dining-room door."

Kirsty turned to her landlord.

"What a blessing you came home with me," she said. "I think you had better speak to Bill in the tone that you use at court martials and things, for nothing I say has any effect. It's ridiculous to be beaten by a child of that age."

"It's Bill who ought to be beaten," Colonel Home said.

Kirsty's face got pink at the suggestion. "Oh dear me, no. It isn't as if he were really bad, as if he told lies and cheated. It's only that the things that occur to him to do have such disastrous results. There was no real harm in him being an alligator, but what induced him to be one inside the dining-room door?"

"I expect he remembered that the tray would be coming in, and, like an alligator, he waited."

Kirsty began to laugh. "Poor Miss Wotherspoon! And poor Aunt Fanny! Whenever I go out something like this happens . . . Here is the little scoundrel!"

Along the path by the Hope Water came a small figure in blue. The sun shone on his yellow head, and his blue eyes were as innocent as the speedwell flower they so resembled. He showed no guilt on seeing Kirsty and her companion, but greeted them cordially:

"Hullo, Pie! Hullo, Colonel Home!"

Pie gazed at him reproachfully, while Colonel Home said, "Hullo, Sykes!"

Bill did not seem to mind the reproach of the name, but slipped his hand confidingly into the tall man's, as if he found him a kindred spirit.

"Bill, *what* have you been doing?" Kirsty asked.

"*I* have been doing nothing," said Bill, "but Miss Wotherspoon's broke a lot of glasses and things."

"But you made her, you wretched child!"

"I was only a nalligator," Bill said blandly. "And people who walk on nalligators are sure to get bitten."

"Bill," almost shrieked Kirsty, "you didn't bite Miss Wotherspoon?"

"Only a little," said Bill lightly, "not nearly as bad as a nalligator generally bites: she had such *thick* stockings."

Kirsty gazed despairingly at her landlord.

"I'll fly home," she said, "and see how things are. You'll bring Bill, will you?"

It was much too hot to run, and Kirsty got crosser every step she took. As she neared the house she saw Specky, that patient fisher, diligently casting in his worm.

"Come and watch me, Pie," he invited her, but she merely shouted as she ran, "Stop fishing at once, and come in and wash your hands for tea."

"If there is any tea," she said to herself as she ran across the lawn and entered the house by the drawing-room window.

There was no one in the drawing-room.

Tea was laid as usual in the dining-room, but there was no one there.

Kirsty went up to her aunt's room, knocked, and went in.

Miss Fanny, looking shaken, was reading her Bible.

"Well, Aunt Fanny," said Kirsty in loud, cheerful tones, "isn't it a perfect afternoon! I've been making calls, and I terribly want my tea. Colonel Home is with me. Where is Carty?"

"I believe Miss Carter is in the garden with Mr. Brand. He came about half an hour ago. I saw him pass the window. Miss Carter was getting flowers at the time, and I expect he stayed to help her." Miss Fanny spoke in a resigned monotone.

"Well," said Kirsty, "we'd better ring the bell and summon them all. Are you ready to come down, Aunt Fanny?"

"I think, my dear, I won't come down. I've been rather upset. Bill—"

"I know," Kirsty interrupted. "I hear the little ruffian has been playing some game and frightened Miss Wotherspoon, and I expect she frightened you . . . Never mind, dear Aunt Fanny, come down and have tea, and be cheered up by Mr. Brand. He will tell you all about the Sale of Work they are going to have, and you'll forget all about Bad Bill."

"Kirsty," Miss Fanny said solemnly, "he is not a nice child."

"Oh, my poor Bill! He doesn't mean any harm. He is only five, Aunt Fanny. Were you a model at five?"

"I certainly never bit parlour-maids, Kirsty, at any age, or I would have been severely punished. Poor Miss Wotherspoon has had a great shock. She says such a thing never happened to her before, and I can well believe it . . . You can't mean to let that child sit down to table as if nothing had happened?"

Kirsty stood fingering the little books on the table.

"But he was an alligator," she pleaded. "He would never have bitten her as Bill . . . I shall have to talk to him very seriously tonight. After all, he is very obedient, you must admit. You see, he had never been told not to bite Miss Wotherspoon." She gave a sudden giggle. "I've sometimes felt like biting her myself."

Aunt Fanny bit her lip, and turned, with a patient sigh, to tidy her hair at the glass.

Kirsty proceeded to visit the victim of the assault. She found her sitting in one armchair with her leg on another, a bottle of smelling salts in her hand.

Kirsty addressed her in bracing accents, but it was at once evident to the meanest intelligence that the victim had no intention of being braced. She rolled her head heavily on the cushions, and said that she was "fair done." Easie and Nellie were both ministering to her.

"He *couldn't* have hurt you much," Kirsty told her; "he's so little, almost a baby."

"He's a little callous clown," Miss Wotherspoon said feebly, but with conviction.

"No, he's no," said Nellie fiercely.

Miss Wotherspoon closed her eyes.

"I hope you will soon feel better, Miss Wotherspoon,"

Kirsty said. "Don't you think you should go to bed? Nellie, please make the tea and take it to the dining-room and sound the gong."

"I will that," said Nellie, delighted to have the opportunity.

It was a large and cheerful party that Kirsty looked round at as she poured out tea. Even Miss Fanny, flanked on one side by Mr. Brand and on the other by Miss Carter, and removed as far as possible from Bill, had recovered something of her usual calm. They were just beginning when they heard the sounds of a motor on the drive.

"Visitors," said Kirsty. She caught Miss Carter's eye and groaned. "Only Nellie to open the door, and she knows about as much of a parlour-maid's work as a stot!"

They heard her rush panting through the hall, and presently she appeared, and leaning over Kirsty's shoulder whispered loudly, "It's a wumman. I mean it's twae weemen. I speired at them what they wanted, an' they gied me a ticket." She produced as if by sleight of hand a card, and Kirsty read—

>MRS. DUFF-WHALLEY
>MISS DUFF-WHALLEY
>The Towers,
>Priorsford.

"And where are the ladies?" she asked.

"Standin' on the doorstep. What'll I dae wi' them?" Nellie stood poised, looking ready for anything, however desperate.

"Ask them to come in. No—wait—I'll go," and Kirsty went out of the room and returned presently with the visitors, explaining to them, as room was made at the table and clean cups brought, that the parlour-maid was not feeling well, and that Nellie was still unaccustomed to opening the door to visitors.

"That was evident," said Mrs. Duff-Whalley.

"Let me introduce you . . . My aunt, Miss Gilmour—Mrs. Duff-Whalley, Miss Duff-Whalley. Miss Carter—I expect you know Colonel Home and Mr. Brand?"

Mrs. Duff-Whalley passed over poor Miss Fanny and Miss Carter and Robert Brand with a mere flick of her fingers; but Colonel Home she pounced upon, taking the chair beside him just vacated most reluctantly by Bill.

"Oh, Colonel Home, I am so glad to see you again. It was such a pleasure to meet you at the Manse garden party, but we have been so disappointed, Muriel and I, not to have seen you since. We have been so unfortunate with our invitations to you. You seem a man of many engagements." Colonel Home's face wore a guilty look. "I am so glad you have settled down among us. We are in such need of nice men in this district."

She looked so arch that Kirsty almost feared that she might prod the object of her attention in the ribs.

"Oh—thanks," he said miserably. "It's most kind of you to ask me, but as a matter of fact I—I—Have you come recently to Tweeddale?"

"Oh dear, no. We have lived at the Towers, Priorsford, for quite ten years now, and, of course, we know *everyone*. But Muirburn is a little out of our beat, and rather a dull district socially—and then of course you have only recently come back, so we haven't met . . . Now that you are at Phantasy and Lady Carruthers at Edmonston Hall we shall expect great things of Muirburn. You too, Miss Gilmour, will probably be entertaining as much as you can."

"No," said Kirsty, "I don't expect I shall entertain. I'm what is known as a recluse—Do have one of these scones."

Mrs. Duff-Whalley stared at her hostess.

"A recluse! But what a strange idea for a young woman. Almost as if you had something to hide. Now, I should have thought you would have wanted all the dances and tennis parties and things you could get. You must speak to your niece, Miss Gilmour. Youth doesn't last so very long. My Muriel there is game for anything—" She looked round the table, then addressed Kirsty: "Are these children your niece and nephews?"

"No," said Kirsty, pouring out some milk for Bill.

"Aren't they relatives at all?"

"No," said Kirsty; then, seeing all sorts of questions forming in the ferret-like eyes of her visitor, she said in a low voice, "Their mother was the sister of my greatest friend. She is in India with her husband and couldn't take the children, so I gladly offered to take charge of them for some months."

"I see." Mrs. Duff-Whalley gazed searchingly at each child in turn. "And their father?" she asked.

Kirsty, to her intense annoyance, suddenly found herself blushing. Every moment she got redder, until she felt that even her ears and neck must be scarlet; her very eyes were suffused. She felt Mrs. Duff-Whalley's gaze on her, she knew that Colonel Home had looked at her and had immediately looked away again. She made her voice coldly indifferent as she replied; "He has gone abroad for a time."

"I *see*," said Mrs. Duff-Whalley, and there was infinite meaning in her tone.

Kirsty, furious, and holding her head very high, turned to Mr. Brand and began on the first topic that presented itself to her.

"I called on the Starks today. You didn't prepare me for such a unique couple."

Mr. Brand laughed, and Colonel Home, after a brief glance at Kirsty's still crimson face, broke, surprisingly, into an anecdote.

"Speaking about alligators," he said, with a smile to Bill, "I must tell you what old Stark said to me once. He was by way of giving me good advice, and he finished, 'Eh, Mr. Erchie, dinna marry for love. I yince married for love, an' noo I wud marry an alligawtor, if she'd juist a pickle siller'."

"How quaint!" said Mrs. Duff-Whalley, "isn't it, Muriel? And you speak the dialect so wonderfully for a gentleman."

Kirsty looked gratefully at her landlord as she said, "I like the idea of the 'alligawtor' in white satin and a veil going up the aisle to the strains of the Wedding March."

A silence followed the general laugh, which was broken by Bill saying suddenly and very distinctly:

"Carty, have you ever been drunk?"

It was now Miss Carter's turn to blush.

"No—no. Hush, and go on with your tea."

"Well," said Bill, not rudely, but as if he were making a simple statement of fact, "I expect your father has been—often."

CHAPTER 16

"I should like to set up my tabernacle here . . . I am content."
CHARLES LAMB

"THIS day may be described as a rush," Kirsty said, as she walked one morning in the garden with Miss Carter in the interval between breakfast and lessons. The children had gone off to feed the rabbits, and to get rid of some of their superfluous energy by galloping wildly through the garden. "For a' the warld like young colts," said Easie as she watched them sympathetically.

"What happens today?" Stella Carter asked.

"Why, I'm going out both to luncheon and tea—luncheon at Edmonston Hall, tea at Cherrytrees. Such gaiety almost amounts to excess . . . I'll walk, I think, to Edmonston Hall, and will you bring the children in the pony trap to Cherrytrees? Mrs. Hay kindly said she wanted us all to come, and I meant to order a car from Priorsford, but Aunt Fanny firmly refused to move. Couldn't you persuade her, Carty? It would be a change for her, and if she only would make the effort I am sure she would enjoy going."

Miss Carter shook her head. "I don't believe she would. Not with the children there. She will enjoy much more staying quietly at home, knowing that they are all safely out of the way . . . I'm afraid Bill worries her a good deal. She is always waiting to hear his latest crime—poor old Bill!"

"But, Carty, can you understand any one not liking Bill, in spite of his faults?"

Stella Carter laughed. "I'm ashamed to confess I'm his slave. That little golden-brown face of his is so attractive, and there is so much in the child of affection and kindness as well as pure devilment."

Kirsty laid her arm caressingly on Stella's shoulder.

"My dear," she said, "you adore them all, and I love you for it."

"Oh, well! I defy any one to keep from falling under Specky's spell, and Barbara, dear lamb, so nerve-shattering but so loving—they really are all a bit extra!"

"You're happy here, Carty?"

"Happy?" Miss Carter turned frank eyes on her questioner. "I've never been anything like as happy all my life. I only wish I could stay here always."

"So do I, most earnestly. If only we could continue just as we are now!" and Kirsty sighed as she turned away to interview Easie. Afterwards she wrote some letters and talked to Miss Fanny, then got ready for her walk.

She was glad of the three miles in her own company, for she wanted to think. At home she was seldom alone. Always one or other of the children claimed her attention, or the servants wanted pacifying, or Miss Fanny had to be read to and petted and laughed out of her fears. And Stella and she had so much to say to each other when there were a few spare minutes. And the garden called aloud to her in those mellow August days. So that when night came she was too tired to think, and could only tumble into dreamless sleep.

It was a lovely day for a walk, warm but not heavy. A gentle wind full of sweet scents came in refreshing puffs. Tweed, like a broad silver ribbon in the sunshine, unwound itself, now between yellowing cornfields, and now through green marshy places, while the hills glowed like misty amethysts.

Kirsty felt her throat tighten as she looked at the beauty round her. No grandeur of soaring snow peaks or dark lochs shadowed by majestic mountains could move her as did the pastoral beauty of this her own beloved Border country.

Then she set herself to consider things. Like Charles Lamb she could say, "I am content," and like him she wanted to stop at this part of her life, to keep things unchanged. But in her heart she knew that the present state of affairs could not last; there was no stability in it whatsoever. True, she had Little Phantasy on a lease of three years, but she was beginning to realize that the place would mean little to her without the children, and some day—any day—their father might come rushing home and claim them.

And as Kirsty thought of Alan Crawford she remembered the foolish schoolgirlish way she had blushed at the mention of his name before Mrs. Duff-Whalley and Colonel Home, and remembering, she blushed again from sheer annoyance.

That morning she had received a letter from Alan Crawford, a letter written from some far port in sunny seas. It was a charming letter, giving glimpses of people he met, places he saw, thoughts he had. It was one of many; and

Kirsty was learning to look forward to those letters. The writer had the gift of getting *himself* through the paper and ink, of making his personality felt in the written word. Kirsty had only known him for twenty-four hours in the flesh, and she and Miss Fanny had often smiled together to think how quickly they had become almost intimate with him, and how vivid a memory he had left. But his letters were far more compelling. Kirsty was almost startled sometimes to find how easily and how often her thoughts turned to the traveller.

A sentence at the end of the letter she had got from him that morning kept recurring to her. He had been talking of the picturesque gay port they were calling at, of the warm tropical seas, the blazing stars, the velvet nights. "But," he finished, "somehow I feel apart from it all, often it vanishes, and in its place I see the green glens of Tweeddale, the hills above Priorsford (hear me name them—Hundleshope, Cademuir, the Black Meldon) the woods of Phantasy, its green pastures and still waters (Specky wearing a path with his patient feet), the scarred face of Ratchell Hill, the utter peace of summer nights in the uplands, my sleeping children—and *you* . . ."

"Of course," Kirsty reminded herself, "Mr. Alan Crawford is by way of being an artist, and he sees things in pictures. Also, he is a very fluent gentleman, and probably always says more than he means. You are a fool, my dear, to think that he means anything more than a youngish man with the artistic temperament writing in the moonlight in far-off seas would mean when he thinks of quite a good-looking young (or youngish) woman to whom he feels grateful for relieving him, for a time, of the responsibility of his children."

But still there was a chance that he did mean something, and if he did? It meant that the spectre that so often lay at the back of her mind, the thought of a harsh, un-understanding stepmother, was dissolved, and it meant that the children were hers for "keeps"; but it also meant that Alan Crawford was hers for "keeps," and that was not such a pleasant thought.

But why not? After all, Alan Crawford had much to recommend him. He was what men called a good sort; he was certainly extraordinarily good-looking; he was an amusing companion; he would always be kind and agreeable.

"It's odd," thought Kirsty, "but I don't seem to like that kind of man much."

Then she upbraided herself for selfishness. She who had talked so glibly about "living for others," when a chance lay to her hand feebly hesitated about taking it. Of course, it was going pretty far to marry for the sake of others, almost more than could be expected of any one.

Kirsty, full of such perplexing thoughts, walked so fast in the August sun that when she reached the imposing gates of Edmonston Hall, like Mercy in *The Pilgrim's Progress*, she was "all in a pelting heat," and stood for a few minutes to cool herself and to study the most ornate gateway and gilded railings that guarded the entrance.

"I suppose these are what are known as 'gilt-edged securities'," she told herself, and laughed a little at her own joke.

Two cars passed her in the drive, and realizing that she had been bidden to a party, she wondered if she were smart enough. "Anyway I'm clean," she thought, as she looked down at her fresh white coat and skirt.

A butler admitted her and took her through a hall panelled in light wood to a drawing-room that seemed to extend as far as the eye could reach, carpeted with red carpet with an orange design.

"There must be acres of it," Kirsty thought, as she walked the whole length of the room to where her hostess sat in a large bay window talking to earlier arrivals.

Everything in the room was large—large sofas and armchairs, large oil paintings in large gilt frames, large palms, large cabinets with large Oriental vases standing on them, large polished tables on which were large books with coloured pictures. Kirsty felt crushed beneath it all as she shook hands with her large hostess, with whom were Mr. and Mrs. McCandlish and another couple whom she did not know. It was a positive relief to turn to the small shrinking figure of her host. No wonder, she thought, that Sir Andrew had such a crushed look. To possess such a house and such a wife must be like having a leviathan on a hook.

"I'm so glad to meet you," she said to him. "I hear so much about you from Specky—you know the little boy who lives at Little Phantasy and fishes all the time."

"Oh yes," said Sir Andrew, not in the least as if he desired the conversation to continue.

"You were so good about helping him to untangle his line the other day. And you gave him an artificial minnow which is the delight of his life! He takes it to bed with him every night."

"He's a queer wee chap," said Sir Andrew.

"You are a keen fisher, aren't you?"

"Oh no, I just do it to pass the time."

"Oh," said Kirsty, and conversation died at the fountain-head.

"We are waiting for Mrs. Strang," Lady Carruthers announced when every one had fallen hungrily silent.

Kirsty studied the couple in the window, and decided that she liked the look of them. The man had a delightful shy smile and a scholar's stoop, while his wife was out-of-the-ordinary attractive, with a dark grace that fascinated Kirsty. As the minutes passed, various reasons for Mrs. Strang's unpunctuality were suggested. Mr. McCandlish thought that she might be so absorbed in literary labours as to have lost count of time, while Sir Andrew said gloomily that her car had probably overturned; and while they argued about it Mrs. Strang was announced. Nothing had happened, she told them, except that she had not given herself enough time to come up from Priorsford, where she had been marketing, and she begged humbly to be forgiven. She seemed on the easiest terms with everyone present. The strange couple she called by their Christian names; she gave Mr. McCandlish news of some cuttings he wanted, and said she had got a new recipe for his wife. She turned to her host, and in a trice had him talking in almost an animated manner about some etching he had just bought, and the party went in to luncheon quite jauntily.

Kirsty found herself at the left hand of her host, and

opposite the tall slim woman whose name she did not know. Mrs. McCandlish was beside her. She looked at her host sitting hunched dejectedly in his chair, she looked at her neighbour peeling off immaculate white kid gloves, and felt she was going to have a dull hour.

The strange lady was trying to engage Sir Andrew in conversation, so she turned to Mrs. McCandlish and began on the weather. It was a safe topic, and one that could be made to last a considerable time. From the weather they passed to gardens, and Kirsty waxed enthusiastic about the Manse garden, discussing in detail the herbaceous borders and the joys of a rock garden. Gardens lasted till the sweets, when Kirsty turned to make an effort to converse with her host. His right-hand neighbour had given him up, and was talking merrily to Mrs. Strang. She shot Kirsty a grateful glance when she saw her address him, so evidently her conscience was not void of offence.

"Mrs. McCandlish and I have been talking about gardens," Kirsty began brightly, trying to draw her neighbour in with her. "Didn't you think the Manse garden was beautiful the day of the garden party?"

"Wasn't there," said Sir Andrew, looking mournfully into an empty glass. He drank nothing but water.

"You have fine gardens, I know," she continued bravely. "They must be a great pleasure to you."

"I'm never in them hardly. There is no pleasure in a garden when you're knocking into gardeners at every step. What I like is a little bit of ground where you can potter about and do as you like."

"Oh, I know," Kirsty agreed eagerly, thankful to have got

an opinion out of him. "That of course is the nicest thing. And even when you don't know much about it, and make all sorts of mistakes, it merely adds to the fun. We have a very obliging gardener at Little Phantasy, who doesn't much mind what we do. But of course it is different here: you will need a crowd."

Sir Andrew grunted in evident bitterness of spirit.

"A crowd! That's just what we have. Can't get moving for servants, and gardeners, and visitors."

"Oh," said Kirsty, feeling vaguely guilty . . . "Have you been long at Edmonston Hall?"

"About five years. Five years I've done nothing but eat my meals and take off my clothes and put them on again! Before that we had a villa outside Glasgow, and I went to office every day of my life except Saturdays and a week at the Fair. We had a house down the Clyde too . . . But Maggie—my wife, you know—likes this."

Kirsty felt strongly tempted to ask the little man why he didn't go back to the business life he loved; but, reflecting that it was no part of a guest's duty to sow seeds of insurrection in a host's mind, she was silent.

After luncheon she found herself on a large sofa between her hostess and Mrs. McCandlish.

Lady Carruthers was full of some psychic experience she had had, which she related at length.

"Now, what do you think of that?" she asked when she had finished.

Mrs. McCandlish was drawing on her white kid gloves and pulling down her upper lip. "Well, Lady Carruthers," she said, "you will forgive me saying that I hardly think we should pry into such matters. God will reveal them in His good time."

"Ye-es," her hostess said, somewhat damped, "but it is such a help, don't you think? To be made to feel that the veil between is so thin—so thin," her voice died away in a murmur.

"Take the howling of a dog in the night," Mrs. McCandlish continued. "It seems to me so silly to connect such a thing with evil tidings. Why should the Maker of all things tell a dog? Such a senseless roundabout way of doing things! Mr. McCandlish preached such a fine sermon only last Sunday—I don't think you were present, Lady Carruthers—on foolish superstitions and the harm they do; and he touched on spiritualists, and Saul, you know, and the Witch of Endor. He said to me afterwards that it was borne in on him the need of such a sermon at this time."

"Even in Muirburn?" Kirsty asked, but Lady Carruthers broke in.

"Dear Mrs. McCandlish, I must give you a little book to read that has been such a help to me. It's by Bishop—I've forgotten the name, but it is so helpful. It seems to put one right about so many things, you know what I mean. Makes one see things in their proper perspective—so necessary, is it not?" Then turning to Kirsty—"You and I have had no talk, Miss Gilmour. I want to see so much of you, but life is so full. I'll tell you what, some day we shall meet, and take our lunch with us, and walk over the hills, and talk and talk. I do so love hearing each person's point of view, and I'm sure yours will be interesting. Now tell me, are you more interested in people or things? That is so important to me before I make a real friend of any one—"

She turned away without waiting for an answer, and Merren Strang, at Kirsty's elbow, said, "Mrs. Elliot wants to meet you," and took her up to the lady with the dark eyes, who smiled at her and said, "I hear you have come to Little Phantasy. We have just got back to Laverlaw after an exile of several months, and I hope very soon to call on you. Merren has been telling me all about you, and I long to see the house and the children."

"Oh," said Kirsty, "when will you come? I mean—could you fix a day, for I would so hate to miss you. Any day. It hardly matters to us, we haven't many engagements."

Mrs. Elliot considered. "May I come on Thursday? And may I bring my husband? He will want to see his friend Archie Home, and perhaps you'll let me stay and talk to you."

"Oh, lovely. I shall look forward to that . . . Could you spare time to lunch with us? Forgive me if I'm being a nuisance, for I expect you've heaps of engagements."

Mrs. Elliot laughed. "Not a bit of it! Neither Lewis nor I care much about going out, but we would like to go to you. It's delightful of you to want us. That's settled then. Luncheon on Thursday. Now I must collect Lewis and go. This *has* been nice."

When Kirsty was leaving Mrs. Strang offered to give her a lift. "I know you're going to tea at Cherrytrees. So am I, so we may as well go together."

"Why, it's quite cold now," Kirsty said, as they tucked themselves into the little car. "The wind has gone into the north."

"Our treacherous northern summer," said Mrs. Strang. "Here, put that round you. You aren't clothed for motoring . . . Now, we are too early for tea, and it's hardly worth while going home. What do you say to a run up Tweed? It's only three o'clock now. We could go to Linkumdoddy and back in an hour."

"Lovely," said Kirsty, cuddling into the wide warm scarf that had been handed to her, "and you will tell me about things as we go along."

"What sort of things?" Mrs. Strang asked, as they slipped down the drive and through the "gilt-edged securities" on to the open road.

"First of all about the people who were at luncheon today—that delightful couple?"

"You don't mean the McCandlishes? Perhaps they aren't a delightful couple exactly, but they are a very worthy couple. I like them both. Norman McCandlish is a decent soul, and his wife can talk on the weather for half an hour on end. Of course you mean the Elliots. Hadn't you seen them before? But they have been away. Isn't she a graceful creature? She always makes me think of a greyhound, the lovely swift way she moves. I can sit happily for hours simply watching the way she turns her head, and her hands doing embroidery. They live at Laverlaw, a place, about five miles on the other side of Priorsford. Pamela asked me to take you there. You will love it—a green glen shut away among the hills, and an old whitewashed house. I've known Lewis Elliot all my days. We all thought he had settled down to bachelorhood, when he surprised us all by marrying Pamela Reston. It was an old romance, they should have married twenty years ago. I can't imagine two more utterly contented people. When I get down in spirits and feel that all's wrong with the world, I go over to Laverlaw and take a look at the Elliots."

"How jolly!" Kirsty said wistfully. "They must be very fond of each other. I liked the way they looked at each other now and again across the room, when they thought no one was looking, as if they were signalling 'Cheer up! We'll soon be through with this and get away together.' Marriage must be rather wonderful when two people really care. Most people just seem to jog along more or less tolerating one another."

As they talked they were swinging round the many curves of the road that ran by Tweed. The wind was driving big white clouds across the sky, making shadows on the bare hillsides. Tweed was no longer the silver ribbon it had been at noon, it was a grey and ruffled water. Kirsty shivered a little, and was glad when they turned to go back down the valley, towards tea and the comfort of Cherrytrees.

When they arrived the Little Phantasy pony trap had just driven up, and Kirsty was relieved to see that the children had their coats.

Mr. and Mrs. Anthony Hay were both on the doorstep to welcome them, and led them through the friendly entrance-hall, shabby as to furniture but gay with flowers, into the drawing-room, which was papered, mid-Victorian wise, in white and gold. A big round table stood in the middle of the room covered with a gleaming white cloth. A frosted silver epergne occupied the centre, and held scarlet geraniums and mignonette. Every conceivable good thing in the way of scones and pancakes, buns and shortbread, brandy-scrolls and meringues, were set among ruffled doyleys on white and gold plates. A fire had been lit, and blazed and crackled in a wide steel grate with green and white tiles.

The children stood open-mouthed before the loaded table, and Merren Strang cried:

"I thought a Cherrytrees tea would be a revelation to you. It was to me as a child."

"Ah, Merren," Mr. Hay said, "Cherrytrees has known you for a long time. You used to come when your head wasn't as high as the table. Funny little elf you were!"

"All my life," Merren Strang said, "I've thought of Cherrytrees as the most homelike place in the world, a place to think of for comfort when one is far away. It's about the only place that you get a really decent cup of tea. Don't you agree, Kirsty? I'm so sick of the half cups of tepid tea I get slopped out to me by careless modern hostesses. Mrs. Hay, you're a lesson to us all in how to pour out tea."

"Nonsense, Merren," Mrs. Hay laughed. "Anybody can pour out tea surely; there is no art in it." She was warming each cup with a little hot water which she poured back into the slop basin before she filled the cups with tea. The teapot stood on a little Dutch stand, foursquare, with transparent porcelain sides through which glowed the light of a floating wick; it kept the tea hot without letting it boil. Mrs. Hay had a white lace scarf over her white hair. Her rosy face wore an absorbed expression as she filled each cup carefully with fragrant tea, while a maid, standing beside her with a salver, carried them round one at a time.

Nothing so delighted the Anthony Hays as to entertain young people. Having no children of their own, they adopted the children of the neighbourhood. Neither of these old people found the slightest difficulty in talking to and interesting children. Mr. Hay was already deep in conversation with Specky about fishing; Barbara was telling Mrs. Hay all about their latest pranks, and the two were beaming at each other in high good humour.

In the middle of tea Mrs. Strang jumped up and went to a small side-table on which stood a rosewood box.

"Please, may I have my treat?" she asked, and set going a musical box.

"It's been my special treat since I was Bill's age," she explained. "It's as much Cherrytrees as the green-and-white fireplace, or the silver epergne, or the geraniums and the mignonette, or Mrs. Hay's white lace cap. I can't really enjoy my tea unless it is accompanied by *Oft in the Stilly Night* or *The Last Rose of Summer*."

So while they ate, the sweet tinkle-tinkle went on, making Kirsty think of polite ladies sitting in potpourri-scented parlours, with tatting in their hands and photographic albums beside them: dim dainty creatures long since faded out of the world.

After tea there was a wealth of things to amuse the children—a parrot in the hall that delighted Bill by dancing up and down, singing-

> "Sing hey! the merry masons,
> Sing ho! the merry masons;"

a puppy and a kitten, and outside in the stables other wonders. They were dragged away reluctantly, and only the packets of butterscotch bestowed on them by Mrs. Hay kept Bill from making a scene, so enamoured was he of Cherrytrees and its owners.

"There is no doubt," Mrs. Strang said to Kirsty as she drove her to the turn of the road, "that there was something about the Victorians that is lost to us. It is only among the older women that you find that delightful welcoming way that Mrs. Hay has. There is a coldness and casualness about our modern hospitality. We won't take trouble, and we won't 'put ourselves about.' When the Hays have visitors (as they nearly always have) they make a fuss about them. Everything in the house seems to shout a welcome, and they themselves give of their best to their friends, not only in the way of food and that sort of thing, but time and thought and effort. I must say I do like to be made a fuss of. When I go to stay in a house where I am received by servants and told that the mistress will be back for dinner, and when I have received a casual goodbye from a lady torn from a bridge table to say it, I shake the dust of that house from my feet and never go back."

"I know those sort of people," Kirsty said feelingly. "They think it smart to behave like that. Guests come and go, and are neither welcomed when they come nor missed when they go. Probably they and their hostess know practically nothing of each other. The Hays, I expect, only ask friends."

"Oh yes." Mrs. Strang slowed down to avoid a young collie disporting himself on the road. "Do you know, when the Hays go away for a little their chauffeur has orders to take certain people for drives every day, people to whom a motor-run is a luxury and a treat. Fruit and flowers and vegetables—everything that they have is shared."

"It's nice that there are people like that in the world," Kirsty said slowly. "Most of us are so busy living our own lives, trying to get the very best out of life for ourselves, we haven't time to be kind."

"Live one's own life," Mrs. Strang cried impatiently. "I'm sick of that phrase. It simply means crass selfishness. A girl goes off to live in her own flat and study art or something of the kind, leaving a delicate mother to wrestle as best she can with a big house and servants and entertaining, and people say, 'Oh, but she must live her own life.' If the girl is happy she doesn't deserve to be."

"But surely," said Kirsty, "surely you don't think it was right the way Victorian parents so often victimized a daughter, sometimes making her give up all prospects of a house of her own and a husband to hang round and nurse them."

"I think it was very wrong of the parents, but I think that too much pity is wasted, and scorn poured, by moderns on the meek daughter who allowed herself to be treated so. I'm hopelessly old-fashioned, I know, but I do think there is a tremendous satisfaction in doing what you feel to be your duty, and a great deal of happiness got that way . . . Well, here we part. Goodnight, Kirsty dear. Better keep the scarf, the wind is cold. I'll get it some time . . . My love to Miss Fanny."

As she went to bed that night Kirsty remembered Alan Crawford's letter. She took it from her letter case and read it again. A charming letter. She remembered the writer with his handsome face and easy, friendly ways. Charming, too. No hardship surely about marrying such a man. As she brushed her hair before her looking glass, watching the candles flicker and wave in the air from the open window, she nodded at herself in the glass, promising herself, "I could always encourage him to go away a lot." . . . And as she said it she remembered the couple whom she had so admired at Edmonston that day, remembered the glances she had intercepted between them, the little signalling glances of good comradeship, and more, of deep, satisfied love, and she sighed. The dark lady would not want to encourage her Lewis to go away . . .

CHAPTER 17

"It's rainin'. Weet's the gairden sod,
  Weet the lang roads whaur gangrels plod."
                                    R. L. S.

A POURING wet day, and the Sabbath.

They had all been at church—even Bill. That abandoned character was at his best in the house of God, urbane, gentle, reverent. He liked going to church, and removed his hat in the porch with a solemn gesture. The mere sight of a church enveloped Barbara and Specky in a thick fog of depression, and they sat through the service with blank faces, sunk in profound gloom. Not so Bill. He briskly looked up (or pretended to look up) the psalms and hymns, and certainly sang something very loudly and out of tune. He bowed his head at prayers, and sat all through the sermon staring very hard at the minister, with an absorbed face.

This Sunday there was a strange preacher, very long and *dreich*, and at the end Bill said quite audibly with a sigh, "Oh, what a long preach! I thought he was going on till Monday."

Miss Carter was in bed with a bad headache, and after early dinner, the special Sunday dinner with the children's favourite pudding and an extra allowance of sweeties afterwards, Kirsty wondered how the long wet day was to be put in. Miss Fanny, too, foresaw difficulties, and determined, if the children were to be about, that she would spend the afternoon in her own room. However, there was no need for such extreme measures, for the moment they had been given their toffee the children slipped quietly away, murmuring something about playing a Bible game since they couldn't go out.

Kirsty followed her aunt to the drawing-room where a bright fire was burning, to which Miss Fanny was drawn as a bee is drawn to a flower-bell.

Kirsty went to the window, and stood looking out at the drenched grey world.

"How rain changes things!" she said. "Yesterday it was high summer. Today, with the whirling leaves and the battered flowers, it is autumn."

Miss Fanny had settled herself in her own big chair, and was reading the Old Testament, as she always did on Sunday afternoons. She shook her head mournfully at Kirsty's remark. "Yes, the summer is nearly over. It is such a sad time the fall of the leaf, I always think."

"Oh, would you call it sad? Rather a jolly time, I think, with the days drawing in and winds whistling, and big fires blazing, and the harvest safely in, and the byres full of feeding cattle."

Miss Fanny sighed again. "You are young, Kirsty; you don't see the sadness in things as I do . . . The swallows preparing to go away, and having a desire to depart; the dying flowers—it makes me think of one's own going . . . What an excellent sermon that was this morning. When you went back for Bill's hat, I walked along with that Mrs. Dickson of the shop—a nice, sad woman, she tells me she takes salts every morning—and she said she did not know when she had enjoyed a sermon so much. The very text, *Flee from the wrath to come*, was so refreshing. Ministers nowadays are so taken up with love and forgiveness that they seldom mention the wrath of God. It's a pity."

"Yes," Kirsty agreed. "It's the reaction from Calvinism; they've gone to the other extreme. Doesn't Bill behave well in church?"

Miss Fanny folded her long upper lip over her lower one but said nothing, and Kirsty continued:

"He never moved through that long sermon, though what he made of it I don't know. Perhaps you will live to see Bill a minister yet, Aunt Fanny!"

Miss Fanny gazed at her niece very solemnly and said:

"Kirsty, he came into my room yesterday, and I didn't notice what he was doing till I found he had taken a jar of cold cream and mixed it with bay rum in the soap dish, and stirred it round with my thermometer. He said he was playing at a chemist's shop. I told him how wicked it was to waste things, and to meddle with other people's property—indeed, I took the opportunity to speak very seriously to him about several things, and he listened quite attentively. Indeed, as I talked his face looked quite softened, it lost that arrogant look which I so much object to, and I kissed him, and he went out of the room penitent, I thought, until I found that he had taken the key out of my door and *locked me in!* There is no saying when I would have got out had it not happened to be near lunchtime, and Miss Wotherspoon, coming with my hot water, let me out. She was quite upset about it, and so was I. It was so brazen, just after I had spoken to him so seriously."

Kirsty said, "What a villain!" and tried to look properly shocked (though she was irresistibly reminded of Jonah sitting before Nineveh saying, "I do well to be angry"), and Miss Fanny continued:

"I didn't mean to tell you, for I don't like tale-bearing, but when you spoke of that bad child becoming a minister!—I just thought when he was sitting so quiet in church he was probably meditating evil. There is a verse in this chapter I am reading in Second Chronicles that reminds me of him— *Jehoiachin was eight years old when he began to reign, and he reigned three months and ten days in Jerusalem: and he did that which was evil in the sight of the Lord.*"

Kirsty gave a cry of protest, and went to look over her aunt's shoulder at the verse in question.

"Eight years old and reigning in Jerusalem! Who said he did evil? Not the Lord, I'm sure: the stupid high priests probably. I wonder what he did, the lamb? Ate the shewbread or cut his name on the Ark of the Covenant perhaps! . . D'you see how it goes on? *And when the year was expired, King Nebuchadnezzar sent and brought him to Babylon.* That was better. Jerusalem was no place for a bad little king, but can't you see him ruffling it in Babylon?"

"Kirsty, my dear, I sometimes think you are inclined to be flippant. I don't like the light way you speak of sacred things. At eight years of age this boy was quite old enough to know better. I expect he was just such another as Bill— impenitent." And Miss Fanny returned to the study of the Old Testament, while Kirsty took up a book.

Presently Miss Fanny fell asleep, her hands folded on the

open Bible, a picture of Sabbatarian repose.

Kirsty's book was not very entertaining, and in a little she laid it down and looked out of the window. The rain was still falling steadily. She wondered what the children were doing that was keeping them so quiet. Perhaps Carty would like her tea early. She slipped out of the room.

There was no one in the schoolroom. She went on to Miss Carter's room, and found that lady so far recovered that she had got up and proposed to go downstairs for tea. Kirsty tried to persuade her to remain quietly in her room with a book all day, but she was adamant.

"Where are the children?" she asked.

"Lost," said Kirsty. "After luncheon they went away to the schoolroom (as I thought) to play Bible games, but I've just been to look, and there's no trace of them. They can't be out of the house, and I don't hear them in the kitchen, so I'm going to try the attic."

"Then," said Miss Carter, pulling on a woolly coat, "as Cocky Locky said to Henny Penny when he heard that she was going to tell the King the sky was falling, 'I shall go with you'."

The attic was a large room running the whole length of the house, and was reached from the long passage by a wooden stair with a door at the foot. When the searchers opened the door they knew they had run their quarry to earth. Whispers, giggles, soft thuds, subdued bumpings came down the stair to them—evidently it was quite a Sunday game.

As they reached the head of the stairs they were confronted by a strange sight. The attic as a rule contained nothing but a few old chairs and unwanted pictures and ornaments. These had been stacked in a corner, and the middle of the floor was covered with flowering plants and palms and ferns, all the bushiest things that could be found in the greenhouse. Someone had worked hard.

Behind the largest palm skulked two figures which Kirsty and Miss Carter, staring with amazed eyes, recognized as Barbara and Specky. They were lightly clad in undervests, and had aprons of ivy leaves with ties of red braid fastened on with black safety pins. Specky was devouring a banana.

"What in the world—" Kirsty began, when Barbara flew to her.

"Darling Pie, it's the Garden of Eden. We're Adam and Eve. We ought really to have nothing on but fig leaves, like the picture in Aunt Fanny's big Bible, but they had both long hair, and Specky hasn't, and so we kept on our underthings. And we couldn't find any fig leaves—and anyway, ivy leaves are the easiest to sew. . . I've just got Adam to eat the Forbidden Fruit."

"But that's not an apple," said Miss Carter.

"No," Barbara admitted, "but you see Specky said he wouldn't be tempted except with a banana—he doesn't like apples unless they're stewed. Bill—"

"Yes. Where is Bill?" Kirsty demanded.

Barbara pointed, and there in the "garden," among the flowering plants, on a high chair from which his legs stuck out stiffly, sat Bill. True Elizabethan that he was, he scorned to "dress up." He wore the pale-blue jersey and the brief blue trousers that he had worn at church, but on his gilt head was laid a wreath of tropeolum. His sea-blue eyes were sternly fixed on vacancy; his lower jaw was thrust out, making him look extraordinarily like Lord Carson or a bloodhound; he was heavily scented.

"What is he?" Miss Carter asked.

Barbara gave a frightened giggle. "We didn't want him to be it. Indeed we didn't. We told him we would just pretend something was moving in the bushes, and pretend we heard a voice—but he *would* do it. First he was the Serpent, and went on his stomach (look at his new jersey), and now he's—he is—"

"He's God," said Specky, swallowing the last bite of his banana.

There was a silence, for no one knew what to say next.

Kirsty, shaken by internal laughter, felt thankful that Miss Fanny was safely asleep in the drawing-room. "Evil in the sight of the Lord" indeed!

Miss Carter took the matter in hand.

"Well," she said in a matter-of-fact voice, "it's nearly tea-time, so get properly dressed at once, Barbara and Specky, and remember another time that you are not to undress in the day-time. And when you are dressed, carry all these plants carefully back to their places. Bill, come with me and learn a hymn."

Bill turned on his governess a cold glance, but seeing that she was evidently not in a mood to be trifled with, he took her hand and trotted meekly away.

At tea Miss Fanny asked Barbara innocently, "Had you a nice quiet Bible game, dear?"

"Yes, thank you, Aunt Fanny," Barbara said demurely, and Kirsty quickly changed the subject.

After tea the children lounged about the drawing-room for a little, taking out books, glancing through them, and leaving them about in a way that greatly annoyed Miss Fanny, but in a short time they slipped unobtrusively away to their favourite refuge, the kitchen.

Easie and Nellie were their boon companions, and Miss Wotherspoon with her stern ways and long face had a strange attraction for them.

It was Nellie's day out, but Easie was sitting by the fire, and Miss Wotherspoon sat in the window, with her spectacles on, reading the *Missionary Record*.

The Little Phantasy servants had a very comfortable sitting-room with a couch and wicker chairs filled with bright cushions, and a piano, but they seldom used it except when they had a visitor. It is true that Miss Wotherspoon liked to sit there in state of an afternoon and write letters, but for real cosiness there was no place like the kitchen, especially on a Sunday afternoon when Easie laid down a cherished rug and brought some chairs from the sitting-room.

"Weel, here ye are," Easie greeted their entrance. "Are ye wearit, puir bairns? 'Straight lines are tiresome like lang Sabbath days'."

Specky sat down on the floor beside Easie and the fire, with a bit of wood in his hand to whittle into a boat.

"Were you ever in England, Mrs. Orphoot?" he asked.

The question seemed to amuse Easie. "No' me," she said, "it's a place I never set fit in."

Specky studied his bit of wood with his head on one side. "Well, I don't think you've missed much," he assured her.

Easie laughed again, then yawned frankly.

"Eh, hey hech um! an auld wife an' a strae brechum. I dinna like a wat Sabbath. See how dark it is, an' it no' near six yet!"

Barbara was dancing Bill about in the middle of the floor trying to work off her high spirits, and she now made a playful dash at Miss Wotherspoon, caught her round the neck and kissed her.

"Tuts, give over, lassie." Miss Wotherspoon shook herself free like a nervous horse. "You're that violent. Ye should try to be more ladylike, such a great girl as ye are."

Barbara was unabashed, and wanted to know what Miss Wotherspoon was reading, and if there were any pictures.

Plenty pictures, she was told, but not the kind she would like.

"But how d'you know I wouldn't like them?" Barbara asked. "Show me one." But on being shown a group of dark gentlemen in European costume posing before the camera her interest was quickly quenched.

Bill went and seated himself firmly in Easie's capacious lap. He put up one hand and touched her very gently under the chin (a favourite action of his if he wanted to coax someone), and said, "Mrs. Orphoot, tell us a story."

"Me! I dinna ken nae Sabbath stories."

"All the better," said Bill. "Tell *The Red Etain of Ireland*."

"Ye've heard it a hunner times."

"We don't mind," Specky said handsomely, whittling away hard at his boat.

They gathered round Easie prepared for a treat, for Easie had a great sense of drama, and could drop her voice thrillingly when she was the beggar wife begging the King's son for a bit of his bannock and offering him her benison, and on being refused, bestowing on him her malison—but today there was to be no Red Etain, Easie's conscience would not allow it.

"It's no' the thing," she said, "to tell lees on the Lord's Day. I'll tell ye aboot the Prodigal Son."

"Must you?" Specky sighed. "I don't like him much."

"Or aboot the pigs rinnin' doon the hill into the sea."

This promised better. "Bible pigs?" Bill asked.

"Ay. Ye mind when Christ was on earth, and walkit aboot makin' sick folk weel, He cast devils oot o' folk. An' the devils didna ken whaur to gang when they werena allowed to torment folk ony langer, an' there was a herd o' swine feedin' quite quiet there on the hillside (juist like sheep would feed here in Muirburn), an' they gaed into the swine, an' the puir beasts ran doon the steep hill into the sea, an' were never mair heard tell o'."

"It was hard on the swine," said Specky.

"Ay, I think that masel', but better swine than folk, if somebody's got to be drooned."

"Were the devils drowned?" Bill asked.

Easie stared at him. "Eh, d'ye ken, I never thocht o' that. I doot if ye can droon devils, that's to say if they're ony thing like witches, but I dinna ken."

"Do you know any more Bible stories?" Barbara asked.

"Plenty, but they feenish awfu' quick. Ye've hardly begun when ye're done. Miss Wotherspoon'll read us something oot o' the paper, mebbe."

Miss Wotherspoon did not seem to hear, and went on reading.

"Sing to us, please," Bill said. "Sing *Kitty Bairdie*."

There was nothing the children enjoyed more than to get Easie to sing her store of old songs and rhymes to them. She could tell how

> "Kitty Bairdie hed a coo
> A' black aboot the moo,
> Wasna that a denty coo?
> Dance, Kitty Bairdie."

And not only had Kitty Bairdie a "coo," but she had a "grice that could skate upon the ice," also a "hen that could toddle but and ben." And about "the wee bit mousikie that lived in Gilberatie-o, and couldna get a bit o' cheese for cheetie-pussie-cattie-o." And the ballad of *Willie Wud*, whose clothes were surely the strangest ever seen, for "his buttons they were made o' the bawbee baps," and "his coat it was made o' the guid roast beef," and "his breeks they were made o' the haggis-bags."

"Sing," Bill commanded.

Easie cast a glance at her fellow servant, who seemed deep in the *Record*. "I canna sing thae sangs the day," she whispered. "Wait till the morn."

"I shan't want them 'the morn'," Bill pointed out.

Easie hesitated, and then began to sing softly in her sweet high voice the song that seemed to her most Sabbath-like:

> "Alla-balla-balla-balla-be,
> Sittin' on his Mammy's knee,
> Greetin' for anither bawbee
> To buy Colthart's candy.

> Little Annie greetin' tae,
> What can patient Mammy dae,
> But halve a penny atween the twae
> To buy Colthart's candy?"

At the conclusion of the song Miss Wotherspoon rose in her wrath. "What ongoings on the Sabbath day! Are ye not ashamed, Easie Orphoot? Put that laddie on his feet, and we'll all sing a hymn, one we all know, *The Old, Old Story.*"

There was something strangely compelling in Miss Wotherspoon's personality. In a trice she had each one supplied with a hymnbook and sitting demurely on chairs round the fire. A little later, when Kirsty softly opened the kitchen door, she found a devout little gathering. Miss Wotherspoon was singing loud and clear, her eyes shut, her head wagging in time with the tune. The light from the fire lay rosy on Bill's gilt head and serious face as he sang with unction:

> "Tell me the same old story
> If you have cause to fear
> That this world's empty glory.
> Is costing me too dear . . ."

As Kirsty slipped away unnoticed she remembered with a smile the bad little king who had "done evil" in Jerusalem. Had there been no Eastern equivalent to Miss Wotherspoon for Jehoiachin?

CHAPTER 18

> "Whaur sall I enter the Promised Land,
> Ower the Sutra or doun the Lyne,
>
> . . . . . .
>
> Or staucherin' on by Crawfordjohn
> Yont to the glens whaur Tweed rins wee?
> It's maitter sma' whaur your road may fa'
> Gin it land ye safe in the South Countrie."
>
> J. B.

IT WAS with very distinct annoyance that Kirsty found, in the middle of September, that she must go to London to see her lawyer.

"It means almost a whole week away from Little Phantasy," she complained. "Mr. Haynes says five days, but you know what the law's delays are."

Miss Carter sought to console her with talk of the plays she would see, the shops, the people, but Kirsty would have none of such consolation.

"It's no fun going to plays alone," she said, "and I don't believe any one I know is in London just now. There are the shops, of course, but one day will finish my shopping—I do need some new clothes badly, though. All my white woollen skirts have washed in, and my white silk jumpers have washed out, so they'll all have to go to a Jumble Sale. There will be Wednesday, Thursday, Friday to get through, for I don't suppose Mr. Haynes will want me for more than an hour at a time. It is horribly tiresome of him to want me at all. Tell me, Carty, would you like to leave

Little Phantasy just now, in this glorious weather, and go to town? I thought not. Well, anyway, I'll be back on Saturday at the latest. I leave everything in your charge. Be good to Aunt Fanny and keep Bill away from her, and don't grudge the children an extra sweetie at a time: you are just a little inclined to be parsimonious with the sweets. And soothe Miss Wotherspoon if she is fractious, and if you can find time, go up to the Castle and see Nannie Tait. I shall write to her from London, and send her something . . . That's all, I think . . . Oh, and don't let them set the house on fire."

When in London Kirsty and her stepmother had always stayed in a private hotel in Albemarle Street, and Kirsty went there now. The first night she found herself woefully homesick. Her bedroom was as fresh and comfortable as it is possible for a town bedroom to be, but the smuts fell thickly through the open window, the air felt thrice breathed, the constant passing and repassing of traffic made her head ache, the houses on the opposite side of the street seemed to be trying to crush her. She tossed about and thought of the blue and white room at home, with its wide windows letting in the hill air, the garden so gay with autumn flowers, the woods of Phantasy, still green but touched here and there with flame, the sound of running water which put her to sleep at night and welcomed her waking in the morning. At a distance she saw it all from a fresh angle, and realized as she had never done how much it meant to her.

One night she dined with some friends who happened to be in London, and they told her that they had never seen her look so well.

"Because," said Kirsty, "you never saw me perfectly contented before."

"Contented!" they cried. "Buried in the country, worried by children, plagued by an elderly aunt! What possible pleasure could any one find in such a life?"

Kirsty merely smiled and talked of something else. It was no good trying by word of mouth to convey the charm of Phantasy, of the Hope Water with its green pastures, or the great hills, or Aunt Fanny with her goodness and inconsequence, or the children.

Five nights and four whole days she spent in London.

The days were easy to get through, with visits to the lawyer and much shopping. She had presents to buy for every one, which was something new and delightful, and she expended much thought in getting suitable things. A new biography for Miss Fanny's more serious moments, and a pretty domestic tale for her lighter ones; also a wrap, decorative yet warm, for the fireside. Barbara and Bill were easy to choose for, Carty also. Easie Orphoot and Miss Wotherspoon were to have handbags, and Nellie a brooch. Specky must have something for his favourite sport, and a shop in Bond Street bristling with weapons for the chase lured her inside, where she bought some wonderful blue and silver minnows sticking full of hooks, on the advice of a bored young man.

"Of course, madam," he said, "it depends entirely where you are going to fish."

"I'm not going to fish at all, but is any self-respecting trout fool enough to eat that?" and Kirsty held up one of the minnows.

"Certainly, madam," said the young man coldly.

"But not trout in a burn?" Kirsty insisted.

The young man looked as if he were being asked to descend lower than he considered seemly. With supreme indifference he said, "As to that, madam, of course I cannot say."

"Well, I'll have six of the brightest and most terrible," she said, and thought to herself, "Specky will love them, though I fear they'll scare away every trout from the Hope Water. I wonder if he would appreciate a landing net? He might; it would look so very important, as Bill would say."

The evenings were rather difficult to get through.

Twice she dined with people and went to the play, but three evenings she sat in the drawing-room with a book, not reading much, but taking stock of the occupants of the other armchairs.

There were four women who did not seem to go out much in the evening. One had a girl in a nursing home, and was simply getting through the time until she could take her away. She wrote letters unceasingly.

Two were obviously sisters, and their flow of conversation never for one instant slackened. Kirsty thought that perhaps they had not seen each other for years, and were making up for lost time. When she sat trying to read, not wishing to listen, the talk flowed over her like a stream—a cook's enormities, the impertinence of a housemaid, the extravagance of someone called "Molly," who rushed everywhere and needed continual new frocks, yet would not settle down and marry a really excellent man with money; a husband's dyspepsia, his rage at the household books; a son who was heedless but such a good boy really; the whole interspersed with discussions as to whether Harvey Nichol's or Debenham's was the best place for certain garments, and why their fowls didn't lay when other people were getting dozens of eggs, and whether or not So-and-So was telling the truth when she said Alice's husband drank.

On the whole it was rather entertaining, and Kirsty took swift glances at the couple. One was stout and had a roving eye and a good-natured laugh, and seemed quite happy in spite of owning the extravagant daughter and the heedless son and the dyspeptic husband. The other was thin and yellowish, and was troubled by cooks who were wasteful and hens that wouldn't lay.

The last of the four women interested Kirsty greatly. She sat apart, rather withdrawn, as if sufficient to herself, a handsome woman in middle-age, with the wholesome look of one who spends much time in the open air. Her firm, pretty hands worked at a piece of embroidery, and she had an air of wellbeing and content that was most comfortable to behold.

Watching, Kirsty wove a story round her.

She lived in Devonshire, she decided, this woman with the rose-brown face and quiet eyes, in some old manor-house standing in gardens that glowed with colour, and lawns that went down in terraces to the sea. She had a son at Oxford and two boys at school, and a daughter almost grown up. Serena, the girl's name was, and her eyes were grey. There was a husband who adored her somewhere in the background, but Kirsty could not decide whether he was an ordinary country squire or something rather distinguished, like a retired ambassador. Anyway, she was sure it was a very happy household. There were long summer days when they picnicked together, drank tea in the sunshine, and bathed and climbed rocks; there were autumn days when they went blackberrying, there were winter days when great fires burned in the hall, and carols were sung and old tales told. She wondered if Serena and her brothers knew how lucky they were to have such a delightful sort of mother, who laughed and played with them, advised them, comforted and petted them.

On the last night of Kirsty's stay the woman who wrote letters and the two talkative sisters went early to bed, and she was left alone with the admired lady. She had never spoken to her except to pass the time of day, and she was surprised when the lady looked up from her work, and catching Kirsty's eye raised from her book, said, "Are we late? Or have the others gone early?"

"It isn't late," Kirsty assured her, "not ten o'clock yet."

The lady laid down her work. "I suppose I ought to go to bed too. I go home tomorrow, and start early."

"Why! So do I," said Kirsty. "How odd!"

The lady laughed. "Odd?" she said. "Wouldn't it be odder if we didn't go home, but sat about indefinitely in hotel drawing-rooms?"

"It would," Kirsty agreed, "and how infinitely horrible! I only meant it was odd that we should both be going home tomorrow. I hope you haven't noticed that I've been looking at you a great deal. You were so interested in your work that you hardly looked up, so I thought I might. These evenings have been rather wearisome, and watching you has been the only pleasant bit . . . Perhaps it was impertinent of me, but I've been picturing to myself the sort of home you have."

"But this is very interesting." The lady took up her embroidery and put in a few stitches. "Tell me, what kind of home did you give me?"

Kirsty sat forward with her hands clasped round her knees.

"In Devonshire. Was that by any chance right?"

"Quite right."

"No! How lovely. An old manor house *thick* with roses."

"Too imposing. Say, rather, like the house agents, a commodious cottage."

"Oh!" Kirsty's face fell a little, then brightened again. "I'm not sure about your husband. He isn't a Tory squire, is he? I rather want him to be a man of affairs."

The lady, dropped her work. "But *must* I have a husband?" she asked.

Kirsty stared. "What—do you mean?"

The lady held out her left hand, remarking, "I'm afraid you would make a poor living as a detective."

Kirsty began to laugh. "I was so sure that I never troubled to look for the wedding ring. Oh, but the cheery schoolboy sons and the boy at Oxford, and the girl called Serena, and the beautiful full life I gave you! And you *look* so married, somehow."

The lady laid aside her work, laughing at Kirsty's face.

"You are making me feel very remiss," she said. "But can't

I have a beautiful full life without a husband and family?"

Kirsty considered. "You can, of course, in a way, but I'm so old fashioned—I mean to say there is something more complete in the thought of a woman with a husband and children, don't you think?"

The lady surveyed her with an amused smile.

"I daresay," she said. Then, after a pause: "I'm forty-eight, and I can honestly say I've never envied any woman her husband. I may not realize what I'm missing—that I admit—but I could hardly be happier than I am."

"I know you're happy, that's what attracted me so much and made me like to watch you. You looked so contented, as if you didn't in the least mind a dull hotel drawing-room because you had heaps of nice things to think of. Most people have such a restless look—you looked, somehow, anchored."

"It sounds stolid," the lady laughed, "but I think I know what you mean, and I'm glad I struck you like that. The fact is, I'm contented because I'm always busy; work is easily the best fun in the world."

"What do you do? Is it rude of me to ask?"

"Do? So many things that I can't begin to tell you. Do you live in the country? Then you know how many things there are to occupy one's time. I run my own farm—that is quite a big job in itself—and I help all I can with things in the village. I have a friend who lives with me—Caroline Grenville, a man and a brother if ever there was one, and we work together. Our pet job is taking Anglo-Indian children for school holidays, children who have no relations in this country. That is the most repaying thing to do. It is so pleasant to write to faraway, anxious parents, and send them snapshots of their children, tell them of their pranks and their funny sayings, try to make pictures for them with words that they may ponder over until fresh news comes. Luckily I've got enough money to let me do it for love, though I do take a nominal sum so that there may be no feeling of obligation on the parents' part. We have had one family (one girl and two boys) for two years, and this summer we had in addition two little shy, frightened boys—like mice they were, so small and quiet—aged seven and nine. They almost broke our hearts at first with their goodness and their little white faces, but they brisked up wonderfully, and got really naughty under the able tuition of Betsy and her brothers—real *badmashes* they are! . . I've just been seeing them all back to school and settled down, and now I go home to Caroline, and we shall have a blissful time together until we welcome back (very gladly) our family for Christmas time."

"The two little boys too, I hope?"

"Oh, of course."

Kirsty gave a sigh of satisfaction.

"What fun you must have! Thank you for telling me. It's much better than the life I gave you after all."

"Oh, I shouldn't say that, but if women can live happily alone and make a success of their lives, so much the better, don't you think? And that leaves more men for the women who can't be happy without a husband of sorts."

Kirsty looked interested. "It's quite true. I hadn't thought of it like that, but now, if I don't marry, I shall pat myself approvingly and feel that I've helped someone else to a husband."

The lady laughed as she proceeded to put up her embroidery. Then she stood up, and she was very straight and tall, taller by half a head than Kirsty.

"You've heard about my life—what about yours? Won't you tell me?"

Kirsty shook her head. "There is nothing to tell—much. I've no relations to speak of, and I travelled about with my stepmother till a year ago, and then she died. Now I am at home, in Scotland, and very happy. I've got a home for the first time, and this summer I have three children staying with me. Their mother is dead . . . You can imagine how interested I was to hear of your Anglo-Indians . . ." and she launched into an account of Barbara, Specky, and Bill.

"And how long will you have them?" the lady asked, when a pause came.

"Ah, that's it. Their father will come home some day and want them. He's somewhere about the South Seas now. I try not to think of that day. They are mine for the present, and after all you never know what will happen, do you?"

The tall lady looked at the eager face raised to hers; then she bent and kissed it.

"I wonder if we'll ever meet again," she said. "I should like to hear what happens to you . . . Anyway, I hope life holds much happiness for you. Whatever you do, don't marry a man except for one reason. Remember, there are great points about being single. Goodnight, and bless you."

The next evening, when the London express stopped at the junction Kirsty sprang from it like a bird from a fowler's snare. The snell hill air was an elixir to her; she gazed with rapture at Tinto's purple slopes rising from the brown moorlands. The little train that ambled past Muirburn down to Priorsford was just coming in; a porter was chanting the names of stations: "Change for Lamington— Abington—Crawford and Elvanfo-oot;" Kirsty thought how well his voice went with the sough of the hill wind and the crying of the wild birds . . . Suddenly she became aware that a tall man in a light tweed suit was standing beside her, lifting his hat, and looking up she saw that it was Colonel Home.

"Oh," she said, holding out her hand, surprised at the pleasure the sight of the laird had given her, "are you travelling?"

"Going back to Muirburn. I've been to Edinburgh for the day." As he spoke he bent down and lifted her dressing-bag. "This is our train—you've been to London, haven't you?"

"Yes, seeing my lawyer on tiresome business. I *am* so glad to be back."

"You like Phantasy, then?"

"That," said Kirsty, "is a poor, mild way to put it. I adore it. I'm unhappy every minute I'm away from it. Oh! It has been so dull in London without the children." She leapt into a carriage.

"That's a smoker," Colonel Home pointed out.

"I don't mind. You'll want to smoke, won't you? It's empty. That's the main thing. I have so many packages . . . "

A porter began to stow them away; but Kirsty said, "I wouldn't trouble to put them on the rack. No one is likely to come in, so we can pile them on the seat." She turned to Archie Home. "I've got minnows for Specky, beautiful blue and silver things—and a landing net . . . They're all right, aren't they? The children, I mean. I had a card this morning written yesterday."

Archie Home settled himself in a corner opposite Kirsty.

"My information," he said, "dates from 6 P.M. yesterday. Specky took me fishing in the Hopecarton burn, and afterwards I had tea with Miss Fanny and saw them all. Bill Sykes was urbane to a degree, and there seems to have been no outstanding misdemeanour in your absence—at least I heard of none."

"Not of the glass panel in the passage door that Barbara knocked Bill's head through? The wonder is that he wasn't killed . . . Here is Skarlin. Two more stations and we'll be home."

"You must be tired," Archie Home said, and Kirsty looked up quickly, surprised at the tone in his voice.

"Not a bit," she said briskly, "only longing to see the children."

They were all waiting for her, Carty and the three children, and they put the luggage into the pony cart and walked home, every one talking, no one listening, until, in the dusk, they tumbled into Little Phantasy, to the gentle greetings of Miss Fanny and Percy the cat, and the more strident welcomes of Easie Orphoot and Nellie and Miss Wotherspoon.

Before Kirsty took off her things Bill seized her hand and whispered mysteriously, "Come out to the garden. I want you. I've something to show you. No, tomorrow won't do. It must be now."

He led her quickly across the lawn and through the flower garden to his own little patch.

"There," he said proudly. "It's all dug up for the winter . . . I did it. There were worms in it, long red wriggly ones: lots of them. Now I'm going to plant bulbs; Mr. Tod's getting them for me."

Kirsty admired somewhat extravagantly the plot of bare earth . . . Barbara and Specky had welcomed her with much warmth, Bill had said nothing, but now he thrust his still somewhat earthy little hand into hers, and gruffly said, with his head turned away, *"Good luck you're back!"*

As they returned across the lawn already some windows were lit in Little Phantasy. Through the wide window of the drawing-room they could see the light of the fire leaping up and illumining the long, low room. Miss Wotherspoon was lighting the lamps and exchanging remarks with Miss Fanny as she did so. The front door stood wide open, showing the dark oak-panelled hall bright with firelight, for a fire had been lit in the hall fireplace to welcome home the mistress of the house.

Kirsty gave a great sigh of content. It was home. And never had the children seemed so dear. To keep them she would consider any price small. The lady of the hotel drawing-room had given sound advice, doubtless, but then—she did not know Bill.

As she was falling asleep that night, thinking drowsily over her homecoming, she realized, with an odd little stab, that what had given her most the sense of coming home was not the vociferous welcome of Barbara and Specky, not Carty's smiles, or Miss Fanny's kisses, not even Bill's gruff little sentence, but the unexpected sight of her landlord in his light tweed suit standing beside her on the platform at the junction.

CHAPTER 19

"Whyles o'er the wee bit cup an' platie,
They sip the scandal potion pretty. . ."
ROBERT BURNS

AN event greatly enjoyed in kitchen circles at Little Phantasy was a visit from Mrs. Dickson of The Shop.

It could not happen very often, only when her niece, Jessie Sandilands, came down from the Moors to spend a few days in the riot of life which was Muirburn. Jessie enjoyed keeping shop and exchanging ideas with the customers, and her aunt snatched the opportunity to visit some of her friends.

Mrs. Dickson, strangely enough, was equally friendly with those two widely different characters, Easie Orphoot and Miss Wotherspoon. She was a woman of some imagination and much sympathy, and many-sided. To Easie she talked of cooking and cleaning, of husbands, and of the news of the countryside. She and Miss Wotherspoon met on ministers and kirks and bodily afflictions.

Nellie was out on the occasion of this visit. It was better so. As Easie said, "She's no bad lassie, Nellie, an' she's a fine worker turned, but ye canna rightly enjoy a crack wi' a lassie sittin' hearkenin' a' the time."

Tea was in the sitting-room, a really genteel tea, with a crochet-edged cloth, and a silver biscuit-box. Kirsty had sent in a rich cake as a contribution to the feast, and there was hot toast.

"My!" said Mrs. Dickson as, having removed her hat, she sat down to tea, "ye're comfortable here. A sittin'room to yerselves, an' a piany. I aye say that there's nothing like genteel service for real comfort. Guid wages, an' yer meat juist pit into yer mooths, like."

"Try a bit o' toast," Easie urged. "It's fine an' buttery. I dinna gie a docken for toast when the butter's juist scrapit on—"

"It's easy cuttin' whangs off other folk's leather," Miss Wotherspoon quoted, as she chose a particularly sappy piece.

"Hoots," said Easie. "Miss Gilmour's no' the kind to grudge us onything. An' mind, it is butter—nane o' yer margarine. Eh, I dinna like thon stuff. The knife gangs through it so creeshy-like, it fair maks me scunner."

"It's as weel," said Mrs. Dickson, "that a'body disna think like you . . . for mony a hame sees naething else, an' glad to get it . . . Ay, I'll try yer bramble jeely. I ken ye're a great hand at the jeely-makin', Mrs. Orphoot."

"I wud need to be, Mrs. Dickson. I believe I've made two hunner pounds this summer."

"I wud believe you," Mrs. Dickson nodded. "I've made a gey lot masel'. Dickson canna eat his tea wi'oot it, but it's a queer thing I hardly ever taste jeely except when I'm oot to ma tea."

"How's the indigestion?" Miss Wotherspoon asked.

"No' verra weel. I juist keep on wi' hot water and soda. But Dickson tells me in his cheery way that if it went something waur would come in its place, so I say as little as I can aboot it. How are ye keepin' yersel', Miss

Wotherspoon? I missed ye oot o' the kirk on Sabbath."

Miss Wotherspoon sighed and shook her head. "I could not come, Mrs. Dickson. I hope I'm as good an attender as most folk, and it's a great deprivation to me to miss a service; besides" (Miss Wotherspoon sighed again), "me being mistress of a Manse for five years, I can sympathize with the feelings of the Manse folk when people don't turn out regularly. But last Sabbath I was fair upset. I could not come. Sabbath as it was, that little Bill—I whiles think he's worst on the Sabbath—"

"Tut," said Easie, "he's but a bairn: he means no ill. An' you're that easy upset, it fair tempts a body to try."

Miss Wotherspoon looked sourly at the interrupter, and ignoring the interruption addressed Mrs. Dickson. "If he was ma bairn, Mrs. Dickson—"

Easie munching her toast broke in with a laugh, "Oh, we a' ken what auld maids' bairns are like! Ye've lived over quait a life, ma wumman. If ye had feucht awa' wi' three husbands like me—"

Miss Wotherspoon fixed her fellow servant with a cold eye.

"A lot of husbands is not a thing I would boast about, Easie Orphoot. Juist you mind that the woman of Samaria had seven—"

Mrs. Dickson, a peace-loving woman, gasped. Would Easie rise in her wrath and smite? But Easie either did not understand the allusion, or, understanding, refused to let it ruffle her.

"Oh ay," she said, "but folk were so queer in the Bible that ye canna gang by them. Mercy, look at Solomon!

Seven husbands was a fleabite to his wives. He couldna number them, I've heard tell, an' the Queen o' Sheba (mebbe kind o' jealous hersel') said the half hadna been tellt . . . But I dinna ken hoo we've gotten on to sic a daftlike subject. Pass yer cup, Mistress Dickson, and try a bit o' this London cake . . . What's the news in Muirburn? I hevna seen a soul since Sabbath. I micht hae been oot, for Miss Kirsty's been in London, so there's been nae visitors an' less cookin', but I've been makin' an efternoon dress to masel' for the winter, an' that's keepit me in."

"Ye'll hey to let me see it," Mrs. Dickson said, as she stirred the sugar in her second cup of tea. "Ay, I heard Miss Gilmour was in London. I suppose she'd be up gettin' new goons. It's fine to hae plenty siller. An' Muirburn is bound to be dull for her, used to a' kind o' gay places."

"I dinna think it," said Easie. "She was awfu' sweir to gang an' blythe to come back. She tellt me that hersel'. I must say she keeps hersel' rale happy and contented, an', ye ken, she's fair bigoted on thae bairns. If she was their mither she couldna be mair attentive to them, an' as for that little Bill, she canna see daylicht for him."

Miss Wotherspoon sniffed. "If she lickit him it would be better for him. She laughs at him, and encourages him in his evil ways. It's time his faither was here to take him in hand. He gets the better of women."

"Is there nae word o' his faither comin' back?" Mrs. Dickson asked. "Is he aye rangin' yet aboot foreign parts?"

Miss Wotherspoon shook her head gloomily. "I've heard no word of him coming, an' it's a pity. He came here, ye ken, afore he started on his travels (that would be in April), an' I thought a lot of him. A real personable gentleman."

"Ay," said Easie, "a braw fellay. I could hae taen a fancy to him masel'." (Here Miss Wotherspoon shivered ostentatiously to show her disapproval of Easie's regrettably free, almost rollicking style of speech.) "An' I'm thinkin'—of course this is juist between oorsel's—that Miss Kirsty hersel' hes a notion o' him." She nodded her head and smiled happily. "He'll be comin' hame one o' thae days, an' then Miss Kirsty'll get the bairns for keeps. An' a gude thing it'll be for them, puir lambs, an' for their faither too, for Miss Kirsty's a nice cratur, an' a real bonnie yin, an' rich forbye."

Mrs. Dickson nodded agreement. "Free wi' her money too, an' that canna be said of a'body roond here . . . I heard tell that she wanted to send puir Nannie Tait awa' a voyage to see if it would help her—an' her mither wi' her."

"A daft-like proposal," said Miss Wotherspoon. "Mrs. Tait kent fine, poor soul, that no voyage would help Nannie. And if there's one thing a body wants it's to be allowed to die at home. That's one thing poor folk need never envy rich folk—the money to drag about the world seeking health."

"Still," Mrs. Dickson said, "it was kind of Miss Gilmour to think o't. Mrs. Tait canna say enough aboot how kind she's been, carryin' books and pictures to Nannie to amuse her, and sendin' for everything she could think of to tempt her to eat."

"Ay, that's true," said Easie. "An' mony a fowl do I roast to send to Hawkshaw, an' light cakes an' jeelies an' things—but I doot they are nae guid."

Mrs. Dickson shook her head sadly. "I was up at Hawkshaw the ither nicht—just ran up efter I shut the shop—an' d'ye ken I was fair vexed. Mrs. Tait that cheery by way of tryin' to keep Nannie up, an' aye sayin', 'Oh, but she's better, Mrs. Dickson. She hardly coughed at a' last nicht, and see the fine colour she's got.' An' the lassie sittin' there wi' daith in her e'en—enough to break a body's hert. Me that has seen them a' go—Bella an' Aggie, an' noo Nannie. They were a' bonnie an' terr'ble fond o' pleasure, an' it vexes ye mair to see that kind gang. It seems unnaitural somehoo . . . I dinna ken."

Miss Wotherspoon primed her mouth. "I hope Nannie's prepared, Mrs. Dickson."

"Eh, I hope so, Miss Wotherspoon, but I did not feel it ma place to say a word. Puir Mrs. Tait's that anxious for ye to tell her that she's gettin' better."

"An' she's right," said Easie defiantly.

"A fool's paradise," Miss Wotherspoon said. "She would be better to prepare the girl's mind for what comes after death—the Judgment Seat."

Easie rose from the table, her rosy face clouded, her eyes fixed angrily on Miss Wotherspoon.

"You and yer Judgment Seats! It makes me grue to hear ye. I wonder what kinna shape ye'll mak at the Judgment Seat? Did ye ever let yersel' enjoy onything in this bonnie warld? D'ye think the Lord likes folk to gang roond wi' soor faces glumchin' at their fellow craturs? I warrant He's better pleased wi' puir Nannie than wi' you, for a' ye think ye're so perfect—"

Miss Wotherspoon sat dazed under this attack, and before

she could collect her wits and answer, Mrs. Dickson rushed into the breach.

"Ay," she said. "Dickson and me were havin' a crack the ither night, and he was sayin' that it's a solemnizing thing the thocht o' growin' old. He feels it himsel', for he's in his seventieth year, and efter seventy we're on borrowed time."

"Seventy, is he?" said Easie. Her short-lived anger was gone, her face serene. "Wha would think it? But thae wee skimpy men never look their age." Then, seeing Mrs. Dickson look slightly affronted at this description of her husband, she added hastily, "Not but what he's a wise-like man too."

"Oh, I'm not saying anything for Dickson's looks," his wife said, "but I wull say this, he's wonderfu' quick. Nothing passes him. I dinna see things unless they're under ma verra nose, but he's as gleg as a hawk."

"I'm no' verra sure," Easie said, looking doubtful, "that that's a verra guid thing in a man. I like a man to be kinna blind to things—it seems mair naitural like."

"He was tellin' me the ither nicht," Mrs. Dickson went on, absorbed in her husband's quickness, "that there's something atween Mr. Brand and your Miss Carter."

"Never!" ejaculated Miss Wotherspoon.

"He comes here a lot," Easie said musingly, "but I never thocht o' Miss Carter. It's aye Miss Kirsty I think aboot . . . Weel, he micht dae waur. She's a capable lass, and she'll mak a guid wife."

"Ay," Mrs. Dickson agreed, "an' she's rale pleasant. I thocht it wud hae been fine if oor minister had got the rich yin, but that would be ower much to hope. Dickson's got a notion in his head that the laird's fond o' Miss Gilmour, and, mind, Dickson's quick."

"It's not likely," said Miss Wotherspoon. "I've opportunities o' judging, an' when he comes here Miss Kirsty and him are aye quarrellin' more or less."

"Ay, but ye maun mind that bitin' an' scartin' is a Scots courtship," put in Mrs. Dickson. " I dinna think masel' that Dickson's right this time. The laird's cut oot for a bachelor: he wadna fash himsel' to get a wife. But I'm thinkin' Mr. Brand had something in his mind the ither Sabbath when he preached on Martha and Mary. I thocht he was rale kinna tender on Martha the guid housewife. An' ye tell me Miss Carter's that."

"But we have our Lord's word for it that Mary chose the better part," said Miss Wotherspoon.

"A' the same," Easie said, "I was aye vexed for Martha, the cratur. It was awfu' provokin' when she was burstin' gettin' the denner ready to see Mary sittin' there hand-idle."

"So it was," said Mrs. Dickson, "but I dinna think they mak denners in thae warm pairts. No broth and meat, I mean. Missionaries are aye crackin' aboot a pickle rice—but a' the same it was provokin'. I've kent weemen like Mary, useless in the hoose, but grand at crackin' wi' the minister. Dickson thinks a' the warld o' Martha. He canna bide to hear her misca'ed. A strange minister was preachin' ae day, and he was praisin' up Mary for a' that was guid, and then he says, 'There are many Marthas in Hell,' juist like that. Dickson fair jamp in his seat, an' I thocht he wad hae risen and gone oot. It was an awfu'-like thing to say, was't no'?"

"What did he ken aboot it onyway?" commented Easie.

"Ye may say it. But when Dickson thocht over it he said that likely the minister had a terrible managin' wife, yin o' the kind that cleans six days oot o' the seven and winna let a man hae ony comfort, so he excused him, puir soul! There's aye a reason for everything . . . Weel, I maun awa'. I've hed a rale nice crack."

CHAPTER 20

"... Methought they were the perfectest characters
of a contented marriage, where piety and love were
all their wealth."

Letters of Dorothy Osborne

SEPTEMBER over, October burnt itself out in blazing trees and golden bracken, misty mornings, and still, star-filled nights. It was a fit close to a perfect summer. Every day as Kirsty wandered by Tweed and saw the trees shadowed orange and red in the blue depths she thought, "This must be the last: tomorrow the winter storms will break;" but day followed day in beauty.

Again and again through those autumn days the thought came to her that never had she been so consciously happy, so aware of wellbeing. Every hour, from early morning when she wakened and watched the mist drift before the sun from the scarred face of Ratchell, to the drawing in of chairs in the lamplight and the scented blaze of the wood fire, seemed to bear something precious, precious and unforgettable.

She had ceased to look forward. Whatever the future held it must hold change: Alan Crawford was on his way home. A very slow progress, it certainly seemed, but his face was set to the West, and some day he must arrive. From that day she kept her head firmly turned away.

Kirsty was now perfectly at home with her neighbours. Merren Strang was her great friend—there was much coming and going between Hopewaterfoot and Little Phantasy. The kindly couple at Cherrytrees had given Kirsty and her family a standing invitation to any meal, and there was no place she liked better to spend an afternoon than the green and white drawing-room which smelt always of mignonette, being petted by Mr. and Mrs. Anthony Hay, eating an uncommonly good tea, and listening to the faded tinkle of the musical box.

Lady Carruthers descended on Little Phantasy at all sorts of odd hours, impatient to discuss some new and hare-brained scheme, or talk over the latest idea that had impressed her. Kirsty asked the McCandlishes to dinner, and they met frequently at different houses, but there was always a certain restraint between the minister's wife and Kirsty. To Kirsty there seemed a continual question in the eye of Mrs. McCandlish. The good lady could not understand, and it rankled with her, why the Little Phantasy people should have preferred Muirburn church to Netherton, and Robert Brand as a preacher to her own Norman. " It isn't," she said to herself, "as if there was any comparison."

The Elliots came over frequently from Laverlaw, and were very welcome guests, and Colonel Home limped in now and again, and played gravely with the children, who loved him much. "Just like a shy child," Kirsty told herself, "or a frightened dog. Leave him alone and look the other way and he'll make advances."

Colonel Home even went so far as to give a dinner party at Phantasy, to which Miss Fanny went, feeling vastly venturesome, and wearing diamonds with her velvet gown, and only one shawl, and that of lace.

Mrs. Duff-Whalley invited Kirsty once to dinner, twice to luncheon, three times to tennis to The Towers in the space of one fortnight. Kirsty went once to luncheon and found that her hostess, while meaning to be everything that was kind, had a wonderful way of mingling insults with her hospitality, so that her guests wore a cowed look. Feeling utterly unable to keep up with such a stream of invitations, Kirsty asked the lady and her daughter to a luncheon party to meet Sir Andrew and Lady Carruthers, the Elliots, the Anthony Hays, and Colonel Home, and ceased to make any further effort in the matter.

With November the first storms of winter descended on Phantasy, and after three days of violent wind and rain which whirled away the last reluctant leaves, they woke to find a white world.

Breakfast was a restless meal that morning, for the children rushed continually to the window to report as to how deep the snow was, and if there would be enough to make a really good snowman.

Crumbs had to be taken to the birds where a space had been cleared at the front door, and to Bill's delight a robin came and hopped round his feet.

"Look at the darling," he whispered, standing very still so as not to frighten the bird. "He's not afraid of me: he's pecking."

" 'Little hunchback of the snow'," Kirsty quoted, as she watched the valiant bunch of feathers. "We must get a coconut, Bill, and hang it out for them. And at Christmas we'll have a bird's Christmas tree."

"Yes," said Bill, "and I'll tie Percy in the stable."

"Oh, poor Percy," Barbara protested, "then he'll have no Christmas tree."

"You can give him a tree in the stable," Bill said carelessly.

"Shan't, then," said Barbara, and was going on to give her opinion of Bill, when Kirsty broke in, "Who's going with me to Priorsford today?"

"Oh, Pie dear, I should love to," Barbara cried, "but I'm going with Nellie to tea at her mother's. It's such a nice place. They have a cat with two kittens, and a stuffed fox, and potato scones for tea."

"You must certainly not miss those raptures. It is very kind of Nellie's mother to invite you. Well, the boys must go with me, for they both need their hair cut. I wonder if Aunt Fanny would care to go? Or Carty?"

Miss Fanny, when asked, looked shudderingly out at the white world, drew her shawls round her, and edged her chair nearer the fire.

"Not today, thank you, dear. But if you would be so kind as to match this wool I should be so grateful; and ask the bookseller if my *Life of Faith* didn't come last week, and get me a few more of those lozenges at the chemist's—perhaps you had better take the bottle to be sure of getting the right kind. You won't be long in being back, will you?"

"Oh dear no! We'll leave just after luncheon, and be back by four o'clock. Carty, would you care to come? Have you anything that wants doing in Priorsford?"

"Oh, thank you." Miss Carter hesitated. "As a matter of fact, I thought of going to Hawkshaw with those papers and things you laid out for Nannie Tait, but . . ."

"No, no. Don't change your plans. I shall be so glad if you will go to Hawkshaw. I like Nannie to have something every day. Her mother says it helps her through wonderfully to have something to expect. You don't think it will be too difficult getting up the hill in the snow? Well, our capacious hired car will only have to carry the boys and myself. I wonder if Rebecca Brand would like to come. No, I believe this is the afternoon of her Mothers' Meeting. Somehow I can't imagine Rebecca at a Mothers' Meeting, but still . . ."

Specky's eyes were glued on Tweed all the way to Priorsford, and he was rewarded by the sight of a heron. Bill sat cocked on a little seat—he had asked as a special favour to be allowed to sit there—wearing his new winter things, a powder-blue overcoat with a velvet collar, and a black velour hat that gave him an oddly ecclesiastical look. Buttoned under his overcoat, with the head sticking out, was an old crimson Teddy bear which he had feared might be lonely if left at home. Bill was on his best behaviour, pleased with the outing, and proud to have his hair cut along with Specky.

"We'll go first to the hairdresser," Kirsty decreed, "and I'll leave you there and do my shopping. Have you anything you want to do?"

"Yes," said Specky, "I want to go and look in at the window where all the fishing things are."

"But you won't be fishing in winter," Kirsty reminded him.

"Oh, I know, I only want to look at all the rods and

minnows, and flies and things, and Barbara gave me sixpence to buy her something."

"I see. And Bill?"

Bill's face was eager. "Could I see the Muirburn engine turn round at the station?"

"Yes, that is to say if there is a train in at the time." It was an agreeable surprise to find that the Priorsford pavements were dry.

"Miss Wotherspoon is right," thought Kirsty, remembering how that lady had remarked, after ploughing through the muddy roads round Phantasy: "There's a lot to be said for plain stanes."

She took the boys to the hairdresser, and did the list of errands given her by Easie. She procured from the chemist the right kind of lozenge for Miss Fanny, and visited the bookseller to retrieve the *Life of Faith* and get some new books and magazines.

When she went back to the hairdresser's she found both boys ready and waiting for her, their hats looking uncomfortably large for their shorn heads. They were sitting solemnly on high chairs in a glass-enclosed compartment, never exchanging a remark, companioned by a stout man who breathed heavily.

Out on the street Bill marched a little in front (like the cat he preferred to walk by his wild lone), but Specky, put his hand in Kirsty's.

"I don't much like having my hair cut," he told her. "It was a boy who did me, and he asked if I wanted it short. I said I didn't know, and he said, 'What did your Maw say?' He meant you. He thought you were our mother."

"Did he?" said Kirsty. "I'm afraid he has made it too short. It was stupid of me not to tell him, but, you see, I never took boys to have their hair cut before."

"Oh," said Specky, "it'll last the longer. There was a card hanging in the place telling all the prices—8d. for a haircut, 4d. for a shave. The dearest thing I could have done was to have a shampoo and my beard trimmed. If I had had everything it would have cost 4s. 9d., and if I had had everything twice it would have cost—" Specky made a laborious calculation—"it would have cost 9s. 6d. And if I had had everything done three times it would have cost—" but this was too difficult, and his voice trailed away.

Kirsty's hand tightened on the small hand in hers. The boy in the shop had thought she was their "Maw." If only that were true, if only she might keep them forever—Specky with his gentle ways, Bill so bad, and Barbara such an affectionate destroying angel . . .

It was almost dark when the car bore them back to Phantasy. As they passed the drawing-room window Miss Wotherspoon was in the act of drawing the curtains, and the light streamed out on the snowy garden.

Miss Fanny was feeling a little aggrieved. When a meal was at a fixed time she liked to have it then. Tea was at four, and it was now half-past.

"No one has come in," she told Kirsty. "I can't think where Miss Carter is. She went out just after you did, and it isn't a long walk to Hawkshaw. She may be lying with a broken leg, who knows? And when you didn't come I was sure there had been an accident; it is so dangerous motoring in snow. I was just wondering what steps we could take—women alone are so helpless—when I heard the car coming . . . Are you going to have tea as you are, dear?"

"If you'll let me, Aunt Fanny. I know you don't like people to sit in the house in outdoor things, but it was really rather cold driving, and I would like to get thawed. Carty perhaps has met someone—Merren Strang, maybe, and gone home to tea with her."

"And had you a pleasant afternoon?" Miss Fanny asked presently, soothed by the hot tea and a particularly good toasted muffin

"Very," said Kirsty, her feet on the high brass fender, her cup on the table beside her, a muffin in her hand. "The boys were angelic, almost frighteningly good. Specky studied all the fishing things in Watson's, and Bill (that's what kept us) met the three-thirty train from Muirburn and watched it turn—I'm not quite sure that that black hat is a success. He looked like a small dissenting parson, I thought. I'd better get him a blue one to match his coat—oh yes, we enjoyed ourselves greatly. I think if I didn't live at Phantasy I would choose to live in Priorsford. Today as we came round the corner of the Old Town, and saw the white shoulders of the hills humped above the grey houses, and Tweed running dark and *drumly* under the wide bridge, and when we walked in the clean little town with its bright shops (I love to shop in Priorsford, they serve you with such interest) and watched the people greet each other all like members of one big family, I felt the charm of it as I never did before. There is something about a summer place in winter—the drawing together of the real inhabitants after the migration of the mere visitors (like the robins and the others when the swallows go), the settling down to the short days and the long nights, the thought of all the little festivities, the cosy talkative tea-parties, the informal dinners, the dances, the preparing for and rehearsing theatricals, all the hundred pleasant things that people amuse themselves with through the dark days—Doesn't it seem to you all very attractive?"

"Oh yes, dear, quite. At Harelaw we had very happy winters, though, of course, it was only a small village."

"And I expect Muirburn has its own social life—why, Aunt Fanny, it must be quite dark outside. Where can Carty be?"

Miss Fanny looked troubled. "The newspapers are so terrible now, it hardly seems safe to walk about. And if anything did happen it would be so upsetting for us all—one would never feel really comfortable again."

Kirsty laughed. "Then I hope for all our sakes that all is well. Happily, an athletic young woman isn't likely to come to grief. I don't know why one's mind should always rush to an accident when any one is late, there are so many perfectly simple things that may have happened. She may have stayed at Hawkshaw, and let Mrs. Tait go out. She may have gone home to tea with someone. She may—oh, anything. But if she isn't in soon Nellie and I will take lanterns and go out and meet her . . . Hullo! Here she is. Why, Carty, we pictured ourselves going out with lanterns, tracking your footsteps in the snow like Lucy Grey . . . Were you kept at Hawkshaw? How is Nannie?"

Miss Fanny looked at Miss Carter, and it struck her that

the girl was looking rather odd. Her face was brilliant with colour (that, she admitted to herself, might be the effect of the frosty air), and her eyes were shining with a light that surely a visit to a sick girl could not have put there. Her manner, too, was odd. She stood back as if unwilling to come into the bright light round the fire.

"Nannie is much the same," she said rather hurriedly. "I sat with her while her mother ran down to the shop for some things. We looked at the pictures in the magazines you sent, and she was quite looking forward to her tea; the cake with the icing and the violets gave her an appetite."

"By the way, have you had tea, my dear?"

"Well—I haven't, as a matter of fact, but please don't trouble about getting any; it doesn't matter."

In Miss Fanny's eyes DEAR ME was writ large. Out till nearly six o'clock and no tea. Where in the world . . ?

"Of course it matters," Kirsty said, ringing the bell. Miss Wotherspoon after an interval answered it with her usual aggrieved air, but Kirsty was bold now.

"Fresh tea, please, Miss Wotherspoon. Miss Carter has been detained."

Stella Carter came forward, pulling off her thick gloves. "I'm ashamed to give you all this trouble . . ." She sat down near Kirsty and held out her hands to the blaze. "Had you a nice drive?"

"Very. The boys were models, and are now shaven and shorn in a most priestly way . . . I caught a glimpse of Mrs. Duff-Whalley's opulent car rolling along the High Street. Otherwise the afternoon was uneventful."

Miss Carter said nothing more, and an odd restraint fell

on the, three women.

Miss Wotherspoon brought in fresh tea. Kirsty poured out a cup, and Miss Carter drank it thoughtfully.

"You're not eating anything," Miss Fanny said.

"I only want the tea, thank you."

"Carty," said Kirsty, "I hope you haven't got a chill. It was bitterly cold out today."

Stella Carter put down her cup and said, rather shakily, as she rose to her feet, clutching her fur gloves as if for support, "Oh no. I haven't got a chill or anything, but I don't know how to tell you. You have been so kind, both of you, and—I don't know what you'll think of me—but I met Mr. Brand coming from Hawkshaw, and he asked me to go for a walk, and he—and he—Well, I've promised to marry him some time."

She stood looking at once so proud and defiant and beseeching that Kirsty rose and flung her arms round her neck and hugged her. Then, half laughing and half crying, they subsided together on to the sofa.

"Well, of all the nice things," Kirsty said, turning to Miss Fanny. "I confess such a thing did enter my mind, but it seemed too good to come true. I like Mr. Brand so much, and you will be such a nice couple in the Manse. Oh, Carty, won't it be fun doing the house up?"

"Oh, but nothing is settled like that. We can't be married for ages. Perhaps I shouldn't have said anything, but I couldn't keep you in the dark even for an hour—but no one else is to know for ages. We are both so poor, and there are so many things to think of, we can't call ourselves engaged even—but I wanted you and Miss Fanny to know at once."

"I should think so. We would never have forgiven you if you hadn't told us, would we, Aunt Fanny?"

Miss Fanny smiled acquiescently, and Miss Carter, gathering her belongings, murmured that she must go and change, and fled from the room.

"Aren't you pleased?" Kirsty asked her aunt. "Don't you think it's a good thing for them both?"

Miss Fanny looked into the fire. "It's a good thing for Miss Carter. She's a nice girl, of course, and will do her best, but she is English, and how can a girl brought up in the English Church understand a congregation like Muirburn? Of course, she could play the harmonium and save a salary . . . I don't suppose she has a penny. It is so like a minister to marry someone with no money."

Kirsty was amazed at the bitterness in her aunt's tone.

"I think it is very nice of him," she said. "I wouldn't have much respect for a minister who married for money. What's money after all?"

"A great deal. You have never known what it is to be scrimped for money, so you don't realize its value. I don't say that it is necessary to happiness, but it certainly helps enormously—especially in a minister's house. A minister is always seeing cases where a little money would make all the difference, he can make such a good use of it, smooth so many rough bits for people—it is a great blessing when he or his wife have more than they need."

Kirsty nodded. "I suppose so, but it isn't essential . . . Just think, Aunt Fanny, if we had never come here this would never have happened. It's a great responsibility in a way, but it's splendid to have been the means of making two people happy."

"Yes," said Aunt Fanny. "Yes. But what about Miss Brand? Will she be pleased?"

Kirsty stared at her aunt for a moment.

"Rebecca " she said. "Rebecca! I'd forgotten about her."

"She will lose her home."

"I hadn't thought of that. I suppose she couldn't go on living at the Manse. We must think of something . . . and make it up to Rebecca somehow . . . Oh, but, Aunt, just think of these two creatures wandering about in the dark, in the snow ('We went for a walk,' said Carty), utterly unaware that they were tea-less and cold and wet, lost to everything but the fact that they were together, these two out of all the world." She leaned forward pleadingly. "Don't damp me, Aunt Fanny. I am so happy . . . I must be very feminine, for I absolutely glow with interest over the first love affair that has ever come close to me. When you see people lost in happiness like that, do you never regret that you didn't marry?"

Miss Fanny neatly folded aside her knitting, and prepared to go upstairs to her warm bedroom, to change her daytime costume for the striped grey silk with the old lace, which was her usual dinner dress.

"*Never*," she said, with quite unusual firmness. It was obvious that Miss Fanny did not glow.

CHAPTER 21

> "Brightness falls from the air;
> Queens have died young and fair;
> Dust hath closed Helen's eyes."
> THOMAS NASHE

IT looked as if the hard weather had come to stay. For three days it was bright keen frost, then the sky was overcast, a wind came strongly from the north, and snowflakes fell falteringly at intervals.

"It's going to be more snow," Kirsty said, as they stood giving the birds their breakfast. "Easie calls it 'a feeding storm,' whatever that may mean."

"Oh, good," said Specky, "I hope it will snow and snow until the glen is filled up level."

"And how would we get food?" Miss Carter asked. "The vans wouldn't be able to get up from Priorsford, and we would get no meat or bread."

"Easie would bake scones and cakes," Specky said comfortably.

Bill was shunting up and down in his Wellington boots, making the snow fly round him like spray.

"I'm taking the golden journey to Aberdeen," he announced.

Kirsty laughed. "Surely they are brave," she quoted, "who take the golden journey to—Aberdeen. Carty, you hear? Bill listens to the reading after all . . . Oh, my dear, aren't the white hills strange and lovely against that sullen sky?

I'm not at all sure that winter isn't even more beautiful than summer."

She turned to go into the house, and found Easie in the hall. Her smooth round face was distressed, and she twisted her clean apron in her fingers.

"Miss Kirsty, mem, we've juist been hearin' that Nannie Tait slippit awa' early this mornin'. The cauld spell hed juist nippit her aff, puir lass!"

"Oh, Easie," Kirsty cried, and fell silent, amazed almost at her own feeling of sorrow. Nannie, so pretty in the shadows of the old Castle, gentle, eager, pleased with everything that was brought to her. To have her no longer to think of, to carry little presents to—it would be strange; she would miss her.

And what of the mother who had watched her last child die?

Easie was wiping her eyes with her apron.

"Weel, she's won awa'. An' if there was nae betterness for her here it's mebbe juist as well. It's the road we maun a' gang, but to gang at twenty is sad and sad."

Kirsty nodded, not trusting herself to speak, and followed by Miss Carter went into the drawing-room, where Miss Fanny was already ensconced beside the fire. She was knitting—she never allowed herself to read before luncheon—and presently she meant to write a few letters. She looked up as the two girls came in, and said chidingly, "Did I see you out in the snow, Kirsty, with nothing on your head? And Miss Carter, too. It's extraordinary how reckless young people are. You won't value your health till you lose it."

"It is cold," Kirsty said, going over and standing by the fire. "There's a wind like a knife; but out there where we feed the birds it's quite sheltered . . . Aunt Fanny, Nannie Tait is dead."

Miss Fanny at once assumed the expression she kept for news of death and disasters; it made her face seem unnaturally long.

"So she has got away," she said solemnly. "And I was just hurrying to finish this shawl for her as the weather had got so cold . . . But in such an hour as we think not . . ." She sighed deeply. "She won't need shawls or anything we can do for her now. *Poor* Nannie!"

"Why 'poor'?" Kirsty asked.

Miss Fanny looked up, startled at her tone, and Kirsty went on: "It's a very stumbling thing to me in my path through life to find that the best people—I mean the goodest people, who believe most firmly in the next world and the joys that there await the blest, have so small a desire to arise and go to them. They call the blessed dead 'poor.' Another funny thing they do is to send flowers with deepest sympathy. Who are they sympathizing with? The flowers are, I suppose, a last gift to the one who has gone, a last token of affection, and sympathy seems sadly out of place. Last night, Aunt Fanny, at prayers you thanked God that we had been spared while so many had been called into His presence . . . I wish people weren't so . . . so illogical."

Miss Fanny knitted rapidly for a minute, and then said in a hurt but dignified tone, "I did not mean to irritate you, Kirsty, with my remark. I meant nothing when I used the word 'poor': it was simply a word, an adjective, perhaps, as you say, inappropriate. If Nannie Tait had been in our own class—I mean a friend—I should have said 'dear' instead of 'poor'—would that have pleased you better?"

Kirsty, already ashamed of her impatience, dropped on her knees beside her aunt and cried in her impulsive way, "I'm the rudest of wretches, and you, my dear, are the funniest of aunts. Forgive me, please."

But Miss Fanny drew away, affronted.

"I don't see why you should say I am funny. I have no intention of being so, I assure you, and as for what you say about good people not wanting to go to Heaven, I'm sure it isn't true." Her voice quivered with self-pity. "No normal person wants to die; even St. Paul said, 'Not that I would be unclothed, but clothed upon,' and it is a step in the dark no matter how you look at it . . . But I always remember what my dear friend Christian Johnstone said—you've heard me speak of her?—Mrs. Arnold Johnstone: we were at school together. It was such a lovely place, Darnshiels, and she had everything to make life pleasant: an enviable social position, a family that adored her, most successful grandchildren, perfect health—her teeth were like a girl's. And when I was staying there two summers ago, we were having tea in the rose-garden, and the children were round her treating her as if she had been a queen, and the sun shining, and I said to her, 'Oh, Christian, you are a fortunate woman, you've everything in the world your heart can desire.' And she smiled at me, and looked at all the beauty round us, and said, 'Yes, but I am so looking forward to the next world.' Of course, she may have meant her husband—she adored his memory. Anyway, she died of influenza the following winter. She was the best woman I ever knew." Miss Fanny knitted silently for a minute, and then said somewhat irrelevantly, "I can't see why anyone would want to be cremated. I do so dislike cremation and divorce."

"But surely," Kirsty said, "there isn't much connection between them?"

Miss Fanny laid down her knitting. "Perhaps not, but they give me the same jarred feeling—both so unnatural . . . My dear, I quite forgot I meant to ask Miss Wotherspoon to put an extra cover on my bed. She will be in my room now."

"But let me," Kirsty cried, but Miss Fanny had pulled her shawls round her and fluttered from the room.

Kirsty went over to the window to where Stella Carter stood looking out. She turned as Kirsty approached. "I can't get it out of my head," she said, "the thought of that poor mother in that grim old place, sitting beside her dead child . . . Oh, why is Nannie finished with everything so soon?"

Kirsty shook her head, smiling sadly. " We ask and ask . . . D'you remember Bill when the beloved puppy died? 'Oh, Pie, why did it wear out so soon?' . . . To have finished joy and moan at twenty!"

Miss Carter wiped her eyes. "I feel mean to be so happy," she said.

"Don't feel mean. It's life—some weep and some dance. It's your turn today to be happy . . . You've worked a miracle in Rob Brand. He looked a different man when I saw him yesterday."

"I'm not half good enough for him, Kirsty. It isn't that he talks religion, for he doesn't, but you can't know him without realizing what his religion means to him. I should so hate to feel that my companionship should even the least little bit in the world make him less keen. I mean to say, I'm afraid marrying me might somehow lower his ideals—you see, I wasn't brought up in that atmosphere, and it must make a difference, don't you think?"

"No, I don't," said Kirsty stoutly. "You are bar gold yourself, my dear, and the two of you will make a splendid combination. You are so practical that you will keep his feet straight on earth when his head is in the clouds; and he is so full of his visions that he will be able to carry you with him on his flights—has Rebecca written to you or sent any message."

"Not yet. You see, I expect it was a surprise to her, and not a pleasant one, and she will want time to get used to the idea. I know if Rob were my brother I should detest any girl he cared for. I'm just hoping that when she sees how happy we are she won't mind so much."

That Stella was happy there was little doubt. There was a shining look in her eyes and a spring in her step, and always about her mouth a little secret smile.

Kirsty looked very kindly at her as she said, "I'm sure Rebecca is too good a woman to grudge her brother happiness. When one person is happy he or she helps all the people round. It's like a fire lighted . . . Do you think I might go to Hawkshaw this afternoon? Would it seem an intrusion? I want to take some flowers—I was very fond of Nannie."

Miss Carter nodded. "I think Mrs. Tait would like you to go. She told me the other day that Nannie 'wearied on your visits.' Well, I must be off. By the way, Barbara said I was to remind you that they are going out to tea today, and she wants to know if they might have their reading after luncheon instead of after tea; they don't want to miss it."

Since the days had shortened Kirsty had begun to read aloud to the children every evening for an hour after tea. Their mother, it seemed, had always read to them.

"Yes, of course, but what shall I read today? Can you suggest something with lovely words? That's what Barbara likes. We've had the *Morte d'Arthur*, and *The Golden Journey to Samarkand*, and some of Kipling and Newbolt, also some of *Puck of Pook's Hill*, and various fairy books. Yesterday I read them about Flodden from Jean Lang's *Land of Romance*. They loved that, but were terribly inflamed against the English. Jean Lang makes such pictures with words. Do they know about Mary Queen of Scots?"

"A little, not very much. You see"—Miss Carter gave a small deprecating smile—"it's rather delicate work for me, a mere Englishwoman, to attempt to teach Scots history to such perfervid patriots."

Kirsty laughed. "Well, admit you English didn't come well out of that chapter of history, but I'll soften it down for Barbara."

Kirsty gathered all she could find of beauty in the greenhouse and devoted the rest of her morning to making peace with Miss Fanny, who was inclined to be pensive and quiet, obviously brooding over Kirsty's unfortunate remarks.

After luncheon she retired with the children to the schoolroom. "What shall I read?" she asked.

"Poetry," cried Barbara, thrusting a book into her hands.

"No," protested Specky, who was lying on the floor tidying his fly-book, "it's that beastly Queen of the May thing, and she only wants to cry. Read *Huck Finn*."

Bill, who was as usual walking by his "wild lone" at the other end of the room, said, "No, I want *Toad he went a-pleasuring—*"

If you can't agree," said Kirsty, "I'd better decide. I'll read to you about poor Queen Mary."

"I've seen her," said Bill airily.

Barbara giggled. "He means our Queen Mary. He saw her once driving in the Park and he wouldn't lift his hat, not all we could do. Go on, Pie, read about Queen Mary of Scotland. Here's the Romance book."

Kirsty turned over the pages. "I don't know how much of this you would understand," she said, but impatient Barbara assured her that, for herself, she preferred things she didn't quite understand.

"Well—here is the sort of spelling that will appeal to Specky. Whistle—*quhissel*. That is almost as good as *yph* for wife. And listen, Barbara, when Queen Mary was at Jedburgh getting better of an illness, she whiled away the time, she and her four Maries, doing beautiful needlework. This is what she ordered 'in all possible haste' from Edinburgh, 'twenty ells of red champit chamlet of silk, with twenty ells white plaiding, four ells white taffety, three ells fine black velvet . . . six ounces black stitching silk, with a pound of black thread'—"

Barbara gasped. "Had she to sew up a pound of black thread? How awful! Go on, Pie. Read about Rizzio being murdered and about her being locked up in Loch Leven."

"I wouldn't mind being locked up in Loch Leven," Specky said thoughtfully, as he sorted out tangled casts. "That's where the Loch Leven trout come from. Did she ever get out?"

So Kirsty read to them the tragic story: plot following plot, prison following prison, hopes budding only to be blasted, but always the unhappy Queen carrying wherever she went that golden key that unlocks hearts. *Would that I had died at Jedworth* was her bitter cry, and well for her if she had. But at last it was over, the lonely hours, the insults, the misery of mind and body were finished; the tragedy of Mary Stuart was ended.

"Surely that night," read Kirsty, "sighing spirits must have held court at Holyrood. The winds sobbed and wailed through the glens and cleughs of snowclad Teviotdale, the flooded rivers moaned. Did there, perchance, ride out from the grey house in the Backgate of Jedburgh a slim girlish figure on a white palfrey—Death's pale horse—making the wild things on the Liddesdale hills fly in fear as horse and rider galloped past across the dark moors, down the valley to Hermitage?"

Barbara gave a sigh of impotent fury as Kirsty finished.

"Pie," she said solemnly, "I shall never forgive the English, never. Miss Strong, at Clapham, taught me a song about, 'England, homeland,' but I just shut my mouth tight. I didn't sing, for it's no home of mine."

Kirsty put her arm round the child.

"But, Barbara dear, these are old unhappy far-off things. You are as bad as Pet Marjorie, who consigned Queen Elizabeth straight to 'her very great friend the divil'! You don't know 'Pet Marjorie'? Tut-tut, this'll never do. I've a spare copy you shall have . . . Now isn't it about time you were getting ready for Cherrytrees?"

"It's a party," said Barbara, her tears for Queen Mary already dried. "Won't it be fun?"

"No, it won't," Specky said. "Not if there are girls. I do hate girls."

"Oh, Specky, think of Barbara," Kirsty protested.

"Well, she can't help it, but she doesn't like being a girl. If they dance I'll look at the stuffed seal and the big trout in the case . . . Aren't you coming, Pie?"

"I'm not invited. I'm going to Hawkshaw now. You know," she looked round at the three faces turned to her, "you know that Nannie Tait died this morning?"

Instantly it was as if a shutter had been let down in the eyes of each child, and they looked uneasily away. This was something they did not understand, and did not wish to discuss.

"Run, my darlings. Mr. Dickson is coming for you at half-past three. You'll be very good and reflect credit on Little Phantasy, I know. You will be good, won't you, Bill?"

"I'll play with the musical box," was Bill's non committal reply.

When Kirsty reached the old courtyard at Hawkshaw, the door of Mrs. Stark's cottage opened, and Agnes came out to shake the crumbs out of the teacloth.

"Miss Gilmour," she said, then as her glance fell on the flowers, "You'll be for Mrs. Tait's. Eh, puir body, puir body."

"Bring Miss Gilmour in, Agnes," came a voice from the kitchen, "an' dinna stand hingin' there lettin' in the cauld."

"I really can't stay, Mrs. Stark," Kirsty said, stepping into the kitchen that Agnes might shut the door. "I must get back before the darkening."

"Tuts, sit doon for a meenit. What's a' yer hurry? Agnes'll mak ye a cup o' tea. We've juist feenished. I like ma denner aboot eleeven an' ma tea afore three o'clock."

"Whiles it's no much after two when ye have it, Mother," Agnes said.

"Why, Mrs. Stark," Kirsty exclaimed, "at that rate you'll soon have all your meals over in the forenoon. When do you have supper?"

"We get our parritch aboot five when Wullie and his faither come in, and then they get their tea, an' we're a' beddit on the back o' eight o'clock. It saves fire and licht, and what is there to sit up for?"

Kirsty agreed that it was a good plan, and rose to go.

"I'm taking these flowers to Nannie. Do you think Mrs. Tait will mind me calling? I only want to tell her how sorry we all are."

Mrs. Stark drew her hand over her mouth as if trying to smooth away the lines.

"Gang if ye like and tell her ye're vexed. It'll dae her nae harm, but it's juist poorin' water on a drooned moose . . . They cam for me this mornin' afore it was licht. I kent a' the lassies, but Nannie was the bonniest o' them a' . . . Ye'll find Mrs. Tait verra colleckit. She's the sense to say naething when there's naething to be said."

The snow was beginning to fall as Kirsty went up the flight of worn steps to the doorway of the Castle, tiny hard particles that blew off the hard surface of the trodden snow, and lay in little heaps in sheltered nooks. A hareskin hung on a nail by the door, the wind blowing the fur apart . . . Where had she read of a hare hanging in a bitter wind with its fur blown? . . . The tall trees that sheltered one side of the Castle bent in the wind, soughing eerily, and far down below Tweed ran in spate between its white banks.

She shivered partly with cold, and partly with the feeling of gloom that seemed to encircle her. The words of the unhappy Queen that she had been reading to the children still rang in her ears: *Would that I had died at Jedworth*.

Mary the Queen had known the Borders and loved the silver voice of Tweed. Her slim feet had mounted those same worn steps that Nannie had run up and down so lightly—what was it that she had overheard Easie say of Nannie in her days of health and lightness, "She wasna ower guid a yin." And Mary? Frail and lovely, frail and lovely . . .

Up the steps she went into the brooding quiet of the old keep. The white-panelled room seemed more uncanny than ever in the half light as she stepped through it carrying her burden of flowers. Almost it seemed to her that she heard the whisper of a silk dress, the ghostly tap of high-heeled shoes, the sigh of a fan . . . If she stayed and peered into the shadows would she see the Queen and her four Manes sitting at their tapestry: *twenty ells of red champit chamlet of silk, four ells white taffety, three ells fine black velvet—*

The living-room, dim in high summer, would have been quite dark in the winter twilight had it not been lit by the flicker of the fire.

The table was laid ready for tea; the brass candlesticks on the mantelpiece shone, everything was very tidy. Mrs. Tait sat by the fire, her hands idle in her lap.

"It's you," she said, making a half-effort to rise. "Come in to the fire, it's cauld the day."

"Yes," said Kirsty, "it's very cold today."

Mrs Tait went on looking into the fire, and Kirsty sat in silence opposite to her.

It was very still. Sometimes a branch of ivy tapped against the narrow window, sometimes a cinder fell on the hearth; through the silence ran the rushing sound of water far below.

Suddenly Mrs. Tait rose. "I'm gaun in to her; I canna bide to leave her lang. Will ye come?" and Kirsty followed her through the door beside the fireplace to the little room beyond where Nannie lay. She shrank back for a moment as the mother lifted the sheet from the dead face, but there was nothing to shock or alarm in the frozen peace that lay there—"a lily in a linen clout."

Kirsty sank down beside the bed, crying softly, while the mother stood straight and stern, looking, looking, as if she could never look her fill.

Presently in a flat even voice she began to speak, never taking her eyes from her child's face:

"Nannie and me 'greed awfu' weel: we never flayt. Last

nicht—it's queer to think that it was only last nicht that she spoke to me, for it seems lang, lang since I heard her voice—she was sittin' by the kitchen fire, no' nae waur ye would hae said, but aboot twal o'clock she got awfu' restless an' she said, 'I dinna ken what's wrang wi' me, Mother, I'm sae wearied.' I kent by the look in her face that she was for off, an' I said, Nannie, are ye gaun to leave yer mither?' an' she gaed me sic a look, as if she were seein' me for the first time, an' she said, 'I wish I had de'ed when I was a wee bairn,' an' turned her face to the wall."

Would that I had died at Jedworth!

Kirsty caught Mrs. Tait's hand with a sob. After a minute she went on:

"I got kinna frantic to see her look at me like that, an' I cried, 'Hes yer mither ever failed ye, ma hinny?' an' she turned an' lookit at me, juist as if she was sayin' she was vexed she had ever hurt me, an' she smiled, but she never spoke again . . . Ay weel, we'd better gang ben to the fire. Tait'll be comin' in, puir man—he's been down at Priorsford seein' aboot things, an' he'll need his tea—Dinna greet, ma lassie."

But Kirsty wept sore, for on the "drawershead" she saw standing Nannie's little silver slippers.

CHAPTER 22

"If the barricades went up in our streets and the poor became masters, I think the priests would escape, I fear the gentlemen would, but I believe the gutters would be simply running with the blood of philanthropists."

G. K. CHESTERTON

THE next morning when the children had left the table (Miss Fanny was breakfasting in bed) Miss Carter did not follow them at once, but sat fingering a letter that had come for her by the morning's post.

Kirsty, looking up from her own correspondence, asked, "Any special news, Carty?"

"I have a letter from Rebecca Brand."

"Oh!" Kirsty laid down the letter she was reading. "A nice letter, I hope?"

"Well—a little curt, perhaps, but she's handsome about Rob, and says what a good brother he has been." She pushed the letter uncertainly towards Kirsty. "I don't know whether you would care to read it."

"No, I'd better not. Rebecca isn't one of those almost professional letter-writers who like their epistles to be circulated. I expect it cost her something to write, and remember, Carty, a little from her goes a long way. If she says, however curtly, that she will welcome you it means a lot."

"Oh, I know, and I think it's very decent of her to write to me at all. Hadn't I better go and see her? I'm scared to death of her, really."

"You must go, of course," Kirsty decreed, "but I think perhaps I had better have a talk to her first. In a way I'm responsible for the whole thing . . . I'll go this very morning. Mr. Brand will be in his study: it's a chance."

The news of her brother's engagement had come to Rebecca as a complete surprise. She was not a suspicious creature, and it had simply never occurred to her that there might be anything between her brother and Miss Carter. "And yet," she told herself bitterly, "I might have known. He was always hanging about Little Phantasy, and it's just the sort of ridiculous thing that does happen. A minister with nothing but his stipend and a penniless governess! And the girl English and can know nothing about the Presbyterian kirk; young and sure to be flighty, probably never has attempted to keep house, and will race through the whole year's income in a month."

In her heart she had no blame for the girl, she had liked anything she had seen of her, and Robert was a man and therefore could not be expected to be sensible; but against Kirsty Gilmour, who, Rebecca shrewdly suspected, had made the match, her anger was hot.

This morning Rebecca sat by the dining-room fire—a small fire depressed by a backing of dross—mending household linen. That had to be done though the skies fell.

She took a sheet and held it up to the light, revealing a worn patch in the middle. Taking up a large pair of scissors she cut the hem and tore the sheet up the middle. It meant overcasting the outer edges, and hemming the sides after the worn part had been cut away, and when it was finished it would be a poor mutilated thing, fit only for an emergency, "to kep a strait," as Easie Orphoot would have said.

As she sewed she reflected on her position: it seemed to her as dreary and futureless as the worn sheet.

Robert had said, "Of course we shan't be married for ages, and, anyway, your home is always at the Manse." That was absurd. The Manse was no place for her when Robert brought a wife to it. But what was she to do? That was the rub.

"If I was really fitted for anything," Rebecca said to herself. "If I could make dresses and trim hats really well—but I've no head for dressmaking, I can only gorble away and mend. Or if I had a good business head and had learned typing and shorthand." She gave the sheet a vicious tweak. "I'd be no use as a companion, for I'm not tactful . . . I'm a good worker in the house—that's an idea; I might be a housemaid. It would be better to be a thoroughly competent housemaid, valued and considered by a mistress, than a companion never quite sure what her position was, and always prepared to ooze out of sight in case she was in the way. I would be a little like Miss Wotherspoon at Little Phantasy, but I wouldn't hang on to shreds of gentility by asking to be called 'Miss'. They might call me Brand or Rebecca just as they pleased."

She had just finished the middle seam, and was preparing to attack one of the sides, when the creak of the garden gate made her lift her head and listen. Presently the doorbell rang, and the small maid could be heard in easy conversation with someone.

"A caller," Rebecca said resignedly, "I hope I may be spared Lady Carruthers, for if she . . ."

To what reckless lengths Rebecca might have gone if it had been that well-meaning woman will never be known, for it was Kirsty Gilmour that entered.

The two women stood looking at each other for a moment before anything was said in greeting. They made a striking contrast: Kirsty in soft golden brown with a great collar of beaver framing her face, Rebecca in her old brown jumper and shabby grey skirt, her straight mouse-coloured hair pulled firmly back from her round red face, the old sheet which she was mending trailing round her. The becomingness of Kirsty's clothes did nothing to soften Rebecca's feelings towards her.

"How d'you do?" she said. "Come near the fire, though," she gave the big lump of coal a push with her foot as she spoke, "the poor thing is almost too discouraged by dross to give much heat."

"Oh, don't touch it, please, it's such a thrifty fire," Kirsty said as she sat down near it. "It would rejoice the heart of Miss Wotherspoon; she simply can't bear to see coals burning away . . . It's a lovely morning for a walk, though it looks so cold."

She took a seat near Rebecca and they proceeded to make conversation. "Is Miss Fanny well?" Rebecca asked politely.

"Quite well, thank you. Of course she feels the cold."

"Muirburn," said Rebecca, "is very cold in winter."

"But so lovely."

"I'd rather," said Rebecca, "live in a less lovely place and have a milder climate."

"Oh," said Kirsty, "really," and a silence fell which Kirsty broke, after a minute, with an anecdote about Bill.

To Rebecca, sitting placidly sewing her long seam, and waiting to be told what had brought her visitor to the Manse at such an early hour, the situation was easy, but Kirsty was finding it hard.

"We were so interested," she burst out at last, "I mean I was so very glad when Stella Carter told me the great news."

She stopped.

Rebecca tore off a long strip of worn sheet and bent down to recapture the reel of cotton which had rolled under her chair.

"I do hope," Kirsty went on rather falteringly, "I do hope they will be very happy, for I feel in a way responsible. If I hadn't come to Little Phantasy they would never have met."

Rebecca snipped a thread. "You must feel quite a providence," she said pleasantly.

Kirsty flushed. "Well—I confess I did hope this would happen: it seemed so suitable somehow."

"Why suitable?"

"Oh, because they are both so nice, so sincere, and keen about the same things—and then poor Carty hasn't got much of a home, and it is so delightful to think of her settled in Muirburn."

"And you didn't consider that settling her in Muirburn meant turning me out."

"No," Kirsty admitted, her voice dropping, "I never

thought of that."

"That's the worst of you sentimental people, you never think—you only feel." Rebecca was sewing so fiercely that her thread snapped. She threaded her needle as she continued. "I've suffered all my life from sentiment. I always cared for music and might have played really well if I'd had a chance, but my music teacher was chosen for me by my parents because she had a sad love affair and it was thought that it would give her an interest in life to teach music: she had no qualifications whatever for the job. Your great idea is to have every one pleased and happy around you so that you may feel pleased and happy. It's a form of selfishness."

"You never liked me," said Kirsty.

"Is it necessary that *everyone* should like you?"

Kirsty winced at the tone. "Of course not," she said quickly, "only—did I ever do anything to hurt you? If I did I never meant to."

Rebecca sewed diligently for a minute, her eyes on the seam; then she said, "You're not the sort of person who would ever mean to hurt any one. You would always want to shower gifts on people and be kind to them and pet them, but did you ever think how irritating unwanted kindness can be to the recipient? Did you ever think how much more grace it requires to be a receiver than a giver? From the first I could feel you saying to yourself, 'Oh, the poor plain good little thing! I must be kind to her and try to brighten life for her a little.' You thought, because I was dumpy and had a red face and uninteresting hair, that I must want brightening. And you talked away about how you loved living in a homely, simple way, trying to put yourself on a level with me, and raved over servants and housekeeping details as if it were some new game invented for your special amusement. What do you know about keeping a house? Have you ever got up on winter mornings and lit fires and washed front doorsteps? Do you know what it is to wash dishes and scrape pots until your hands seem to smell of dishcloths, and you can't keep decently tidy, and life is one long preparing of meals and clearing them away? You said hotel life was so sickening, so unhomelike . . ."

"Oh," cried Kirsty, stricken, "what an affected idiot you must have thought me."

"At first I did," Rebecca owned. "Then I saw that it wasn't affectation, that you really were enjoying what I thought you were only pretending to enjoy, that you were like a child playing at 'houses.' Oh, but *I* needn't pretend—what annoyed me was just the difference between us. You had everything I hadn't. I never knew how plain I was till I saw you. And your clothes! I've always longed for good clothes, but you can see for yourself I've no notion of how to dress. Other women can make pretty things out of little, but I'm at the mercy of a fifth-rate dressmaker, so that I haven't even the chance to look as decent as I might. You have perfect clothes for every occasion, so you can't begin to understand how sick one gets of wearing a tweed coat and skirt day in and day out; and every one turned to you and liked you and admired you, and I was nowhere. Not that I ever was anywhere, but that didn't make it any easier."

Rebecca bent her head over the sheet and sewed as for a wager, while Kirsty sat like a penitent on a stool, the picture of abject misery.

"And now I'm losing Rob. It's a long time since we were children together, and we've always been great friends. I don't want to grumble about him marrying; it's right and it's natural, and I haven't a word to say. I've tried to be decent to him about it, though, mind you, I think he has made a foolish choice. I know nothing against the girl, but she's young, and she's English, and not likely to know much about housekeeping, and as for managing a kirk—! I'm not much good myself, for I haven't a taking way, but anyway I can understand the people."

"Couldn't you help her?" Kirsty asked timidly.

"Me? I won't be there to help. When Rob brings his wife to the Manse I walk out. I'm thinking of taking a 'place' as a housemaid."

Kirsty moaned.

"Why not? I wouldn't have to work as hard as I work now." She stopped, and then said cruelly, "I'll be like your Miss Wotherspoon."

Kirsty rose to her feet. "I'm going," she said. "I suppose it's not much good asking you to forgive me? I seem to have done nothing but hurt you all the time."

"As to that," Rebecca said, sticking the needle into her seam and rising, "I ought to apologize to you for my rudeness."

"You were honest, anyway, and that's something. No, don't rise. I'll let myself out. Good morning."

Rebecca sat still after the door closed behind Kirsty,

feeling more than a little ashamed of herself.

"Was I honest?" she asked herself. "I doubt it . . . But I was very rude. It's a great mistake to let oneself go."

Near Little Phantasy Kirsty met Merren Strang, who proceeded to walk homewards with her.

"Well met! I would accept an invitation to luncheon if you thought of giving me one. I couldn't work this morning. I never can work when the sun shines; I wanted a trudge in the snow . . . You don't look very bright, my friend. Anything troubling you?"

"Lots," said Kirsty. "I've just been hearing the truth about myself."

"That should have been interesting, but it seems to have depressed you . . . I'm in great spirits myself this morning. I've just got news of a legacy—an utterly unexpected one from the widow of an uncle. I was hardly sorry at all when I heard she was dead, for I hadn't seen her for years, but I wish now I had grieved a little. But I rather think she left it not from any feeling of affection for me, but from a feeling of loyalty to her dead husband who was fond of me as a child. Anyway, the legacy is quite considerable. D'you know what I'm going to do with some of it? I'm going to Italy."

"When?" Kirsty asked.

"Immediately after Christmas. I arranged it all with myself this morning when I heard from the lawyer—Italy first, Rome—oh, glorious! Then other places—Sicily, perhaps—sunshine, flowers . . ."

"Oh," Kirsty shouted suddenly, "*will* you take Rebecca

Brand with you?"

Merren Strang stood still in the snow and stared.

"What in the world would I do with Rebecca Brand in Italy? Do talk sense, Kirsty."

Kirsty grabbed her arm. "Wait till I tell you. Rob Brand has got engaged to Carty, and Rebecca says she will be a housemaid like Miss Wotherspoon, and somehow or other it seems to be all my blame. I'm perfectly *miserable*. Merren, couldn't you say you wanted a companion and ask her to go with you? You would need to be very humble about it, because she is hurt in her feelings and suspicious of everyone . . . If you could make her feel you *need* her—"

"But I don't," Merren interrupted.

Kirsty gave an exasperated stamp. "Oh, but couldn't you *try* to need her, seeing how serious it is and all my fault in a way?"

"But what is your fault?"

"Well," said Kirsty, "it isn't really, because if they hadn't been prepared to fall in love with each other nothing I could have done would have made them. But I did think it would be nice to have Carty settled here, and I did give them every opportunity to meet, and I did forget all about Rebecca. And a trip to Italy would be such a treat to her. She has been nowhere, poor Rebecca . . ." Kirsty stopped short, remembering Rebecca's own words about the "Poor plain good little thing." "And I do think you would enjoy having her. It would be so amusing to show her things. Of course I would pay for everything, but she wouldn't need to know that. If she got a hint of such an arrangement her pride would be up in arms. Everything must seem to come from you—do you think that is an underhand way to do things? It's all very difficult, but do, do help me to give Rebecca one good time in her life."

Kirsty was so urgent and so distressed that before Little Phantasy was reached Merren Strang had consented to go meekly to the Manse and beg for Rebecca's companionship on her trip.

But she sighed as she said, "Your living for others, my dear, makes life very difficult for your friends. There's nothing I enjoy so much as going about alone, following my own free will, and Rebecca, I know, will gloom disapprovingly at the pictures, and in Rome she will say rude things about the Pope. She is just like the Edinburgh man who said to the two devout Catholic ladies who offered to pray for him, 'I'll thank you not to mention me by name to the Virgin Mary.' Well, well, so this is all my legacy has brought me! Let me go in and have a talk to Bill, and let some of Aunt Fanny's serenity slide into my soul. I often wish I had, as she has, a refuge of shawls from this bleak world."

CHAPTER 23

> "You promise heavens free from strife,
> Pure truth and perfect change of will;
> But sweet, sweet is this human life,
> So sweet, I fain would breathe it still;
> Your chilly stars I can forgo,
> This warm kind world is all I know."
> WILLIAM CORY

LATER, when Mrs. Strang had been warmed and fed, and had somewhat recovered from the shock of Kirsty's proposal, she remembered what had brought her to Little Phantasy.

"I knew there was something," she said. "I knew I hadn't just arrived aimlessly to beg a meal. Meeting you on the road, Kirsty, put everything out of my head. Now, listen. Which of you will come with me tonight to Priorsford to a concert?"

She looked round the table as she spoke, then addressed Miss Fanny. "Won't you come?"

"Oh, my dear Mrs. Strang!" Miss Fanny retreated into her shawls at the very suggestion. "I never go out in the evenings—at least very rarely; and the long drive in the snow, and the draughty hall and the dark . . . Thank you very much for thinking of me, but I really could not."

"It won't be dark," Mrs. Strang pointed out unfeelingly. "There's a moon."

"Oh, a moon!" Miss Fanny's tone seemed to convey that she thought poorly of the moon. "No—please don't think me ungrateful, but I would be much happier at home."

Merren patted her hand soothingly. "No, I didn't really expect that you would go out at night. But somebody *must* come. I've ordered a closed car, and if that isn't luxury I don't know what is. Kirsty, you don't seem to jump at my invitation. 'No' is written all over your speaking countenance."

"It would be lovely," Kirsty began, but was immediately interrupted.

"I know that beginning. 'It would be lovely, but—' It is too discouraging to try to give people pleasure and have the wretched people with one accord begin to make excuses. What were you going to say, Kirsty? *I have married a wife and therefore cannot come*, or something equally likely."

Kirsty laughed. "It's very rude, I know, and certainly not the way to treat an invitation, but I was so looking forward to an evening by the fire—that sounds as if I dined and danced every night of my life instead of—oh yes, Merren, I'll come. I'm getting to be an oyster; it will do me good."

"No, I don't want you. I hate to do people good. I tell you what, Barbara and Specky will come, and if Carty wouldn't find it too much of a bore—" She looked at Miss Carter, who replied with fervour:

"I would like it above everything; a concert is always a treat to me." And there was no doubt about the joyful acceptance of Barbara and Specky.

"Well, that's settled. Come to Hopewaterfoot about six and we'll have a tea-dinner before we start, a solid meal, and then you'll only need a hot drink when you come in."

The two children were almost speechless with delight,

and found a vent to their solemn joy by rubbing their foreheads like two friendly ponies, while Bill stared fixedly at the tablecloth. Kirsty knew that he was on the point of crying, a humiliation which would have vexed his proud soul, and without looking at him she slid her hand over his small, clenched fist and said:

"What a splendid plan! And when we get rid of them all, Bill, I want you to help me open the big box that came this morning." She turned to Miss Fanny "I thought I would order the Christmas toys for the school children in good time, and we must see what they are like, and if none are broken . . . Bill, d'you think you could find a hammer and chisel, so that we'll quite ready to open it whenever they go away."

Bill nodded. "In the kitchen table drawer." He slipped from the table, mightily important, to see about it at once.

Specky looked rather regretfully at the retreating form of his brother. "I'd like to help Bill open the box," he said. "I don't think he knows quite how to work a chisel, and he might hammer his fingers. I don't want to stay at home, for I do want to see Tweed in the dark but I like opening boxes too. Couldn't we open the box before we go away, Pie?"

"I'm afraid not," Kirsty said gravely. "That's Bill's treat and you are having yours—Carty, you would need a very early tea to be ready for supper at six. Shall we say tea at three-thirty? Children, you hear? Be in shortly after three, and we shall have time for our reading before we need get ready. What are you going to do now? Toboggan? Well, don't be rash, darlings. I'll be out to look at you in a little. Dear me, this is a terribly busy day . . . Come along,

Merren, to the drawing-room fire."

Mrs. Strang stood up and began to prepare to depart.

"Don't tempt me, girl, with drawing-room fires—where did I leave my coat?—I must get home and put in some grim work at the book I'm finishing. I only realized this morning that I had mislaid one of the characters entirely."

Kirsty looked sympathetic. "Is it going to be good?" she asked.

"It is not," said the author shortly. "And I've taken such a dislike to my heroine that I thwart her at every turn. She is a well-meaning creature, but she takes after Bunyan's creation 'the deplorable young woman named Dull.' I'm bound to get it done before I go off on my jaunt—but that's largely spoilt for me too, thanks to you. As I said before, the vicarious kindness of one's friends is a great nuisance. And who acquires merit by it, I should like to know? You, I suppose. Yes, you may well look penitent—"

Some hours later Miss Fanny and her niece sat reading by the fire. The chintz curtains were drawn across the wide low windows—a reading lamp stood on the table by Miss Fanny's side, another stood near Kirsty's chair, and two tall standard lamps helped to make a bright glow round the hearth; the corners of the room were in shadow.

Miss Fanny laid down her book, looked at Kirsty's absorbed face, and sighed deeply.

Kirsty heard her sigh and lifted her head.

"Tired, Aunt Fanny? No? Merely bored, then?"

"What are you reading, dear?" Miss Fanny asked in her gentle voice.

Kirsty lifted a little book bound in red leather and held it up for her aunt to see.

"One of my favourite stories—*The Children of the Zodiac*. I don't know whether you care much for Kipling?"

"Not much, dear; such a swearing sort of writer, except for *The Recessional*, which, of course, is very nice."

"There is no swearing in this story. It's about the Children of the Zodiac—Leo and the Girl, the Bull, the Twins—who were gods and became mortal. When they first realized that some day death would come for them, Leo and the Girl sat down in despair, then they looked at the people round them who did not know what day they would die, yet laughed and were cheerful, till for shame's sake they had to learn to laugh too. And the story goes on, Aunt Fanny, that the two went about singing among the country people and collecting pence for their daily bread. They sang that whatever came or did not come the children of men must not be afraid. It was heavy teaching at first, but as the years went on, Leo discovered that he could make men laugh and hold them listening even when the rain fell. But sometimes they got very tired and Leo would say, 'Let us stop singing and making jokes,' but the Girl said 'No.' And other singers sprang up and Leo hated them for dividing the applause, and sometimes Leo's songs would be broken and the jokes fall flat, and the children would shout, 'Go home, and learn something worth singing'."

Kirsty fell silent, and after a minute Miss Fanny asked what happened to Leo and the Girl.

"The Girl died, and as she was dying Leo cried in

bitterness, 'Surely we were gods once.'

" 'Surely we are gods still,' said the Girl, '. . . but we've forgotten what we were singing for—we sang for pence, and oh! we fought for them—we who are the Children of the Zodiac.' And the Girl died, and Leo, remembering her, sang more beautiful songs than ever he had done, and did not forget that he was a god—though he had to die . . . Don't you think it's a beautiful story, Aunt Fanny?"

"Yes," doubtfully, "I suppose it is, but very fanciful—are you afraid of death, Kirsty?"

"It's hard to say," Kirsty said, surprised at the question.

" The ways of Death are soothing and serene,
And all the words of Death are grave and sweet . . .

so the poet says."

"That's nonsense," said Miss Fanny, sitting up and becoming unexpectedly definite. "It's poetry, of course, and poets say anything so long as it sounds pretty. I ought to be ashamed to say it, but Death seems to me a terrible thing. I fight against the feeling. I read little books about Heaven, and hymns, but I don't seem to get much comfort from them. When the sun shines and I feel very well, and cheerful people are round me, I seem to have a firmer faith, but at night when I am alone and not sleeping and remember that in four years I'll be seventy . . . To be nearly at the end of the span and to be so unwilling to leave this world. You said, Kirsty—you know you did—that it was a stumbling-block to you to see how little the good people wanted to leave this life for the life everlasting, but I can'thelp it. I shrink from such a step in the dark. Perhaps it's because I've always been so comfortable all my life, fires in my bedroom, and fur-lined slippers, and shawls . . . and the River will be so cold . . ."

She ended on a frightened sob, and in a second Kirsty was kneeling beside her, stroking her hand, comforting her as if she had been a frightened child.

"Dear Aunt Fanny—poor darling. Why should you of all people worry yourself? I am sure you have hardly ever had a hard thought of any one, much less done any one harm."

But Miss Fanny refused this comfort, pushing Kirsty away with one hand while she wiped her eyes with the other.

"I don't say I've done much active harm, but I sometimes think I have lived too much to myself, that I haven't troubled myself enough about other people, although I always did give quite a lot to Missions and had the work-party in my own drawing-room every week at Harelaw. But all our righteousness is as filthy rags and it won't help at the last . . . I've always been timid, afraid of so many things—burglars and mice and thunder, and I never could bear to go anywhere alone, I always took a maid with me, and to set off at last *alone* . . ."

Kirsty had a vision of Aunt Fanny's soul, very small and shrunken, no shawls to comfort, no maid to lean on, setting off in the cold and dark, and her arms tightened round the poor lady.

"Oh, Kirsty, I fear I'll never see the Celestial City."

"Dear heart," said Kirsty, "you would be sadly out of place anywhere else . . . Why, darling, leaving the body is just like leaving an old garment one doesn't want any more."

"Yes, yes. I know that, but somehow I don't believe it. There's the River to cross."

"But there is no real river: it's just a beautiful imagining; and don't you remember how Much Afraid, who dreaded everything, went through the water singing—though none knew what she said."

"You get comfort from poetry," said Miss Fanny, "I never could."

Kirsty laughed a little. "But you like your religious little books, Aunt Fanny, so we each have something . . . It may be an incurable lightness in my nature, but I can't say I ever worry much about death. I just trust to be given strength to behave decently when my time comes. It's amazing, I think, how philosophically we all take it when it comes to the end, for we never really believe that death will come to ourselves. Like Bill when I said we would do something next year if we were all spared.

" 'Perhaps you'll be dead,' he said calmly.

" 'Perhaps you will,' I retorted.

" 'Oh no, I'm always spared,' said Bill.

" . . . Aunt Fanny, did you ever read (no, this isn't poetry) a letter written by Lewis Carroll to the children who loved 'Alice.' He describes a child wakening from a frightening dream, to find a mother's hand drawing aside the curtains and letting in the sunshine of a spring morning, and he goes on to say that death is like that, a morning when God's hand shall draw aside the curtains and we shall see the Sun of Righteousness. That is all it is, just sleeping to wake where everything that frightened us and vexed us will be finished with . . . And here comes Miss Wotherspoon with the kettle and the spongecakes."

As they sat sipping hot water Kirsty smiled at her aunt and said:

"Aren't we blest beyond compare? To have a house full of life and peace (I don't mean stagnant quiet, but peace in the real sense) and beautiful things. Age and youth and middling ones like Carty and me, it all makes for happiness and completeness. You *are* happy here, Aunt Fanny? Say you are."

"Oh yes," Miss Fanny sighed as if it were almost wrong to admit to happiness. "You keep house very comfortably, my dear, and the children are sometimes a pleasure—even Bill."

"Oh," Kirsty cried, "did you ever know anything so delightful as Bill tonight? Trotting about so earnestly, struggling with hammer and chisel and little paddy-paws to open the big box. A busy child is always a good child. In fact, I'm beginning to think that the only reliable prescription for happiness is to have lots to do."

Kirsty munched her spongecake contentedly, and nodded at her aunt. "I hope you and I will sit here like this a long time o' nights."

"Ah, my dear, I hope you will have a better companion than a dull old woman, and I can't expect it to be very long at the longest. No Gilmour ever lives much past seventy."

"Dull old woman!" Kirsty scoffed. "I tell you what, if you go on suggesting to yourself that you'll die at seventy, you'll do it. It's an uncanny thing the power of suggestion. There's no reason why you shouldn't live to be ninety, especially now that you've begun to have spongecakes and hot water! You take such good care of your health that you'll likely be going strong when I'm either dead or a withered old dotard at fifty—Oh, I had forgotten. I was lent such a nice little book today. It belongs to Merren Strang, and she loves it—a book of religious poems by B. M. I've just glanced at them, they look lovely. Merren thought you might like to see them."

She took from the table a small book bound in dark green and gold, and turned over the leaves for a few minutes, till she found what she wanted. "This now. Doesn't it say something to you, even if it is poetry? It is called *The Desire to Depart*.

> "And thus our hearts appeal to them
> When we behold our dearest rise
> And look towards Jerusalem
> With strangely kindling eyes.
>
> For ah! the Master is so fair,
> His smile so sweet to banished men
> That they who meet it unawares
> Can never rest on earth again.
>
> And they who see Him risen far,
> At God's right hand to welcome them,
> Forgetful stand of home and land,
> Desiring fair Jerusalem."

Miss Fanny sat forward in her chair.

"My dear, let me see that book. I used to know it so well. B. M. is Barbara Miller—I haven't seen it for years, indeed I had forgotten all about it. Yes, this is the same book. Dear me, the very look of it brings so much back to me . . ." She gloated over it for a little, and then, "Let me take it up to my room," she begged, "those are sweet words . . . I'm sure I wish it could be said of me that I desired fair Jerusalem!" She gave a small rueful smile, and Kirsty hugged her.

"I certainly don't want you rise with 'strangely kindling eyes' and leave us. We can't do without you, my dear. Now, are you going to sit up for these merry wanderers of the night, or will you go to bed now?"

"Well, dear, if you don't mind sitting up alone . . . I'm rather tired."

"Of course not. Let me help you with your shawls. Yes, I'm coming up to see if your fire is good and everything cosy."

Kirsty picked up various trifles, a gold-mounted magnifying glass, a bottle of smelling salts, a small devotional book or two, and said:

"D'you know, I was rather badly depressed this morning after hearing some home truths about myself from Rebecca Brand, and didn't see much light in life. Then I met Merren Strang and she seemed to cheer things up wonderfully, and it has been such a happy evening with Bill and the toys, and this peaceful time talking to you."

"Well, I don't know what right Rebecca Brand has to tell you home truths," Miss Fanny said resentfully; "but I do know," here the voice softened, "that you are a great comfort to me. I don't know how I ever managed without you."

CHAPTER 24

"What would you, ladies? It was ever thus. Men are
unwise and curiously planned."
                    JAMES ELROY FLECKER

IT IS POSSIBLE to go to bed filled with noble thoughts, and a tender tolerance to all humanity, and a not entirely dissatisfied feeling about one's own conduct, and to waken feeling more or less at war with the whole world.

After hearing a full account of the wonderful concert, and the even more wonderful drive by Tweed in the snow and moonlight, from the two excited children, having stayed them with spongecakes and comforted them with hot cocoa, and seen them warmly tucked up in bed, Kirsty had gone to her own room, her heart within her like a singing bird. To be needed by someone was the breath of life to her, and here she was the centre of a warm, snug home, here was a household of old and young depending on her. She fell asleep with her mouth curved in a smile.

She woke, struggling out of an unpleasant dream, and looked at her watch. Seven o'clock. It wasn't worthwhile snuggling down again, for her tea would be coming in half an hour, so she lay and thought of her absurd dream. She had been in a large and crowded church where a wedding was about to take place, her own, it seemed, but she was most unsuitably attired in a tweed skirt and a Shetland jumper. She had begged plaintively for a veil, and someone had torn a sheet from the *Scotsman* and handed it to her and she had pinned it on, knowing it was entirely the wrong thing; but, with the terrible impotence which oppresses one in dreams, unable to help herself. Nor could she see the bridegroom anywhere. As she wandered through the church she had met Mrs. Norman McCandlish and asked her if she knew anything about him, and that lady had replied in her primest accents, "I believe he belongs to the far north." (Kirsty lay and laughed to herself as the absurdity of the dream struck her.) Finally she had seen him—a small, timid man with side whiskers and a slight pink rash on each high cheek-bone, and immediately he faded away, with the church and the people, and only the voice of the Rev. Norman McCandlish remained, asking pathetically if Kirsty would lend him a shilling as he was tired of selling rhubarb.

As Kirsty thought over her dream she became aware that she had caught a cold, and that her head felt fuggy and heavy. All the pleasantness and comfort that had filled her being the night before seemed to have vanished. Now she could only remember that Rebecca Brand disliked her and thought that she had done her an ill turn. Also, any day, she might get a letter saying that Alan Crawford was on his way home, and then there was bound to be a crisis of some sort.

She sat up and lit the lamp that stood on the table by her bed, and in doing so held the match too long and burned her fingers, and then, letting it fall hurriedly, burnt a small hole in the sheet. Lamps, she concluded, were a nuisance.

It was very cold, the tip of her nose felt quite frozen; she pulled the covers over her and lay and looked out of the window. It was beginning to get light, and she could just make out the bridge that marked the meeting of Tweed and the Hope Water. There was a light in one of the narrow windows of the old Castle. John Tait would be getting his breakfast and going out to his work, decent man, leaving his wife to her lonely days, for now she scrubbed floors with an empty heart. Well, Nannie was away from it all, away from the hard work and the small pleasures, away from the bitter winter mornings and the long light summer nights. She would never feel dissatisfied again.

"She's not missing much," Kirsty thought morosely, "for half the time one's alive one's making a fool of oneself. I'm sure Miss Wotherspoon's late this morning. I don't know why I lie here and expect her to bring me tea. She's probably a Socialist and loathes me for the trouble I give her . . ." She yawned and wondered how it was that even in snow Ratchell Hill had such a worn, scarred look.

A tap at the door.

Tea.

Kirsty pulled a soft Shetland wool jacket over her shoulders.

"Oh, *thank* you, Miss Wotherspoon," she said gratefully, remembering that she had no right to lie in bed and drink tea while older women (probably with headaches) got the house warm and comfortable for her.

Miss Wotherspoon, with a firm hand, pulled down the blinds to the very foot, to remind her mistress that the lamp was exposing her to the gaze of the public.

"Nobody could see me but a sheep on the Ratchell Hill," Kirsty pointed out, but Miss Wotherspoon primmed her lips and said that to her way of thinking it was a very daft-like thing, indecent, too, to lie in bed with a light and the blinds up.

Kirsty tied the broad blue satin ribbons of her dressing-jacket and looked thoughtfully at the white tray with its fragile blue and white china, got to match the blue and white room. Rebecca Brand had put many things in a new light. Hitherto Kirsty had taken it more or less for granted that every one lay in bed till morning tea was brought to them, and then went into a well-warmed bathroom smelling of the best kinds of bath salts, and bathed and dressed at leisure. Now she had a picture in her mind of the austere little Manse, with its one small shiftless maid-servant, and Rebecca rising at all hours to sweep and dust. No wonder, thought Kirsty, that Rebecca felt soured when she looked at her. Some people were so constituted that they liked hard work, liked nothing better than to rise early in the morning and rush about putting things straight, but Rebecca was not one of them. She had hankerings after luxury; without a glimmering of knowledge how to dress, she loved beautiful clothes. Well, Kirsty thought, she would see to it that now Rebecca had some colour in her life. As she rose and put on her dressing-gown she smiled to think that if she went on collecting people and providing for them at the rate she was doing, the fortune her father had left her would soon cease to be a burden, and the thought cheered her and made her forget her cold.

The post arrived early at Little Phantasy, and, as Kirsty was generally down first, she often had read her letters before the others put in an appearance.

This morning there was quite a pile by her place, not bills or circulars, real letters, thick, addressed in interesting writing.

She turned them over with a pleased smile: they were from old friends, welcome letters but not exciting. The last one she took up made her heart beat with heavy thuds. It was from Alan Crawford, the letter she had dreaded.

There had been no letters for some little time, which had made her fear that he was on his way home, but—she tried to reassure herself—this might be a reprieve: it might be saying that he had decided to winter abroad. She tore it open and tried to read it at one gulp, to get the meaning with a glance.

The first page was merely thanks for her letter and snapshots, and compliments about the children's improved looks. She turned that over impatiently. What was all this about a fellow-voyager, also bereaved—comforted each other—a mother's care— *What!*

She felt as if her heart had turned to ice within her, but Stella Carter had come into the room followed by the children with their shining morning faces, and she had to greet them, and stroke their heads as if they were ponies (the two boys strongly objected to kissing), and admire Bill's new stockings, and laugh and be gay as they had always seen her.

"Kedgeree," said Specky, who liked his meals. "Good!"

"Are you sure there are no eggshells in it?" Bill asked, having a horror of finding even the minutest fragment of shell in his food. "Try it with your fork, Pie." So Kirsty pounded it with her fork until he was satisfied.

"When I was a little girl," Miss Fanny told him, "I got nothing to breakfast on weekdays but porridge, and some thick bread and butter. Only on Sabbath morning we got ham and eggs, and only on Sabbath afternoon we got cake for tea. Nothing is a treat to you children."

"Yes," Barbara corrected her, "toasted cheese, Aunt Fanny. Easie gave it us once, and it was lovely. When I'm grown up I shall have it for tea every afternoon."

Kirsty's eyes strayed back to the letter. She had made no mistake. Her eyes had not played her false. There it was in his beautiful clear small writing. He had met a lady who, he felt, would be a mother to his poor children. They were coming home in the same ship and would be married quietly in London on the 15th, and a few days later would come for the children.

There was much more. Profuse thanks for her goodness, promises of lifelong gratitude from himself and the children; some details about the lady who was to be his wife. She was a widow, it appeared, Scots, and had a place in Perthshire.

Kirsty merely glanced impatiently at what was written. All that mattered was that in a week the children would be gone.

It was a still, intensely cold morning. The sun was shining on the Hope Water, and on the yellow chrysanthemums in the yellow bowl in the middle of the table. Bill was wearing a yellow jersey, and with his gilt head looked rather like a canary. There was an air of jollity about the whole party. Even Miss Fanny greeted the sun with a pleased blink of her eyes, and Miss Carter's mouth turned up all the time in a happy smile.

Kirsty sat at the head of the table, and made a pretence of eating, and listened and laughed and made plans for the day, and, after what seemed hours, the children ran out and she and Stella Carter followed Miss Fanny into the drawing-room.

"Any news this morning?" Miss Fanny asked, settling herself placidly into her chair.

Kirsty knelt down before the fire.

"Yes," she said, "somewhat startling news this morning—don't go, Carty, please. It concerns you a lot . . . I have a letter from Mr. Crawford telling me that he is coming here in about a week's time with a new wife"—she stopped for a second, and then went on in a hard, clear voice—"to take the children away."

There was no comment from either of her hearers, and she continued: "It sounds rather an ideal arrangement. The lady, evidently wealthy, has lost her husband, and is childless. I expect their loneliness drew them together . . . Quite a romance, isn't it, Aunt Fanny?"

"I suppose so." Miss Fanny's voice sounded uncertain. "Meeting on board ship like that—I wonder if he knew much about her. I do hope she will be good to the children."

"Oh dear, yes," Kirsty said lightly, springing to her feet. "Well, Carty, later on you and I must have a tremendous discussion about things . . . Perhaps you had better say nothing to the children in the meantime. It's a sudden uprooting, but, as Easie often says, 'Changes are lichtsome'." She turned away with a laugh, but Miss Carter went out of the room with tears in her eyes.

"I'm not going to think," Kirsty told herself as she went upstairs. "I must keep myself occupied every minute of the day." So she did every small disagreeable task that she had been putting off to a convenient season, wrote letters to people she had neglected, tied up magazines to send to a hospital, and (a job that always irritated her) sent postal orders for fiddling little bills. So the morning passed, and at luncheon she told the children so many ridiculous stories, and laughed so much, that Miss Fanny thought to herself, half pleased, half disappointed:

"Kirsty seems actually glad that the children are going away, and I was sure she would be brokenhearted. It's just as well, of course, but I thought she had deeper feelings."

"Are you going out, Kirsty?" she asked later as her niece came into the room with her out-of-door things on. "Isn't it very cold?"

"Yes, but it's a fine day for a walk. I was thinking I had better call on those new people who have taken Carton Place. Something-Thomson, they're called, I can't remember what. Merren Strang says they are appallingly dull, but that's all the more reason why they should be called on."

"Because they are dull?" Miss Fanny asked, puzzled.

"Well, they won't know they are dull; and coming to a new place they will expect to be made a fuss of, and it's a pity to disappoint people in this short world. Don't you think so?"

"Yes, dear, but don't overtire yourself."

Kirsty set off at a swinging pace along the frost-bound

snowy road, bidding herself enjoy the beauty of the white world; but, struggle as she would, she could not keep her thoughts under control. Whatever she tried to think about seemed to lead her back to Alan Crawford's letter.

"It's so frightfully funny," she thought. "I can't think why I'm not more amused. Here was I dreading, yet prepared to accept, an offer of marriage from a man who hadn't a thought of me. His letters meant nothing evidently: it was only my silly imagination. I'm like Miss Baxter, 'who refused the captain before he axed her.' Really, to be prepared to sacrifice oneself and then find that no sacrifice is required is a dreadful letdown. I feel bruised and bumped."

About three o'clock she reached the gates of Carton Place, where the Griffith-Thomsons had taken up their abode. "I expect they'll be out," she told herself hopefully, but the servant who opened the door said Mrs. Griffith-Thomson was at home, and showed Kirsty into a small room at the back of the hall, where the lady herself was discovered running up curtains on a sewing machine.

She rose with an annoyed expression at the sight of Kirsty and said severely, "Take the lady into the drawing-room, Agnes, and light the fire, as it's beginning to get chilly."

"Beginning to get chilly!" Kirsty repeated to herself. The sun was already going down, and the cold was intense. The window of the drawing-room was thick with frost-flowers and the atmosphere was like a vault.

Mrs. Griffith-Thomson, a small woman with a pinched mouth and a nervous manner, followed her into the room, and sitting down on a sofa began to make conversation, while Kirsty sat on a slim hard chair and tried to keep her teeth from chattering. The fire as yet was only one anaemic flame fastidiously licking a piece of coal, and had no effect on the icy air of the room.

"I'm afraid I'm rather an early caller," Kirsty said, feeling that an apology for the fire was necessary from someone, "but the days are so short now that I thought I would come directly after luncheon. I do hope I'm not disturbing you."

"Oh no," said Mrs. Griffith-Thomson, obviously lying. "I was only doing a little sewing. A new house needs so much."

"Indeed it does. I live at Little Phantasy, and I only came last spring."

"Indeed! It seems a pretty neighbourhood."

"Oh, it is." Kirsty was getting colder and colder; her breath made a white cloud before her every time she spoke. How long must she sit? Ten minutes, anyway.

The door opened and admitted Mr. Griffith-Thomson. He too was small and pinched, with a sparse black moustache. Kirsty felt she could have borne it better had he been a stout red-faced man. As it was, he seemed to lower rather than raise the temperature of the room.

They began again, together, on the beauty of the neighbourhood, while Kirsty tried to puzzle out why such a couple should have taken Carton Place. They were obviously intended to live in a suburb and go into town for shopping and concerts and theatres. They appeared to have nothing within themselves.

"I hope you won't find it too quiet here," she ventured. "I expect in winter almost nothing goes on."

"It seems a little cheerless," said Mr. Griffith-Thomson in his bleak voice, "with so much snow about, and the hills. We have always lived in a good suburb, so we shall miss a lot. But the Tweed is a nice stream. I fish a little, and Mrs. Thomson is fond of the garden."

"One need not lack for occupation," his wife said, "not even in the country."

"No, indeed," Kirsty agreed, and a silence fell.

Mr. Griffith-Thomson cleared his throat but said nothing. His wife watched the one flame flutter against what was evidently a stonyhearted coal, but made no effort to help it with the poker.

Kirsty rushed violently into the first subject that occurred to her. "There are two swans on Tweed. They swim about and look so pretty . . . In spring they built a nest and we so looked forward to baby swans, cygnets, I mean. I've never seen a cygnet and I always loved *The Ugly Duckling*, didn't you? But there was only one egg and the mother swan sat on it for weeks and weeks and then she got discouraged— no wonder!— and it was never hatched at all."

"Indeed!" Mrs. Griffith-Thomson said coldly, as if she thought the subject not a very nice one, and again her husband cleared his throat, but said nothing.

A wild desire to laugh seized Kirsty. What in the world had made her talk of swans? The very thought, of them, swimming coldly, or resting on the snow-covered banks, chilled her already so chilly body.

She got up to go, glad to take leave of the dreary little couple sitting in their so cold and lifeless room. They betrayed no emotion at her departure, as they had shown no pleasure at her appearance, and she went out feeling that her call had been entirely mistaken kindness.

It was glorious outside with the sunset sky pale green barred with rose-pink, and Kirsty, in her relief, skipped with delight. To go home to the warmth and comfort of Little Phantasy, the generous fires, Aunt Fanny as comfortable as a tea cosy, the children—she stopped, and all the life and vigour seemed to go out of her. The children! It was a warm nest, Little Phantasy, but it would soon be an empty one.

Colder far than the breasts of the swans on Tweed's wan water, colder than the comfortless drawing-room with its bleak little inhabitants, came the remembrance that she was losing the children. It took every vestige of pleasure out of the present, and left her without hope or spirit for the future.

Oh, if only that letter had not come, what fun to have gone home and made Aunt Fanny and Carty laugh at the odd reception she had got at Carton Place! How interested they would have been in the new and very queer little couple! How she would have hugged the fire after being nearly frozen! Now she had to go home and read to the children as if nothing had happened. To look at them, to laugh at their funny ways, knowing that in a week she would see them and hear them no more.

On the highroad, near the bridge, she met Colonel Home with his dogs. He turned and walked by her side, merely remarking, "D'you mind my pipe?" and then relapsing into silence.

"Are you coming in to tea?" Kirsty asked as they neared

Little Phantasy.

"Are you asking me?"

"Not really, only politely. You see—I'm not feeling very happy today. We heard this morning that Mr. Crawford (the children's father, you know) has married a new wife and is coming to fetch . . . to fetch Barbara and Specky and Bill."

To her deep disgust Kirsty found her voice breaking. "As if I were asking for sympathy," she said to herself.

But whether she asked for it or not, she did not get it. Archie Home looked at her in silence for a few seconds, then, "Taking them away, is he?" he said . . . "We're going to have hard frost tonight. It looks like being a long hard winter. It's begun early. Goodnight, Miss Gilmour."

As he walked away, whistling to his dogs, Kirsty looked after him with dim eyes.

"He might have been a little sorry. I thought he was fond of the children. He doesn't care a pin what happens to any of us . . . I wish I'd never seen this place!"

CHAPTER 25

> "Parting is all we know of heaven,
> And all we need of hell . . ."
> EMILY DICKINSON

KIRSTY never knew how she got through the week that elapsed between the coming of Alan Crawford's letter and the arrival of himself and his wife. It always dwelt in her mind, a nightmare recollection. To be with the children, hearing them make plans for Christmas, arranging little festivities, and deciding what they would do with their gardens in the spring, was acute torture.

She had the prospect before her of telling the children, and of telling them in such a way as to make them like the thought of a stepmother and a new house.

Stella Carter, with whom she talked it all over, said: "I think you are very unselfish."

Kirsty scoffed at the motion. "Why, it's sheer selfishness on my part, for if the children went away miserable I would be miserable too. And naturally I don't want to be that."

They were together in Barbara's room looking over the children's clothes.

Kirsty was kneeling on the floor beside a pile of frocks.

"What a child Barbara is! She treats her frocks exactly as an otter treats a salmon, takes a bite out of each and throws it aside. None of these things are soiled, but none of them are quite fresh."

"I know. I've spoken about it to her often, but she has a passion for putting on fresh frocks. All those white knitted things had better be washed to go away clean."

Kirsty nodded. "We mustn't let the new mother think we didn't look after them well. That would never do, Carty. If only we knew what kind of woman she is, but we haven't an inkling. The best I can hope for is that she will let them alone. But promise me this, Carty, promise me solemnly that you won't leave them till Bill goes to school. Barbara and Specky could go at once, and Bill is six. Only two years, Carty, and you're young."

"But," Carty objected, "I couldn't insist on staying if they wanted to get rid of me."

"I suppose you couldn't," said Kirsty gloomily, "but I refuse to think of such a thing . . . Remember, you must come here always for your holidays, and if—if you should have to leave the children . . . come straight to Little Phantasy. I hear from Merren Strang that she has arranged to start immediately after Christmas with Rebecca. Miss Wotherspoon is going to look after your Rob. Nellie has a sister who can come here in her place for the time. Oh, Carty, if only Mr. Crawford had stayed away! Men are the most uncomfortable creatures . . ."

Mr. and Mrs. Crawford were expected on the Wednesday, and on the Sunday night Kirsty told the children.

They particularly loved Sunday evening for two reasons, one being that they did not have a bath but only a wash ("grubby night," they called it), and the other that Kirsty told them stories all the time from tea till bedtime. They were supposed, in deference to Miss Fanny's wishes, to be

Bible stories, but there is a limit to Bible stories, and as the children ceaselessly demanded something new Kirsty was forced to adapt secular tales to Sunday purposes by providing them with a moral. Rider Haggard's *She*, without losing its thrills, became a tale of missionary zeal, while Alan Breck, that bonnie fighter, would hardly have known himself as a *colporteur* hawking Bibles.

This Sunday evening they were gathered round the schoolroom fire. The children preferred it to the drawing-room, for Miss Fanny was there, occupying the best chair and looking pained when Barbara laughed too loudly, or Bill and Specky told each other home truths. There was no one to shock in the schoolroom, and nothing to spoil. You might pull the furniture about as you liked, and rumple the rugs and leave cushions on the floor.

Bill had a footstool of his own on which he liked to sit close to Kirsty's feet, while Barbara enjoyed the stories best when she drew pictures as well as listened. Specky gloated over his fly-book.

"Do tell us about Huckleberry Finn," he said, looking up. "The bit about the raft."

"I like the bit about Moses," Barbara said, "about 'I don't take no stock in dead people'."

"I'm going to tell you a true story," Kirsty said. Bill turned a suspicious glance on her and said warningly:

"Not about me." True stories, in his experience, had a nasty trick of bringing in names of delinquents to point the moral.

"Pie, we prefer stories that aren't true," Barbara said with dignity, as she sharpened a pencil preparatory to beginning on a work of art.

"Well, we'll try a true one today," said Kirsty, "and I want you to listen very carefully. Are you listening, Specky? Once upon a time there were three children, not bad children as children go, and they lived with their father and mother and were always very happy and sometimes fairly good—Barbara, my dear, do you think you should suck these crayons? They can't be wholesome—but their mother had to go away and leave them—"

"Is it us?" Specky asked.

"Yes, it's you. You remember how very sad you were when your darling mother couldn't play with you and tell you stories any more because she was so weak and ill? And God saw that she wanted a rest, so He took her away to His own country where nobody is ever ill or tired or sad. But she never forgets her Barbara and Specky and Bill. She loves you more and more as the years pass—always remember that, darlings—and some day you will go to her, and you will all be together again, and that will be a lovely day . . . But what pleases your mother most is to know that you are happy and good on this earth, and you have been happy, haven't you, my mice, at Little Phantasy?"

"We're not going away?" Bill asked quickly, before the others could answer.

"That's what I'm telling you about. Just listen for a minute and you'll hear. You missed your mother, I know, missed most dreadfully not having her to sing to you and play with you, and come and cuddle you up, and all the sweet names she called you, and the way she ran to you at night if you gave the slightest little frightened cry. But poor

Daddy missed her much more than you did. He missed her so much that he couldn't bear the house without her, so he shut it up and went away to see if he would get any better travelling about the world."

She paused, but no comment was made, so she went on:

"Now, while he was travelling about he met a lady who had lost her husband, and she was very lonely and sad. And because they were both lonely they talked a lot to each other, and they liked talking to each other, and found that when they were together they weren't so lonely, so they agreed that they would marry each other."

She stopped and looked at the children, almost dreading what she would see in their faces, but they remained perfectly calm.

Bill said, "Is that all? *Now* tell us about Huck Finn."

"That was quite a nice story, Pie, but not very exciting," Barbara said as she finished putting wings on a fairy she was drawing. "Did you say Daddy had married some lady?" Her tone was supremely uninterested.

"I think," said Kirsty, feeling that all her tact had been wasted, "I think you are the most heartless children I ever knew, quite without natural affection. Sit up now and listen. Your father has married this lady and they are coming here on Wednesday. You are going away with them to Perthshire, where the lady has a lovely place. Who said this story wasn't exciting?"

For answer Barbara cast all her drawing materials violently on the floor, and flung herself at Kirsty's feet, clasping her round the knees, and sobbing bitterly, "I shan't go. I shan't go."

Bill merely folded his mouth to a straight line of obstinacy, while Specky said gently, "I'll stay with you, Pie."

Kirsty had no longer any need to complain of indifference.

It was some time before Barbara could be quieted sufficiently to listen to the tale of the joys that awaited them in their new home, and Kirsty's explanation of the position regarding their stepmother. "She doesn't want in the least to take the place of your own mother, you understand that, don't you? She only wants to make you happy, and to make your father happy."

"Why can't she make Daddy happy and leave us alone?" Barbara wanted to know.

"And when we all go to God's country," Specky said in his grave way, "and get our own mother back, what will Daddy do with this lady? He won't need her then, will he?"

"No-o," said Kirsty, nonplussed. Then she had an inspiration. "Of course the lady will get her own husband back then."

"Will she?" said Specky doubtfully; "it all seems very queer."

"Specky," said Kirsty, "the world is full of queer things which you and I can never hope to understand, but in the next world there will be neither marrying nor giving in marriage, and that's a comfort . . . Now I'll tell you about your new home." She shut her eyes as if she were seeing visions. "What times you will have! I shouldn't be in the least surprised if you have a pony."

"We've a pony here," said Bill coldly.

"Ah, but a Shetland pony, all shaggy, and so small that it doesn't matter how often you fall off, because you can't hurt yourself, you are so near the ground."

A spark of interest came into Bill's gloomy blue eyes which, however, he quenched instantly, while Barbara tossed her long plaits and said, "I'd rather have Phantasy than all the beastly ponies in the world."

Specky sighed and asked if there were any burns in Perthshire.

"Burns! My dear son, there are rushing mighty rivers. The Tay, the Tummel, the Garry. Salmon leaping all over the place, and trout! Perhaps your father will take you out in a boat to fish. How you will love it!"

"If he loves it," said Barbara viciously. "I'll kick him."

"I shan't love it," poor Specky protested. "None of them could be as nice as the Hope Water. The trout are so friendly to me now."

The door, which was not quite shut, creaked a little, and Percy, the cat, walked in a stately way across the floor.

The three children immediately flung themselves on him, to tell him the story of their wrongs.

Percy lay on Barbara's knee looking infinitely wise, while Specky and Bill each held a paw.

"Percy, Pie says we're to go away from Little Phantasy," Barbara told him. "Daddy's found some sort of lady to marry, and we've got to go to live with her."

"In Persia," supplemented Bill.

"Perthshire," corrected Kirsty.

"It's all the same to Percy," said Specky, "he comes from Persia anyway."

"Put down Percy and come and sing hymns to Aunt Fanny," Kirsty suggested mildly.

"Sing!" said Barbara, looking at her out of swollen, reproachful eyes.

"Why not? It would be better than making poor Percy uncomfortable by dropping salt tears on his fur. Ah, here is Carty. She will cheer us all up."

Stella Carter came forward to the fire and knelt down to stroke Percy. She did not look at any one, but began to talk in an even cheerful voice about an exciting book she had been reading; and presently Kirsty rose and slipped away.

She went up to her own room, not feeling able at the moment for Miss Fanny's conversation.

Her fire was burning brightly, the curtains drawn, the room made ready for the night. She lit the candles on the writing-table, and sat down with notepaper before her.

She meant to write to Blanche Cunningham, but she bit her pen for many minutes before she wrote a word. When she did begin she wrote with a lagging pen. Nothing seemed of enough interest to put down on paper.

"Such a lot of things have happened, Blanche, my dear, since I wrote last; though it isn't much more than a week, it seems an age. Firstly, Carty has got engaged to Rob Brand. They are so happy and I am so glad for them. They make the nicest sort of lovers, quite natural and friendly in the public eye, but really very much in love. They won't be married for a year or two, anyway. Carty is young and Rob has no money to speak of. Also there is the question of Rebecca Brand. Naturally, Rob won't marry until she is comfortably settled somewhere—and all that will take time.

"And dear Nannie Tait is dead. I suppose we expected it, but it somehow came as a great shock. The courage of that stricken little mother was something to wonder at.

"I expect you will have heard before this reaches you, that Mr. Alan Crawford is being married shortly—tomorrow, I believe—and he writes that he and his bride are coming here on Wednesday to take the children away.

"I am trying not to make a fuss, Blanche. I've had them for nearly seven months, longer than at first I hoped; and I always knew I held them on an uncertain tenure. If only I knew what kind of woman the new Mrs. Crawford is, if I were certain that she would make a real home for the children, I wouldn't be so *sweir* to let them go. But I hope and believe it will be all right. Whenever I see her I shall write and tell you how she strikes me. It is harder far for you.

"I'm so frightfully stupid tonight I can't write at all, but I love you, Blanche.

"Your KIRSTY."

" . . . Don't, please, be sorry that the children came here. I wouldn't for worlds have missed having them. I am sending Rose Macaulay's new book. I know how you enjoy her. This one, *Told by an Idiot*, is brilliant. But she sums up life—'a story told by an idiot, and not a very nice idiot at that, but an idiot with gleams of genius and fineness. No achievement can matter, and all things done are vanity . . . but the queer, enduring spirit of enterprise when it animates the dust we are is not contemptible or absurd.'

"Tonight I almost believe it, that life is a tale told by an idiot, I mean, but that is only because I'm down and out at the moment. In a little my heart will jump up again. As Easie would say, 'I'll be better gin mornin'.' "

CHAPTER 26

"The popular preference for a story with a happy ending is not a mere sweet-stuff optimism; it is the remains of the old idea of the triumph of the dragon-slayer, the ultimate apotheosis of the man beloved of heaven."

G. K. CHESTERTON

MR. and Mrs. Alan Crawford arrived about eleven o'clock, stayed to luncheon, and left, with the children, immediately after.

Easie Orphoot, who had wept at intervals for two days, remarked on the day of departure, "Weel, weel, better a finger off than aye waggin'," to which piece of philosophy Nellie responded with a howl like a wolf. Miss Wotherspoon said nothing, but looked, if possible, more disapproving than ever of the world at large, and of the particular corner which she found herself inhabiting. The children alternated between moments of excited anticipation and hours of deep gloom.

Kirsty had never dared to allow her thoughts to centre on the new Mrs. Crawford, but unconsciously she had in the back of her mind the picture of a pretty posing creature, very feminine and clinging, rather like her own stepmother, the sort of woman that would be likely to appeal to a susceptible man; and she had had very little comfort in thinking of the children's future. So sure had she been of the correctness of her surmise, that when Mrs. Crawford came into the room she felt in a bewildered way that there had been some mistake, that the real Mrs. Crawford had failed to appear.

Alan Crawford's new wife (widow of one Robert Weir of large fortune) was what is known as a fine woman. She was dark and tall and inclined to be massive. Her face looked somewhat forbidding, until she smiled, but her eyes were the eyes of a nice dog, honest and anxious, and a little beseeching. When Kirsty met those eyes her anxious heart lightened: here was no ordinary stepmother.

Alan Crawford greeted Kirsty in the most enthusiastic way, holding both her hands, gazing at her with the frankest admiration in his eyes, appealing to his wife to know if Kirsty was not all he had told her, pure gold hair and all, and Kirsty, looking at him, tanned by sun and sea-winds, debonair, graceful, handsomer than she had remembered him, realized with complete certainty that she could never have married him.

"The children are in the garden somewhere," she told him, after they had talked for a few minutes. "They are saying goodbye to all their favourite haunts. Perhaps you would like to go and find them yourself."

Mr. Crawford went with alacrity, and Kirsty sat down and tried to think of something to say to the new wife.

Her manners were rather awkward, and it was evident that she was not quite at her ease (probably, thought Kirsty, the late Robert Weir had risen in life and had married while he was still down), but she made no effort to appear anything but what she was, a simple good woman.

"I just hope he'll make her happy," thought Kirsty. "But some men are born husbands, and I think he's one; and she will always be grateful."

Kirsty spoke pleasantly about nothing till she found that her companion was not listening, when she stopped.

"Were you surprised to hear about our marriage?" Mrs. Crawford asked abruptly.

"I was, rather," said Kirsty.

There was a pause, then Mrs. Crawford spoke again.

"I don't wonder. I was surprised myself. In fact, I can't believe it yet. We met on board ship, you know? The doctor sent me for a voyage because I was all run down, first nursing my husband, then my mother-in-law. I was left alone, you see, and I think that great big house got on my nerves . . . I'm older than he is, six years older, and I look more. Of course I've got lots of money—but I don't believe that was why he married me." She looked almost defiantly at Kirsty, who said, "Of course not."

"You've been very good to the children. He couldn't say enough about it, and about you—that you were like something out of a fairytale, you know how he talks? It's all new to me that way of talking. Mr. Weir never talked like that, but of course he was a businessman, and that makes a difference. You expect artists to have queer ways . . . Did Mr. Crawford—did Alan know you well that he left the children with you?"

"Oh no, I only saw him once, when he came to arrange about the children coming. He stayed a night then. It is the children's aunt, Blanche Cunningham, who is my great friend, and it was through her the children came to me."

There was a silence, and then Mrs. Crawford said, "Will you not be very sorry to let the children go?"

Kirsty laughed. "Well, I shan't be as sorry as I would have been if I hadn't met you. I can trust them to you."

The dog-like eyes suddenly filled with tears.

"I've never had a child of my own. It was a terrible vex to Mr. Weir, but it was worse for me . . . I promise you, Miss Gilmour, that they'll never be sick nor sorry if I can help it. Everything money can get they'll have. Are they—are they easy children to get on with?"

"You'll adore them," Kirsty assured her. "Hasn't their father told you about them? They are the happiest creatures. Specky, the elder boy, you will find a positive delight to do anything for. He purrs when he is pleased—I mean to say he always tells you when things are nice, and is so conscious of his own happiness. Barbara is a great dear, and as for old Bill . . . By the way, I'm afraid I've promised them a Shetland pony in your name."

"Oh goodness yes, as many as they like. But do they want to come? Aren't they terribly sorry to leave you?"

"Oh, they are," Kirsty acknowledged. "We've been very happy together. But you know what children are. Once they are in a new place and surrounded by new interests they so quickly forget. And a great blessing it is, the easy forgetfulness of childhood."

"But what about you?"

"I must get new interests too. Here they come. You see they are as pleased and excited as possible at having their father again."

Mrs. Crawford joined Kirsty at the window and watched the children come across the lawn with their father.

"What if they don't take to me?" She moistened her lips

nervously. "I haven't much way with children. I thought they were wee tots; I didn't realize they were so big, especially the girl. Perhaps she will think me . . ." She stopped and looked apprehensively at Kirsty, who said reassuringly:

"Barbara's very young for her age. She's only about eleven though she is so tall, and is the simplest child; you'll get on together splendidly."

The door opened and Alan Crawford cried eagerly, "These are the children."

Barbara and Specky came forward and allowed themselves to be kissed, but Bill stood stock-still in the doorway. He wore his "bloodhound face," and glowered at the newcomer.

Kirsty went to him and led him forward, and, still holding his hand, knelt beside him before his stepmother.

Bill looked at his father's wife—a swift glance—then turned and looked into Kirsty's eyes. That look told her all that his tongue would fain have uttered, told her that he liked people slim as willow wands, with shining hair, and detested such as filled their clothes impressively, and had large swarthy faces.

Kirsty quailed for what he would do or say next, but he took another look at his stepmother, met her eyes, saw in them what Kirsty had seen, something gentle and anxious and beseeching—and of his own accord he put his hand in hers.

They left after luncheon. Large crystal tears rolled slowly over Specky's face and he held on to his fishing rod as his only comfort; Barbara sobbed aloud, and clung in turn to

Miss Fanny, Miss Wotherspoon, Easie, Nellie, and Kirsty; Bill hugged his melodeon and said nothing.

When they were all gone Kirsty walked slowly upstairs. She felt strangely tired.

It was all over. The door of the Stable stood open. Miss Wotherspoon had been cleaning it, and a large heap of outgrown garments and discarded books and toys were piled on a chair, ready to be given away, or sent to a jumble sale. On the top was the red plush Teddy bear that Bill had carried about with him everywhere.

Kirsty seized it. It must be sent after him, he would be missing it terribly, he loved it even better than his melodeon. She remembered how he had carried it buttoned under his new overcoat, with the head sticking comically out, the day they had gone to Priorsford to get the boys' hair cut. What a long time ago that seemed already! Then she had felt quite securely that the children would be with her indefinitely. She had held their hands with a proprietary air. She had been looking forward to Christmas trees and planning all manner of amusements. She had been thinking of spring and the delights spring would bring. A length of happy days had seemed to stretch endlessly in front of her. And now—the two little beds stood straight and smooth. An air of prim tidiness was over everything. There was no one now to kick the rugs about and scatter things on the floor. One could now lean back in a chair without being impaled on a hook, and cease to fear to find tumblers of dirty water belonging to Barbara's painting operations in every place where they were most likely to be knocked over. Books would remain on shelves, cushions in chairs; the mantelshelf would no longer he [be] decorated with stones believed to be agates and treasured by Bill, or forgotten tins of worms owned by Specky.

Kirsty shivered. It felt as if someone had died.

Outside the sparkle and gaiety of the frost and snow had gone. Ratchell top was in the mists, Cardon was invisible, Cademuir and Hundleshope and the Black Meldon were dim shapes, and rain was falling with melancholy persistence.

Kirsty wandered back to the drawing-room. Here things looked more cheerful. Outside were the driving rain and the swaying trees, but within the fire was reflected in the shining old mahogany, the parrots swung gaily among the tulips on the chintzes, tall chrysanthemums made the room fragrant with their fresh spicy smell, Miss Fanny, soft and comfortable in her fleecy shawls, dozed in her armchair, and Percy, the cat, lay curled on the fender-stool.

And in her sick heart Kirsty hated the comfort of it.

Three-thirty! The children would have been coming in (they had never regarded the weather) to change their wet clothes and come down brushed and dry and ready for tea. It had always been such a gay meal, more especially since the early darkening; eating by lamplight had pleased the children mightily.

Miss Fanny sat up and delicately rubbed her eyes.

"My dear," she said apologetically, "I must have dropped asleep. I woke rather early this morning. A departure always unsettles me. I wish the dear children had got a more cheerful day to go. Travelling in the rain is so depressing . . . You will miss them, Kirsty."

"Yes," said Kirsty.

"But of course," Aunt Fanny continued, "it is the proper thing that they should be with their parents, and it is so fortunate that Mrs. Crawford is rich and seems inclined to be generous. Had the first wife money? I never heard, but of course Mr. Crawford must have a good private income or he could never career about the world as he does and do no work. The children will lack for nothing. I could see that Mrs. Crawford was quite prepared to make herself a slave to them. She will probably spoil them completely with adoration, and her husband too. Dear me, how plain she is! It seems a pity deliberately to marry a plain woman; the prettiest have their ugly moments, but to begin with someone frankly ugly is simply . . . however—"

Miss Fanny was feeling very content. She had been sorry in a way to see the children go, but she was thinking pleasantly that there would be no more sticky fingers on her work, and that Kirsty would be much more with her now that she had not the children to take up her attention. And tea would be coming in presently, and tea on a wet November afternoon was very welcome. Kirsty, poor child, was out of spirits, but she would get over that.

The bell rang, and Colonel Home was shown in.

Miss Fanny felt rather annoyed. She would have enjoyed her tea better without him, and Kirsty was in no mood for a visitor.

But Kirsty, to her aunt's astonishment, at once began to talk with great animation.

"Have you come to condole?" she asked, laughing lightly. "Aunt Fanny and I are feeling very bereft. Yes, they went just after luncheon. Oh, in excellent spirits. They are enormously interested in their new life, and the thought of all the glories of Inchtay—that is the name of Mrs. Crawford's place, bought by her late husband, who did something mysterious with bottles. I can't quite make out what it was, but it must have been very large and very paying, for he seems to have left her exceedingly well off."

"You like her, I hope?"

"Oh yes," said Kirsty. "She's a little, how shall I say it? There's a slight flavour of the bottles about her, perhaps. . ."

Miss Fanny glanced at her niece. Kirsty saw the glance, and remembered also the beseeching look in the honest eyes of the woman she was discussing, and hated herself.

"There is something big about her," she went on. "I don't quite know what made Mr. Crawford marry her. I mean, I don't think he had the sense to do it himself. It must have been instinct that made him choose so wisely twice running. I am glad for the children."

Miss Wotherspoon came in to make preparations for tea.

"You will feel your hands empty," Archie Home said to Kirsty.

He seemed to be in a surprisingly gentle mood.

"For a day or two," Kirsty said lightly. "I expect we shall go away soon for the winter. One can't always stay in the same place—" She rose abruptly. "Aunt Fanny, will you give Colonel Home tea? I've just remembered something I ought to do."

In a second she was out of the room.

She felt she must get into open air, away from the talk and the comfort in the drawing-room. Throwing a coat round her she opened the door and slipped quietly out.

The wind met her, buffeting her, blowing her hair over her face, but she caught her coat round her and ran through the sodden garden, down to the side of the Hope Water.

> ". . . Gie me a Border burn
> That canna rin wi'oot a turn."

The words brought back to her mind a sunny summer day in a green glen where a hawthorn tree had shaken white petals on the turf, and children's voices had mingled with the song of the water.

"Pooelie, pooelie," the whaups had cried . . .

The Hope Water had come down from the hills with their melting snow, and ran high in spate. There was no little grey figure now wandering up and down the banks. Specky and his fishing rod had gone, but the path in the grass that his patient feet had trod was there, and it was too much for Kirsty. She had kept up bravely, but now the full blast of her loss struck her, and she sank to the ground sobbing like a broken-hearted child.

"Specky," she moaned, as if summoning him to her aid, "Specky!" But Specky was speeding every minute farther from her, and the water rushed unheeding past.

She had sobbed herself almost quiet when she became aware that her landlord was standing beside her. Raising herself on one hand she glared at him. "Why have you come here?" she said. "Go away, please. I want to be alone."

There may be people who can look pretty in tears, but of

a certainty Kirsty was not one of them. Her eyelids were swollen, her face had lost all its delicate colour and was blotched and disfigured, her hair was bedraggled with the rain. But to Archie Home she had never seemed so human and so lovable.

She dabbed her eyes with a futile little damp ball of a handkerchief, and he gravely held out his own large one, still in its folds.

There is nothing more annoying than to have people assume that one is going to cry indefinitely, and Kirsty indignantly refused the proffered handkerchief.

"What's that for?" she asked coldly. "I've got one of my own—thanks." Then shakily, "I know you're laughing at me. You think it's silly and sentimental to cry like this about—about—"

Archie Home shook his head in denial, but she heeded him not.

"I was so happy," she went on; "I thought I had made a home all secure and warm, and now it's a *harried* nest—the birds all gone."

"They were cuckoos, Kirsty."

Kirsty gave a mixture of a laugh and a sob, which resulted in a sort of snort. "Y-you're getting mixed in your bird knowledge. Cuckoos aren't invited into a nest, are they? If Bill heard you call him a cuckoo—Oh, Bill, *Bill!*" She dropped back in a crumpled heap on the wet grass, all attempt at dignity gone.

Her companion made no attempt to comfort her, but simply stood beside her and waited.

Presently she looked up at him with something of

apology in her face.

"I don't know why I'm behaving like this, but, anyway, it isn't very nice of you to come and spy on me . . . Why aren't you having tea comfortably with Aunt Fanny?"

"Why? Because I'm standing by the Hope Water with the rain running down my neck, trying to summon up courage to ask you to marry me."

Kirsty sat with her handkerchief halfway to her eyes and stared incredulously.

"Will you, Kirsty?"

Utterly demoralized, Kirsty began to cry again, and as she cried she said:

"You don't know what sort of woman I am or you wouldn't ask me that. I was prepared to marry Alan Crawford, not caring for him in the least, simply for the sake of Bill."

Archie Home seemed unimpressed by such infamy.

"Well," he said coolly, "Bill's a better reason for marrying than most people have."

But Kirsty was down in the depths, walking in the Valley of Humiliation, unable to see a ray of daylight.

"When I came to Little Phantasy I meant to do so much," she moaned, "and I've been such a hopeless failure. I was going to be a mother to the children, and I wasn't wanted. I was going to cherish the village people, and they won't be cherished. I tried to save dear little Nannie Tait, and I couldn't. I was going to make Carty and Rob Brand happy, and I've done Rebecca out of a home. And now," she turned reproachfully on her suitor, "and now you come and offer to marry me out of pity."

Archie Home's temper was always inclined to be brittle.

"My dear girl," he said, "for goodness' sake don't talk nonsense. I'm not standing here in the rain for pleasure. Get up now and come home and get dry. I don't want to have you down with rheumatic fever."

He stooped, and putting his arm round her, pulled her to her feet, and still keeping his arm round her, he said, "Pity, you silly child! Haven't I adored you for the last six months, and had no hope because I thought you cared for this man Crawford . . . Is it possible that you can ever care for me, Kirsty?"

Kirsty was finding it strangely comfortable to lean her weary head against a shoulder in a wet burberry.

"How can I tell?" she said. "I haven't had time for anything but trying to make myself think I could marry Alan Crawford—who never gave a thought to me." She stopped suddenly, remembering how extraordinarily happy she had been all through the summer and autumn. Had there been some secret fount of joy that she had not suspected?

"I was so happy," she went on. "I thought it was because the children were there . . . *Could it have been you?*"

"My dear, if I could dare to think so."

Kirsty thought for a minute or two. It was wonderfully natural to be standing here leaning on her landlord's shoulder. She could not understand it.

"But"—she suddenly slid from his encircling arm and faced him—"how could you care for me when you hardly ever spoke to me? Have you forgotten how you disapproved of me, how you always scolded me? We each seemed to make the other cross. I'm not quarrelsome with other people as I am with you . . . Have you forgotten what kind of creature I am? I'm not going to change if I do marry you—don't think it. I'll always be full of sentiment. I'll always like what you call the 'pink sugar' of life. I'll always be doing things to irritate you . . ."

"Such as?"

"Oh," said Kirsty, "like—" she remembered suddenly an incident that had provoked her stepmother, "like running back and giving an extra tip to a waiter if I think he looks consumptive! I simply can't help trying to make people pleased. Even if I don't at all like a woman, I find myself telling her nice things I have heard people say of her simply to make her purr. Rebecca Brand says it's a form of selfishness, and I daresay she is right."

Archie Home caught her in his arms and kissed her, kissed the wet hair, and the tear-stained eyelids, and the mouth that trembled half with laughter and half with grief.

"You ridiculous darling," he said, "don't you suppose I love pink sugar for your sake?"

After a pause. "Well," said Kirsty, "I'll try to quarrel with you a good deal for the sake of variety. Otherwise, you might find life with me rather like supping syrup."

They walked homewards oblivious of the rain and the gathering darkness.

"What will Aunt Fanny say?" Kirsty wondered. "She must stay on at Little Phantasy with Easie and Miss Wotherspoon, if you don't mind, Archie—that's the first time I've said your name—Archie! . . You know, although she looks so placid and comfortable and buttressed with shawls, she is really dreadfully frightened of being old and having to die. Isn't that pathetic? I would like always to stay near her so that I could hold her hand if she goes first out of Vanity Fair . . ." Kirsty stopped and added, "Not that this world has been much of a Vanity Fair to her. More like Paternoster Row with so many hymnbooks and religious weeklies and little books about Heaven! You do like her, don't you, Archie? I wish you would talk to her as much as you can and ask her advice about things and just try to make a fuss of her a little. I know it isn't your way, but it would please her."

"I'll try," Archie Home said meekly.

As they came up to the lighted house he suddenly felt her shaken with a sob.

"Still grieving for Bill, darling?"

"Not really," said Kirsty, now well out of the Valley of Humiliation, and inclined to be impertinent. "When I have you I haven't lost old Bill, for men, even when, like you, they are middle-aged and rather cross, are only little boys at heart."

CHAPTER 27

"For tragedy Dorothea had no aptitude at all. She did what she could—tidied up." *The Westcotes*

AS a rule there was not much to talk about in Muirburn. Mrs. Stark had once amused Kirsty by recounting to her that, "When the coo died Robert and me juist sat and crackit about the Other World."

Now Little Phantasy supplied sensation after sensation. First, the sudden arrival of Mr. Alan Crawford with his new wife, and the departure of the children; next, the rumour that the laird was going to marry Miss Gilmour; and then that the minister was engaged to the governess.

The kitchen folk of Little Phantasy had never known themselves of such importance to the district. It was amazing how many people found it necessary to call at the kitchen door, and were hospitably haled in and entertained to tea and talk.

Mrs. Dickson from The Shop ran round in the darkening with a shawl round her head, leaving her husband behind the counter (where he was no ornament, and almost entirely useless), so that, as she put it, she might hear Easie's breath on it.

Easie was making a pudding for the dinner, and asked her visitor to be seated, and excuse her going on with her work. "Makin' the denner as usual," she said, "though to tell ye the truth, what wi' yae thing and another, I feel mair like fleein' up i' the air than makin' this pudden." She beat butter and sugar vigorously for a minute, and went on—"*Hard labour* pudden I ca' it, for it needs sic a beatin' to mak it richt. Eh, but wark's no' the hertsome thing that it was when oor bairns were here. It was a pleasure to cook then, wi' Specky rinnin' oot and in askin' for raisins to eat and empty tins for his wurrums, or wantin' a troot weighed. He was that disappointed, the puir bairn, when the scales hardly moved. I hed aye to tell him that the weights were wrang. Bill was a caution, for he aye wantit to help me, and patted awa' at jam turnovers—sic nate wee hands he hed. An' Miss Barbara could mak pancakes no' sae bad at a'. She's growin' up a braw lass, she'll mak somebody sigh and set by their supper—Ay, they gaed off on Wednesday. Is that only twae days they've been awa'? Mercy! It's mair like a month."

Easie turned to inspect something in the oven, and Mrs. Dickson seized the opportunity to ask, "What like's the new wife?"

Easie closed the oven door, and standing with her hands on her sides, said solemnly:

"A muckle blackaveesed wumman. A great hoose end o' a wife. A sulky-lookin' cratur. Oh, I tell ye ma hert was sair for thae bairns, but Miss Kirsty says I'm no' to say that. She says Mrs. Crawford is a fine body, and that she'll be rale guid to them, and mebbe she's richt, but I canna help feelin' vexed for Mr. Crawford—sic a blythe fellay to get sic a dour-lookin' wife!"

"An' what's this aboot Miss Kirsty and the laird? Dickson says—"

But what Mr. Dickson said Easie was not to hear, for at that moment Miss Wotherspoon came in, and behind her Mrs. Stark.

"My, Mrs. Stark," Mrs. Dickson greeted her, "it's no' often we meet you in onybody's hoose. We'll need to strike a hack in the post."

"Ye may say it," Mrs. Stark said, taking the chair Miss Wotherspoon offered her. "I'm no' likely to be cursed for failing to withdraw ma fit from ma neebor's hoose—Agnes came in wi' a story that the laird was gaun to mairry your Miss, an' I juist cam richt doun to see if it was true."

"Loosen yer cloak, Mrs. Stark," Miss Wotherspoon advised, "an' ye'll feel the good of it when ye go out. I've been down at the post office, and I'm fair out of breath . . . Ay, it's true. They're engaged. It's to be in the papers the morn's morning."

Easie was still beating her "hard labour" pudding, and she continued to beat as she broke into the conversation with, "Miss Kirsty came in yesterday mornin' as usual to speak aboot the denner and things, and says she, 'Easie,' she says, 'I've got surprisin' news for you. I'm going to marry Colonel Home'—juist like that. Surprisin' news! Ye could ha' knockit me doon wi' a feather. I never thocht that soor-lookin' customer would hey the sense to seek a wife, nor the luck to get sic a denty yin."

Mrs. Stark gave a snort of wrath. "Whae are ye ca'in' a 'soor-lookin' customer,' Easie Orphoot? The laird? D'ye no' ken that he could hey the pick o' the hale countryside, an' Lunnon and a'? The laird o' Phantasy! Ma word! Miss Gilmour's done weel. She's ca'ed her yowes to nae silly merket. She kens what's what, if ye dinna, Easie ma wumman. A braw man and a braw place and an' auld name—what could lassie want mair?"

" 'Deed, Mrs. Stark," said Easie, surprised at the wrath she had aroused, "I'm no' lichtlying the laird. It's true what ye say, but for a' that I wadna fancy him masel'. I aye likit an easy-tempered blythe kinna man. But," she gave her broad laugh, "a' this talk o' marryin' is fair gaun to ma heid. If Jimmie wud write frae Canada and send me an address I wud juist bundle awa' to him."

Miss Wotherspoon closed her eyes for a moment as if in pain, her usual protest against Easie's too rollicking way of speaking; then she said with more than her usual prim superiority of manner:

"You'll take a cup of tea, Mrs. Stark, you and Mrs Dickson?"

"No' me," said Mrs. Stark. "I'm gaun hame this verra meenit to ma parritch;" and Mrs. Dickson also refused, but more politely, the proffered hospitality.

"There's nothing but changes," Miss Wotherspoon said, folding her scarf carefully. "Miss Carter and Mr. Brand—ye would hear aboot that?"

"Ay," said Mrs. Dickson. "Wasn't it queer that Dickson should have seen that first? Ye mind I tellt ye what he said yae day I had ma tea here?"

Mrs. Stark demanded to be told what news this was about her minister.

"Miss Carter, the governess," she said. "Ay, I ken her. She went often to see puir Nannie Tait. A likeable lass. We whiles hed a crack in the passin' . . . But what aboot Miss

Brand when the minister taks a wife?"

"As to that," said Miss Wotherspoon, "I could not say. But next month she's going for a trip abroad with Mrs. Strang. I ken that, for I'm to go and look after the minister in her absence."

"Ay, I heard that," Mrs. Dickson put in. "And how lang will it be for, Miss Wotherspoon?"

"Three months at least. Ay, I'll feel it queer to be back in a Manse again, and not in my old position," Miss Wotherspoon sighed.

"So you will," Mrs. Dickson agreed sympathetically. "Fancy Miss Brand awa' to the Continent! She's comin' oot. My, d'ye ken, I'd like fine to see her get a guid man. Mind you, she deserves it. I've kent her a' her days. Strangers dinna tak tae her, she's no way wi' her to mak hersel' liked, but she's good a' through . . . Weel, she'll mebbe meet wi' somebody on her traivels."

"I doot it," said Mrs. Stark. "She'll be a dour crop to lift . . . Will ye be losin' yer place, Easie, when the Miss marries?"

Easie turned from the fire, her face flushed with her efforts, but serene and smiling as usual. "Na," she said, "we can bide here as lang as Miss Fanny bides. But I never look far forrit. There's no sayin' whaur I'll land." She straightened herself up, a handsome woman with her comely face and fine shoulders and smooth round arms. "I'm no' auld. I daursay there's a heap o' living afore me yet, an' I'm fit for onything."

"Oh, wheesht," cried Miss Wotherspoon, "and mind what an uncertain thing this life is."

Easie laughed in kindly scorn. "There's some folk creep

through this warld wi' their hands aye ower their heids for fear they get a skelp. What's the use o' that? It's a graund warld if ye tak it the richt way. I've naething but ma twa hands to work for me, but I'm no' feared."

Mrs. Stark gave a short laugh as she rose to go. "Ye're a cheery yin, Easie," she said.

Rebecca Brand heard the news from Lady Carruthers. They met on the Friday morning on the road near the Manse, and Lady Carruthers flung herself exuberantly on the unwilling Rebecca.

"Isn't it delightful, this news?"

"I haven't heard any news," said Rebecca.

"Not about Colonel Home and dear Kirsty Gilmour? I simply must call her Kirsty. In the face of great happiness one cannot be formal, and besides, of course, she will be settled here for good now. Of course I saw it from the beginning. It was too suitable not to come true: the money and everything . . . I only heard this morning, and I'm on my way to Little Phantasy now. I want to be one of the very first to wish her joy. A love story is so precious to happily married people. As Sir Andrew said to me when I told him, 'If they are as happy as we are they will be happy indeed.'"

"Did he say that?" said Rebecca unbelievingly, remembering Sir Andrew's gloomy speechlessness.

Lady Carruthers flitted from that subject and alighted on another.

"And I hear your brother is engaged to Miss Carter. So suitable in every way. And you are meditating a flight to

Rome with Mrs. Strang? How our little community is stirring and spreading its wings! Oh, isn't life wonderful? That's what I always say, 'Isn't life *wonderful?*' "

She went, and Rebecca turned and retraced her steps to the house. She had meant to do a variety of things, but they would have to wait for a more convenient season; at present the refuge of her own little room was what she felt she must have. The news was not unexpected; she had been prepared for it. She had thought she did not care, that she could hear it and be calm. But now that it was come it seemed to drain her strength, to make her feet heavy and unwilling, to leave her exceeding comfortless, and worn, and old.

She locked the door of her room and sat heavily down in the old wooden chair with arms that stood before the writing-table in the window.

Anyway, nobody knew. How amused every one would be if they knew that she, Rebecca Brand, the little, plain, ill-dressed, unattractive sister of the minister, had been dreaming dreams about the laird of Phantasy. Kirsty would not be amused—she did her the justice of believing that—but she would be worse, kind beyond enduring.

Well, it was all over. It had been very innocent and unharmful, and surely Archie Home was none the worse that all unknown to him someone had been thinking of him, caring for him, praying for his wellbeing. And she would never let her thoughts wander to him again, he who was soon to be another woman's husband. Rebecca had the unswerving morality of the girl in the old song:

> "I daurna think o' Jamie,
> For that wad be a sin . . ."

She opened the shabby desk, and taking out the photograph that she had cut from a paper and mounted clumsily on pasteboard, sat with it in her hand. It was all she had to show for her romance.

Presently she lifted her head and looked, as she had so often looked, across the fields to Phantasy. In the low meadow over the hedge from the Manse garden, a man and girl were walking—Archie Home and Kirsty.

It was a bright mild morning, and the two were walking slowly in the sunshine, stopping every now and again when the conversation became too absorbing. Through the open window Rebecca could hear Kirsty's laugh, and see the way they looked into each other's eyes.

She sat and watched them till they climbed the stile and passed out of sight.

"I could have loved him," she told herself, "but that's all I could have done. I could never have amused him or delighted his eyes. I could have lain at his feet and adored him. He will be the grateful, adoring one always—and that's how it should be. It's much better so."

But the fact that it was better so made her bow her head on the writing-desk and weep a few hot difficult tears. At first her thoughts were bitter. She felt defrauded. Her youth was passing, well-nigh gone, and life had so far brought her nothing but a fight with poverty and hard work. Why should one have so much and another so little? —Then her own common sense came to her aid. The good

God would have it so, some must pipe and some must dance. What right had she to question when she had so much—health, steady nerves, a respected name, the remembrance of honoured, loved parents, work to do and strength to do it. As she thought of all she had she began to feel ashamed. She need envy no one. Compared with Kirsty's her life seemed dull and meagre, but it was in her own hands to make it rich.

Rebecca had always been somewhat complacent about herself and her actions. She had never really doubted that she was a thoroughly estimable person, hard-working, conscientious, honest almost to a fault, greatly to be esteemed. It was not for her to cultivate the flowers of politeness and gentleness, and the desire to please. She was strictly utilitarian, like a vegetable garden. She could have said with *Weir of Hermiston* that she had no call to be bonnie, she got through her day's work.

But now Rebecca was not so sure. She had never quite forgiven herself her rudeness to Kirsty. Might there not be a happy mean? Kirsty was all sweetness and grace: she was like a flower garden, something fair and pleasant to delight all comers—something fragrant to be remembered. Rebecca knew that she could never be like that. "But," she thought to herself, "why shouldn't I be like the cottage gardens round here, useful with berry bushes and cabbages, but brightened with a few hardy common flowers, sweet-williams, say, and candytuft, and some bushes of the little prickly yellow Scots roses . . ?"

She even smiled to herself at the thought. Had she not rather forgotten about the hardy simple flowers? . . This room now—she seemed to see it with new eyes. Those thick crochet mats, grown yellow with repeated washings. That shell box. Those bottles of coloured salt. They were ugly, they were useless, but she had kept them all these years. Anybody else would have managed to buy some pretty things for her own room . . . With something like a shock Rebecca realized that it was self-complacency that had made her keep everything as it had always been—a feeling that she had a soul above mere prettiness. She reflected, "It will all be changed when Stella Carter comes to the Manse. Rob will no longer be cheated out of the pleasant things of life. She'll make it bright and gay for him. If you are clever about that sort of thing, beauty costs no more than ugliness."

She stood up and straightened herself before the little dim looking-glass, pulled down the jumper she wore, and tried to make her hair a little fuller round her ears.

"I'll have to get some clothes to go to Italy," she said to herself, and the thought awoke, almost shamefacedly, a little gasp of anticipation. Italy! Three months of wonderland—no meals to plan for, no dishes to wash; rest, freedom, beauty . . . When the three months were over she would have to work. But what did that matter? Somehow the sudden breach in her complacency had stiffened her courage, had even given her a new sense of exhilaration. She was determined now to take hold of life with both hands and to keep hold of it.

She went back to the dressing-table and lifted the crochet mats and the shell box and the bottles. Out of a drawer she took a piece of Chinese embroidery that Mrs. Anthony Hay had once given her, and which she had put away as a useless sort of present, and laid it on the dressing-table. She was amazed at the effect of the rose and blue and gold on the mellow old wood. The thing, the act, seemed to her symbolical, and she stood for a little looking out of the window with eyes which were both bright and thoughtful.

But the morning was passing, and it was after twelve o'clock. She turned to the table in the window, locked the writing-desk, and picked up the photograph which lay on it. With head erect and shoulders squared, she marched downstairs to the dining-room, where she knelt before the fire, and, tearing the photograph into small pieces, poked each piece carefully into the flames and watched them burn.

Then she went into the kitchen and made a pudding for the early dinner, not a plain rice pudding as she had at first intended, but a bread pudding with jam on the top, and switched white of egg to make an ornamentation.

Also published by
Greyladies

THE DAY OF SMALL THINGS
by O. Douglas

"To you and to me this is the day of small things – Who said that? Someone in the Bible, wasn't it? And the small things keep you going wonderfully; the kindness of friends; the fact of being needed; nice meals; books; interesting plays; the funny people in the world; the sea and the space and the wind – not very small, are they, after all?"

Old friends and new in the Borders and Fife: Nicole and her mother, Lady Jane Rutherfurd; Mrs. Heggie; Mrs. Jackson; and Barbara Burt, now Mrs. Andrew Jackson, of Rutherfurd.

Originally published in 1930.

THE FAIR MISS FORTUNE
by D. E. Stevenson

Never before published, this charming story was originally written in the 1930s, when it was thought to be too old-fashioned to appeal to the modern market.

Jane Fortune causes a stir when she arrives in Dingleford to open a tearoom. Charles and Harold both fall for the newcomer, but her behaviour seems to vary wildly – first she encourages one then the other and at other times barely recognises them.

This edition also contains fascinating letters about the book between D. E. Stevenson and her agent.

EMILY DENNISTOUN
by D. E. Stevenson

Emily Dennistoun lives alone with her elderly tyrannical father at Borriston Hall on the Scottish coast. She has few friends and lives through her writing. Then she meets Francis, and despite vicissitudes of fortune, despite uncertainties, loneliness and unhappiness, Emily holds steadfast to a love she knows is true.

Originally entitled *Truth is the Strong Thing,* the themes of truth and honour pervade this rich multi-layered novel. Written at the beginning of her career in the 1920s, it has never before been published.

This edition includes an introduction by D. E. Stevenson's granddaughter, telling the story of the finding of the box of unpublished manuscripts by this much loved author.

PORTRAIT OF SASKIA
by D. E. Stevenson

Kenneth Leslie, needing money to start a new life in Canada after a broken engagement, answers an advertisement in the Daily Clarion –

Retired Army Officer offers a large sum of money to a Young Man who wants Adventure. Must be of good appearance and free from dependents

– and finds more than he dreamed of: fishing, art, family skullduggery, rogues, thieves and fisticuffs, friendship – and romance.

Also included are four short stories: *Moira, The Mulberry Coach, The Secret of the Black Loch, The Murder of Alma Atherton,* and a novella, *Where the Gentian Blooms.*

Previously unpublished, these are some of the manuscripts 'Found in the Attic' by the author's granddaughter. They were probably written in the 1920s, and foreshadow her later romances and family stories with that little humorous twist of something extra.

JEAN ERSKINE'S SECRET
by D. E. Stevenson

This is one of the early unpublished D. E. Stevenson manuscripts recently 'found in the attic' by the author's granddaughter. Probably written c.1917, it opens in 1913 with the Erskine family moving from Edinburgh to the Scottish east coast village of Crale, where Jean's life is transformed by her friendship with Diana MacDonald of Crale Castle. She writes a book telling Diana's story; of friendships and love affairs, of family and village life, all shadowed by the much darker themes of the Great War and devastating inherited conditions. And at the heart of the story is the secret, known only to Jean, that threatens Diana's hard-won happiness.

FOUND IN THE ATTIC
by D. E. Stevenson

A selection from the unpublished papers 'found in the attic' by the author's granddaughter: short stories (including a gentle revenge on critics), an eccentric maid, a ventriloquist desperate for work, a very human burglar); verse (a burlesque, some war poems and a long narrative verse); two delightfully witty one-act plays, and articles and talks on books and writing. Illustrated with family photographs, including the one on the cover, which shows the author at work in her Moffat hoe, where she wrote in a room overlooking the Scottish Border hills.